Dead End Poverty

To my dear friend Kitty
from Roland Charley
   Charley -13-03-2014
Kiss Kiss Kiss

DEAD END POVERTY

Roland Charley

authorHOUSE

AuthorHouse™ UK Ltd.
1663 Liberty Drive
Bloomington, IN 47403 USA
www.authorhouse.co.uk
Phone: 0800.197.4150

© 2013 Roland Charley. All rights reserved.

No part of this book may be reproduced, stored in a retrieval system, or transmitted by any means without the written permission of the author.

Published by AuthorHouse 11/23/2013

ISBN: 978-1-4918-8467-6 (sc)
ISBN: 978-1-4918-8466-9 (hc)
ISBN: 978-1-4918-8468-3 (e)

Any people depicted in stock imagery provided by Thinkstock are models, and such images are being used for illustrative purposes only.
Certain stock imagery © Thinkstock.

This book is printed on acid-free paper.

Because of the dynamic nature of the Internet, any web addresses or links contained in this book may have changed since publication and may no longer be valid. The views expressed in this work are solely those of the author and do not necessarily reflect the views of the publisher, and the publisher hereby disclaims any responsibility for them.

For my late brother, Anthony Charley, and the rest of the family

Acknowledgements

I owe a huge debt to everyone who helped with my work and went that extra mile to make this book a reality. I must extend special gratitude to my wife, Abibatu Jalloh-Charley, for pushing me—albeit in loving, tender ways—to complete this book. I welcomed her bright smiles and encouragement when writer's block set in, and the constant trips to the kitchen to make sure I was never hungry or thirsty were always appreciated. I also thank Chris Charley, my elder brother, for making me believe in myself, regardless of how I tried to put myself down; Abdul, Atu, and Fatima, for constantly interrupting me with questions and making sure that my laptop was charged; my good friend, Temitope Osho, for his much-appreciated advice and help determining the title of this text; AuthorHouse, for their high standard of professionalism, transparency, and dedication that enabled me to get this work to print; and everyone else not mentioned who helped (consciously or not) to prepare this book.

Prologue

With devastating speed, a large, thick, black cloud glided towards me. As it sped towards me, I realised how phenomenal its sheer volume was, and it immediately forced me into a defenceless position. Even as I watched its intimidating approach, the cloud evolved into different but equally frightful things.

It transformed into a distinctive, malevolent face with grotesque features, and it changed colours like a chameleon hunting for prey or hiding from predators. Although I was frightened, my eyes remained focussed on the peculiarity that had invaded my space. I was convinced that the apparition I perceived wasn't there to cuddle with me. Somehow, I knew its aim was to hurt me. I didn't know how, but I knew all the same.

The flaming, red eyes of the malevolent face penetrated my entire being. The blazing eyes looked out and were accompanied by a fierce, protruding, red-spiked tongue that drooped over a thick lower lip. I was sure the creature could see through me. Instinct alerted me to the fact that it could read my mind. I reckoned there would be no escape from the monster. Disgusting blobs of slimy, greenish stuff dripped from its mouth to the ground. As the blobs reached the ground, they glowed bright yellow and bubbled delicately like soup left to simmer at a low temperature. The face advanced towards me, seemingly uttering unearthly sounds that made it doubly terrible to behold. By that point, I was truly afraid. Suddenly, I was shivering due to the fear brewing inside me. I felt my limbs weakening and my strength waning, and I knew I was helpless in the face of the force. Irrespective of its intentions, the feeling that it sought to hurt me remained. But my focus didn't waver from the strange phenomenon; I was afraid it would strike when I wasn't looking.

I felt its aura coil around my body in a powerful grip resembling that of a python. It was squeezing me, trying to crush my bones and make my life ooze out of me. I felt the immense power of its mighty grip as it coils tightened further around my now-ravaged body. I felt powerless to resist the intense contraction on my rib cage. I panicked and tried to cry out for help. I felt my mouth open and shouted at the top of my voice, but I couldn't hear my own voice. And the apparition wouldn't go away.

I hung in there as darkness began to creep over me like rising floodwater over a riverbank. It became darker and darker until I couldn't see a thing. I felt the apparition would crush me to a pulp. I was in a sorry state, but I willed myself to defend against the powerful intruder. I violently thrashed my body around in an effort to thwart the evil being. I managed to keep some of my sanity, mustered my remaining strength, and put up more resistance against the force. As I struggled, the powerful constricting pressure on my rib cage continued to increase. With a deafening noise, I heard my ribs crack. Even as I willed myself to stay awake, I slipped into a semi-unconscious state. Eventually, I felt someone shake me awake vigorously and call out my name several times: "Yandi, Yandi! Wake up, Yandi! Yandi, wake up!"

1

I woke up with a jolt, terrified as a frightened buffalo, believing I was still in the grip of the face-like cloud. I was ready to resist anything it threw at me; I was not prepared to die. Although I was rattled, a little groggy, and a bit disoriented, I recognised my father's voice. I realised then that I had been having a nightmare.

"You were shouting in your sleep," said Joe Weggo, a patronising smile on his face. "You must've had a bad dream. You should tell me all about it when I get back from the farm. I am going ahead; you'll find me there . . . if you desire to come. You've been avoiding the farm for several days now."

Without waiting for a response, Joe Weggo walked out of the semi-dark hut with his razor-sharp machete clutched under his armpit. The hem of his faded blue gown trailed behind him, sweeping the dusty ground of the floor in my room.

My father believed in dreams and claimed that he could interpret any dream ever experienced. Fellow villagers believed in and respected his interpretations without question. They had to one way or the other; after all, he was the village's fortune teller and witch doctor.

I knew I would not follow my father to the farm. Lately, I had come to hate the farm and everything it represented. Thus, I continued lying in my bed. In time, my eyes adapted to the semi-darkness in the little, mud-floored veranda room. Rays of golden light from the early morning sun penetrated the room through the holes in the old door and window bored by hungry woodworms. Each golden ray resembled an awesome, wriggling creature struggling to burst out of some kind of restraint, as if eager to devour me. Maybe my imagination was playing tricks on me or I was still under the spell of the nightmare. I felt cold, but I was also sweating. Incredibly, I stopped being afraid, but the pleasure only lasted moments before the fear returned.

Still lying on my back on the crude bed, I made out the thick beams that supported the old, corrugated iron and zinc roof that kept the elements out of the antique house. In its heyday, the house was the pride of my father and the entire village. As I lay there watching the beams and rafters, a strange feeling came over me: I felt unusually tired and helpless. It was as if someone had just walked over my grave.

Previous nights had been quite warm as compared to last night. In fact, it was still cold. However, I sweated profusely as if I were standing directly in the sun. I attributed this condition to the incident I in my dream. The turbulent sleep and terrible nightmare had left me badly shaken. Even though I realised that it'd only been a dream, I felt ashamed of my fear. I felt cold air gush into the room, and I quickly covered up with my inadequate, country cloth.

An unusual chill ran through my entire body as the sweat oozed out of my skin pores. In fact, we were on the threshold of the harmattan season. It was the time when nature, as if in vengeance against the people, unleashed cold, dry winds over the Sahara Desert and into all of West Africa. These winds were unusually cold and harsh due to the fine particles of sand they carried. They created painful, small, bloody cracks on already very dry lips. People inhaled sand particles with every intake of breath, and their nostrils became overwhelmingly dry, making them hurt and sometimes bleed. It was the time when skin itched. And when one scratched to relieve the itch, it left a kind of chalky residue on the body. The harmattan also caused skin to wrinkle and form elaborate, spidery patterns that were often found on patched clay soils, especially in high areas during droughts.

I was still lying in bed, a very basic affair rigged from four sturdy, forked pieces of wood. Several strong sticks made up the flat surface that held the abundant, evenly spread dry grass. The grass was concealed by lots of used brown rice sacks and additional flimsy material. This served as a mattress. Somewhere, a hard blade of grass within the mattress penetrated the covering and pricked me sharply in the small of my back. I jerked up in pain, readjusted my position, and continued to lie on my back quietly. My mind was engaged with all sorts of things. Prominent among my thoughts was the desire to review the last few years in my village, Simbaru. Here, I was Yandi Lenga. I was seventeen years old, extremely poor, and illiterate. There were no schools in Simbaru. In fact, no one from my village had ever been to school. A few had lived in Mano Junction or Kenema and could speak Krio, the lingua franca in the area. My friend Mila and I had managed to learn that fact from people who had returned from those towns to settle back in the village.

All seventeen years had been spent in the village, except when my father, compelled by business, took me along to the commercial town of Mano Junction or the provincial headquarters town of Kenema. The only other places I had ever been were nearby villages, which were even smaller than mine. And the farm. Yes, the farm. The farm has always been there, and as far as I could see, it would still be there a hundred years hence. I had worked the land since I was five years old, as expected of every man, woman, and child who lived under the auspices of my father. There was nothing more important than working on the farm. It was what almost everyone did in Simbaru.

Working on the farm was not easy. It was manual labour, back-breaking work. Daylight never met you in town, and night fell on you on the farm or on your way home. Farming was a daily dawn-to-dusk task. We worked Monday through Sunday, all year long, rain or shine. We used primitive tools such as the machete, axe, and hoe. These were the most important tools in subsistence farming. There were no machines to make the work easier.

We used the machete to clear all the undergrowth of the forestland used as farmland. The axe was for felling all the big trees in the area and cutting them into sizable logs for use as firewood. We used hoes to do most of the back-breaking work of ploughing, sowing, and weeding. Farming was an annual activity, and there was no end to the work involved. Moreover, every year, the farm relocated to a new area to allow used farmland to fallow.

We never cultivated enough food to meet the requirements of the family. This annual problem was hard to avoid. It became customary for father to take loans in advance from the local trader in order to survive the rainy season, when food was scarce. Of course, father always repaid the loans with interest in cash or in kind, normally from the proceeds of the very first harvests. Failing to repay a loan meant one was untrustworthy. Getting a loan from the local trader was a matter of trust; if one abused that trust, one would be out in the cold with no one to turn to for help.

Father had to sell most of what we produced, including the cocoa, coffee, kola nuts, and other cash crops. Still, there was never enough money. We never wore nice clothes, and we were often hungry during the rainy season. I had tried working harder and longer, putting in my best efforts to help the family increase its financial status, but I failed miserably. The family remained poor and hungry. Father was responsible for scores of people in his household (most were extended family members). There were simply too many mouths to feed—too much responsibility, not enough income.

While still in bed, I shifted onto my stomach. I was comfortable with my right hand supporting my chin. My head was slightly raised above the single pillow. I remained completely silent for a while, but one question kept nagging my conscience: What have I achieved to date? Every time I engaged this question in the past, I had a ready answer: nothing. As of late, I felt like nothing, a nobody, a helpless nonentity.

I've achieved absolutely nothing. If I remain in this village, I'll always be nothing. Deep down, I don't believe I was cut out for life on the farm. I want to do something else with my life other than farming—something I can be proud of, something to make my parents proud, something that can help me break the poverty cycle afflicting my family. But I'll never achieve that in this village. I'll have to leave. I must seriously think of it and . . . I did not complete the sentence in my mind. I suddenly thought of something more alarming than my present plight. *Come the dry season, my parents will arrange a marriage between Kona, one of Mila's sisters, and me.* The thought provoked a wince on my solicitous, youthful face. I felt sweat break out on my forehead. *There is no way I'm going to get married. Whatever happens, I must leave this village before the dry season; otherwise, I'm forever doomed. Once married, it will be children and more children. And then it will be a second wife and more children. And then a third wife and even more children.*

The scenario seemed grim. It was completely unacceptable. I vowed then to leave Simbaru sooner than I had anticipated. It was going to be my little secret; I would tell no one. Actually, I would be obliged to tell someone: I would tell Mila. I would invite him to take a plunge into the unknown—take a chance—take his life into his own hands. If Mila accepted, it would be thrilling. If he did not, I was prepared to leave without him. I believe that one must be in control of one's life and destiny before one can succeed. I believe that I took charge of my destiny the moment I started thinking about a change of scene. If he declined to leave, Mila could do whatever he fancied with his destiny. After all, it was his life. However, I was hopeful that he would agree to leave with me.

Sitting up on the coarse affair that passed for my bed, I peered through the holes in the door. It was just before dawn. Early risers sought to keep the morning chill at bay by huddling around little fires, hands extended over the naked flames and embers. Unless one dressed in heavy clothing, the warmth gained never lasted long. But most people in Simbaru did not dress heavily—they couldn't afford to. They wore cheap, second-hand clothes, clothes that did not provide adequate warmth. The villagers wore clothes more to avoid going naked than to keep warm.

I peered through the holes in the door again while thinking, *This is no life for me. I must try to leave this village. I must try to leave Simbaru very soon.*

2

I threw my inadequate, threadbare cotton cover to one side and got out of bed reluctantly. And then I started towards the fires in the village square. Kindled from dry logs, condemned vehicle tyres, and other combustible materials, the little fires burned brightly in the open air. The jumping yellow flames threw ghostly shadows on the clean, sandy ground and the surrounding fruit trees. The flames danced according to the direction and strength of the ample morning breeze. I watched as they swayed solemnly at one moment before lurching to and fro like a well-fed, singing lark. I made my way to one of the groups around the fires. It was my favourite group, and I knew all the people present. I saw Pa Gibril, the carpenter; Saidu Korah, the driver; Lansana Kpaka, the blacksmith; Jaya, the mason; and others. They all murmured, "Good morning," and I knew they were genuinely happy to see me. I replied in equal fashion.

My best friend, Simila Jabba (*Mila* for short), was also there to greet me personally and heartily. "Yandi Lenga!" he shouted with visible pleasure as he got up to join me. We walked a few yards away from the others. "I suppose you'd a good night. Anything new under the sun?" he asked.

"Not really," I replied, "I thank God that I'm alive and well, but every day seems to be the same. No changes. Nothing will ever change for us here."

"There you go again. Why be so pessimistic?" said Mila with mock horror. His face was so comical that I had to try hard not to laugh. "All is not gloom and damnation. Optimism is the word. It leads to those positive changes that are so evidently lacking in your miserable life," he observed with finality. It was as if he would be the one to oversee those changes.

This was proper Mila speaking. Apart from himself, everyone in his circle either lacked optimism or was shy of what he referred to as positive optimism. I couldn't even begin to conjecture the number of intense arguments he had had with people he branded pessimistic, myself included.

I knew he was trying to trick me into an argument, but I was not ready for one so early in the morning (or anytime else, for that matter). I just took a deep breath and denied his accusation. "I'm optimistic," I protested. "What positive changes are you talking about anyway? The positive aspects of working on the farm all day long with no personal rewards? Or the positive qualities bound up in waiting on our parents to provide us with basic food, clothes, and shelter? Is that how man must live? There is nothing here for me—for us, Mila. I hate this life. I must do something about it, and I'm going to do it soon. I'll have to leave this village. I'm seriously considering making a long journey away from this place."

"That's good news!" Where'll you go—on a journey to join your great ancestors?"

"That would be far better than staying in this place," I replied.

"Count on me to be punctual and very loud at your funeral. Because you are my best friend, I may even wear my green T-shirt with the "Boozy Big Joe" caption on the front? On the back it says, "Only here for the beer." I may even wear that to make sure you go in good humour," he concluded as he erupted in rolls of laughter. Mila, like me, was illiterate, and he had memorised the captions on his T-shirt after a friendly visit by a student from Kenema. The student read the words to Mila and made him repeat the slogans hundreds of times until he knew them by heart.

I smiled at the joke but I was determined to make him listen with some degree of seriousness. "You're the same old Mila," I said solemnly, "Even when I'm being absolutely staid, you never take things seriously. Look at our parents and their parents before them. What did they achieve, what quality did they add to their lives? We found them poor, and we'll forever be poor if we remain in Simbaru."

Mila shrugged his shoulders but didn't say a word. Nevertheless, his facial expression revealed he was still amused by my idea. I ignored his jolly face and continued talking: "Anyway, I meant I'm thinking of leaving this village for good to begin a new life in a place where no one knows me, where I can find something fulfilling and rewarding to do. In fact, I'd be happy to go to any place as long as it takes me out of this miserable town. Even if you're not thinking about what to do with your life, I think about what to do with mine. I think of what to do with mine every day, and I try to do something about it."

After reflecting, I realised I was being a little uptight with my friend, so I attempted to put him at ease: "As for dying, God decreed that you'll die before me. Make no mistake about that, man, you'll definitely die before me." We both laughed and walked further away from the fires, towards the river almost a mile away from the village. I believe the rebuke I rained on Mila affected him deeply. Maybe it touched something in his personality because he sounded apologetic.

"I'm really sorry," he said. I thought you were just larking about." I said, "I've never been more serious in my life. You may come with me if you wish. I would love it if you decided to come along. It would be fun."

Mila didn't say anything until we cleared the village. We'd taken the wide footpath that led directly to the river. Lined with cocoa and coffee trees, the ripe fruits and slightly damp vegetation vented a combined odour of the sweetest smelling flowers I could imagine.

"I'll have to think about this one," he said suddenly. "The proposition is fine, but it's too sudden. I can't make a decision now. I need some time, but I'll let you know my decision soon. Right now, though, Mama is expecting me to help her prepare for market this morning. I have to go."

"It's all right, you've to go, but remember: I expect an answer from you soon. I don't have much time to linger around here anymore."

"Oh, give me a break," he said, "You'll get your answer sooner than you expect. There's no need for worry. One more thing you must know: you really are going to die before me, you know. You're." He guffawed as he hurried away to his mother's house.

I continued towards the River Woa for my early morning dip. As usual, regardless of the season, the water was very cold but equally refreshing. Afterward, I felt like a different person, but the strange dream still lingered in my mind.

3

The day passed quickly for me. Maybe it was the dream: the vision lurked in my mind, refusing to go away, usurping my thoughts. The dream kept resurfacing whenever I tried to confine it. It penetrated my thoughts one too many times for my comfort. Though I fought against it vehemently, it repeatedly tried to creep out of its confinement to torment me. Somehow, however, I managed to incarcerate it in a corner of my brain that kept it concealed for long periods of time. Due to that stroke of luck, I was able to put together a tentative plan of action for the journey I'd resolved to undertake. I decided to meet up with Mila to ask about his decision. If he agreed to go, I would tell him my plan.

I was home, back in the little, mud-floored room where I experienced that terrible dream. Even after so much time passed, I still envisaged that distinctive creature with unblinking, flaming, red eyes. I recalled its protruding, flaming, red tongue drooping over its thick lower lip. I shivered and huddled my legs together. *It was only a dream,* I told myself. *There's really nothing to it.*

Evening arrived as the moved slowly beyond the distant range of mountains known as the Kamboi Hills. Its last golden rays rained on the village, creating a bright, yellow glow in the village and on the vegetation. With a cacophony of different calls, birds were already hurrying to roost. Some of the domestic birds continued scratching the ground frantically, trying to get a last meal of insects or grains of rice that inevitably fell from the housewives' cooking utensils. Ducks, followed by their fluffy ducklings, waddled over to the nearby banana trees to huddle in little groups in preparation for nightfall. Thin, hungry dogs wandered around the cooking areas; they picked up and devoured scraps of discarded food. At times, they gulped down fresh feces recently excreted by a poor toddler. Occasionally, the dogs got lucky and snatched pieces of meat or fish from the baskets of the women when they were not looking. This theft caused the women to throw things at them and scream obscenities.

From the woods surrounding the village, chattering, cheeky monkeys descended and attempted to steal fruits and other goodies from the women's baskets. Shrieking women and children armed with their voices, sticks, and stones chased them away. Sometimes, though, the monkeys succeeded: they raided whole baskets of fruits when security was lax or not very efficient. They bolted into the woods with their trophies, and in seconds, they were high up in tree branches, greedily munching the fruits and chattering excitedly. As soon as the stolen goodies were consumed, the monkeys started the process all over again. Eventually, the women decided to store the baskets inside their houses. This was a daily exercise for both parties. Nevertheless, the women and children never learned. Maybe they just loved the distraction that the invading animals provided. After all, such escapades were more entertaining than the long hours spent on the farm in scorching temperatures or under incessant rain. They always dumped their baskets of food haphazardly on the clearance used as an open kitchen, and the monkeys never failed to grab some food.

Joe Weggo, my devoted dad, had returned from the farm along with many other inhabitants of the town. I knew this fact because of the buzz evident in the little town. Wives, children, and other family members were rushing out to greet and welcome fathers, uncles, and mothers. Everyone wanted to see what had been brought home for the evening meal. I could hear the dissonance of voices at our front gate and the distinctive calls—"*Ngoh*"—from the wives. The children cried out for their fathers.

I got up from my rickety bed and went outside to greet my father. By the time I reached him, the women and children were already on their way to the backyard, chattering excitedly about some dead animal Papa had brought home. By the shape of its head, horns, and feet, I reckoned it was a gazelle. The animal's throat was already cut. Thick, black, clotted blood (almost the colour of marmite) crusted around its limp neck. Papa must've caught the animal in one of his numerous traps. My father didn't own a gun. He and the other men of the village went hunting with dogs, nets, sticks, and cutlasses. In fact, only Pa Saffa owned a gun. That gun was the ancient kind that needed to be stuffed with gunpowder and lit before it could be fired.

"Hello, Papa," I said as I reached him. "Welcome back. How was the farm?" Without missing a beat, he smiled at me and said, "I want to see you now. In my room. Follow me."

I followed Papa meekly, wondering what the issue was. I reckoned it was about the dream. He was going to give me an interpretation. My father never had time to waste; he tackled things quickly and effectively.

"Sit over there by the foot of the bed," he ordered. Magbindi, his youngest wife, was also in the room. She was pretending to be busy with something. "Go help the others with the cooking," he commanded in order to get rid of her. Magbindi left the room quicker than lightning. Though she was quite young, she had realised quickly that she must obey her husband and show no signs of dissent.

I sat down by the foot of the bed as Papa instructed. He sat close to me and cleared his throat. He withdrew a whole red kola nut and divided it neatly in two before giving me one half and keeping the other half for himself. He raised his half of the nut and gestured to me to do the same. He recited some incarnations after which he took a bite from the bittersweet fruit. I followed suit and remained quiet while I chewed. Only the crunchy sound of the fresh kola nut was audible until his voice startled me: "Where're you planning to go, my son?" he asked solemnly. "I know you're planning to go somewhere, so don't deny it."

I was too surprised to answer the question immediately. Only one thought came to mind: *Mila must have betrayed me. But Mila has never betrayed me. We've done so many naughty things together and never betrayed each other. Why should he betray me now?* I willed that thought out of my mind. After all, father was a fortune teller and should know everything. In my confusion, I managed to blurt out an answer: "I'm not planning to go anywhere, Papa"

"Yandi, you mustn't lie to me. You must tell me if you've plans to go anywhere, to leave this village. You must tell me."

"I'm going nowhere," I repeated stubbornly.

"All right. I know you're planning to leave this village, but I'll bring myself to believe you for now. Tell me about the dream you had this morning."

"They say it is bad to interpret dreams at dusk or at night."

"So who's the witchdoctor here? I don't suppose it's you, do you? Tell me the dream now."

"Well it was like this," I began. I then proceeded to tell him the dream just as it happened. When I finished my narration, Papa sat for quite a while. He was motionless and quiet. He appeared troubled.

"Hmm," he grunted at a last, "that was a strange dream. And not a good one at all. It spells danger. It means you'll fall into danger and may even lose your life."

He paused for a while to look at me intently before he solemnly continued: "The thick, black cloud you saw rushing towards you means danger, and it is not far from you. The cloud changing into a horrible face also means danger. Its aura, which you felt squeezing you, signifies that you or someone close to you will die soon. This is an important and revealing dream, and you must take it seriously. You must tell me where you are planning to go, my son. You really should."

Though tempted to tell him the truth, I resisted because I feared that he would forbid and physically restrain me from leaving. "I'm not going anywhere, Father," I lied. "If I were, I would tell you. You don't have to worry. I'm going to stay in this village and take over when you get old or when you cross over to the other side."

"That would be a long time yet, crossing over to the other side," he said with great confidence. It was as if he knew when he would die. "I believe you, my son. However, something tells me that you're going to do something stupid. Whatever it is, Son, it may lead to some serious consequences. You may lose your life in the process." He paused again for a while before continuing, "The best I can do is to offer sacrifices to the gods for your protection and leave all else to fate. You may leave now." He reached for his old transistor radio on the small table at the head of the bed and switched it on.

Taking great care to avoid looking apprehensive, I left him and returned to my room where I waited for the evening meal. I was deep in thought and pacing like an angry lion in confinement. I kept going over what had transpired between Papa and me. *How did he know I was leaving? And the dream's interpretation, that's not what I expected. It is too severe an interpretation, and now I'm having second thoughts. Second thoughts aside, why would I want to remain in a village where there is no future for me? I don't want to walk in my father's footsteps. Look where it landed my ancestors after all these years. There is nothing worthwhile to show for it, only poverty, suffering, and illness.*

Someone knocked on the door. It opened to reveal my seven-year-old cousin, Morie. He was carrying a bowl of rice and vegetable soup for me. I took the bowl from him and opened the lid. The delicious smell of fresh gazelle meat wafted into my nose. I immediately washed my hands and began eating. Morie was still standing and grinning sheepishly, very sure of himself. I knew what he wanted. I dipped my hand in the soup bowl and handed him a piece of meat. With the meat safely in his hand, he turned round and sprinted away from the room. As he ran, he shouted a gleeful *thank you* back at me. I closed the door and enjoyed one of the best meals I had eaten in days.

4

I found Mila eating a sizable portion of rice and vegetables cooked in palm oil in his mother's house. "Join me," he invited cheerfully. I declined, murmuring, "I've just eaten." He didn't try to persuade me. He was a glutton, but he refused to admit it.

He was eighteen, sturdily built, good-looking, and strong like an ox. He was also a little thick in terms of intelligence. He was easy-going and avoided confrontations and intense arguments unless he was accusing people of pessimism.

I was the exact opposite: tall, lanky, thin, and a bit odd (I had a large, crooked nose that I inherited from my father). I was a little arrogant and stubborn, but I got on well with people. I was sharp, clever, and very willing to work profitably. I was handsome in my own way and didn't find it difficult to pull girls; they seemed to be attracted to me. I think they were attracted to something unique in me.

Mila finished eating. He unabashedly cleaned the bowl with his tongue. The bottom gleamed as if it were freshly polished. I wondered where all that food went. He washed his hands and drank a good quantity of water as if he were still hungry. He produced an enormous belch that I suspected most of the village heard. He laughed loudly and thanked his mother, Nyallay, who had moved her makeshift bench into a corner. Armed with a self-made spindle, she set about the skilful task of transforming fluffy, treated cotton into yarn.

Mila literally dragged me out of his mother's house. We strolled towards our favourite spot in the village square. We were silent until we arrived. The exposed roots of the big cotton tree served as our seat. There were little groups of people around the vicinity, but they were not too close to overhear us.

I didn't want word filtering back to my father about our intentions. That would confirm his suspicions that I was on the verge of leaving for good. If he heard anything, he would make sure to stop me. The thought alone was very depressing. Somehow, I managed to wriggle out of it and bring myself round to ask Mila about his decision.

"Well," I said, "have you made a decision yet?"

"Yes, I've. I'll go with you. I'm sure about that. However, we must go tonight. We must leave tonight. I'll have to answer to the elders' council tomorrow evening."

Although surprised that he wanted to leave almost immediately, I laughed about his meeting with the elders. Mila was a horny one. In fact, he was always horny. He had scored with many women in the village, regardless of age or beauty. He was always in trouble with husbands and other young men. He was a very well-known customer at the elders' council. There was a girlfriend, but he made sure to remain on the good side of other women in case his girlfriend failed to cater to his high sexual demands. Having bedded Adama, Saidu Korah's youngest and favourite wife, the elders were out to get him. They saw him as an imminent threat to their wives, too. Before his latest exploit, they warned him that if he continued pleasuring other people's wives, he risked exile from the village. Evidently, he hadn't heeded their warning. His poor mother was always crying and begging for forgiveness on his behalf. His father was deceased; the man died a couple of years prior when a tree he was chopping down fell on him. As was customary, Mila's uncle inherited his brother's wives and property. Unfortunately for Mila, his uncle, Marrah, didn't like him at all. He had never liked him. Nyallay, his mother, was the one who always cared for him. *Maybe Mila wants to give his poor mother a little break. That could be another reason for his decision to agree to leave with me,* I thought.

"What's so funny?" Mila asked in good humour. "A man's got to water gardens as much as possible if the flowers are to grow pretty. With the old, cunning lizards grabbing almost all the young ones available, what do you expect? We bachelors have to have a share in their marital investments. But they'll be pleased when I'm gone—correction: they'll be ecstatic!" He laughed heartily at his words.

"Delighted you're coming," I said. "However, I wasn't planning on leaving tonight. I've made no preparations, and I've no money."

"Leave that to me. I've already raided Uncle Marrah's bedroom." He removed some weak notes folded into a small ball. "At least this will take us through the first phase of our journey . . . wherever that may be."

I took the balled notes and carefully separated them. The money was barely enough to get us out of the village. I reckoned the money would only take us to the big commercial town of Kenema and said, "This money may only take us to Kenema. That's too close to home. But as you already implied, it's a start. We must think of other ways to raise money and decide on our destination."

Mila didn't have an immediate answer. He ruffled his knotty hair, giving the impression he was searching for one. I stated that his uncle reared many animals. His face brightened as it transformed into a conniving grin. "I should've thought of that myself," he said, tapping his forehead loudly as if that constituted thinking of it himself. On the other hand, he could have been punishing his brain for not coming up with the idea.

"It is a fabulous idea," he continued. "I guarantee you that I'll get the fattest one." He looked at me quizzically as a belated thought formed in his head. "You must bring something too, Yandi. Your father raises animals."

"You needn't worry about me. Of course, I'll bring something. I've now seen the sense in leaving tonight or very early in the morning. It is important that no one sees us leaving. You mustn't tell anyone about our plan. Not even our parents or girlfriends."

"Are we actually leaving tonight or early in the morning?" Mila asked.

"Early in the morning, perhaps," I said. "Papa suspects that I'm up to something. However, I think I was able to convince him otherwise."

"How come he suspects?" asked Mila.

"Never mind," I said. "As I was saying, you mustn't tell anybody. If you do, we'll be doomed; we'll be going nowhere. That would be a disaster, especially for you. You have the elders on your case."

"They can go rot in hell for all I care. Anyway, I'll not tell anyone, believe me."

"Good. When you return home, behave as usual. Get the animal as soon as you can and keep it safe. Don't get caught. The blacksmith's workshop would be perfect for a rendezvous. It's a tad out of town. We'll meet there when we're sure everyone is asleep. We'll set off from there. Only bring your most necessary things. And don't leave it too late. We wouldn't want to be caught red-handed with stolen animals, would we?" I added the last question for good effect.

"Rest assured: I won't be late."

"You may go home now. Remember to keep your mouth shut," I cautioned.

Mila turned around like a soldier, and without another word, he set out in the direction of his house. I believe he was more anxious to leave Simbaru than I was. I reckoned he was not going to tell anyone about our intentions. Satisfied, I started for home. I was feeling pleased but apprehensive at the thought of leaving everybody and everything I had ever known for an unknown future.

5

Stealing an animal was no easy feat, especially when chickens, goats, and sheep were kept together in one place. Walking home slowly, I thought of and planned a suitable way to make a sheep disappear from my father's yard. Papa was a light sleeper. He walked the compound at least three times per night to make sure everything was in order. Removing an animal as big as a sheep was going to be very difficult. However, it was very essential to our escape plan. For our trip to work, we needed more money than Mila had provided. The animals were going to provide that.

Father and mother were just about to retire to bed when I arrived at our compound. We talked for a while, exchanging greetings and small talk.

"Welcome, Son," Papa said. "We were just preparing to go to bed."

"Hello, Papa. Hello, Massey," I said. I've always called my mother by name, against tradition Fortunately, she didn't take offence (and neither did my dad).

"May God save you," Massey said, touching me affectionately on my upper arm. "I hope you're all right. You're not hungry, I suppose?"

"No, Massey, I'm full. Thanks anyway."

"Then we're going to bed," threw in my father with finality. "Good night, Son. Sleep in peace; no terrible dreams this time. Check the compound gate to make sure it's locked properly. May God look after you and have you in his safekeeping."

"Sleep well, Son," Massey said. "We'll see you in the morning, God willing. Sleep well."

"Good night, Papa. Good night, Massey," I returned with a heavy heart, aware that it might be the last time I would see them. "Sleep well."

They retired for the night as I said a final, silent goodbye silently. A feeling of guilt crept over me. I loved my folks without question; they cared for me my whole life. But I was about to disappear from their lives with no clues as to my whereabouts. That would be cruel and heartbreaking. But man must live. Staying in the village was not going to improve my lot in life. Telling them I wanted to leave for greener pastures wouldn't go down well, either. I know Papa would try to stop me by any means. He would even disown me if I refused to stay. As for Massey, she would be devastated. She would cry infinitely until I changed my mind.

I arrived in my room feeling sorry for my parents and for myself. However, there were still things to do if I was going to make the journey that night or early in the morning. I looked around to see what was worth taking with me. There wasn't much. I had just a few articles of clothing and other necessities to my name. I neatly folded my clothes and packed them in a raffia bag. Afterward, I lay flat on my back on the hard bed. The dream of the previous night invaded my brain again. But I wasn't worried about it (or Papa's gloomy interpretation of it). Still, the mental replay irritated me immensely. It took some time before I was able to force it out of my mind in order to concentrate on the urgent matter at hand.

Failure to get the sheep would mean being delayed, and a delay would mean Mila would endure the wrath of the elders council. Neither of us wanted that. I was resolved to get the sheep at any cost. I would just wait until my parents were asleep and all was completely quiet. Satisfied, I shifted into a more comfortable position and closed my eyes. I slowly drifted off to sleep, but I kept thinking of the best way to kidnap a living and noisy animal.

I woke up panicking, thinking that sleep had usurped my plan. I wasn't sure how long I was out. However, I noticed quickly that everything was quiet save the occasional bleats of sheep in the backyard and some night birds and other creatures on the hunt. I knew there were still many hours before dawn and that Mila wouldn't be at the meeting point yet. Like me, he was likely preparing to grab an animal. The thought spurred me on. I sprang up from the bed. Barefooted, I walked the short distance to the door and quietly opened it. I walked over to the window of my parents' room and listened. I heard my father's heavy snoring backed by the much quieter snoring emanating from Massey. Both snored regularly. I realised that they were fast asleep. Back in my little room, I put on my flip-flops and grabbed the raffia bag that contained my meagre belongings. I also took a strong rope from under the bed and put it in my pocket. I stood there for a while, looking around the place I had called home until that moment. I felt sadness and loneliness creep over me. I wondered whether I would ever see the place again. I wondered whether I would see my siblings and other relatives again. And my mum, I wondered what would happen to her. I thought, *She might even die due to heartbreak*. I felt fat tears roll down my cheeks before I realised I was crying. I wiped the tears away with the back of my right hand. With a heavy heart, I stepped outside gingerly. The operation to escape had begun.

Rigged out of reeds, ropes, and sticks, our backyard fence was easy to penetrate. I made up my mind that the reed fence would be my escape route once I secured the animal. The sheep were in the far corner of the yard. There was just enough moonlight to see them huddled together. I made out the big ram with its majestic, crooked horn. I decided against it; rams were difficult to handle. I might even get a butt up my ass for my trouble. Instead, I decided to go for the biggest female. Its coat was black and white. The moonlight from above made it outstandingly beautiful.

I easily caught and secured my quarry. It wasn't as difficult as I'd anticipated. I just took some sweet potato leaves from the thatched roof of the makeshift kitchen and walked up to her with the leaves. She was eating from my hands in no time, and I was able to put the noosed rope I'd retrieved from under my bed around her neck. While I was securing the big female, the other sheep bleated every now and then. My heart was in my mouth. With every bleat, I half-expected my old man's voice to inquire what was going on. That would be a total disaster. Fortunately, I wasn't interrupted. The sheep and I eventually left the compound through a hole I made in the reed fence. Once out, I repaired the opening as neatly as I could. With my trophy chewing cud behind me, I led it out of town, towards the isolated blacksmith's workshop.

6

Mila wasn't at the blacksmith's workshop when I arrived. I soon had the creature tied to a shrub and waited anxiously for Mila to show up. However, I was determined to leave on my own if he failed to appear. Thankfully, that wasn't to be: he emerged from the bushes with the biggest ram I'd ever seen and a small raffia bag slung over his left shoulder. His right hand pulled vigorously at the rope that was noosed round the reluctant animal's neck. He beckoned me closer so I could help him secure the animal. I took the ram from him, and with much effort, I tied it on the other side of the workshop. I didn't want the animals together because they might start bleating, and that would surely alert the villagers to a potential problem.

"I'd no problem catching this big brute from the farm," Mila quipped as he brushed off leaves, small twigs, and insects from his clothing. "My younger brother, Jayman, helped me."

I couldn't believe what I was hearing. How could he have let his brother help him? His brother would definitely tell their father in the morning. I was angry that he had allowed himself to be so careless, but I was in no mood to reprimand him—that would only delay us further. "We must be going now," I said. "If we don't leave, we will probably be discovered with these stolen animals."

Mila made no answer. He went straight to the ram and removed a rope from his pocket. He knelt down beside the animal, grabbed both its hind legs, and tied them together. He repeated the same procedure with the forelegs before untying the ram from the spot where it was tethered. He manhandled the animal and draped it round his neck like a loose cloak; he held the drooping, tied limbs over his shoulders to secure the animal from falling off.

"Come along, then," he called cheerfully. He started along the windy footpath out of the village and added, "I'm ready."

I copied Mila. I soon had my animal draped over my neck as well. With mixed feelings, I followed Mila meekly. I was afraid I would never see the village again. I felt very sad, and as if on cue, both animals bleated feebly in a way that echoed my sadness. It was as if they knew that our lives were never going to be the same again. I turned around and gave the village one last look, and then I trotted to catch up with Mila who was already scores of yards ahead.

We did the uneventful five miles to the main road in just under two hours. Not long after arriving, we were able to board a goods vehicle to the big commercial town of Kenema. Once we were in that vehicle, Mila expressed his jubilance: "I'm free!" he said. "There will be no more idle, old men to reckon with."

I agreed, but I reminded him that our parents and relatives were going to be very sad. He became less jubilant. In Kenema, after a long and colourful haggling that involved lots of bluffing and swearing to the Almighty, we sold the animals to an animal trader. Somehow, we reckoned the trader knew that we'd stolen the animals and were desperate to sell. However, in the end, he paid us enough money to cover our travel and other expenses for a while. I added it to the money that remained from Mila's initial donation. I hoped we would find something to do before the money ran out.

We decided to go to Kono while we were in the goods vehicle. We heard many intriguing stories about Kono. It was the place to go if your ambition was to get rich. It was no secret that the place was full of diamonds, and sometimes, when it rained heavily, lucky people found the precious stones on the surface of the newly eroded ground. We had also heard stories of people getting rich from mining diamonds.

Mila was very excited and happy that we were going to Kono. As far as I knew, he had only left our village a few times before. Even then, he had only managed to get to Mano Junction, a town much smaller than Kenema. "We'll soon be rich people," he said when we reached Kenema. He was smiling with satisfaction.

"I hope so," I replied, praying that his prediction would come true. "Then we'll have no fear of returning to the village."

7

The journey to Kono was long. It took more than six hours before we arrived. Luckily, we were travelling in style. We were lodged cosily within the confines of a beautiful Hino bus with about two scores of passengers all heading for Kono. The views along the unpaved road were spectacular, especially as we got closer to our destination. The thick forest vegetation that had been the main source of scenery began to change into a savannah landscape as we drew closer. There were long elephant grasses covering vast areas; a few bushes and a great many palm trees dotted the landscape. The eye could see far. We were amazed. We had never seen anything like it before. In our part of the country, we had a solid jungle amid the hills.

The houses along the road also became different. The language was different, too, and it sounded foreign to us. But I was not discouraged because Krio was the common language spoken throughout the country. Judging by the contentment visible on Mila's face, I guessed that he was not discouraged either. I believed that we would love it in our new city. I believed we'd succeed or die trying.

About five hours into the journey, the driver slowed down and stopped by the side of the road. He climbed down from his driver's cab and came to the main section of the bus, where all the passengers were concentrated.

"In half an hour," he announced with a lit cigarette clenched between his lips, "we'll arrive at Mamoudu checkpoint. So if there is any male in this vehicle without a resident or entry permit, you must see me now."

He got off the vehicle and walked a few yards. Mila and I had never heard about permits, and we had no idea what would be required to enter Kono. We didn't have any of the documents the driver had mentioned, so we walked the short distance to meet him. Three other men joined us. The driver explained that, because the five of us didn't have documents, we needed to contribute money to bribe the officers to let us in. "Without doing that," he cautioned solemnly, "it is almost impossible to get in."

All five of us gave him the money he requested and boarded the bus again. We drove for a little while before the bus stopped at a long bamboo pole. It was laid horizontally across the width of the road as a barrier; there were two empty drums used for support on either side. The driver went to meet the officers in charge in their makeshift hut. He came back with two police officers who promptly boarded the bus and started inquiring for permits. When they got to Mila and me, they didn't ask for anything. I noticed, too, that they didn't ask the three men who had contributed money with us. The police officers finished checking the permits, and at last, they raised the long bamboo pole to allow the bus to pass through. We were safe. I was relieved.

The next phase of our journey saw us passing through many villages, some that were very small, others that were quite big. They all seemed to be overcrowded and bustling with activity. The inhabitants were better dressed than the people in our village. In most villages, there were many stalls by the roadside selling a variety of goods ranging from food to mining paraphernalia. Mila was very impressed; I was, too. "Yandi," he said brightly, "there's evidence of money in this place. Look at all the things they have to sell in the shops. I'm glad we came."

"God willing, Mila," I replied with equal enthusiasm, "we'll soon be counted as one of those people."

"Are we there yet, Yandi?"

"How would I know? I've never been to this place before."

"Then we should ask," he promptly returned.

"You are free to," I said.

Mila turned to a man sitting behind us. The man was like a chimney: he smoked a cigarette every five minutes or so. Mila and I didn't smoke, but we didn't mind the man and others smoking in the small confinement of the vehicle. Besides, even if the other passengers didn't like it, we couldn't do anything.

"Have we arrived in Kono yet?" Mila asked politely. The man took a cigarette out of his mouth, smiled, and answered informatively, "Yes, young man. Actually, you have been in Kono since the checkpoint. Where are you going? Kono is a big place and has many towns and villages."

"We want to go to the largest town," I answered.

"That must be Koidu Town. It is the district headquarters, and this bus will be terminating there," said the man, returning the cigarette to his lips and puffing fervently to keep it glowing. "We'll be there in less than an hour, but that depends on the driver."

8

Almost an hour after the checkpoint, the bus came creaking to a stop in a crowded space full of people, other vehicles, and different types of handcarts. It was just after midday. Koidu turned out to be sprawling and busy. The streets, most of which were riddled with deep potholes and pungent, muddy waters, were full of different types of motor vehicles and lined with attractive houses and shops. Most of the shops, as Mila and I would learn later, belonged to Lebanese or Fulani traders. They sold everything from sweets to safety matches to the specially treated circular wood used to make the big sieves used in diamond mining.

Here we were, two ignorant, young men in a strange town. We knew no one. We didn't even know what to do or where to begin. For more than an hour after our arrival, we stayed in the same place, observing and admiring all that we saw. We grew hungry and made some inquiries about eating houses. A smartly dressed woman in the traditional attire of Docket and Lappa pointed out a place a little farther up the road.

"There's a nice one just down this road," she said cheerfully. You can't miss it; it's painted bright yellow."

The food was nice, and my hunger was satisfied before I finished the contents of my bowl. Mila, however, continued eating until his bowl was completely empty. I passed him my unfinished bowl, and he ate ravenously, like a very hungry animal.

The woman who sold us the food looked like a kind person. At first, I couldn't decide whether to tell her about our plight, but without consulting Mila, I opted to walk over to her. Speaking in Krio, I explained that we were newcomers, homeless, and hoping to work in the mines but didn't know where to begin.

"Oh!" she exclaimed, "Is that all? You don't have to worry any longer. On Main Motor Park, you can find anything you want. My name is Finda Bondu, but everyone calls me Mama Finda. I would like you to call me that, too."

"Thank you, Mama Finda," I said dutifully and politely.

Dead End Poverty

I wondered why she was called Mama Finda. In my eyes, she was just a young woman who was very pretty and merry. She had a captivating, sexy, lopsided smile. She didn't deserve the appellation *mama*. In my mind, *mama* referred to a middle-aged or old woman, and Mama Finda was not an old woman by any means.

"Now as for the mining thing," Mama Finda said, "I know many people who are involved in the diamond trade. I'll definitely set you up with someone as soon as the opportunity arises. People are always on the lookout for healthy, strong, young men like you. By the way, what are your names?"

"I'm Yandi, and that's Mila over there."

Laughing gaily, she said, "Good. Wait over there with your friend while I try to sort you out. As soon as I get things arranged, I'm sure you'll be okay. So don't fret yourselves anymore, you'll soon have work and a place to stay."

By late afternoon, Mama Finda and a well-dressed man came to meet us. "This is Mr Kalilu, the local yullaman and supporter," she explained. "He mines and buys most of the diamond in this area."

We stood up to greet the elaborately (but oddly) dressed man. He had on a three-piece, yellow suit, a bright red shirt, and a purple necktie that almost reached his groin. His shoes were bright green and his socks were brown. He looked like a cheerful, colourful, and active person. His disposition seemed quite friendly. He was a big man, too, and we felt his physicality when he shook our hands with vigour and enthusiasm. His grip was very strong and a little painful.

"I'm very glad to meet you," he said in a booming voice.

"Yandi and Mila," said Mama Finda in her sweet, quiet voice. "I want you to go with Mr Kalilu. Don't be afraid; he will take good care of you and help you get into mining, which is what you want to do."

Mama Finda was a crafty businessperson. She had affiliations with most of the prominent people involved in mining. There was a concrete arrangement in place: they paid her a little for any new hand she found for them. However, she negotiated with each miner and dealer separately. She knew Mr Kalilu would return sometime the next day to give her the two hundred leones he owed her for her latest finds. She smiled contentedly.

"Yes, Mama Finda," Mila and I said in unison, glad that we found someone so soon to help us lock down employment and lodging.

"Well don't just stand there, grab your things and go with him before it gets very dark," our female benefactor said. "Before you know it, you may be richer than you have ever imagined. Hope you remember me when that happens," she concluded while laughing.

Her melodious laughter was still ringing in our ears as we followed our showman benefactor to a battered Land Rover he had parked down the road. We drove along the rough roads of the town, weaving our way among various vehicles, people, cats, stray dogs, and handcarts known locally as *omolankes*. The evening was bustling with activity and full of life. There was loud music blaring from powerful speakers in various shops. Little crowds of children, young men, and young women gathered at the sources of the blaring music. They wriggled their bodies to the rhythms, employing different forms of provocative gyrations. It was chaotic but noticeably peaceful. The girls seemed to be prolific dancers. They wriggled their bottoms in a variety of sensuous, sexual simulations that left many red-blooded, young men hot and flushed.

Mila and I had our eyes glued to the side windows of the old Land Rover, missing nothing of interest. Some of the things we saw were actually new to us, such as the beautiful, elegant Opera Cinema building.

"That's the Opera Cinema," said a proud Mr Kalilu, as if he were the owner. "It has more than five hundred seats inside. It's the most beautiful and expensive of the two main cinemas we have in this town. I know you'll want to go there when you get your first diamond money. You may want to go to the Hollywood Cinema, too. But the Opera is more beautiful and most comfortable. No bed bugs."

Mila and I were impressed with the building, as well as many others we saw. We were also happy to learn that we could go there one day if we had money. To think that I, Yandi Lenga, and my friend, Mila, could grace such a building with our presence was unbelievable. Nevertheless, we believed that we would go there one day. Hadn't the bigwig, Mr Kalilu, predicted it himself?

A mixture of concrete and mud houses lined both sides of most of the roads. Mesmerisingly decorated with murals depicting cultural activities and occupations in the area, the houses were a source of pleasure for the eyes. Although the light was fading, I was able to see the murals quite clearly. There were paintings of men in diamond pits, women carrying children on their backs or breastfeeding them, and mature women with cone-like, naked breasts that jutted out from their chests like the peaks of mountains. There were also scenes of police officers arresting miners and other interesting events. The colours were great and seemed to be a mixture of all hues imaginable. I enjoyed them immensely and assumed Mila did too given his unabashed gawking at the murals.

"I see you are enjoying the view," said Mr Kalilu. "You'll enjoy it even more when you get to know the town better. There're lots to see. If you are interested in women, you've come to the right place. As long as you have money, you've got them."

Mila, who did not appear to be listening, piped in, "Did I hear you say women?" He wore a mischievous smile on his face. "I love this place already. Did you hear that Yandi? Women!"

We all laughed like old friends. The Casanova in Mila couldn't stay put for a long time. We drove past a big building from which blasted the loudest noise I had ever heard apart from thunder.

"That's the power station," our benefactor pointed out. "The generators producing that noise supply this town with electricity. And the other big building you see on your right is the police station. We simply call it Tankoro. Everyone knows Tankoro."

It was a big, high, brown building with a huge cotton tree in front of it. An equally huge roundabout that circled the tree allowed vendors to sell a variety of foodstuffs, cigarettes, and other commodities from the centre. Several police officers were engaged in different activities short of police business. Some were openly flirting with the female vendors or passers-by. Others were talking among themselves or buying something.

"Tankoro is where they take you when you are arrested," said Mr Kalilu. "Arrested?" Mila and I asked in unison, alarmed. Mr Kalilu answered, "Yes, arrested—by the security forces of the NDMC. That's short for the National Diamond Mining Corporation. Anyone arrested for illegal mining or another crime will be thrown in jail in Tankoro. It's the miners who make up the majority of those arrested."

"Why are the miners arrested?" Mila inquired. "Because most bosses of the miners don't procure mining licences in the first place," Mr Kalilu explained. "Those bosses who procure licences don't get their miners arrested as long as they mine on the sites the licenses indicate."

"But I'm sure you have a license," I said hopefully. Mr Kalilu laughed cheerfully. In our ignorance, we looked on with confusion and embarrassment. "The answer to your question is *no,*" continued Mr Kalilu. "I don't have a license. Not everyone has one. Very few people bother to get one."

"We don't want to be arrested," said Mila. "We only want to mine diamonds. We don't want to be arrested at all." There was a hint of apprehension in his voice. "No need to worry about that," said Mr Kalilu. "Even if you were arrested, there's a way to bring you out almost immediately. In this town, money is the key to many problems in all walks of life."

I assumed Mr Kalilu knew what he was talking about. We cleared the town and joined a beautiful tarmac road. It was the best we had seen since we started the drive. Mr Kalilu hit the controls, and the old jalopy (with a grinding noise and a slight shudder) responded at once. I felt a change in the speed. The old tub was actually overtaking newer-looking vehicles on the road. Our host seemed to be satisfied with the vehicle's performance. He burst into a song, singing the actual words for a while and then whistling along. Mila and I just sat there, digesting the scenery and wondering what would become of us.

It was night when we arrived at a town. We left the main road and took a dirt road that led us directly to the town. It was very dark along the road, but the headlights of the old jalopy danced across the surrounding vegetation as it bumped its way to our destination. Once, we saw a troupe of monkeys crossing the road with tiny youngsters clinging to their backs for dear life. We also forded two small streams where some antelope that had been having a drink galloped away majestically, like kings on their horses. Mr Kalilu coaxed the old vehicle until the dirt road suddenly terminated in what appeared to be the town square. The wailing sounds of music coming from tape recorders and transistor radios greeted us. Some people had their radios close to their ears; others held them in their hands like handbags.

The town was a small one, but it was a couple of times bigger than Simbaru. Mr Kalilu drove slowly between the houses, and before long, he stopped in front of a very big compound that was fenced all around with sturdy sticks and palm fronds.

"We've arrived," announced our host buoyantly. "This is where I was born and bred. I've lived in this town all my life. Wherever I go, I always come back to Yengema. I can never stay anywhere else for long."

"It looks like a nice town," I ventured, wanting to please.

"It is a nice town," he said simply but with real feeling.

"Yes, it is," I agreed.

I saw the semblance of a smile appearing on his big jolly face. He added, "I am beginning to like you. You'll enjoy it here; this is home now. We've to find Sahr. He'll make you comfortable. I'll be placing you in his gang."

We climbed down from the vehicle, our sorry raffia bags slung over our shoulders. We followed Mr Kalilu through the open gate and were amazed at what we saw. Our heads were wagging from side to side, trying to take everything in at once. The compound was very big and well lit. Somewhere in the background, I heard a generator moaning, hard at work to supply electricity to the big compound. I counted more than thirty houses in plain view. They were built along the four walls of the fence, and they left a big, spacious area in the middle of the compound. Also visible were smaller structures behind the houses. I assumed they were latrines. The compound was like a big workshop, and there was a huge well in the centre of the yard. Several rubber buckets made out of tyres were nestled on the broad, concrete structure that formed the mouth of the well. Attached to long, thick, twined, nylon ropes, the rubber buckets enabled people in the compound to draw water.

Seemingly, the space provided a communal venue for many daily activities in the village. The women and children were engaged in cooking the evening meal and other household chores. The men were busy making new (or mending old) sifters, locally known as *shakers later*. Eventually, we learned that the name derived from the shaking and wriggling actions involved in washing gravel to discover diamonds. Some of the younger men stood by, talking among themselves. Sometimes, they teased the women who passed by. Some played card games and other traditional games. I noticed that some people sat idle, dreaming away or fortifying themselves for the heavy work ahead. Whatever they were engaged in, the men in the compound looked strong and rough. That fact was evident in their physical features and demeanours.

We followed Mr Kalilu obediently. We meandered across the yard through people, things, and animals (including dogs, cats, chickens, goats, and sheep). We stopped in front of a large, mud-brick house. Several hammocks hung from sturdy rafters along the long veranda. Bodies leisurely whiling the time away until it was time to leave for work occupied some of the hammocks. I had never seen so many hammocks hung along one veranda.

"This is where Sahr lives. You will be staying here, too," Mr Kalilu explained. "Sahr will make you comfortable and teach you all you want to know. He's a good teacher, that Sahr. You'll see in good time."

9

Sahr was a tall, sinewy, bird-like man with a pleasant face. He was wearing neat khaki shorts and a blue, satin smock decoratively embroidered in golden thread around the neck and long sleeves. As Mr Kalilu introduced us, Sahr smiled and looked at us encouragingly, welcoming us with his solemn eyes as if he had known us for a long time. Pointing at us with straight, strong fingers, Mr Kalilu said, "This here is Mila; this here is Yandi. I'm putting them in your care to complete your work gang."

Sahr appeared to be very pleased with the news. He laughed and revealed a set of white, even teeth when he offered his hand to greet us.

"Hello, Yandi and Mila," he said as he shook our hands. After turning to our benefactor, he grabbed his right hand and pumped it profusely, gratefulness showing in his eyes as he thanked him: "And thank you, Mr K. What would I do without you?"

For a moment, Mila and I were confused by the name. Soon thereafter, Mr Kalilu, sensing our confusion, explained, "All my friends call me Mr K. You can call me that, too. You are my friends now. Good luck, and show me some diamonds soon, my friends."

Mr K, with nothing more to say, turned his back to us and walked away briskly. We stood looking after him until he disappeared into one of the other houses.

"He's a good man, that Mr K," commented Sahr. "Please come inside the house so we can see how best to make you comfortable."

We followed him through the front door and entered a big parlour with two doors on each side. There was also a back door leading outside to the kitchen and the latrine. There were mats and bundles of different sizes containing what looked like sleeping gear. Everything was packed and stowed away against the walls of the parlour. Evidently, we were in the huge sleeping place for the miners. Sahr educated us as if he knew what I was thinking: "This is where some miners sleep," he said. "Three of these rooms are occupied by my three wives and my children. I occupy the fourth room. You'll have to find a spot here to sleep. Put your bags in the place where you would like to sleep. You can use any spot as long as no one is sleeping there at the time. I'll ask one of my wives to supply you with sleeping mats. Meanwhile, you can go have a wash. There is a little stream just at the back of this compound. One of my boys will take you there. See me when you come back."

A young man not much older than us appeared shortly thereafter to lead us to the stream. His name was Tamba. It was much darker by the time we began walking, but he came prepared with a torch that he used to help us navigate the terrain leading to the stream.

"Are there crocodiles in this stream?" asked Mila, his voice portraying alarm.

"There're no crocodiles," Tamba replied. "The children spend lots of time here. To my knowledge, no one has ever reported seeing a crocodile. Besides, if there were, they would have been hunted and eaten by the locals a long time ago."

The stream water was cold but refreshing. Back at the house, Tamba took us straight to Sahr. We found him lying in one of the hammocks in the veranda. Sahr instructed Tamba to take us to his third wife, Sandivah, so that she could feed us. The food was nice (though slightly different from what we ate in Simbaru). We finished everything in the bowls and Sandivah was pleased. Mila, however, was licking his fingers so much that Sandivah asked whether we wanted some more. "Yes, thank you!" replied a very eager Mila before I had the chance to decline the offer.

I gave my friend a murderous look as Sandivah went to fetch us another helping. It was our first night; I didn't want anyone to draw any negative conclusions about us. Despite the fact that I was already full, I was determined to join Mila to divert attention from his greed. Sandivah brought another bowl of rice and vegetable soup in palm oil. We thanked her and fell to. I toyed with each handful, but Mila stuffed himself as if it were the last time he would eat. Sandivah noticed. She held my eye and smiled discreetly and brilliantly, but she didn't comment. Her eyes and smile sent a lovely tinge through my body. After the meal, we thanked Sandivah again and went to meet Sahr on the veranda.

"I see you've eaten," he said cheerfully. "I've sent Tamba to fetch the rest of the crew so that I can introduce you before we leave for work."

"Are we going to work with you tonight?" I asked.

"Not at all, young man," he replied. "You'll stay here tonight and have a good rest. Tomorrow afternoon, I'll give you a verbal orientation of what we do here and how we do it. But come now, here comes the clan."

A group of young men led by Tamba crowded the veranda and stood directly under the single electric bulb. It illuminated them very well, allowing us to see most of their features. There were five men; all of them seemed to be as old as we were. I was delighted to find that we would be working with cheerful, toughened, young men. Sahr did not vacate the hammock. He simply shifted into a sitting position to face us and started talking.

"Hello, everyone," he said after noisily clearing his throat. The clan murmured something in return and waited.

"As you know," he continued, "we've been struggling with our work because we don't have enough men. This evening, Mr K brought me two new men. They'll be working with us. I believe you'll give them the best help you can. Now step over here, Yandi and Mila."

We left the group and stood very close to him. Pointing at me first, he said, "This is Yandi." And then he pointed to Mila and introduced him.

Clothes ruffled and voices mingled as the five young men moved to shake our hands. They shook our hands warmly and made us feel welcome. Sahr waited until all the handshaking was finished. He then used his index finger to point at each of the young men and told us their names quickly: "That is Dowu, Samson, Boima, Sumaa, and Francis. Tomorrow afternoon, you will be acquainted with each other properly. For now, duty calls. We're heading for the pits. You try to get some good sleep—you'll need it. Good night."

10

They turned off the electricity as soon as the gang left for the diamond fields. The parlour was dark save the dull glow of a single, makeshift lamp located in a corner. Already, there were some mats laid out neatly against the walls of the big parlour. Mila and I went to the spot where we'd left our bags. We found two mats covering them, on top of which lay two threadbare, cotton wrappers to serve as covers for sleeping. We carefully laid out the mats and positioned our raffia bags so that we could use them as pillows. Tiredness eventually caught up with us and we drifted into deep sleep.

I was up very early the next morning, feeling refreshed and cold. The harmattan wind was blowing harshly through the doors. Somehow, they had been left wide open at both ends. But even the cold wind couldn't wake up Mila. When I looked at him in the grey morning light that drifted into the parlour, I saw that there was a trace of a smile on his lips, which gave his whole visage a kind of sanguine appearance. I looked around the big parlour with the help of the dawn light and noticed that there were very few bodies still sleeping. I shook Mila awake; he was not very happy about my actions.

"Leave me alone. Let me get some sleep, man," he protested in a sleepy voice.

"But you must wake up," I insisted firmly.

"Why should I? I'm not going to the farm today. I am too tired to even carry a hoe."

"You are no longer home, Mila, and you'll not be going to the farm for a long time," I said and laughed quietly so as not to disturb the other men still trying to gain a few more minutes of precious sleep.

He shot up from the mat as if catapulted by an unseen force. He was rattled only for a moment before he realised where we were. He smiled apologetically and sat down quietly on his mat, disarmed of all protests. His demeanour changed to that of concentration and worry . . . and probably regret. I could tell he was thinking about home and the folks we'd left behind. He sighed sorrowfully, but then his demeanour changed again. This time, a wilful smile appeared on his face as he talked: "Our parents must be very worried and angry.

I feel for them, you know? Are you sure it was the right thing to do, leaving the village?"

This is a tricky one, I thought. *I should handle it carefully. I must make him believe that we did the right thing or he won't want to stay. This is the first time he has ever left his family. Besides, I knew he was missing his mother considerably.* Bearing all that in mind, I answered him judiciously: "Yes, Mila, we did the right thing. Here, we can make big money and return to the village as respectable people. Even the elders' council—"

"The elders' council," Mila repeated, interrupting me. "They must have been very mad when I failed to appear before them. I know they'll pursue my wicked stepfather to settle the damages on my behalf." A cynical laugh erupted from his throat, obviously satisfied that the consequence of his philandering would fall upon his wicked stepfather.

"Better him than you, Mila," I said, quickly seizing the opportunity to convince him further that we were right to leave. "Consider how long you worked for him. Did he ever do anything for you? The man's got a heart of stone."

He was about to say something when we noticed that Sandivah heading towards us. "Good morning," she said and gave us a dazzling smile.

"Good morning," we answered together, very pleased that she was finding time to talk to us.

"You must get up now or you'll be late for the morning meal. We never provide for latecomers. Off with you now to the stream. And don't stay too long unless you want to miss your breakfast."

We got up and started reaching for our mats so that we could fold them and stack them safely against the wall.

"Stop that now and get going. I'll take care of that," she said. "But you will have to get up earlier than this."

We assured her we would take her advice. Grabbing our precious bags, we raced to the river to clean ourselves. We returned to the house to find breakfast served in four giant, plastic bowls of varying colours. The meal consisted of boiled cassava in palm oil soup with lots of freshwater fish, onions, tomato, herbs, and spices. Everyone was busy eating. Sandivah saw us and instructed us to join in. On average, there were five people at each bowl, including the women and children. I looked around and saw Tamba eating from one of the bowls with two other members of the gang: Dowu and Boima. Tamba saw us, too, and he beckoned to us with his hands to join in. We needed no second invitation. We walked over eagerly.

The men did a lot of talking during the meal. Apparently, breakfast time doubled as news time. Discussions of overnight occurrences in the diamond fields and current affairs in the village took place during the morning meal. Everyone was there except for Sahr.

"Where is Sahr?" Mila asked. Does he not eat with us?

"Sahr never eats here," Dowu replied quickly, laughing as if the inquiry was very funny. "Would you eat in the backyard if you were a gang master with three wives? One of his women takes his food to him in his room."

"It's true," confirmed Tamba, "he must be a happy man this morning. We bagged one and a half carat of blue-white diamond last night."

"And a pit collapsed on some workers not too far from ours," Boima volunteered.

"But we were able to dig them out and save their lives," Tamba said quickly, realising that such news was not the best for newcomers who hadn't even been deployed in the fields yet.

I was very grateful for Tamba's timely intervention. Anything more about the topic may have spooked Mila, and I would've been left with the task of reassuring him. I looked at him and saw a man gorging on the cassava and soup. It didn't seem like he heard Boima's bleak news.

"But I'm happy," I heard Tamba say. "We'll be getting some money today after we sell the stone to Mr K. We'll be doing that as soon as Sahr is ready."

"I can't wait to go to Koidu when I get my share," said Boima. "I've been missing the life—the women especially."

Mila's food-laden hand stopped halfway between the bowl and his mouth. His favourite topic had crept into the conversation. He recovered in time to finish putting the food into his mouth. He chewed slowly, ears pricked, apparently hoping to hear more on the topic. He was disappointed: Boima didn't say anything else about women.

Dead End Poverty

We finished eating, washed our hands, and followed Tamba, Boima, and Dowu to the veranda. The hammocks were empty and inviting. We took full advantage of the situation. Tamba, Boima, and Dowu wanted to catch up on the sleep they'd missed the previous night, and Mila and I contemplated our new lives.

11

We had hardly settled into our swinging hammocks when Francis appeared. "No need to get too comfortable," he announced as he looked directly at us, "Sahr wants to see his new boys. Now."

"What about us?" Dowu inquired on behalf of the rest of the gang. "I thought he sent you to get us for the diamond sale."

"Patience, Dowu. You've to be patient. Koidu isn't going anywhere. And for that matter, neither are the girls," said Tamba.

We all laughed and followed Francis into the huge parlour. He knocked on the first door on the right. Sahr's voice was strong and laced with a ring of jubilance, probably because of the diamond find. "Come in," he said, "the door's open."

We entered the room and found Sahr sitting on his prayer mat, his feet folded underneath his body. He was holding red prayer beads. Sahr was a Muslim and it seemed like he had just finished one of his five obligatory prayer sessions for the day. He remained sitting when he gestured for us to have a seat. He politely asked Francis to leave, but he instructed him not to go far because he would need him after he was finished with us.

Sahr's room was big, beautiful, and impressively furnished. In fact, I had never seen a room so exquisitely furnished as his. The chairs were gorgeous: red leather upholstery complemented by three-legged, black Formica stools on each side of the armrests. In the far corner stood the biggest pair of speakers and component stereo set I'd ever seen. Tuned to some local station, the radio blared music in a dialect I couldn't understand. The walls of the room were plastered with cement and painted light blue; they matched the meticulously designed, white bamboo ceiling. We were still standing, afraid to sit down on such lovely seats (even after Sahr had invited us to do so). We reckoned such seats were not for people like us.

"Sit down," Sahr stated again, emphatically pointing in the direction of to the three-sitter against the wall by the window. I gingerly sat down on the edge of the chair. Mila hesitated, but encouraged by Sahr, he overcame his reservations. He sat down on the edge of the chair just like I had. I conjectured that we were afraid that contact with the beautiful piece of furniture would contaminate or destroy it. Sahr instructed us to sit farther back in our chairs. Having noticed the softness and comfort the chair provided, we needed no further encouragement. I felt like a newly crowned chieftain, pleased to be chief but anxious about the job.

"Hope you slept well," I heard Sahr say. I nudged Mila to gain his attention. I'd noticed that he was still admiring his surroundings. We slept very well and told him so. We even thanked him for the hefty breakfast his wife had given to us. He was pleased by our words.

"I won't keep you long. Just want you to know a few things about how we operate here. Rule number one: I'm the boss, and the boss is always right. Rule number two: if the boss is wrong, remember rule number one." He laughed and continued: "Friday's prayer day, a day to rest. My gang doesn't work on Fridays, but some other gangs do. The day is yours, and you may use it how you see fit. Understood?" We nodded, but he was already on to the next topic.

"Now listen carefully," he said. "My wives, Bondu, Yei, and Sandivah are out of bounds to you and everyone else. Anyone who interferes with them interferes with me. They would have to settle with me. And believe me, young men, no one wants to cross with Sahr." He said the last part of his sentence with just enough venom for Mila and I to realise that he was not making an empty threat. Still, Sahr didn't look like a hard man.

"Another important thing I want to warn you about is the cardinal sin when mining: theft. No one steals from me. No one steals from Mr K. And when I say *steal*, I mean diamonds. It'll be at your peril that you steal. We'll find you out; make no mistake about that. The punishment would be severe. You could be killed. In the fields, everyone else is watching the others at all times. You'll never know who is watching you. Do you understand?" We nodded our heads in acknowledgement.

"Very well, then, so long as we are clear on that. You will be going out with the gang tonight. You'll be learning the basic skills of the trade. Can you dig?" We nodded affirmative again. If only he knew. If there was anything we were expert at, it was digging. We had been digging all our lives. Back in the village, digging was a natural part of everyday life.

"Good," said Sahr, "now I'll tell you how we share the money we earn. First, you need to know that Mr K is our supporter. This means that he's the one that provides us with tools, food, and accommodations. He also makes sure that we sustain our good health. When we get diamonds, we sell them to him (or together, we sell to someone else). Regardless, the proceeds are always shared in the same way: supporter, shovel, work gang."

"I don't understand," I ventured.

"Never mind," he returned, "you'll understand all right as time goes by."

The supporter gets a third of the share for supporting us; the shovel gets a third of the share to maintain tool supplies and other necessities; the work gang, which means you and the others, get one third for your hard labour, which is equally divided among you. I'm not included in the work gang's share. As your leader, I get half of the shovel's share."

"That's very nice," said Mila. "I'm sure we would be pleased to work under such terms. There're no problems at all, right Yandi?"

I shook my head from side to side. "No, no problems at all," I said.

"Most of the time," continued Sahr, "the money you get amounts to nought, especially if the stones are relatively small. However, sometimes you land bigger stones and earn more money. Seldom, you get the big, clear, blue-white stones. But if you do, you'll be in real money. All the miners in this village dream of landing a big, clear stone one day."

Somewhere in my head, I visualised that big stone. In my mind's eye, it was a clear, blue-white gem with perfect corners that reflected light from every angle. How I wished that we would find such a stone quickly.

"Tamba will look after you for the first few days," Sahr was saying when I returned from my visualisation. "After that, you'll be on your own. Remember, in the field, you look after yourself. If you prove cowardly and lazy, others will see you just like that. They will probably bully you. On the other hand, if you prove strong, hardworking, and witty, you'll become the darling of the fields."

"We'll do our best, Sahr," said Mila with confidence. "We are not scared of work. We are strong, hardworking lads."

Sahr smiled and said, "I can see that. And I like what I see. You belong to my gang, and we all work for Mr K. Your loyalty is to Mr

K, myself, and the rest of the gang. We're not the only gang in the field. There're hundreds more from other areas, and we all meet in the fields. Be careful of what you say. People are easily annoyed, and there are no prevailing laws in the fields. It's more like survival of the fittest. Therefore, you must take good care once you get out there. You can leave now. Tamba will fetch you later to teach you a few things more. Hope you enjoy the work."

We had been quite comfortable in the big chairs, but with some reluctance, we rose and walked towards the door.

"And one last thing," I heard Sahr say, "when you are at the shakers, never pass your hands near your mouth."

"Why?" I asked, turning around to face him.

"Doing so may cause your death."

"I don't understand," said Mila.

"Other gang members will assume you've put a diamond in your mouth and swallowed it."

"Suppose I actually swallow a diamond, what happens then?" asked Mila.

Sahr laughed and said, "Simple. They'll assign some people to watch you, especially when you feel like shitting. If that doesn't bring the diamond out, they'll operate."

"Operate?" I asked.

"Yes, operate. But not as they do in hospitals. Here, they will literally split your stomach open and rummage through your guts and organs until they get the diamond back. If they find nothing, it's your loss. No one cares whether you live or die when it involves stolen gems. You must never pass your hand near your mouth when you are working at the shakers. I've seen a few people lose their lives by doing that. Hope you remember these words of caution."

"What happens if you feel like scratching around your mouth?"

"Simple: you die. Unless you've a death wish, don't do it. Always ask someone to do it for you," he said with finality.

We walked out and closed the door behind us. We had nowhere to go. We decided to stay put in the big veranda until Tamba came to fetch us. Fortunately, there were two vacant hammocks. We took the opportunity to occupy them. We lay there idly, swinging gently to snatch some sleep.

12

Tamba patted me awake, startling me in the process. Mila was already awake but fared no better; I saw him vigorously rub his sleepy eyes. Tamba said, "You must wake up now. There're things you must know before we set off for the diamond pits. If you come with me now, we'll soon be done."

We followed Tamba to his quarters in the huge compound. He led us to a mango tree that was in bloom with yellow-white flowers. The flowers would eventually evolve into those exotic, fleshy, and luscious fruits so appreciated in the tropics. The mango tree was a giant one, and it had large, exposed roots snaking in different directions. The tree was quite leafy and provided ample protection from the hot, piercing sunrays that penetrated through thick, white clouds and a lucid, blue sky.

I noticed that a large area around the tree was swept clean in readiness for the day's task. There were a few young men engaged in one task or another, mostly tasks related to mining. One young man was wholly engrossed in repairing shakers (used for washing gravel in order to separate precious diamonds from worthless stones. Another was repairing his work shoes and clothes. A huge man, naked down to his waist, was busy sharpening a vicious-looking machete on an improvised whet stone. Sweat was glistening on his bare back like miniature diamonds. He kept rubbing the tip of his finger on the sharp edge of the machete to ascertain whether the tool was sharp enough for his liking. As we passed him, he grunted a lazy, almost inaudible greeting. We responded cheerfully. Nearby, a group of about five men were busy gambling with dice, oblivious of all other things around them. Occasionally, they shouted and scuffled with each other, but no one seemed to mind.

Tamba stopped by one of the big roots of the mango tree. It was as smooth as a baby's bottom, having served as a seat to countless bottoms for many years. Tamba sat down on the root and indicated that we should take a seat. We sat facing each other. Looking at him closely in the late morning sunlight, I noticed he was a handsome, fair-skinned man who was slightly older than we were. He was tall, huge,

Dead End Poverty

and strong. His hair was jet black, which matched his bushy eyebrows. For someone so big, he had a soft, melodious voice.

"Sahr asked me to tell you about our work and the tools we work with," said Tamba. "If you listen carefully, it won't take long. Some of what I'll tell you is very important. The information might help save your lives one day."

We were a little confused but ready to absorb the crucial lesson in diamond mining. Tentatively, I started having doubts. *Will I be able to cope with the demands of the job? Maybe Mila is feeling the same.* I looked at him, but he didn't seem bothered. He was lost in admiration; his eyes intensely fixed on our new instructor. He looked at me, too, and our eyes met. I knew then that Mila was ready to have a go. That knowledge boosted my wavering confidence. All doubts disappeared from my mind.

"Diamond mining is a very difficult and dangerous job. I've been doing it for six years now, so I should know," continued Tamba. "Sahr is my boss as well as yours. Any issues you're not comfortable with must be taken up with him. Sahr, in turn, will talk to Mr K if need be. However, I'm sure he must've told you this already." We both nodded our heads in agreement as he continued talking. "All right, so we're clear on that." He passed his hand nervously through his thick ebony hair when Mila interrupted him: "Sahr also told us that we must never steal diamonds in the field or anywhere else," said Mila. "He said we must never pass our hands near our mouths when working with shakers. He said we might be killed if we do."

"He's right," Tamba said, "but you'll learn on the job. Did he also tell you how we share diamond money?"

"He did. We agreed to the terms," I said.

"Good," he said, seeming satisfied. "Next thing to know about is the diamond fields. We mine anywhere we suspect diamonds to be. There's no prospecting; we prospect with our instincts. We dig on dry land, in swamps, in rivers, and even in cemeteries. As long as we believe that we could find the precious stones, we dig there. Nowhere is sacred in terms of diamond digging, as I've come to learn. I heard that people in Koidu town even dig pits within and under their houses to look for the precious stones."

We sat there dumbfounded. *I wondered, How could anyone dig within or under his own house for diamonds? Where would his family stay during the process? It seems so impractical. No one should be mining in a house.*

"We always mine near some sort of water source so we can wash the gravel, clean the tools, and freshen up our bodies," Tamba continued. "We use sacks or buckets to carry the gravel to the nearest water source. Water isn't hard to find. Old pits always have abundant water in them. We use that water most of the time. We don't mine very close to the village. People mined in that area long ago. The site we're mining on now is about three miles from the village. It becomes very wet and soggy during the rains."

"We're used to working in the rain. In fact, we've been doing that all our lives," I said. Just then, I stood up to scratch my groin from what I suspected was an ant bite. This amused Tamba and Mila; they laughed as I tried to get rid of the little monster. It didn't bother me, I continued regardless of who was watching. I managed to get the bugger off, though, and squashed it between my fingers. Satisfied, I sat down on the root again.

"You must really be careful with those ants," Tamba said in a matter-of-fact but jocular tone. "The ants are the price we pay for enjoying the tree's shade. You'll encounter ants that are even more vicious and numerous in the diamond fields. You'll get used to them."

"What do we need to work in the fields?" asked Mila.

"That was my next topic," said Tamba. "You really don't need much in the field, Mila. Generally, we use tools as the need arises. Mr K, our supporter, provides most of the tools for us. They include sifters, konkordus, machetes, battery-loaded torches, spades, buckets, sacks, and pickaxes. Sometimes, we take hoes."

"Hoes are easy to use," I quipped. "Being a farmer all my life, I should know."

"Glad to hear that," Tamba said quickly as if he didn't want his lecture to be interrupted. "Now let me tell you about the rest of the tools. The sifters or shakers are for washing the gravel in order to extract diamonds from the ordinary stones. It's a difficult process: it involves standing in water for long hours. The sifter is called a shaker because of the way the user's body shakes when using the tool."

"Will we be able to work with shakers soon?" asked Mila. It seemed like he was very eager to get to work.

Dead End Poverty

"Sure," Tamba replied, "you have no choice. You'll have to work with shakers. The earlier you become adept with them, the better for us all." Tamba was being candid.

"How do they make them?" I inquired.

"That's not important," Tamba replied sharply. "As I said before, you'll learn on the job. Right now, I want you to have the knowledge to use these tools. For your own good, learn quickly. You may be using some of these tools tonight."

"So what does a konkordu do?" I asked him.

"We use the konkordu for digging soil on dry ground and in the pits. It is like a hoe with a curved blade, almost like a sickle. It has a very short handle to help you work in underground pits."

"Ah, underground pits. Sahr told us about those and how they normally collapse," said Mila knowingly.

Tamba didn't want to encourage conversations about pit cave-ins. He feared that it might spook the new-comers. "True, but that's not in our discussion at the moment," said Tamba before continuing his explanation. "The pickaxe is also used for digging hard-surface soils and penetrating rocks that block paths leading to the gravel."

"What is gravel?" I queried.

"Gravel is precious and comes in three colours," Tamba replied without effort. "Gravel is the clay within which we find diamonds. It can be blue, green, or a combination of both."

"Are diamonds hard to find?" I asked

"That depends entirely on luck. Let's get back to the tools please," he coaxed.

"The spade are used for digging and scooping, the sacks are used to transport gravel to the nearest available water source for processing. The bucket is used to retrieve gravel from the pit and carry it to a pile. Do you get that?" We nodded our heads in agreement.

"And as we work at night," Tamba resumed, "it is necessary to have torches. Without a torch of some kind, mining will only be possible by moonlight. That's about all you need to know for now. The rest you'll learn on the job if you keep your eyes and ears open."

"I'm sure we'll soon be adept at using all these tools. We are fast learners and want to learn. Right, Mila?"

"Yes," Mila said confidently, "it'll be a piece of cake."

"Only when you use your brain," Tamba said. "Your wits must be about you in the mines or the Joe Khakis will get you." He laughed and displayed his white teeth.

"Who is Joe Khakis?" I inquired.

Tamba laughed again. "The Joe Khakis are the NDMC security force. They protect the interests of the company. They raid illegal mines like ours to arrest illegal miners like us. In the fields, when you see Joe Khakis, grab what you can and run for your freedom."

"We'll remember that," Mila stated.

"I have to go get some sleep now, my friends," said Tamba. "I worked the whole of last night. You could go back to the house if you prefer."

Tamba got up and started to walk slowly away from the mango tree, looking tired. Suddenly, though, he stopped and said, "Before I forget, Sahr asked me to supply each of you with a battery-loaded torch, a machete, and some working gear. You'll pay for the torches and batteries when you get your first diamond money. The torches will belong to you permanently. The other tools will be hidden for gang use."

"We'll pay for the tools as soon as we earn some money," I said reassuringly.

"No problem there," Tamba said in a jovial tone. "You will pay all right; Sahr will deduct the money from the source." He laughed and displayed ridges of worry lines on his forehead.

"But what is a diamond? How do we recognise one when we see it?" I asked.

"Simple," said Tamba, and he smiling in a patronising way. "A diamond is unlike any other stone you've seen. When you see one, you'll know it's a diamond. You'll just know."

"But how would I—" Mila began.

"Enough about diamonds now," Tamba, interrupted. "If I were you, I would be looking for a nice, cool place to sleep. Nights in the mines are exceptionally long and cold. Do you smoke?" We shook our heads. "You will. Trust me," said Tamba. "In the fields, almost everyone smokes something. You'll have to, the cold will see to that. Don't bother smoking cigarettes alone. They won't help you. Only djamba can help you."

"What's djamba?" asked Mila.

"This," he said, dipping his hand into his pocket and withdrawing a small parcel wrapped in brown sugar paper. "This will keep you warm through the rains and the hard, cold nights."

We still didn't know what it was, so Tamba carefully unwrapped the brown sugar paper to reveal a small quantity of what looked like crushed, dry leaves.

"This is marijuana. People have different names for it. Here, we call it djamba, taffi, or ganja."

After he showed it to us, we knew what it was. A few people in Simbaru smoked it. The elders used to say anyone who smoked it was a dangerous psychopath, so we'd stayed away from it.

"I'll let you have some tonight when we are in the fields," said Tamba.

"I think we'll pa—" I began, but Mila interrupted me.

"Thank you very much, Tamba. We are looking forward to it."

"Yes," I managed to say, "thank you."

"Make sure you are with one of the boys when it's time to leave for the fields. We wouldn't want you getting lost. And don't forget to look for a nice location to get some sleep. Trust me, you'll need it."

Without another word, he turned on his heels and left briskly. I felt like I had imagined his tiredness before.

13

We found a pleasant location to take a nap before going back to the big house, our new home. Fortunately, we found a couple of unoccupied hammocks side by side. We jumped gratefully into them, joining several overnight miners hoping to get some sleep before work commenced at dusk. The veranda wasn't a quiet space: some hammock occupants snored loudly and released loud, pongy farts. Others preferred to talk instead of catching up on sleep. Still, we managed to get comfortable in our slightly swinging rope beds.

"Are you ready to go to the fields tonight, Yandi?" Mila inquired in a low voice.

"Sure. Is that not why we left our village in the first place?" I answered.

Mila knew it was a rhetorical question, but he answered it anyway: "It's just that we only arrived yesterday evening. Now we are ready to work in the fields. I think it's too soon. We are simply not ready without experience."

"So how do we get the experience? By staying in town? You worry too much. Get some rest; I'm sure you you'll be eager to go once night falls."

Mila smiled nervously and scratched his head. He said, "If it's okay with you, I guess it's also okay by me."

"Don't worry," I said, "it'll be okay for us." And then I changed the topic—I didn't want him to get spooked. "Did you tell anyone that we were leaving Simbaru?"

"Not a soul," said Mila. It was a lie. He felt ashamed for lying to his friend. He'd told Jayman, his younger brother, when he helped him snare the sheep back in Simbaru. He hadn't revealed their destination . . . partly because he didn't know at that point. He knew Jayman wouldn't betray him. But his shame was so overwhelming that he decided to tell the truth: "Well I did tell Jayman about it," Mila admitted."

"You shouldn't have told him," I replied.

"I know. But Jayman wouldn't betray me," he said. "No, never. In fact, I reckon he was happy I was leaving. Jayman even said that he would be getting a little fuller since I was leaving."

"He is just like you: gluttonous and not ashamed of it," I observed judiciously.

"It runs in the family, take it from me," Mila pointed out, laughing merrily as if he had just said the funniest thing in the world.

I laughed with him, but concerns for our parents' given over our sudden departure still lingered in the back of my mind. I would've told them my plans if I believed they would've let me go with their blessings. I knew my father wouldn't have played ball. Considering the workload of the family and the fact that I was his first born, he would've done everything to keep me in Simbaru. He would've pleaded with me not to leave; he would've used everything in his power, including my major weakness: my love for my mother. If that didn't work, he would've resorted to ordering me to stay. And failing that, he would've gone a notch further and threatened to disown me. Though leaving the village may have caused him some embarrassment, I reckoned that I'd also saved him any added anguish by disappearing in that manner. I figured he may even claim that he sent me away to forge a better life for the family. Of course, no one would dispute that. No one knew whether I'd left of my own volition, due to his orders, or through other arrangements.

Apparently, Mila was in the same position as I was. His stepfather, being the original redneck, wouldn't want it known that Mila had absconded with one of his best-bred animals for company. He would prefer to keep it a secret. Anyone who chose to probe more would upset him. Such a nosey person would certainly get taste of the foul side of his tongue, temper, and enormous strength. I looked at Mila in a new light. We were in a strange location. He was all the family I had, and I was all the family he had.

"What do you think your father did when he discovered you'd left?" Mila asked abruptly.

"Nothing, I suppose. But I know he would be very disappointed in me. How do you think Uncle Mariah reacted when he realised you'd finally escaped his clutches?"

"Forget the old sod," he said and laughed before continuing in a sombre tone, "He's not even my real father. Why should I care how he feels? The man is an arrogant bully. He'll remain exactly that for the rest of his miserable life."

"Do you miss the village?" I asked.

"Not at all," he answered after a brief silence, "but I miss my mother." Mila laughed, his faced etched with pleasure as he reminisced about the numerous good times he had had with his mother. I miss my beautiful girlfriend and the extras, too, but I miss Massey the most."

"Nevertheless, we're out of there now. We must concentrate on where we are. It is vital for our success," I said. "What do you think?"

"Yes, we must concentrate on the here and now," Mila agreed. "And that reminds me, we'd better get some sleep; otherwise, we'll be worse for the night."

I agreed. We didn't talk again and had no idea when sleep overcame us in our swaying, rope beds.

14

Immediately after the evening meal, we set out for the diamond fields. By then, it was quite dark. Tamba and five other members of the gang—Dowu, Samson, Boima, Sumaa, and Francis—came along with us. Sahr remained in the village. He was not a day labourer. He was the boss and only visited the mines to surprise his boys and oversee the gravel washing. Tamba represented him as the boss on most occasions. Everyone in the gang, in and out of the fields, respected Tamba. The gang also listened to his instructions and respected the decisions he made. The gang realised he was acting for the boss and that the boss must be obeyed. If Tamba complained about anyone, Sahr wouldn't take it lightly. Sahr rejected any worker who attempted to usurp the team and would return such a worker to Mr K. Recently, he sacked two gang members who weren't pulling their weight. It was the reason why Mila and I were members of his team.

True to his word, Tamba supplied us with battery-loaded torches, machetes, and some working clothes. He taught us how to operate the torches and said, "You should use your torches wisely," he said. "Torch batteries are very expensive."

Once it was confirmed that we would work in the field that night, we changed into our working gear like everyone else. I felt proud as I held the torch in my right hand and waved its rays along the windy path. I had never owned a torch in my life. I knew Mila hadn't either.

"Even at work," Tamba continued, "we use makambos to provide light while we dig. If you use your torch unwisely, it'll run low on batteries and you'll have to buy more batteries yourself. Sahr only supplies batteries once a month."

"What are makambos?" I asked as I switched off my latest prized possession.

"Look around you. What are Suma and Boima holding?"

"Lighted bottles with naked flames," said Mila.

"Those are what we call makambos," Boima stated. "Just put some kerosene or palm oil in an empty bottle and insert a twisted, dry piece of cloth for a wick. Make sure the piece of cloth at the mouth of the bottle fits tight, shake the bottle well until the fuel flows to the top, and then light it. There, you've your makambo lamp. You'll see loads of them once we arrive in the fields."

Using makambos to light our way, we trudged along the footpath. A couple of miles later, we entered an area filled with the din of men at work. We saw numerous small fires, apparently from lighted makambos. The sounds of konkordus and pickaxes falling on hard-caked earth were audible above the voices of the miners and those noises mingled with the soft thuds of earth hitting the ground. The infinite rattling of the shakers against water resembled a kind of melodious music to me. I dubbed it the music of the mining fields. Apart from the makambos and the occasional glare of torches, it was pitch dark. There was no moonshine. Nevertheless, the little flames provided amazing lighting. I could see my immediate surroundings almost clearly.

Tamba led the way as we weaved our way between the pits, tools, mounds of mud, and men to get to our work site. Upon arrival, he sent Francis and Sumaa to fetch the hidden mining tools. As an afterthought, he instructed Mila and I to go with them.

"You need to know where we hide the tools," Tamba said. "Starting from tonight, you will be hiding and retrieving them when we come to work."

When we came back with the tools, I noticed Tamba and the others already had five lighted makambos around a big hole full of muddy water. The flames danced across the surface of the stagnant water to the tune of the wind and threw silhouettes of various shapes all around us.

"Did you bring all the buckets?" asked Boima. "This pit is full of water. We have to get rid of all the water before we start digging."

Francis passed him a stack of six locally made, metal buckets. The pit Boima was referring to was not the size of a water well pit. It was huge and terraced, and it could accommodate at least three working adults flipping out shovels full of wet, heavy earth. The terracing was used to facilitate the removal of water, earth, and gravel from the pit. There were already three terraced platforms within the pit. Two of the terraces were completely under the muddy water, and the third, the highest of the terraces, remained partially free of water. To remove the water from the pit, miners stood in the water. Dowu positioned himself on the lowest terrace. By the time he got proper footing, he was already waist deep in the water. Samson took the next terrace, and Francis took the highest one.

A man would have to stand up fully in order to pass a bucket to someone on any of the terraces. Tamba stood near the pit on the ground level, and the rest of us positioned ourselves in a straight line, ready to receive the full or empty buckets. We stood in a single-file formation that allowed us to pass along the buckets of water scooped from the pit without the need to walk to the next man. We had to work with both hands: one hand to receive a full bucket and the other to receive an empty bucket on its way to Dowu in the pit. When an empty bucket reached Dowu, he scooped up a bucket full of water and placed it within reach of Samson. Samson, in turn, passed it on to Francis who passed it on to Tamba. This process continued along the single-file line. The empty buckets returned the same way, but in reverse.

It was a hard job, but we were up to it. Apart from the initial stutter we experienced from the weight of the loaded buckets, we held our own among our new workmates. They were impressed and let us know by commending us frequently. After a half hour or so, Boima relieved Dowu from the pit and the process continued. I watched Mila take his turn in the pit without hesitation. He seemed determined to show the gang that he was up to the task. The speed with which he collected the empty buckets from the side of the pit and dispatched the full ones was greater than that of those who had already been in the pit. Without a noticeable change in his breathing rate, he kept at it longer than the recommended half hour. It was only with the intervention of Tamba that we got him to relinquish the job to another participant.

"You must climb out," Tamba instructed. He approached the pit to make sure Mila would climb out. "If you go on like that, you'll get burned out before we are halfway through the night."

Removing water from flooded pits was as important as digging for the gravel. Water flooded the pits every two hours or so. And working the pits would be very difficult, if not impossible, unless they were free of water. The water level receded as buckets raced in and out of the pit. Almost all the water was gone before Tamba instructed Boima to start taking the sludge out. We took turns scooping the slimy sludge and throwing it directly out of the pit. Sometimes, however, we loaded the muck in buckets and passed the buckets via a single-file line, exactly as we did with the water in the pit.

About three quarters of an hour later, Tamba instructed those in the pit to stop scooping up the sludge and start clearing the water out again. A sizable quantity had accumulated at the bottom of the pit throughout the sludge operation.

"This would be faster with a machine," said Tamba with yearning in his voice. "The only one we had broke, and it has not been repaired yet. Mr K promised to buy us a new one if we got worthy diamonds, but those are still eluding us."

After a while, it was my turn to get into the pit. The water was cold, but after the first few shudders, I had buckets going down the line as if I had been doing such work all my life. By the time the half hour expired, there was not much water left in the pit to interfere with digging and shovelling out the earth. Tamba elected Dowu, Boima, and himself to start digging and shovelling out the wet earth again. Three makambos in strategic places within the pit provided sufficient light to see what was going on.

The rest of us remained above ground chatting and looking out for any Joe Khakis on raid patrol. Watching out for Joe Khakis was a communal assignment for everyone in the fields. Gangs mined a large area of land; lookouts were supposed to raise the alarm by blowing a cow's horn loud enough for everyone to hear. It was one of the golden rules of illicit mining: every gang member alerted everyone else when they spotted Joe Khakis.

Once down in the pit, the men were hidden from view, but the wet earth from the pit flew out regularly in three different directions. Unlike when we were ridding the pit of excess water, the digging phase of the operation only required operatives to change places when they felt tired. Because it was a harder job, it was difficult for any of us to work continuously for more than three quarters of an hour. The earth was heavier than usual because it was wet. Throwing it high and far from a seven-foot pit was equally demanding. Only a strong fortitude and the fear of letting others down kept most of us working throughout the night.

I went down the pit before Mila. Nevertheless, his body language was all impatience; he wanted to have a go and experience the actual digging and shovelling actions. Tamba was exhausted before the other two, and I took the opportunity to replace him quickly. Dowu and Boima grinned when they realised it was one of the new boys down in the pit.

Dowu immediately put his spade down and came to my side. "It is easy when you do it this way," he said. He took my spade and slowly demonstrated the method. He positioned the spade on the soggy earth, put his right foot on the metal blade, and exerted pressure until the blade disappeared into the soil. He then slanted the spade to separate the scooped earth from the rest, raised the loaded spade as he pivoted on his left leg, and sent the earth flying out of the pit. "Do you think you can do that?" he asked as he repeated the procedure. He did it very quickly, which impressed me.

"I'll try," I said, taking back my spade. I was determined to reproduce his technique. For a beginner, I felt I was doing fine. After the first few throws, I got used to the weight of the loaded spade. I also adopted a convenient posture to help me dig and throw out the earth without much trouble. I stayed in the pit when Boima and Dowu decided to climb out. Mila and Francis took their places and the work continued. Mila didn't need any demonstration to start. Once in the pit, he executed the procedure of getting rid of the turned up earth as if he had done it all his life.

"You are a natural, Mila," said Tamba who came to the edge of the pit to check on the status of the job.

Mila just grunted and continued his task. He worked as if he were possessed, never stopping for a breather, digging and shovelling doggedly. It seemed as if he didn't want to relinquish his place to anyone. On the other hand, I realised that I was exhausted.

"I'm tired now, Mila," I announced and laid down my spade to get out of the pit.

"Meet you up there soon," he replied without missing a beat.

I climbed out of the pit and someone else immediately took my place. We worked in that manner until dawn, when it was time to leave. We washed all our tools and washed off some of the mud on our clothes and bodies. Tamba instructed Mila and I to join Boima to hide the tools. Once the tools were hidden, we joined the others and began the long walk back to town.

15

"Tonight, we expect to reach the gravel," Suma announced as we trudged along the semi-dark path towards the mining fields. "We might even start taking it out tonight."

He was leading the way, and I was right behind him. The lit makambo held at chest height and arm's length belched out thick, black smoke and provided ample light to see where we were going. Some people used their torches. The lights from a few of the torches brushed against the sides of the thick grassland and leaped far in front of us to scan the path for any surprises ahead.

"You'll be earning your first diamond money soon. Let's hope it's a lot," continued Suma. He was quite excited.

"How do you know that we'll reach the gravel tonight," asked Mila. He, too, was right behind me. Mila and I had formed an unspoken agreement to stay close to each other. We both knew there was no one else to turn to if things went horribly wrong. We were in a strange land and survival was wholly dependent upon what we did. We figured that staying together and supporting each other was our best bet. After all, we came from the same village, grew up together, became good friends, knew each other's family well, and even left together to seek our fortunes. It was only natural that we remained united; anything else would be a disaster to our progress and well-being.

Suma snorted a quick, derogatory laugh, probably reserved for novices like us. But he proceeded to explain, "I'm sure you saw the greenish, hard clay we removed from the pit yesterday. When that greenish earth—incidentally, we call it *cake*—turns up, it implies that gravel is close by. We've worked like jackasses over these few days to reach the precious gravel. The gravel is normally blue in colour. Sometimes it appears green, though nowhere near the green colour of the cake."

These few days, according to my count, amounted to exactly fifteen nights of continuous, hard labour. And the gang had started the pit before our arrival! "Fifteen nights are not a few days," I protested.

Suma grunted, "Sometimes gangs work a pit for a month or more only to discover that the gravel can't be reached," he said. "You guys are lucky. We are now at the threshold of reaching the gravel," he continued with the air of someone who knows a great deal about mining. "The previous pit we worked on took us thirty two days. Guess what? We never reached the gravel."

"Why was that?" Mila asked.

"Because we hit the fucking chimpanzee's ass," offered Dowu a little down the line. I wasn't aware he was listening. "Yes, we hit a damned chimpanzee's ass.

"Chimpanzee's ass," I inquired, "What's that?"

Dowu laughed and said, "A chimpanzee's ass is when you come across an impregnable rock that entirely covers up the gravel."

"Yes," agreed Suma quickly. It was as if he feared losing his spot as the centre of attention. "I believe you know what a chimpanzee is. Have you ever touched its bottom? It's as hard as a rock. That's why the impenetrable rock covering gravel is called a chimpanzee's ass." He touched his backside and mimicked a chimpanzee's cry. No one was amused.

"What do you do when you hit a chimpanzee's ass?" Mila asked.

"Move to another spot and begin a new pit," answered Suma promptly.

"You mean you do nothing more about it? You just let all your hard work go to waste?" Mila persisted.

"There is nothing anyone can do once we land a chimpanzee's ass. The stuff is so hard that it bends or breaks the strongest heads or blades on pickaxes. Wait until you see one. We never waste time on them; we just take the bad luck on the chin and move on to another spot," said Suma.

No one spoke for a while. I used the interlude to reflect on the way we broke even the largest boulders at home. We just set huge fires on them. Heat from the fire cracked them after a considerable period. I wondered whether we could use the same technique on a chimpanzee's ass in the near future. I didn't reveal my idea to anyone, however.

"We are almost at the mines," Tamba shouted to us. "Mila and Yandi, you will get the tools on arrival. Make it fast. We will be removing some or all of the gravel tonight."

It was a cold night. It became even colder when we removed the excess water from the pit. As it was, there was no way to work in pits and stay dry. One always got wet from one thing or another. All of us were completely wet, but we nevertheless started clearing the cake out of the way. After a couple of hours' work, Suma (who was in the pit with Samson and Francis) announced that all the cake was removed, that the gravel was ready to be dug and taken out of the pit. It was very good news.

Tamba instructed us to remove the gravel immediately.

"First, bring all the buckets you can lay hands on and put them close to the pit," he said. "For you, Yandi and Mila, the procedure of retrieving the gravel is almost the same as removing excess water. But the gravel is much heavier. Therefore, whoever is digging mustn't overload the buckets. The gravel must always stop in the middle of the buckets. Do you get it?"

"Perfectly," I replied. Mila appeared to nod his head.

"We will store the gravel near that termite hill under the guava tree," Tamba said. "It's very close to our pit. We will use the water in the pit to kick the gravel in the shakers." As if he knew I was going to ask what he meant by *kick,* he went on to explain: "To kick is when you actually have gravel in a shaker and are washing it to retrieve the precious stones from ordinary pebbles." He paused, scratched his cheek, and continued. "There'll be no time to waste on trivial matters anymore. We must start now. The pit will soon be flooded again."

Having said that, he collected the stack of buckets and descended to the bottom of the pit. Samson and Boima, being old hands at the job, also descended into the pit. Boima stopped at the terrace nearest Tamba, and Boima stopped on the second highest terrace. Mila also descended into the pit, but he stood on the last terrace, near the entrance. The rest of us stayed out of the pit, ready to receive the buckets of gravel, convey them, and store them under the designated guava tree. We were also alerted to be on the lookout for any Joe Khakis or any other danger.

"Some people with eagle eyes pick diamonds straight from the unwashed gravel," said Dowu on one of our many trips to the guava tree. "However, that rarely happens."

I didn't say a thing, but I was grateful for the information. Thereafter, whenever I emptied my bucket of gravel on the growing pile, my eyes roamed around, searching for a diamond. The funny thing was that Mila and I only had the vague descriptions given to us by the veterans. We knew they were shiny, waterproof, unbreakable, and recognisable to the most stupid novice. I was no stupid novice, yet I wondered how I would recognise a diamond when I saw one. Still, every time I emptied another bucket, my roaming eyes scanned the top of the growing pile of gravel.

Tamba stayed in the pit about half an hour. During this time, we managed to deposit a reasonable pile of wet, bluish gravel under the guava tree. When he climbed out of the pit, Samson replaced him. Mila, in turn, took the place Samson vacated, and Suma replaced Mila on the terrace nearest the mouth of the pit. This was how we worked the entire night, replacing each other in an organised manner. However, each time we changed places, we removed the excess water that inevitably settled at the bottom of the pit. That wetness made us wetter and colder.

Sometime during the work, Sahr appeared at the pit. He was not dressed for work. He was simply visiting the site in order to boost the morale of his boys and to see what progress we'd made. When he came back from inspecting the little pile under the guava tree, he was impressed and genuinely hopeful. "The gravel looks promising," he announced. "I'm sure this one will yield us a few precious stones, better stones than we've had lately." Several of us murmured, "amen to that" and placed our open, right palms on our foreheads, a gesture believed by the locals to make predictions happen.

Sahr didn't stay in the mines for long. He and Tamba walked together towards the town engrossed in deep conversation. The work continued in Tamba's absence. Those in the pit exchanged places, and soon, we were throwing away buckets full of water from the pit. After that, the gravel kept coming. The pile under the tree increased steadily.

The Joe Khakis were busy, too. They made frequent raids on the fields and made several arrests as well. They also confiscated tools they found lying around. Altogether, the NDMC security personnel raided the fields six times since we started working there. Luckily, Mila and I managed to evade capture. However, several of our gang members weren't so lucky, especially when a raid took place while they were down in the pit. The Joe Khakis were on them before they cleared the first of several terraces in the pit. The Joe Khakis took all the miners they arrested to Tankoro. However, the arrested miners returned the same day or a couple of days after. Indeed, Mr K made sure, like all other yullamen, that the Joe Khakis released the men as soon as possible. Money did all the talking. The underpaid Joe Khakis and police officers did not really care about protecting NDMC's mining concession interests; they just needed to earn enough to take care of family and other matters. Selling and receiving money for captured illicit miners was a means of doing just that. In short, bribes changed hands or palms greased each other and miners returned to their laborious tasks until the next time they were caught. Mr K was never tired of boasting that he could get anyone out if arrested. Nevertheless, Mila and I were wary of how far his power or influence reached. We decided we shouldn't be caught in the first place.

Tamba returned. He continued to supervise us before we executed the next change. The gravel was coming up fast. The pile beneath the guava tree was already a good size. A second pile started close by and was growing by the minute. Tamba was pleased with our progress. "If it goes on like this, we may start washing or kicking the gravel by tomorrow," he said in a jovial, excited voice. We agreed with him.

The first light of dawn was peeking out when Tamba instructed us to stop work and prepare to go back to town. We cleaned the tools, hid them, and washed some mud off our bodies before we headed back to town.

16

We learned of the diamond theft—or *swallowing*, to be exact—when we were equidistant between the mines and the village. The news arrived through our single-file configuration as we walked down the road towards the village.

Apparently, an overly enthusiastic Maina (Maina was the halfwit in town) couldn't wait for us to arrive; instead, he came out to meet us and give us the information. He seemed excited and happy, deriving pleasure from the occurrence as if he'd been bestowed all the wealth in Kono.

"Samuka the giant is being accused of swallowing a diamond," Maina said to the first miner he encountered. Thereafter, the bush telegraph took over. News of the alleged diamond theft travelled down the line like wildfire, reaching us seconds after the first miner learned about it. The news created a buzz among the returning miners; everyone seemed to have something to say about it. The din of voices increased as miners closest to each other discussed the punishments they anticipated Samuka would get. The incident galvanised our effort to trek into town.

"So who's Samuka?" Mila inquired. "I believe I must have met him. What are they going to do with him?" There was a hint of trepidation in his voice. Apparently, he was thinking of the consequences Sahr and Tamba had outlined for a diamond thief.

"Never mind," Tamba replied seriously. It doesn't matter who Samuka is; he's practically done for anyway. At least four burly men will constantly watch his every move. I'm sure, by now, he has been roughly handled and savagely beaten in an effort to force him to divulge the whereabouts of the diamond. If he doesn't, they'll tie him up against the big, ant-ridden, orange tree—the one near the big mango tree in the village square. The savage ants will waste no time getting all over him, and that will be very painful, especially if the ants invade his private areas and other sensitive crevices." I shuddered at the thought.

"What happens after that?" I asked.

"They'll keep him tied up," Tamba patiently explained. "However, they'll also feed him generously with a powerful herbal laxative to act as a catalyst to make him empty his bowels within the hour. Of course, when he feels the need to go, he will be marched to a specially prepared place near the river or the swamp. Under stringent, watchful eyes, he will be forced to sift through his own feces with his bare hands. I wouldn't want to be one of the people watching a grown man play with his own shit. That's not my idea of fun."

"And if that also fails?" I asked.

"He'll get some more beating," said Dowu. "He could even be killed during the process. That would be pleasing to his gang master and the members of his gang; it would be much easier to search the guts of a dead man for stolen diamonds."

"You mean they would actually kill him?" Mila asked.

"Yes, to get the diamond out of his guts," said Tamba. "It's nothing personal, and it has never been personal. In this business, that's just the way things are done. Once accused of swallowing a diamond, your life is in great danger."

I took a moment to digest the information. I thought it was an evil practice to kill a suspect for swallowing a diamond, for stealing a stone. I felt that the laxatives alone could do the job effectively. All they would need to do was wait. It would be a matter of sound reasoning and patience for the problem to be resolved without torture or bloodshed.

"Killing a diamond thief is a last resort practice," I heard Tamba say. "There're many other things to do to force a diamond thief to speak the truth, to reveal the location of a stolen stone."

"Such as?" I asked.

"Hanging him upside down and subjecting him to more physical abuse," Tamba replied.

"And don't forget, Tamba, there's that psychotic Yaya and his Gaandoe," shouted Boima, from somewhere in the line.

"Yes, Yaya and his Gaandoe," repeated Tamba. "The Gaandoe is what he would be hanged on. Upside down."

"Does he really have a real Gaandoe?" I asked in awe. We were learning the local lingo fast and knew that *Gaandoe* meant crocodile.

Almost everyone within hearing range laughed at my apparent naiveté. I was not offended because I was used to the spontaneous goading and laughter that every witty or daft comment seemed to provoke among miners. Besides, the ever patient Tamba (as soon as the laughter subsided) explained the meaning of the phrase *Yaya and his Gaandoe.*

"The Gaandoe is a special torturing device you won't wish to be put on," said Tamba. "Old Yaya operates it. You'll see it when we get to town. I'm certain that Yaya is sadistically relishing in its preparation by now. It is the last torture before a diamond thief is murdered. If he's still uncooperative, the same Gaandoe device will disembowel him. No thief ever survives the Gaandoe unless he cooperates and divulges the whereabouts of the stolen gem."

"What's it like, this Gaandoe?" I persisted.

"I told you: you'll see it when we arrive in town," Tamba said. "In fact, we're almost in town now. Look! There're the coconut trees by the river. Once we pass those, we'll be in the village."

We were a hundred yards away from town when we heard the first din of an excited crowd. The sound confirmed something exciting was happening in town. Since starting work in the mines, we had always returned to a sleeping village or one just on the brink of stirring. Our pace quickened, and within a few minutes, we were part of the crowd and watching a half-naked, bloody Samuka being interrogated by members of his own gang in the dawn light.

The accused was sitting on the ground, hands tied in front of him. He was covered in dust and blood. A slap accompanied every question asked, a kick or a cracking whip abused his naked back. At least he was not yet tied to the ant-ridden orange tree Tamba had mentioned. But some people in the crowd were already demanding that he be put on it. It seemed as if, in Yengema, no one was the friend of a diamond thief.

A loincloth the locals called vomii scarcely concealed Samuka's groin. The vomii was a unisex type of primitive local dress. It was a piece of cloth normally worn between the legs and secured by a cord around the waist that concealed the genitals but left the thighs and buttocks bare. No one in the crowd missed the bulky bulge under Samuka's vomii. Almost all the women present had a wistful smile on their faces, especially when part of Samuka's crown jewels became visible due to his position.

Mila and I forced our way to the front of the little crowd to see whether we could recognise Samuka and to observe the punishments that would be inflicted on him. The man we saw sitting on the ground was in a sorrier state than we had imagined. There was hardly a space left on his naked back without huge, swollen, bleeding welts. Because the whip used to flog him is first immersed in a mixture of soil and half-soaked sand, the blood meandering down from his upper body was more brown than red.

A closer look revealed that he was someone we had seen several times. We'd even spoken to him occasionally. On the few occasions we'd interacted, we found him to be good company. He made us laugh and gave us lots of advice on many things, including diamond theft. "Never steal a diamond," he said to us, "It's the worst crime to commit here, and no one will feel pity for you." I assumed that Samuka was a cheerful, mild-mannered, and honest person. Evidently, I was wrong. For the bloodied pitiful soul I was staring at was not cheerful any longer. He didn't look like the honest character I assumed he was. Pity, Samuka the generous adviser hadn't followed his own advice.

Another crack of the whip landed on his already-damaged back. He yelped and twisted in agony, but he remained seated on the ground. As another lash connected with his body, he yelped even louder and raised his head. Our eyes connected and held for a moment, his penetrating through my concentration as if sending me a message. It was almost as if his eyes were saying, *I told you so. Never steal diamonds. Now look what's happening to me.* I felt sorry for him then, but not enough to make me shy away from watching the harsh methods employed to recover the stolen diamond.

"Tie him to the ant-infested tree," ordered Kemokai."

He was the leader of Samuka's gang, just as Sahr was our leader. He was personally overseeing the procedure to recover the stolen stone. Such an important and sensitive matter wasn't deputised. A gang leader's reputation depended upon it. The village's chief had nothing to do with it. It was diamond business, and only people who knew about diamonds dealt with it. Kemokai would work within the *diamond law;* he wouldn't be lenient. He believed that diamond thieves should be punished harshly to limit further thieving.

At the command, two pairs of arms stepped forward, shoved a hand each under Samuka's armpits, lifted him up, and dragged him like a full sack of potatoes towards the ant-ridden tree. The excited crowd followed in their wake.

"Untie his hands and use the rope to tie him against the tree," Kemokai bellowed. "No, don't do that," he countered almost immediately. "Leave his hands tied and get another rope. Make sure you tie him where the most ants are concentrated. He will soon be singing when the ants start partying in his groin, in his body crevices." He laughed as if he had just stated the funniest joke. Some people laughed with him. I didn't.

Samuka succumbed silently as the rope went round and round his body, his already tied hands, and the tree. Samuka was gyrating and stamping his feet. It seemed that the ferocious ants were already at work. When they were sure he was securely tied to the tree, the men retreated from him and rubbed off the vicious ants that had climbed onto their hands.

"Someone tell Sama to bring me her most potent concoction," said Kemokai.

Sama was the most senior of his four wives. Kemokai had specifically asked her to prepare a laxative from a blend of local leaves, roots, and herbs as soon as he learned that Samuka had swallowed a diamond. She appeared shortly, gingerly carrying a small calabash full of slimy, green leaves. The little crowd parted for her as she approached the tree. She went directly to the tree and stood before the ant-tormented Samuka, muttering strange words under her breath.

"Give it to him," ordered her husband. "Ensure that he drinks it all. We want him to defecate as soon as possible."

Sama held the calabash to Samuka's mouth. He eagerly drank the foul concoction—eagerly because he knew what would happen to him if his tormentors noticed any hesitation. He finished the content with three long draughts and belched loudly. Sama turned the calabash upside down so everyone could see that the accused had drank the last drop. Unceremoniously, she disappeared from the square as quickly as she had appeared.

Drinking the laxative didn't stop the goading, abuse, and physical beating. More lashes rained on Samuka as Kemokai unsuccessfully tried to discover whether he had swallowed the stolen diamond. He even tried to wheedle and cajole him: "Samuka, just tell me what you did with the diamond. I promise your punishment will stop immediately." But his words didn't yield a positive result either.

Samuka just looked at him as if he were speaking Greek. He knew what was going to happen. It infuriated Kemokai to the point that he took the whip himself, and in quick succession, delivered more than six killing lashes to his already over-bloodied body. But he still didn't get the desired result.

Samuka knew he had broken the sacred rule of miners and would suffer the consequences. Secretly, in his pain-filled mind, he prayed that the laxative Sama administered would work effectively. He was hoping that the stone he swallowed would come out on the first attempt because that would stop them from disembowelling him and killing him. He also knew that if he admitted swallowing the diamond they might choose to "operate" on him at once. Though his mind and nerves were almost deadened to pain, he decided to resist them regardless of how he was tortured. Even though he still felt pain, he believed he was close to reaching the point where pain was no longer painful. The ants from the tree had certainly made sure of that. They were all over his body and private parts, biting everywhere at the same time. They even bit into the bloody wounds on his body.

The whip descended on him again, this time with a ferocity that matched the frustration of Kemokai. It was as if he was using all the strength in his body to inflict the blows. However, true to his belief that he was over the pain threshold, Samuka didn't even yelp. All he did was wriggle against the ant-ridden tree. The lack of a cry provoked his tormentors to deliver more vicious blows.

"Tell Yaya to bring the Gaandoe immediately," ordered a still-exasperated Kemokai. "And you," he continued, waving his hand at the men in charge of Samuka, "be ready to take him to the Gaandoe if he endures all the other punishments without telling us what happened to the diamond. You and Yaya know what to do. I'll be watching."

17

The Gaandoe was a mean device designed exclusively for torture. From whichever warped mind the invention had originated, it had served the community effectively over the years. Rumours say the Gaandoe was designed a long time ago, before my great grandparents were born.

The story goes that an earlier chief (called Mbormborlai) designed the menacing tool to punish a daring, young man who openly dared to sleep with one of his favourite wives. Chief Mbormborlai considered Amadi to be his sacred property. As was the case with his other wives, Amadi was off limits for other men. For her to be corrupted and contaminated by an underling was an affront to his pride. It would lower his esteem in the eyes of his subjects, especially if he did nothing about it. It's said that Chief Mbormborlai was so incensed at the gross disregard for traditional values that he decided to make an example of the young man. Thus, he summoned his advisers and devised a way to punish the miscreant that had dared to eat where he ate. Enter the Gaandoe!

The public punishment dished out to the man proved a brilliant success. Such a situation never occurred again during his reign and long after he died. All those who witnessed what happened that day knew better than to interfere with any of the chief's wives. The young man died when his body was ripped open from his anus to his head. The process produced a terrible tearing noise. The gruesome sight of internal body organs flying in different directions scared even the bravest of men.

The Gaandoe was a simple, crudely designed torture device. It was called *Gaandoe* because its two stout prongs looked like the open jaws of a crocodile. Made out of highly flexible guava tree wood, the device was like a giant catapult frame. It was a little larger than a grown man. It lacked the normal trappings of a catapult; instead, the base of the forked angle was rigged with a size-adjustable basket made out of virgin, treated rattan. The basket was used to hold a man's head securely. The two forked prongs, slightly mortised to make space for several corresponding levels were rigged to accommodate the feet of any victim. Two sturdy, twined ropes made out of the bark of trees were attached at the highest level of the notches, and they could be readjusted to secure the legs of the victim. There were no notches to secure the hands, so they normally hung limply, drooping towards the sturdy base of the device. A third rope was deployed to help tie the forked points in order to splice the victim's legs.

Samuka silently acknowledged the arrival of the torture device with subdued apprehension. He had seen a man—Onemanday—placed on the dreaded device a couple of years ago. The consequences were devastating. Eventually, the man was split open like a watermelon. Samuka had resolved then that he would never steal a diamond. He failed miserably; he became a diamond thief. Short of a miracle, nothing would save him from his predicament. He had stolen a diamond and swallowed it. He had been caught. He had to suffer the penalty, brutal as it may be.

Why did I steal the diamond in the first place? he pondered silently. *I've never been a thief. I haven't stolen anything since I arrived in this village. I never even intended to steal the bloody gem. But it was so beautiful, lying there among the other stones in the shaker, its brilliant, blue-white hue glittering under the half-muddy water.* Even in his agony, Samuka admired the marvellous stone that sat somewhere in his intestines. He resigned himself to the fact that what would be, would be. He knew he would never admit to the theft of the stone. He would never give it up voluntarily either. Somehow, he believed that the stone was the most important part of his life, his destiny. It was as if he had been possessed by the stone and didn't care what happened to him. As long as the stone was with him, part of him, nothing else counted—not even the excruciating pain his punishers would inflict on him or the possibility of death.

When it was first used on the unfortunate lover boy, the village's blacksmith, on Chief Mbormborlai's orders, commissioned a two-foot metal tube to hold the base of the Gaandoe. This was inserted into a hole in the centre of the village square to securely hold the two-foot "tail" of the Gaandoe. The metal tube, still in the same place where it was first inserted into the ground, would accommodate one of its several successors: Yaya's Gaandoe. In fact, Yaya and his team were gathered around the metal tube in the ground, trying to insert the base or tail of the Gaandoe into it.

Samuka had swallowed the gem more out of instinct than desire. At the time, he thought that no one saw him. He had furtively watched the watchers, the men whose task it was to ensure that no one hid or swallowed diamonds while at the shakers. His moment arrived when fighting broke out between Mori and Sellu. Mori and Sellu were fellow gang members, but they were quite disagreeable to each other. They were two of the three watchers that night. No one knew how the fight started. All of a sudden, the two men ceased being workmates and became ferocious enemies.

Two watchers were fighting. The third, naturally, attempted to stop the fight. Thus, none of the watchers were paying proper attention to him. He pounced on the opportunity. He carefully retrieved the stone from the shaker and dumped it into his mouth. No one had challenged him at the time, and he felt that he was safe. In fact, he was satisfied that he had pulled it off with no one the wiser. He was very wrong, though, as later events proved.

Samuka and his workmates had returned from the fields a little early that morning. He was very surprised when he received word that gang leader Kemokai wanted to see him immediately. He was apprehensive as he followed the burly messenger to Kemokai's residence. He wondered why Kemokai was summoning him soon after they got back from the fields. Besides, Kemokai hadn't requested to see him since he started work with his gang. He was extremely worried and thought someone may have seen him put the diamond in his mouth. He immediately dismissed that line of thinking, though. He was convinced that no one had observed him steal the stone. He reckoned Kemokai might want to see him for some other reason, but try as he might, he couldn't think of another reason. Nevertheless, he bravely followed the burly messenger into the gang leader's room.

What he saw startled him. Senesie, one of his gang mates and closest friend, stood cosily beside Kemokai as if they had been buddies all their lives. The messenger shut the door and stood behind Senesie, cracking his knuckles in a rather frightening manner. Samuka suspected that he could be in deep trouble. Senesie, with an aloof stance, avoided eye contact with him. He'd been one of the three watchers that night, and he was the one who had stepped in to end the scuffle between the other two watchers. He was his friend and confidant, but his demeanour indicated otherwise.

"Where's the diamond you stole at the shaker?" asked Kemokai, his voice barely audible but loaded with venom. He was one of the good ones, and he was as strong as a buffalo. Nevertheless, the boy was a diamond thief, and Kemokai knew he had to show toughness to deter potential diamond thieves.

That was it. Samuka knew for sure that he was down shit creek; he was in deep trouble. There was no good morning, no smiles, and no invitation to sit down . . . just the one question about the diamond. Even Senesie was acting as if he had never seen him before. He felt lost, but he strengthened his resolution: he would never admit to the theft of the diamond, no matter what they did to him. He experienced a false sense of relief as he mentally reinforced his stance.

"What diamond?" Samuka asked, surprised at his own voice, which sounded controlled and fearless. "I didn't steal any diamond."

The slap came from behind him. The sound loudly resonated in the confined space, and the sting paralysed him for a moment. It was a vicious, unexpected slap. He hadn't expected it so soon, but he knew it was coming at some point. He turned round to see the dispenser: it was Kemokai's burly messenger boy. He'd been ferociously cracking his knuckles all the while he stood behind the accused man. Samuka had another vicious blow delivered to the middle of his face, just above the bridge of his nose and right between his eyes. Blood started trickling down his nose instantly. He instinctively put his left hand to his nose in an attempt to stem the blood flow, but the blood kept dripping from his battered nose and onto his shirt.

In a sour tone, Kemokai ordered the eager beaver to stop. "By the way things are going, you'll be having enough time for that yet." And then, turning to Senesie, he continued, "I'll ask you one more time. After that, you get the whole works. I believe you know the score, so please don't mess me about. Do you understand?"

Samuka nodded comprehension and then continued soothing his broken nose, which was hurting terribly. In his pain, he noticed his nose was swelling up as well.

"Now where is the diamond you stole?" Kemokai asked in a bellowing voice that startled even the burly messenger.

"I already told you, I didn't steal any diamond."

"So you are determined to play it tough? All right, then, we'll play it tough," said Kemokai. "Do you remember what happened to Onemanday? Do you wish to go down the same route?"

"I didn't steal any diamond," Samuka insisted.

"I didn't steal any diamond," Kemokai repeated in a mocking tone. He turned to Senesie, who was still standing beside him like a static bodyguard and said, "Tell us what you saw Samuka do at the mines last night."

Senesie, without a glance in the direction of his friend, recounted what he had recounted to Kemokai when they returned from the mines. Senesie's accurate narration of the event surprised Samuka. The rat seemed to have been watching his every move.

"And when he thought no one was watching him," he heard Senesie say, "he retrieved the stone from his shaker and threw it in his mouth. I should know. Regardless of the fight, I was fervently watching him, as I always do with people at the shakers. A beautiful woman can't distract me, let alone a mere fight between friends. You're well aware of that."

Kemokai and the messenger exchanged wry smiles. They knew very well that Senesie had never been an admirer of the opposite sex.

"Hear that?" asked Kemokai. "Do you still deny stealing the diamond?"

"I didn't steal any diamond. He is lying."

"I pity you, then," said Kemokai, "because I believe him, and so would any diamond worker. We all know that allegations of diamond theft don't come lightly. The accuser is aware of what happens to him if an allegation proves to be false." Kemokai paused, and in short, guttural bursts, he giggled twice before he resumed. "But you don't really want to wait for that, do you? You'll be permanently damaged or long dead by the time we realise your accuser was mendacious."

Kemokai stood up then, his massive, six foot eight frame towering over everyone in the room. He'd taken a step towards Samuka then stooped so his eyes could look straight into Samuka's eyeballs. Samuka maintained intense, unblinking eye contact for a few seconds before lowering his eyes. Kemokai didn't blink once during the staring competition. He stood up to his full height again and said, "Take him to the tree in the village square. Get him ready for the works, like we do with all diamond thieves. I'll join you shortly to oversee the rest of the procedures myself."

That was how the punishment had begun. And tied against the tree, his body aching all over, his wounds beginning to scab over, and the ants seeking industriously to reach the wet tissues underneath, Samuka needed all his courage to avoid bellowing. The excruciating pain of a thousand and one ants devouring him alive was no easy feat to experience. And the torment didn't stop there: there were the flies to reckon with, too. They were huge, shiny creatures in shades of green and blue. They swarmed around him, hovering and landing on the raw tissue the ants exposed. They buzzed round his head with unbelievable speed and agility. They looked like a halo, albeit a harrowing one, over his head. There wasn't much he could do about the ants and flies except vigorously shake his swollen head and stamp his already weakened, sore feet on the ground.

Samuka felt his stomach rumble and he knew the smelly concoction Sama administered would have its desired effect soon. He wondered whether the diamond lodged deep in his stomach would come out with the first wave of defecation. He smiled in his mind. If it did, his gruelling endeavour would be for nothing. His stomach rumbled again, and he knew he would have to go soon.

"I want to go to the toilet," he said to the men in charge of him.

"Thought the day would never come," one of the men said as he laughed.

"He says he wants to go to the toilet," another repeated loudly for the benefit of Kemokai and the crowd.

18

The excited crowd watched as they peeled Samuka away from the ant-ridden tree before the rope attaching him was completely removed. Samuka groaned in pain. One of the burly men minding him kicked him viciously on the shin. "You shouldn't have stolen a diamond," he quipped as he delivered another kick into Samuka's stomach. Some people in the crowd laughed.

"Take him to the diamond thief latrine," ordered Kemokai.

The illicit diamond mining industry was a hard and cruel one. It required savage strength, perseverance, hope, and (predominantly) luck in order to survive.

Unlike the National Diamond Mining Company (NDMC), illegal miners didn't prospect mining sites. Therefore, there was no guarantee of finding diamonds on a site after several weeks of twelve-hour days. Under the circumstances, if a man were accused of stealing diamonds, he was already dead. Diamond theft was like stealing the combined efforts of the strength, perseverance, hope, and luck of the gang in one go. The accused personally stole from all the gang members and everyone working on the mines. They would demand justice, and that justice would be achieved through the traditional customs of the mines. Samuka had dared to gamble with his life, fully aware that he could lose it in the process.

Kemokai was actually feeling sorry for Samuka and wondered whether he was going soft. *The boy must be a plain moron. Probably reckless and very greedy with little regard for his life,* Kemokai thought.

Amid shouting and taunting that excited the crowds even more, they unceremoniously dragged Samuka to the diamond thief latrine.

"Make sure he gets a taste of his shit, the thieving baboon," shouted a miner from the crowd.

"Yeah," returned Marie, the village whore, "make us see him whole. Nothing would excite us better than seeing his ding dong." Marie wasn't one with many inhibitions. She spoke and did things the way she liked, regardless of what everyone else thought.

A few women in the crowd laughed at the joke. Many more didn't. They despised Marie. They didn't want to be associated with a loose woman, one who openly cavorted with men. Men may like her because men liked every kind of woman, but to the women of Simbaru, Marie was like Siberia, a place everyone knows but no one wants to visit. Every woman knew Marie, but no one wanted to get close with her. They didn't want their good characters contaminated. They had good reasons to be afraid: the majority were aware of the lewd things she was up to with their husbands or boyfriends. They couldn't ever forgive Marie for that. But for their men, they would've chased her out of town a long time ago. Still, some women planned vengeance against her. They knew their opportunity would arrive one day.

The crowd followed. They knew what to expect. They were going to watch a man shit. They were going to watch a man smell his own shit while rummaging through it with his bare hands to recover the allegedly stolen gem. The crowd was aware that they wouldn't merely smell Samuka's shit, they would see it as well.

The latrine was a crude, shallow hole in the ground. It was the size of a small bucket and located on the swampland near the village. A small-sized shaker particularly designed for such a purpose lay at the bottom of the hole to catch the feces. Samuka would be rummaging through that shaker to recover the stolen gem. The crowd watched as Samuka squatted over the hole. As he did so, his huge penis escaped from the loin cloth and hung in full view of the people at the scene.

"God, he's big," Mila whispered hoarsely, prodding me in my left ribs at the same time. I guess he wanted to draw my attention to what had induced his comment. He must have thought I hadn't seen Samuka's monster of a dick fall out.

"Is there much difference between his and yours?" I asked while grinning.

"I should've known better than to depend on you to have a laugh." Mila seemed a little embarrassed but didn't comment again.

The women were ecstatic. It showed on their faces, even as their men looked on. Some had their hands covering their mouths in gestures of surprise and awe. "That's too big," commented a thin, bony, old crone. She spoke loud enough for those nearest to her to hear. In all my life—mind you, I've been with many men—I never came across something like that. That's the real yamakopoi!"

Yamakopoi was what the locals called a very large dick. It meant *go back with your money.* Many of the women laughed at the old woman's comment. Some of them didn't; they would do anything for such a yamakopoi to water their gardens.

"Come visit me any day, sweetheart. If you survive this," said Marie, smacking her lips loudly and unabashedly in anticipation of the sensations she imagined she would get from such a tool. "It will be on the house, as you already know. It would cost you nothing, absolutely nothing."

"She has no shame," commented Sandivah to a pregnant woman with a child strapped to her back.

"Yeah, tell me about it," said the pregnant woman in a sarcastic tone. In a stern candid tone, the woman continued, "But why must she? At least she's brave enough to let everyone know who she is and what she does, unlike us. I must say, she is a very brave and honest woman. Don't you think? I am sure many of us would like to be like her." She gave Sandivah a knowing look."

Sandivah declined to answer. She immediately moved several paces away from the woman, but she kept her eyes firmly glued on Samuka's huge appendage, which was hanging down towards the latrine hole like a short, thick snake. *It is true what the other woman said,* Sandivah mused. *We are all hypocrites. We keep our thoughts and feelings wrapped up within ourselves, but they are no different from Marie's. She makes them public. I bet most women would like their men to have a lunchbox like Samuka's. But none of us would dare to admit it in public. For instance, what wouldn't I do if I had such a tool to give me a daily workout? I would probably worship it every day.*

While yearning for Samuka's one-eyed snake, Sandivah felt hot inside. She squirmed as she felt a trickle of warm liquid run down her right thigh. She looked around nervously, for a moment confused and wondering whether others were aware of what was happening between her thighs. She continued looking carefully at other women in the crowd to determine if they, too, were feeling the effect. In the process, she saw her husband, Sahr, engaged in an intimate conversation with a young girl of about sixteen.

It was common knowledge that Sahr was determined to make Martha his fourth wife. That made his other wives jealous, Sandivah included. She immediately forgot about her fantasy as a murderous jealousy overwhelmed her. She wanted to thrash the insolent baby who was flattering her husband. *Yes, the girl is only a baby, and yet she's already determined to eat from the same bowl as her elders and betters. It was just yesterday that she stopped running around dirty and completely naked. Now she wants to usurp my status as the favoured wife. If Sahr marries a fourth, all the attention, endearments, and love I am getting now will be lavished upon Martha. I should know: that's what happened when Sahr took me as his third wife.*

Sandivah turned around, determined to head in her husband's direction. She took a few steps forward and then realised her position was helpless. She couldn't stop Sahr from marrying another woman if he chose to do so. His first two wives were unable to stop him when he wished to marry her. Now she knew exactly how the other women must've felt. It was her turn, and it broke her heart. Like it or hate it, she had to accept the situation. She turned round again and returned to her place in the crowd. She banished the thoughts of her husband and the young girl from her mind to concentrate on the poor diamond thief still squatting over the hole. She noticed that his penis had grown even bigger. It was fully erect, and it looked enormous. She became happy again and smiled brilliantly within herself. She wished Samuka hadn't stolen a diamond. She would have found a way to get into his trousers. Because she knew that Sahr would basically abandon her when his latest princess joined the harem, she was determined to get a sideshow.

Sandivah thought about what the man's tool would do to her, the thrills she would get from touching it and caressing it, and the ecstasy she would experience when he was deep inside her. She also thought about what it would feel like when he finally exploded inside of her, the mind blowing orgasm that she would experience in turn. She felt that wet feeling between her thighs again, but it was a lot wetter than before. Sandivah smiled, contented. Sahr could do whatever he liked. He could marry all the women in the village for all she cared. She really was tired of caring anymore.

She believed she had found something to occupy those empty nights when one of the other wives was sleeping in Sahr's bed. It didn't matter whether Samuka survived or not; the image of his huge appendage would forever be implanted in her mind. She had discovered something she could latch onto to fulfil her fantasies. She realised she didn't need to have the real thing to experience pleasure. All she had to do was think about it and fantasise. The mere thought of Samuka's magnificent, almost adorable manhood would, for the rest of her life, make her swoon and be fulfilled. She looked at it once more and sighed regretfully. *If only he hadn't stolen a diamond! Now he will be dead or maimed forever.* Nevertheless, what she saw would forever stick inside her mind. She would treasure it forever and use it effectively, especially with a fourth woman in the wing.

The unmistaken pong of human feces wafted over the heads of the people closest to the crude latrine. The foul odour diffused and reached the rest of the crowd. Even in the open air, the smell was overpowering. Some people pinched their noses. Others didn't mind. They were too intoxicated by all the excitement to bother about the smell of shit. After all, they seemed to reason, everyone shits, and shit smells.

"He has dropped," one of the men guarding him proudly announced as if anyone needed the commentary. Everyone knew that Samuka had dropped; the pungent smell in the immediate atmosphere verified that.

The crowd stirred excitedly. Two of the burly guards yanked the poor fellow from the makeshift latrine and onto his feet. They handed him a blue and white striped plastic kettle full of water. No one told him what to do; he already knew. Graciously resigned to what fate would dish out to him, he prepared to sift through his own feces with his bare hands.

On his feet, Sandivah realised that she had wrongly assessed the size of Samuka's penis. Fully erect, it was an outrageous, provocative, enormous monstrosity. Her juices really began to flow. Her underwear got wet, and she felt hot fluid flowing down her thighs, right down to her knee. Only the cotton wrapper she wore from her waist to feet spared her any embarrassment. Nevertheless, she shivered from the unique sensation she was experiencing.

"Are you cold?" asked Marie.

She'd noticed Sandivah shiver and assumed correctly that it was from the sight of Samuka's penis. She had experienced the same effect when Aiah Kamanda had purchased her amorous services. She couldn't comprehend how a man could get as big as that. But at the time, she'd loved every minute of the monstrosity lodged in the abyss of her throbbing, hot pussy. She loved the experience of him exploring and ravaging her soft, erotic tissues. She kept coming until she lost count. Afterward, she wondered how she was able to accommodate all of him, especially when Aiah Kamanda had insisted on sampling her asshole with his tool. She had obliged; she couldn't refuse. After all, she was a mere commodity bought by men. And when men bought her, they expected to be serviced any way they wanted. Besides, she figured that if she could gain such pleasure from Aiah Kamanda's tool in her pussy, she could get even more satisfaction when he was in her asshole.

"I could swear I just saw you shiver," Marie continued, smirking. "Is something wrong with you?"

"No, I'm not cold. What if I'm cold? What's it to you?" Sandivah answered curtly, failing to cloak the embarrassment and anger in her voice.

"You don't have to chop my head off," replied Marie heatedly. "I only inquired because I was concerned. What do I care any—" Marie began before being interrupted by the sight of pointed at Samuka's penis. "Now wait a minute," she said knowingly, "don't tell me the sight of that has turned you on so much that you're shivering?" She asked and laughed boisterously.

At that moment, Sandivah wished the ground could swallow her on the spot. She was visibly blushing, and she felt more embarrassed than she had ever been. She was sure other women heard Marie's comment. Some of them turned round to look at her. She knew she had to say something quickly or everyone would think Marie was right.

"Does Sahr know you have the hots for that thief?" asked Marie, more to ridicule Sandivah than to get an answer. The other women laughed and slapped their thighs.

"Don't be daft," returned Sandivah. "I'm a married woman, unlike you," she added in an unconvincing voice. "You are free to have him. You could even go over to the latrine and have him right there." Some of the women laughed.

"Would you lot shut up your lousy mouths?" requested a very plump woman. "You are all very naive. Let me tell you this straight: only a hypocrite woman would deny she's not captivated by the man's size. So please shut up and let's enjoy what we are here for."

Sandivah was grateful for the plump woman's intervention. No one pursued the topic again and peace reigned. However, Sandivah decided it was best to wait a while before leaving. She didn't want anyone else commenting on her disposition. She didn't want anyone knowing about her latest secret, her fantasy about the naked man who was now sifting through his own shit for some damned diamond.

Diamonds! Diamonds! Why did God ever make them? The damned things are cursed. As beautiful and expensive as they are, they undo the very people that work with them. One can't be involved with diamonds and claim to be very honest. There was always a percentage of dishonesty in the most honest diamond man. Most diamond men managed to keep that particular vice under their cloaks as long as possible, but it always came out in the end. And when the vice did show up, it always led to scenes now unfolding. Savagery and humiliation are the main tools for recovering a stolen gem. What a waste, what a disaster!

Sandivah watched the accused man sift fervently through the hot feces in the shaker. If he hesitated for a second, one of the giants flanking him delivered a blow or a crack of the whip. Somehow, she felt his pain. Watching became too much for her. She turned around in disgust to make the short walk back to the village and straight to her house. Inside her room, she broke down and grieved for the man she knew was going to die. Unless they recovered the gem he was accused of lifting, Samuka was a dead man. It was only a matter of time. The next step would be the Gaandoe. No men put on the Gaandoe survived. Sandivah was on her bed and watching the ceiling intently. Tears blurred her vision, and she continued to grieve for a man she had never felt anything for before that day.

19

"There is nothing in it," announced one of the burly men put in charge of Samuka. "And he seems to have finished emptying his bowels. What a stench!" He was referring to the search that had just taken place in the shaker.

"The Gaandoe it is, then," declared an impatient Kemokai. He had stood by without interfering as Samuka shifted through his own shit. Kemokai had hoped that the stolen gem would turn up in the mess. It was not so much about the stone or what it was worth, it was for the sake of Samuka. He liked the boy; he was a hard worker and as strong as a buffalo. He didn't want him to die over a bloody stone. However, he had no choice other than to go through with the process to recover the stone. Otherwise, he would be regarded as a weakling. He would lose respect and support among all the miners. He didn't want that to happen; it would be like committing suicide. So he had no qualms with ordering Samuka to be taken to the Gaandoe.

"They are now taking him to Yaya and his boys," Samson gleefully announced. I was woeful and standing motionless. My eyes were wide open, but almost vacant.

I couldn't understand how anyone could be so happy to see a man savagely beaten and publicly humiliated, violated, and shattered. Suddenly, I did not like Samson anymore. Samson had just become a monster to me. I was determined to let Samson know exactly what I thought of him: "You are a monster," I said. "Do you realise that? You are a complete pervert if you take pleasure from this unfortunate situation."

"I'm no pervert, Yandi," returned Samson a little heatedly. "He deserves it, all of what he's undergoing. He should never have stolen the diamond."

"You don't even know or have any proof that he stole a diamond," I argued. "No proof at all—other than someone's claim that he saw him swallow a—"

"Save your breath," interrupted Samson. "You know nothing about this. You are new, and that explains your naiveté. Anyway, Senesie said he saw Samuka put the stone in his mouth. Senesie is his best friend. I believe him."

"Why would only Senesie see him when there were other watchers? No other watcher saw him."

"Leave it, would you," Mila said to me softly. "As Samson said, we are new here. Come, let's get out of here and find a comfortable spot to see all that takes place on the Gaandoe."

"You mean you enjoy it, too, Mila?" I asked, surprised at his attitude. Suddenly, I didn't feel like watching anymore.

"No, I don't enjoy it at all. I only want to see and learn everything about diamond thieving. I see this as a catalyst to strengthen my resolve to never steal diamonds. Hell, man, if this doesn't deter a potential thief, nothing will."

"Samuka saw it all before, but that didn't stop him from stealing one (at least according to his best friend, Senesie)." And of course, that monster Samson," I added sarcastically.

"Anyway, let's go," insisted Mila as he pulled me gently by the arm. I allowed myself to be pulled away, and we headed back to the village square.

"If you are so sorry for him, why don't you offer to exchange places?" Samson asked loudly in our wake.

"Don't let him get to you, my friend," said Mila. He patted me slightly on my left arm. "Samson is a poisoned prick, and you were right to call him a monster and a pervert. Indeed, he is both and more as far as I'm concerned. He's also got the evil eye."

"How do you know that?"

"I don't. I'm just trying to placate you, pigheaded fool"

We laughed merrily as we arrived on the square. All thoughts of the evil, perverted monster that was Samson disappeared. It was as if our laughter became an antidote for that vile person. Nevertheless, it wasn't the sole antidote. We also caught a glimpse of what was being done to Samuka, and that alone was enough to erase any thoughts of Samson.

Samuka's feet were fully strapped to the highest notches on the prongs of the Gaandoe, and his hands drooped almost lifelessly towards the base. His head was safely nestled in the adjustable rattan basket that was rigged in the Y-base of the frame. The vomii he was wearing proved useless to protect his modesty when he was hung upside down on the crude device. His hands were miles apart from the vomii, yet his private parts found a way to escape the loose prison. His penis and scrotum were on show, drooping down past his belly button and towards his massive, hairy chest. His huge appendage was still long but a bit shrivelled, and it behaved like a wriggling snake every time he moved. His eyes were extremely red but devoid of emotion, and his face conveyed the expression of one who didn't care about what lay in store for him. Nevertheless, the young women appeared to care . . . not for the pain and humiliation he was enduring, but for his huge tool. Their eyes never wavered from it as they smiled knowingly at each other. They were fantasising and regretting the fact that his magnificent tool was going to waste.

As Mila and I squeezed and pushed our way to the front, we sensed the excitement among the crowd. There was a cacophony of voices discussing Samuka's impending demise. We reached the front just as Yaya, dressed in deep blue satin trousers and a red top decorated with every colour of cowry shells presented an antique-looking bull's horn and tail in his right hand. He had entered from the other side of the square with four of his burly assistants. In his left hand, he was holding a mixture of squashed leaves in a small calabash that had been blackened by grime over the years. We also noticed Kemokai standing in the little group near the Gaandoe.

Leaving three of his assistants behind, Yaya walked ceremoniously to the centre of the square, blew loudly on his bull's horn, and handed it to the assistant. The assistant, per tradition, followed him closely. And then he proceeded to splash the solution of squashed leaves over the crowd with a small palm frond that was hidden until that point. With every splash, he recited some incomprehensible chants to whichever god he was calling upon. Some people cringed as he neared them, but that didn't deter him from splashing the foul, slimy, greenish liquid on them. When he was done, he cleared his throat, and prepared to make a speech.

"My dear people," he began, "we've the unfortunate situation on our hands to brutally deal with one of our own. We are all aware that our community completely depends on the mining trade for our survival. Therefore, we have to protect the industry from unscrupulous people like our Samuka. He knows the golden rule of the mines, and he decided to break it. Samuka is being accused of stealing a diamond.

It means he is being accused of stealing from all of us. He is now going to suffer for his greediness. Once we start working the Gaandoe, there'll be no turning back; the punishment will have to follow its course regardless of the consequence. So before you, all my people, I'll ask the culprit one more time to tell us the whereabouts of the diamond before the Gaandoe starts to devour him."

Yaya stopped so that what he had said thus far would sink in. He passed the mixture in the calabash to one his assistants, transferred the bullhorn to his left hand, and began to manipulate the black and white bull's tail. Slowly, he advanced on the crowd as if in a trance. His eyes were glazed over, vacant, and ghostly. With his left hand, he blew on the horn and tossed the bull's tail high into the air. The tail stayed in the air, floating and shaking vigorously of its own accord. The vigorous shaking of the suspended tail was reflected only in Yaya, not his assistant. Standing in one spot, he effortlessly yet violently shook like the bull's tail. Every fibre in his body trembled like a pneumonic drill operator. The crowd gasped in awe even though some had experienced the mystic occurrence before. Others, out of fear or respect, quickly backed away from the mysterious Yaya.

This little magic of the shaking bull's tail and the shivering man impressed Mila and me. We were at the front of the crowd and not strangers to such magical displays. We'd experienced similar displays in Simbaru, too—something to do with juju or witchcraft. There were two or three people in Simbaru, including my father, who did strange and unexplainable things like commanding noisy weaverbirds to be silent. In fact, Mila and I, on several occasions, had seen my father throw a simple string to the ground that changed into a venomous, spitting cobra with a pink, forked tongue. However, as soon as he picked up the cobra by the tail, it changed into a string again. He did this every time he offered sacrifices to his gods. But a suspended, shivering bull's tail was a first for us.

Both man and tail shivered for over a full minute. In that time, one could have heard a pin drop. And then, a still-trembling Yaya held out his right palm. The bull's tail fell back into it and seemed to be dormant. As soon as the tail was back in his hand, Yaya stopped shivering. But his eyes were still glazed over and vacant. Gradually, he regained his composure and recovered to his original self. He turned to the assistant with the calabash and extended his left hand. The assistant immediately took the few steps needed, handed the calabash to Yaya, and retreated. Yaya put the calabash on the ground, and with his big right toe, he drew an almost perfect circle around it. He then took the palm frond from the bottom of the calabash and started spraying the contents over the crowd again. Once done, he stood erect with his eyes shining and head held high. And then he proceeded to spray the mixture over his shoulders, in front of his body, behind his body, and to his left and right sides.

"The rites of the gods have been performed. The punishment must begin," he said, looking keenly at Kemokai.

"Then commence the punishment," Kemokai ordered. "We must recover the diamond by any means."

Resigned to his plight, and having watched the entire ceremony unmolested from an inconvenient position, Samuka braced himself for what was coming. He had seen it before and was afraid, very afraid. His vision from upside down wasn't perfect, but his ears and emotions were. He wasn't surprised, then, when he heard Kemokai confirm that the punishment must begin.

20

Scenes started playing in his mind. The ancient lover, the first man to die on the Gaandoe according to the oral history of the village, was the first apparition he saw in his tormented mind. He had never seen the man, and he wasn't even there when Chief Mbormborlai sentenced the man to the newly invented Gaandoe. Why was his image tormenting Samuka? Still, in his warped mind, he saw the man tied to the Gaandoe, shouting and bawling his eyes out. The man was begging for mercy that was never forthcoming. He saw an assistant operator of the device let go of the third rope that held the prongs together. The prongs snapped open immediately. He heard a great tearing noise, and then he saw visions of the man's blood, intestines, and other body organs scatter in the dust due to the ferocity of the recoil of the device. He saw the mutilated body hanging on the Gaandoe: each foot was attached to a prong, and the torso was torn evenly in two, from anus to head. Blood was dripping from every part of the man's body. For a brief moment, Samuka believed that it was his blood and organs out there, but he took a look at the ground directly below his head and felt relief that he was still alive. Nevertheless, the event continued to play out in his mind. He shut his eyes to block out the picture, but the equally gruesome image of Onemanday replaced it immediately.

Samuka had actually watched Onemanday die on the Gaandoe. The spectacle that was unfolding in his mind was explicit and personal. Onemanday had also been accused of stealing a diamond. No amount of humiliation and punishment made him admit to the theft. The Gaandoe had been the last resort. The vision playing in Samuka's mind was of a bloodied, shit-pongy, and crippled Onemanday who had been dragged to the torture device. Considering the state that he was in, he put up a good fight. But his efforts only resulted in more punishment, and they eventually got him up on the Gaandoe. Samuka watched as Onemanday was tied to the device. His mind skipped over the ritual and arrived at the scene of the actual punishment on the Gaandoe. Onemanday was completely naked without a stitch on, just as he had come into the world. He was been beaten again, more due to vindictiveness than punishment.

"Where is the diamond?" Samuka heard Yaya ask Onemanday. There was no answer from the unfortunate man, and the Koboko descended on his back in quick succession. All he could do was yelp as loud and as much as his waning strength allowed.

"Just let us know what you did with the diamond, you thick bastard," intervened Kemokai. "Yelping like the coward you are won't help you at all."

And then Onemanday spoke. Everyone was surprised when they heard the man speak, especially Kemokai, at whom most of the filthy tirade was directed. "Go fuck a donkey," Onemanday said. "Yes, you, Kemokai. And that pervert of a witch, Yaya. And yes, the whole lot of you good-for-nothing pig fuckers. Do you think I'm afraid to die? You can kill me anytime you like, but I'm the winner here because you're the ones who smell my—" He couldn't finish the sentence because the whip kept crashing down on his body.

"Loose a little of the rope splicing the Gaandoe's prongs," ordered Yaya. "We'll see who's in control here."

"No," countered a furious Kemokai who looked like he was ready to murder everyone around him. "Go all the way. Right now."

"You heard the man," echoed Yaya to the men operating the Gaandoe, "go all the way."

In his mind's eye, Samuka watched the assistant in charge of the third rope undo it suddenly and let it reel outwards of its own volition. Free from its restraints, the prongs on which Onemanday's feet were still spliced, recoiled with such force that it split him wide open, equally down the middle, from his anus right through his head. Samuka watched as fresh brain tissue and some of Onemanday's insides were sprayed into the brown dust of the town square. Onemanday was dead before he finished the scream that involuntarily erupted from the depths of his thirsty throat. An overwhelming, putrid stench that mixed with the odour of feces and urine filled the air immediately as the device violently disembowelled the unfortunate man. And the smell lingered in the square long after the event. Regardless, the crowd seemed determined to see the end; they pinched their noses to curb the intensity of the terrible smell.

Samuka came back to reality when he felt the Gaandoe's prongs and his feet move apart considerably, causing him major discomfort. He thought it was the end and braced himself for it. He just hoped

Dead End Poverty

that death would be quick and instant. He knew that nothing would save him. Even if he accepted that the diamond was lodged somewhere in his stomach, they would still likely kill him. Kemokai and the men were not going to wait for him to shit out the diamond. The sooner the saga of the stolen diamond was resolved, the better for all. There was still a lot of work to do in the mines. Their impatience would be immense.

But it was not the end, as Samuka had feared. The assistant had only loosened a few reels of the bush rope to cause a little recoil from the device. The prongs didn't expand any further, but he could already feel the strain and intense pain in his legs. He nearly screamed, but he subdued the effort, determined not to die like a a cowering, helpless whelp. He was not going to let his heartless tormentors gain any pleasure from his weakness, even though he was doomed.

"Admit to stealing the diamond so that you can save your life," said Yaya in an imploring tone. "We know it's in your stomach, but we have to get confirmation from you. Now, Samuka, did you swallow the diamond?"

"You're wasting precious time, you stupid, old man. Get on with it," said a very exasperated and impatient Kemokai as he paced up and down the frontline of the crowd.

The crowd gasped when they heard Kemokai call the old man stupid. Kemokai immediately realised that he had made a stupid, terrible error. No one called Yaya stupid or any other derogatory name and got away with it. Before Kemokai could even think of words to apologise or play his verbal abuse down, Yaya was right under his nose, vigorously waving the bull's tail in his face. Abruptly, he released the tail from his hand. With any other man, one would have expected the tail to drop to the ground immediately, pulled down by the force of gravity. But not with Yaya. Instead, seemingly of its own accord, the tail flew around Kemokai's head in an unrestrained manner, brushing his nose, mouth, and face with every revolution. Kemokai was shaken and scared. He tried to move away, but the tail followed him. He realised that he couldn't escape from the bull's tail and stood his ground, resolved to apologise. However, it was almost impossible to talk because he was gasping for breath—the tail kept brushing against his nose. Yaya noticed his discomfort and held his empty hand in the air. The tail immediately fell into his outstretched hand and didn't make any more mysterious movements. Kemokai was grateful to breathe normally again. He tried to talk, but Yaya signalled him not to.

The old man spoke instead: "You have offended the gods." His voice was scary, nasal, and ceremonious. "You must appease them before the day is over. You know what'll happen if you fail. You must take a male goat, a white ram, ten leones in coins, six red cockerels, and six white hens to the shrine. When you've done that, we will talk about how we might convince the gods to absolve your miserable soul for this abomination. Now can you watch quietly while I take care of the job at hand?"

Kemokai didn't argue with the old man. Humbled and humiliated, he returned to his place by the Gaandoe. He was thankful he had escaped almost scot-free. He would take the items to the shrine to appease the gods as soon as the case of the stolen diamond was resolved. Nevertheless, he knew he had been a fool for allowing his emotions to rule over his reasoning power. He shouldn't have called the old wizard stupid. Now it was going to cost him money. It would cost a fortune, and he was going to lose it all because a little bastard decided to be greedy. His greed had him exactly where greedy people found themselves. For all he cared, Samuka could die or disappear. He just wanted to end the saga.

"So you will not tell us where the diamond is?" Yaya asked. "This is your last chance, son. You'd better take it. Maybe it will save your life," he added.

Still, there was no answer from the tormented man. Yet from his unique, upside down position, and with a cheeky smile in his eyes, he held the eyes of the wizard until Yaya turned away in frustration and anger. His semi-wrinkled face twitched to form more worry lines on his broad forehead. Somehow, Samuka implied that he was past caring, that Yaya didn't scare him anymore.

"The old crow must be really angry now. Look at the anger on his miserable face. Samuka's truly finished now," Dowu commented in a low voice. He had managed to make his way through the crowd, and he was standing right behind Mila and me.

"Why is he angry?" asked Mila.

"Because he has defied the great Yaya and shown that he's not afraid of him," Dowu said. "Yaya thrives on fear and loathes anyone who does not submit to his fraudulent scaremongering."

"How do you explain the flying bull's tail, then?" Mila asked. I saw the thing fly and rattle with my own eyes. I didn't detect any engine flying it around Kemokai's head, or anything else for that matter. If he is a fake, he must be a brilliant one."

While having their hushed mini conversation, Yaya gave the signal to release the Gaandoe's prongs all the way by rubbing his scraggy face with the bull's tail. It was a prearranged signal. Those who had watched the Gaandoe consume previous victims before knew exactly what Yaya's little gesture meant. The little crowd gasped as one, and we abruptly cut our conversation so we could focus on the procedure. Everyone knew that the case of the swallowed diamond was going to be resolved at last.

Kemokai thought the order was never going to come, and he was caught by surprise when it actually came. *Now*, he thought, *that son of a goat is going to pay dearly for stealing my diamond and making me lose my animals as sacrifices to the gods. I'm sure he'll rot in hell.* Kemokai smiled to himself and silently willed the assistant to release the rope as soon as possible. For all he cared, Samuka could fly, disappear, or die—he only wanted the saga to be over quickly.

For my part, I immediately felt sorrowful for the plight of my friend, Samuka. Though he wasn't really a friend, he seemed like more than an associate. I recalled, again, that the bloke had actually advised us against what he was now answering for. It was quite ironic! Nevertheless, I felt sad for Samuka because I knew that he wouldn't survive the Gaandoe. I felt two fat tears in the corners of my eyes and used the back of my left hand to wipe them away. I didn't want anyone to notice the tears. I said a short mental prayer for Samuka and hoped for the best—or a miracle. I wondered whether a prayer could really save him. I wondered how people could be so cruel with each other, with people they knew, people they played with and talked to and ate with and worked with. *Are humans really so cruel?* I mused.

Yet people in the town pray five times per day on a daily basis. How could they ask forgiveness from God and other gods if they can't forgive anyone? It was all very confusing for me. The part of the world I came from never practiced such outrageous and sadistic rites for glittering, stupid stones. Nevertheless, I knew people were different and behaved differently. Still, I was disillusioned with the barbarous practise. I was even afraid of it. I made a mental note to talk sternly with Mila about swiping diamonds. For my part, there was nothing I felt I should worry about. From what I had seen thus far, I was resolved not to steal any precious stones. I had never stolen anything before the incident with the sheep, and I knew I would keep my resolution. But I was a little doubtful about my friend who seemed to thrive on danger.

I'll have to talk with Mila as soon as possible, I said silently, turning my head slightly to gaze at my friend. *In fact,* I reasoned, *what better time is there than just after witnessing such an intense experience.* I decided to do exactly that.

Mila was unaware I was watching him. With a sardonic smile on his face, he seemed to have directed his eyes and all his concentration on the incident that was unfolding before him. He had seen Yaya's anger and noticed him give the signal to release fully the prongs of the Gaandoe. Though he knew Samuka would die once the prongs were let go, he felt nothing but pleasure. It was as if he had become someone else. He found himself excited about the prospect of a man being split open like a melon. He had never seen the internal organs of a human.

Back in Simbaru, Mila was always hunting, trapping, and processing bush animals for food. He had seen all their organs, and he used to wonder whether they were similar to humans. At that moment, he had the opportunity to see exactly what they looked like, and he was excited. He didn't even notice when I turned to look at him. He was staring at the Gaandoe, his long neck stretched out, concerned that even the slightest movement of his eyes away from the impending, grisly spectacle would cause him to miss the event. He craned his neck even further, but his eyes remained fixated on the unfortunate man who was on the verge of death, all for a glittering pebble. *It should be ending anytime now,* thought Mila, thrilled and determined to see exactly how it would end.

I turned away just in time to see the last spool of rope reeling off the prongs of the Gaandoe. I held my heart in my mouth and braced myself for the expected. When it finally happened, it was so shocking I couldn't bear the sight. I shut my eyes tightly and silently muttered some prayers that I hoped would get me through the ordeal. As the last

Dead End Poverty

bit of rope left the prongs, I heard some twang from the recoil and a terrible, tearing noise that sounded like a small explosion. That noise was followed by a terrible, harrowing scream that could have come from the abyss of the kingdom of the dead. The unearthly smell that reached me wasn't like anything I had experienced before. It was an outrageous, abysmal smell. It was as if the most foul smelling things had been put together to create an incredibly pungent odour. I smelled it even before the mixture of Samuka's blood, flesh; bones, organs, and shit spattered in every direction and landed on spectators too close to the Gaandoe.

I was one of them, yet I was unaware that there were little specks of the late Samuka's blood decorating my face and clothes. I heard a few people retch instantly, and others followed when they realised that they were covered in bits of human tissue and blood. Yaya seem to have the most blood and body tissue on his person. Perhaps Samuka, even in death, was punishing the man who had ended his young life. Yaya looked to be in a trance, but he was probably satisfied that he had accomplished his goal. The whole episode didn't seem to bother him at all; for him, it was all part of the job.

One thing I was aware of, though, was that Samuka was no longer in the land of the living. The Gaandoe had made it certain that he belonged to the dark kingdom of Hades. He was dead, completely dead. No one would survive being ripped open that way. Samuka's dream of getting rich had died with him, and if we were to believe his accusers, he died with the stolen gem still lodged within his intestines. Half of those intestines were motionless on the ground and presented a very gruesome eyesore. The rest of his battered organs hung separately on both prongs of the Gaandoe. They were all that was left of a man who, only a few hours earlier, was alive and making plans for his future. *What a waste,* I thought, and I shook my head in disbelief and sorrow.

"Don't just stand there," Kemokai bellowed in rebuke to his gang members, "put the guts in a bucket and take it to the river. We must retrieve the diamond. And you, Brima and Munda, get the shakers and sift through the dust in the square. The diamond might have fallen there. Sift as much as you can."

Brima and Munda disappeared with alacrity. They didn't want the boss's anger directed at them. Each armed with a metal bucket, two other gang members (one of whom Yandi knew as Ansumana, though he usually called him Ansu) stepped out into the clear space doing their best to dodge human organs. They stood there confused, not sure where to begin. They were probably wary of doing the gruesome job, or perhaps they were just disgusted that they would use their bare hands to collect the insides of a man. The thought was too much for Ansu, and he promptly deposited a volley of bile over the scattered organs. He was not ideal for the job, and that was not lost on an increasingly agitated Kemokai.

"Get out of there, you thick, yellow bastard," he barked at an embarrassed Ansu. Ansu knew he would lose face among his peers.

"Even toddlers could do the job," Kemokai continued, "yet, there you are, shitting all over yourself at the thought of collecting intestines. The innards at your feet are no different than those of goats and sheep you process to eat. Or are they?" he asked sarcastically. "Get out of the damned place and let our Sheku join Musa."

Ansu left the centre of the square, and as soon as he cleared the small crowd, he disappeared swiftly. Sheku took his place. One look at Sheku, the man who replaced Ansu, revealed to me that he was another impassive one. He was grinning like he relished the job ahead. Without much ado, he grabbed the bucket that Ansu had abandoned and proceeded to gather the guts on the ground. Carefully but disrespectfully, he examined each one before he dumped it unceremoniously in the container. At the same time, he instructed Musa to get the remaining body organs still attached to the prongs.

Sheku collected each piece of organ, held it in the sunlight, and peered at it as if looking for the stolen gem. In the process, he manoeuvred his eyes and facial expressions in such a comical manner that some people in the crowd laughed despite the tragic scene before their eyes. Musa, for his part, advanced towards what remained of Samuka's body and started retrieving body parts from the Gaandoe.

At that point, some of the people in the little crowd began to disperse. It was just after mid-morning, and they all had many daily chores to do. There was nothing for them to watch any longer. The Gaandoe had done its work; the excitement was over. As for the recovery of the stolen gem, it was best left in the hands of Kemokai's gang, whose members they didn't envy at all. Mila and I also left. We wanted to catch some sleep before we were due to return to the mines.

21

Samuka's death affected people in different ways. I firmly believed that it was wrong to kill a man over a stone, regardless of its value. I felt sorrow and anger: anger towards Yaya, who was the master of ceremonies; anger towards Kemokai, who was the heartless dictator; anger towards the inventor of the Gaandoe; anger towards Mila and all who took pleasure in the agonising death of a promising young man. I was sure I would never understand what I had seen. I also started to wonder whether we had made the right decision to work in the illicit diamond industry. A man could easily get killed if he wasn't careful. Considering the manner in which Samuka died, justice was instant, raw, unforgiving, and flawed. And it wasn't necessarily justice.

For Kemokai, Samuka's death was a casual thing. It did not have any profound effect on him; he had seen far too many people die on the Gaandoe. For him, retrieving the diamond and setting precedence was more important. Besides, he earned extra respect as a real man and a leader. Everyone had seen that he didn't waver in terms of his decisions and actions. He could see respect and admiration in the eyes of his men; he could sense it everywhere he looked. He also saw fear, and that satisfied him immensely. Being a tough man had its own advantages: people didn't mess with him, and after a ruthless display of inhuman punishment, that message became easier to comprehend.

For most of the young women in the village, Samuka's death was a total and unnecessary loss as far as the trouser department was concerned, and they secretly lamented it. That was all they could do. Nevertheless, for one young woman, Sandivah, it went beyond that. She was devastated by Samuka's death, but she couldn't really explain why. She didn't know whether she'd fallen in love with him or whether it was just plain, insatiable lust because of his huge pecker. She'd seen Samuka in the village many times before, but she'd never felt anything towards him. However, that perspective had changed. Something within her yearned for the man, even though he was dead. Dead or not, she knew the man had affected her in ways she couldn't understand. She was craving him, praying for a miracle to bring that huge appendage back to life. It was wistful thinking and she knew it.

Samuka would never come to life again. His monster dick would be food for worms; that is, if enough of him were found to bury.

Sandivah hadn't stopped crying since she left the town square after the argument with Marie, the village's whore. It was only when she realised her husband, Sahr, would soon return home that she brought herself to stop crying. She remained glum and withdrawn, sad that she would never experience Samuka's monster dick. Nevertheless, she wasn't put off from it. She reasoned that she still had a clear image of the man's size. She only had to think about it, she reckoned, and she was sure she would be deliciously fulfilled sexually. But she also yearned for a real, physical encounter. Maybe that was why late Samuka's dick affected her so. Sahr hadn't been with her for months. It seemed he only had time for his betrothed, Martha. As it were, Sandivah was almost gagging for it . . . to the point of desperation. But she tried not to make it too obvious.

Samuka's appendage had awoken her sexual hormones. She needed to have a man soon. Fantasising wouldn't be the same for her. She needed to have a man to fuck her or she would go barmy. She would bear the consequences if her husband happened to find out. After all, she hadn't neglected him; Sahr had neglected her. He was confident and secure in the fact that he had other options. Sandivah was aware there were two other wives and his betrothed waiting in the wings. Therefore, the only option left for her was to commit adultery. Sahr had driven her to it. He had stopped sleeping with her without an explanation. She had tried to look extra sexy for him, tempted him with his favourite foods, and asked him directly for sex sessions—a thing nearly unheard of in her community—but all to no avail. In fact, Sahr had laughed at her and pointed out that she was fast developing the attributes of a loose woman.

Sandivah understood that she would have to take some initiative to fulfil her yearning. If she wanted to be entertained, she would have to do something about it. She already had a man in mind. Young Mila seemed like the ideal candidate. She had noticed the way he had been looking at her since his arrival. He always ended the flirtation by rubbing his bulging crotch, which made Sandivah smile with interest. She needed to do something about him, sound him out to see whether he had the guts to cross Sahr. Many in the village feared crossing her husband on any level. The boy might be no different, but he was worth a try. Guts or no guts, she was determined to have Mila, and she was confident that she would succeed. If she didn't, she will try Yandi instead. Contented, she smiled and discovered that she had finally stopped crying.

Marie, the whore, remained unaffected by Samuka's death, though she couldn't vouch for the fact that she wouldn't be missing his penis. His had been the one dick that really rang her bell. With him, there had been no pretences of orgasm. She didn't need to fake anything. Samuka's cock made her come instantly every time he penetrated her, and she kept coming until the end. She shivered in ecstasy just by thinking of the lovely sensations she had had with him. *What a good lover gone to waste!* she thought. Apart from that, in her opinion, he was just another thief whose time had come up. Yes, she would lose some income from a regular like Samuka, but there were still lots of other young men around to offset that. She would see what she could do with Sahr's new boys. They looked like promising clientele, especially the one they called Mila. She figured he was carrying a big load down there judging from the enormous bulge present in his trousers. She had also noticed the way he looked at women, and she knew he would be an easy pick.

She knew and understood types like Mila. Her sojourn in Koidu a couple of years ago hadn't been for nothing. She knew men; she knew all about what they wanted. She would have to work on him—the earlier the better. Of course, he would have to pay for it like all the others. After all, she realised and accepted that she was a whore. It was her livelihood. Maybe he would become a replacement for Samuka, or even surpass his size and bedroom competence. *I must do something about him soon,* she thought. And as she walked back towards her house, she started formulating a plan to seduce him. She smiled to herself and quickened her pace, already feeling victorious in her new quest.

For Mila, Samuka's death was just entertainment. He'd never been exposed to such cruelty; nevertheless, he found himself liking the whole episode of retrieving the stolen gem. He enjoyed the beating, abuse, and humiliation. Above all, he enjoyed the moment when the prongs of the Gaandoe were let go, when Samuka was torn into two like a piece of paper. He loved the way tissues, bones, and blood splattered in the square. In fact, he felt nothing but pure pleasure.

It was the first time in his life he'd ever felt like that. He couldn't understand why, and he suddenly felt afraid. However, fear didn't stop the pleasurable feeling he got from the sadistic punishment. Suddenly, his whole being was involved, emotionally animated by the procedure. An involuntary, sardonic smile appeared on his face. It was at that moment that I turned to look at him. I saw Mila's smile; it was cynical. It made me worry about my friend.

Mila had also learned from the incident. Though he knew that he could enjoy such gruesome incidents, maybe even execute the entire procedure himself, he was not about to be one of the Gaandoe's victims. He noticed the way I watched him from the corner of his eyes, and he didn't like it. He knew me very well, and he was sure he would be getting one of my philosophical lectures eventually. He would welcome it, because he would not take me seriously. I was always worried about him, but I didn't really need to worry. Mila was an adult; he could take care of himself, and I knew that. I would point that out to him again in my impending lecture. I doubted that would change anything on my part, though: I always worried. I figured I would always worry.

22

Back in the swamp, where Samuka had emptied his bowels while being watched over by a seemingly bored Kemokai and a handful of people that didn't mind the foul smell and ghastly procedure, Musa and Sheku emptied their buckets in the bottom half of a large drum. The drum contained some water that would be used to wash what was left of Samuka's guts. Somewhere between the town square and the swamp, Musa and Sheku managed to tie headscarves over their noses to minimise the inhalation of disgusting aromas.

Musa and Sheku proceeded to wash the guts, but they had little hope of locating the diamond. Again, they showed no emotion as they rummaged through the grisly remains. In fact, Musa whistled a tune as he worked as if he were engaged in a routine job. His hands, through to the elbow joints, were covered in watery shit.

Bent over the half drum, Musa and Sheku squeezed Samuka's guts to rid them of the remaining shit. They squeezed down all the shit in the guts into the drum. They then turned the guts inside out to make sure the gem did not remain stuck to the rough wall of an organ. If they found nothing in the guts, they were taken away and buried at once. Finally, they sifted through the watery solution of shit with a shaker (while under the watchful eyes of Kemokai). If they found something during or after the sifting, Samuka's brutal death would have been justifiable. However, if they found nothing, it meant that Samuka was innocent and had been wrongly punished and murdered. That would also mean that Senesie, the initial accuser, would be the next victim on the Gaandoe.

"There's nothing in it," a crestfallen Musa declared to Kemokai when their grisly task was over.

It was an unnecessary announcement; Kemokai had known instinctively that they would find nothing. He'd known even before the last few scoops of the shitty solution were examined. Strangely, he was glad that the gem wasn't found. It meant that he could leave to cleanse his unclean body and airways. He had been inebriated with the smell through the entire procedure to the point that he desperately wanted to delegate his job and leave. He'd decided against it anyway, reasoning that it would make him lose face. Nevertheless, remaining there to see the job done had been a form of self-torture. But with Musa's announcement, he was free to leave whenever he wanted. But before he left, he wanted to make sure the spectators were aware that the search did not recover the diamond. "Are you sure you found nothing at all?" he asked audibly.

"Absolutely nothing," replied Sheku in a loud but disappointed tone.

He had hoped they would find the gem. That would have meant a quick trip to Koidu with his share of the money from the sale of the diamond. Musa and Sheku were no longer bent over the drum. They were standing upright and impatient to get to the stream. The few remaining spectators talked excitedly among themselves as they headed back towards the village square. Kemokai joined them to make the short journey. He was morose, but not for failing to recover the gem, for the futile death of a young man untruthfully accused of stealing. He wondered whether Senesie had lied about the diamond. He did not consider Senesie to be a liar. In fact, he'd no reason to doubt the boy. *But why wasn't the diamond found in Samuka's shit or guts?* he wondered. *Maybe it fell out when the recoil force of the Gaandoe's prongs split him open.*

Halfway towards the village square, Brima and Munda turned up. They told Kemokai their search in the dust of the square yielded nothing. Kemokai grunted his acknowledgement and hastened towards his house. He remembered he owed Yaya and his damned gods. He couldn't forget to take a male goat, a white ram, six white chickens, six red cockerels, and ten leones in coins to the shrine. Yaya's gods didn't accept notes; any money for the gods had to be in coins, regardless of the amount. He would tell Saffa to collect the sacrificial ingredients and take them to the shrine himself. The gods would bring their wrath upon him if he didn't deliver the items himself. Yaya might be a funny, eccentric, old devil, but his gods never joked around. They responded swiftly to his invocations. Kemokai had seen it many times with his own eyes. Just last year, Moijue defied the old crone. He refused to make amends to the gods. He became a virtual invalid: both feet became grotesquely swollen. Kemokai was determined to avoid such a calamity. He would take the items to the shrine as soon as Saffa could get them ready. For the time being, though, he wanted to clean up and think about what to do with Senesie.

Senesie knew his time in the village was over. He felt sad; he liked the village and Kemokai. Kemokai was a good master. That was why he reported the diamond theft to him in the first place. He was sure that he'd seen Samuka put the diamond in his mouth. *What happened to the diamond he swallowed?* Senesie wondered, completely baffled. He'd been present at every stage of Samuka's tragic ordeal. He'd been confident that the stone would be found. He'd even envisaged how Kemokai would lavish praises on him. And above all, he'd pictured the slightly bigger share of the money he would receive from the subsequent sale of the diamond. Senesie had started to worry the stone might not be recovered after Samuka's guts were washed and rummaged through in the drum. He'd become even more worried after a few shifts in the shaker turned out to be fruitless. Worried the tide was turning against him, and aware of the punishment if the stone was not recovered, he left the swamp when everyone was focussed on the recovery of the stolen diamond. He'd gone to his shared room, packed his meagre belongings in a black bag, and taken all his money from the hiding place. He was ready to abscond from the village. He returned to the swamp just in time to hear Musa reporting to Kemokai that nothing had turned up from the search. He immediately made a U-turn and headed out of town, his black bag slung over his droopy shoulder, his gloomy disposition darker than the blackest clouds that herald a storm.

As far as Senesie was concerned, Yengema was history. He knew he would miss the village and his acquaintances, but he had to go. Staying would only land him in deeper trouble, and he might even end up dead. As he crossed the threshold of the village to enter the bush, he turned around to face the village in which he had spent six long years one more time. He looked long and hard at the vegetation and landscape and marvelled at their beauty. Suddenly, he didn't want to leave, but the feeling didn't last. The disadvantages of staying far outweighed the merits. He felt his eyes moisten, and two fat tears dropped onto his shirt. With a concerted effort, he turned round and disappeared into the thick jungle, aware that he was alone and forever banished from Yengema.

23

We were on our way back to the mining fields. We still had some gravel to remove from our pit. According to Tamba, if everyone worked hard, we would succeed in removing the gravel before the night was over. He said we might be able to start washing it that same night. It was good news; everyone was in high spirits despite the sad event of Samuka's violent and unnecessary death. His death kept cropping up in conversations along the single-file formation on the windy footpath.

"Samuka died for nothing, for a stone. I can't understand why," I said to Mila with genuine empathy.

Mila's reply was cynical: "Me either. What a waste of human life! Mind you, I'm not saying that I didn't enjoy or learn things from the episode. Far from that: I'll never forget the experience."

"So what did you enjoy?" I asked carefully. I didn't want an argument, it was just that I found it chilling that my friend enjoyed such a barbaric spectacle.

"It wasn't so much about what I enjoyed," Mila stated, "it's about what I learned. The nail drove home. You don't have to worry about me; I'll never be tempted to steal diamonds. I love my life, and I won't be losing it over some cursed stone, no matter how valuable they may prove to be. It's definitely not for me."

Pleased with his answer, I realised I didn't need to talk to my friend after all. I was shrewd enough to know Mila meant what he said. I decided not to pursue the issue any longer. I changed the topic to the work at hand: "I really hope we can remove all the gravel tonight. I'm impatient for my first diamond money."

"Same here, bro. Imagine what I could do with my share of money! This place has turned me into a monk. If I don't have a woman soon, I'll go crazy." Mila's appetite for the opposite sex seemed undiminished—our new location notwithstanding.

"Patience, Mila, that's what you need," I said. "You will have more women than you can handle once the money starts coming in. As for me, I'm always dreaming about Koidu town. When I get my first diamond money, that's where I'll go. I know I won't be disappointed.

Besides, it will be a pleasure to visit Mama Finda. I'm sure she will be pleased to see us.

"I'm with you on that," Mila said, smiling as a child would when promised a favourite dish. "That's where we'll go, Yandi. We will explore the town and visit places. We'll have as many girls as we like."

We both laughed. At the same time, we realised we'd arrived in the fields. There were scores of people there already. That was the thing about the diamond mines: day or night, the mines were never empty. Some gang members were always at the site, toiling hard, digging, and trying to reach the gravel that may or may not be there. The whole operation was just guesswork. If a pit yielded diamonds, it was wiser to situate another one close by it. The possibility of finding the precious stones in the new pit would be greater than in another untried site.

After the customary ritual of changing clothes, fetching tools, and removing water from the pit, we began the task of removing the gravel in earnest. As usual, gang members rotated to spread out the burden of the job evenly. Buckets full of the bluish-green stuff ascended steadily from the pit and were added to the growing pile under the guava tree. Using makambos and torches, we worked through the night. By dawn, there were three big piles of the stuff under the guava tree. However, the density of the gravel waned. Buckets came up from the pit with more white clay than gravel. The veterans in the gang knew we'd accomplished our mission; the white clay was the harbinger of such a revelation.

"Send up the last few buckets. We've hit the white," said Tamba. "Well done to all of you."

The other gang members cheered, but Mila and I were lost. We didn't join in the cheering; instead, we stood there grinning stupidly, wondering why they were cheering. Boima was closest to us; Mila asked him what hitting the white meant. Boima replied, "It means we finished removing the gravel. When white clay appears in the pit, it indicates that there's no more gravel in the pit. Rejoice! Tomorrow, we may start to kick the stuff."

With understanding dawning on us at last, we joined in the cheering and began backslapping each other fervently. We were also happy: we'd completed work on our first pit. After, the gravel was stored safely and awaited our washing. It all depended upon luck as far as whether the gravel would contain diamonds. The gang members hoped to get lucky.

The noise subsided as Tamba started speaking again: "Now that we have completed removing the gravel, we must cover the piles with palm fronds, twigs, and leaves. We must also collect stones and put them around the piles. There is no sign of rain yet, but it may rain later and wash the gravel away. The palm fronds, twigs, leaves, and stones are our insurance to keep the gravel intact. Everyone, use your torches or makambos to gather these items. Make sure the piles are well covered and protected."

Everyone looked around for the items to cover the piles. It didn't take long before we secured all three piles. Tamba was pleased with the job and declared the work session ended. We carefully hid the tools, washed our bodies, and changed into dry clothes. We were ready to go back to the village. We were so elated we didn't even notice the chilling effects of the cold morning dew on the tips of the long savannah grass that constantly rubbed against us from both sides of the footpath.

Upon arrival in town, Tamba updated Sahr about the status of the pit. Sahr decreed that we should commence washing the gravel when we returned to the fields.

"We must start washing the gravel tonight," he said, pleased that the work was close to completion. "I'll be coming with you tonight. I want to be present for the first wash. Go now, eat your breakfast, and try to rest well. There will be lots of work for us tonight."

Night was ideal for working in the pits. It was during the day that the Joe Khakis tend to raid illicit diamond fields. During the day, it was difficult for lookouts to see the security men in their light green, khaki uniforms. Likewise, it was hard to hear their vehicles approaching due to the natural noises in the area. Night was different: Joe Khakis didn't possess cat eyes that allowed them to see in the dark. They were obliged to carry torches on raids. Illicit miners in the fields (or their sentries) were able to see them from a distance and raise the alarm in time for the miners to escape. Because of that fact, there were more chances for the miners to escape. During the day, the Joe Khakis crept up on the unsuspecting miners and made a few arrests.

Mila and I found our favourite hammocks and installed ourselves in them. We drifted off to sleep almost as soon as our backs touched the hammocks. We woke up in time to join the others for the evening meal. After the evening meal, Tamba shepherded us back to the big veranda. He gave each gang member brand-new torch batteries and a pint full of kerosene for the makambos.

"Sahr asked me to supply them to you," explained Tamba. "He doesn't want torches or makambos to malfunction in the middle of kicking the gravel."

"Is he coming as he promised?" asked Dowu.

"Sahr will be with us tonight," said Tamba. "Nevertheless, knowing him as I do, I reckon he will only grace us with his presence for a couple of hours." He gave us a knowing and comical look before continuing: "Sahr has far too many important things on his hands in town. He prefers to be there instead."

"Such as screwing his three wives and some more?" Suma asked. Like Mila, Suma loved women. We heard that he was sleeping with Yei, Sahr's second wife, so I assumed jealousy and envy were the cause of his dislike for his boss. According to rumours, he hoped the man would drop dead so that he could marry Yei. Suma loved Yei, and Yei loved him. They kept their relationship very discreet. Sahr's redneck image hadn't deterred him at all. Everyone, including Tamba, laughed.

"You'd better not let him hear you say that," said Tamba. "God knows you're not far from the truth. Anyway, we will leave immediately after the evening prayers. Is that understood?"

We nodded our heads in agreement and did as we pleased before departure time.

24

As soon as the gang arrived in the fields, work began in earnest. True to his word, Sahr came with us (though he complained about the distance and the cold wind). He nominated Tamba and Dowu to start washing the gravel. To Suma, he gave the task of transporting the gravel from under the guava tree to the edge of the pit. The pit, up to the topmost terrace, was full of water. Tamba and Dowu, waist-deep in the water, were very busy with the shakers. To Mila, Sahr gave the task of loading the gravel into both shakers when required. Boima and I became lookout men for Joe Khakis on the prowl. Francis and Sahr stood by the edge of the pit with bright torches pointed directly into each of the shakers.

Very close to where the gravel was being washed, three makambos were placed in an arc along the edge of the pit. They provided ample light for the job at hand. The job at hand involved a simple procedure: washing the mud off the gravel, discarding the big stones and other debris, depositing the remaining contents into a specially prepared dry area, and looking through what was left for diamonds. Sorting out the gems from the ordinary stones required strict surveillance to deter theft. If diamonds were found, Tamba kept them until work was over. Except when Sahr was present, Tamba always took the gems of the night back to town.

The first diamond appeared in Tamba's shaker. Rays of light from the makambos and the torches illuminated the stone. He spotted it immediately and cried out, "Spot." It meant that he had found something. He picked up the gem and placed the shaker by the mouth of the pit. He then climbed out and handed the stone to Sahr. Alerted by the cry, members of the gang stopped whatever they were doing and crowded around Sahr. They wanted a glimpse of the object they had laboured to get out of the ground. It was a small stone, approximately three and a half carats. What it lacked in weight, though, it certainly made up for in beauty and elegance. It was a solid hue of sky blue, and it was formed into a hexagonal shape. The blue colour deepened towards the core the longer one looked at it. Majestically lying in Sahr's open palm, the gem beautifully reflected the light from his bright torch in different directions. We all just stood there and marvelled at the little wonder, happy but too excited to talk. Mila and I didn't need to be told that the stone in our boss's hand was a diamond. It was, indeed, unlike any other stone we had ever seen. We had seen our first diamond, and like everyone else, we were elated.

"We must get back to work if we want to finish kicking before dawn," said Sahr, carefully putting the diamond away in a special pouch he carried around with him regularly. "By the looks of things, I'm sure we've a winner in this one. Get back to work if you want to have some money in your pockets sooner."

By midnight, the bigger of the two piles of gravel under the guava tree was carted to the pit and washed. Everyone took turns transporting, loading and washing the gravel. There was always a lookout. Mila and I had two turns at the shakers, but our washes didn't turn up any diamonds. However, we used the shakers so adeptly that even Sahr commended us.

"On your next turn, I'm sure you won't need any instructions. You wash or kick as if you've been at it all your life," Sahr said.

Indeed, on our second attempt, we looked and worked like old hands at the job. Overall, the pit was a productive one. By the end of the wash of the first pile of gravel, Sahr had a hoard of twenty-six diamonds of various shapes, colours, and sizes. He lodged them safely in his pouch, which was secured deep inside his trouser pocket. He constantly kept his left hand over the pouch as if he were afraid the pouch would disappear. The biggest among the stones was the first diamond that Tamba discovered. The rest of the stones were less than or slightly more than a carat. Put together and sold, they would yield enough money to compensate us for our hard work, regardless of the cheating practices of the yullamen and the unavoidable deductions. Sahr hoped the gravel would produce more diamonds and kept muttering Koranic verses so that his God to grant his wish.

Mila was at one of the shakers again and gravel had just being loaded into his crude sifter. He immersed the shaker into the muddy water. In quick succession, he twisted the device clockwise and anticlockwise several times to wash the mud off the contents, sometimes using one hand to remove the stubborn mud. He saw the diamond at once when the muddy water drained from the sieve. It was an oily, glittering stone, and it looked like a big one. His immediate reaction was to swallow the stone, regardless of the mud partially covering it. The thought evaporated from his mind faster than lightning, though, when he remembered the Samuka's ordeal. He began to understand, though, why Samuka stole and swallowed a diamond. Mila concluded that the precious thing was a devil and master of temptation due to its sheer beauty and magnificence. It made you or broke you. It made you if you were honest and patient, and it broke you if you were impatient and dishonest.

It seemed no one had noticed his discovery, but that didn't tempt him to steal it. Instead, he reasoned that everyone was busy doing one thing or another towards retrieving diamonds from the gravel. Everyone had worked hard, and everyone deserved the proceeds from their labour. The decision of one man to steal from the group was completely wrong and immensely immoral. He could see why the punishment for stealing diamonds was so harsh. He also realised that the punishment was the most effective deterrent against diamond theft; it had certainly deterred him from stealing the diamond in his shaker. He resolved again not to make an attempt in that direction. He decided to announce his find. He put the shaker down in a safe place and proudly announced, "I think I've found something."

If Mila was hoping to gain everyone's attention, he succeeded brilliantly. Torchlights and makambos instantly engulfed him and his shaker. Even the other two washers put down their shakers carefully and peered into Mila's sieve. Sahr, with the biggest and brightest torch light, was at the very edge of the pit. His torch was pointing directly into Mila's sifter, and he leaned dangerously close in an attempt to get a glimpse of the stone. "Where is it?" he asked. "I can't see anything from here," he admitted lamely.

"Haven't taken it out of the shaker yet," replied Mila"

"So what are you waiting for?" asked Sahr in a combative tone that provoked giggles among the rest of the gang. The laughter quickly died down when Mila said, "I didn't want to become another Samuka. I wanted everyone to see me retrieve the diamond. That way, I won't be accused of diamond theft and risk being put on the Gaandoe."

Nervous laughter erupted from the small group again, cut short by Sahr as he praised Mila for his brilliant foresight: "Good thinking, my lad. If everyone thought and acted like you, there would never be any need for the Gaandoe. Could you please take the stone out now and give it to me?"

Mila carefully picked up the stone and put it in the palm of his right hand. Even as he did so, minute reflections in colourful arrays of light beamed back from his palm, clearly visible to those in and around the pit. Sahr, as a veteran, immediately knew that they had something big. But whether it was clean and valuable or blemished and considerably less valuable was another matter. He held out his hand towards Mila who had taken the few steps up towards the mouth of the pit, fist clenched over the partially muddy stone. Mila carefully put the stone in Sahr's hand and instinctively climbed out of the pit. Others still left in the pit followed him out.

Sahr anxiously rubbed off the wet mud from the stone using the edge of his shirt, but he couldn't keep his rising excitement secret. Several pairs of eyes watched anxiously and waited as he went through the ritual. Satisfied that he had rubbed off most of the mud, Sahr placed the stone in the centre of his left palm and pointed his bright torch directly at it.

As an old, experienced hand, he was able to analyse the stone instantly. He observed that it was a big, blue-white diamond that weighed about nine carats. He also saw the flaws in the stone at once: minute black dots that ran through it. The latter discovery almost extinguished his excitement. But the stone was a real whopper. It was blue-white, the type of diamond most desirable, but the black dots within it made it much less valuable. If the stone were flawless, they would have come into real money. He knew the diamond would sell for the price of a one-or two-carat diamond. He sighed regretfully and pointed his torch into the little crowd.

"It is a big, blue-white diamond," he announced. The men cheered. "But it is grossly flawed." The cheers died down. "Here, have a look at it yourselves."

The men moved closer and peered over his shoulder as he trained the torch on the diamond again. Even Mila and I saw the flaws at once. "We won't be getting much money for this," said Sahr, "so we'd better get back to work. As usual, I'll keep this with the others."

As the men returned to their duties, Sahr thrust his hands into his deep pocket to retrieve his pouch. Carefully, he opened it, dropped the big and flawed stone inside, secured it again, thrust it into his pocket, and kept his hand over the pouch as before. He stayed with them the entire night. It seemed Sahr didn't have too many important things on his hands in town after all. We resumed working and finished kicking the first pile of gravel. Unfortunately, no more precious stones of any significant value turned up that night. It was a good night's job anyway. We were buoyant men on our way back to town just before dawn. We had twenty-seven stones in the bag already. We were hopeful that the remaining gravel would yield more of the precious stones when we washed it. We were a happy team as we started discussing ways to spend our share once the diamonds were sold.

The following night, we returned to work. Sahr came with us again. He didn't stay the whole night. He was soon bored after several shakers of concentrates came up empty, and he took his leave. Up to the time he left for town, we'd found nothing, but we continued to kick the rest of the gravel. At that point, our morale was a bit low. We washed the entire pile of gravel that night and got a miserable compensation of six flawed stones for our trouble. All the stones were very small. Sold by themselves, they wouldn't amount to much. We were disappointed as we trudged home. But we also knew we had thirty-three gemstones in total to take to Mr K. That cheered us up a bit; we would still get some spending money in our pockets. For Mila and I, the excitement was overwhelming: we would earn our first diamond money and possibly make it to Koidu for some good times.

25

Amadu Bah was a Fulani immigrant from Conakry, Guinea. Like me and Mila, he'd come to seek his fortune in the diamond fields of Kono. He was about forty years old when he arrived. One way or the other, he found himself in Yengema, liked the place, and stayed for about twenty years. Amadu hadn't been a lucky man in the industry. Twenty years of mining had yielded no considerable sum to allow him to retire. Sitting in an old easy chair, constantly snoozing but brooding over his bad luck, he wondered why he had left his country in the first place. He had been learning the hard way that the grass wasn't always greener in another field. Had he remained in Conakry, people would see his condition and wouldn't expect much from him. However, because he had left his home to chase riches, the expectation was that he would return home wealthy.

After all the years he had spent in mining, he never hit it big. His share of monies from diamond sales were not large enough to tempt him to go back home with the family he'd created in Yengema. However, he'd been able to create a small trading stall in the veranda of the house where he lived. His local wife, Konomusu, efficiently managed the shop and fed the family from its profits. Even with the shop, they were only just able to survive the everyday financial hassles. Konomusu also minded the two boys and one girl she had borne for Amadu.

Amadu Bah wondered whether he would ever be able to return to his native country. He worried what his people would say if he returned poor, burdened by three children and a foreign woman. It was the reason why he hadn't returned to the home he missed so much. Besides, his luck hadn't shown any signs of changing for the better. Somehow, he was resigned to his plight; he knew that he would probably never strike it rich. Worst of all, he was an old man, sixty years old. Unless something spectacular happened to improve his luck, he was sure he would die in Yengema. Little did he know, things were about to change for him and his family. But Amadu Bah still believed in Allah, and he never missed any of his five prayers each day.

Amadu Bah's first son, seven-year-old Wurie, could be mistaken for an older boy. He was big for his age, and he could hold his own against bigger boys who tried to bully him when playing games in the village square. Boys in his age group (and even older boys) were wary of him because of his doggedness: he never gave up easily. If someone engaged him in a fight and proved stronger and victorious, Wurie would stalk him for as long as possible, insisting that his opponent would have to beat him to death to get rid of him. No amount of threats or blows would get him to change his stance, so much so that his opponents ended up bribing him just to get rid of him. Despite that fact, Wurie was still a sweet child and much loved, especially by his father, whom he adored. Even at his tender age, Wurie knew his parents were poor. He was aware that his parents were always arguing about money, that his father couldn't afford to buy him or his siblings the nice things that other parents bought for their children. He had since stopped asking and went on with life. He would hunt rodents and birds with his mates when he was not at the local Arabic school.

A couple of days after the public, grisly murder of Samuka, children were again playing in the village square. The square, thoroughly cleaned by Kemokai's men soon after Samuka death, was a social venue again. The torrential rain that fell the night after had further purified the square. All evidence of the brutal murder of Samuka seemed to have disappeared with the rain.

Wurie and his best mate, Komba, were playing a game of marbles not far away from the exact spot where the Gaandoe had disembowelled Samuka. There were other children in the square, too, engaged in different things of interest. A few shouted greetings to Wurie and Komba, and they responded cheerfully but nonchalantly as they continued their game. It was Wurie's turn to have a go. He tried knocking off Komba's marbles with one of his that was out of the demarcated playing circle they had drawn in the dust. For every one of the opposition's marbles he hit, he would win that marble. If he missed twice in succession, he would lose the turn and the marble to his opponent. At that point, Wurie was winning; he was adept at the game and had a generous collection of marbles he had won in a big, tin cup under his parents' bed.

"You're winning all my marbles," Komba lamented. "I've only five left."

Dead End Poverty

"Don't worry," returned Wurie without missing a beat as he knocked out another of Komba's precious marbles. Komba groaned. Wurie noticed and decided to lose deliberately so that they could continue the game much longer.

Komba won back some of his marbles and was happy. He was also determined not to lose his turn. He had already won eight back and was trying to hit the ninth out of the circle. He cradled a pink marble between the tips of his thumb and forefinger, took careful aim, and shot at his friend's marble using his thumb to flick the marble. It was a hit. The shot hit the other marble with such force that it rolled a few yards away from where they were. Komba was straight away after it to retrieve it. It was while he was gone that Wurie noticed the shiny object that was partially hidden by the dust. At first, he thought it was a marble and was very glad to retrieve it for himself. As soon as the shiny object was in his hand, though, Wurie noticed that it was not a marble. It was more beautiful than a marble because it was constantly shining and not quite as big. His friend, meanwhile, returned to resume the game, proudly holding up the marble he had gone to fetch. However, before Komba reached him, Wurie put the shiny object in his other pocket that was not storing any marbles. They continued their game, and Wurie forgot all about the beautiful stone. Soon after, it was mealtime. Therefore, they went to their separate homes, promising to meet again later for another session.

Amadu Bah was snoozing in his easy chair under the big mango tree at the back of his house. He was enjoying the respite the branches provided from the hot, burning, African sun. Wurie found him there, and he sat down beside his hero. He forgot that he had returned home specifically to eat dinner. Amadu opened his eyes lazily. He acknowledged his son with a wink and a pat on the head. "Did you have a nice time playing in the square?"

"Yes, Daddy," the boy answered excitedly. "I won many marbles, too."

"Don't your friends feel bad when you win so much?"

"They do, but I love winning. I don't like to lose unless it is necessary."

Amadu laughed and secretly nourished the opinion that the boy would be a winner. *At such a young age, he is already against losing. He'll surely be a winner, unlike me.* He ruffled the boy's hair again. "Aren't

Roland Charley

you going to have your dinner?" He hoped the child would leave him alone to continue his nap. "Mum and your siblings must be wondering what you're up to."

Remembering that it was dinner that brought him home in the first place, Wurie immediately got up to go, but saw that a few marbles had rolled out of his pocket while he was sitting on the floor. He picked them up to put them in the same pocket. He decided against that pocket, though, because there were too many in there already. He decided to put them in his other pocket instead. That was when his hand touched the shiny object he had found in the dust on the square. "I also found something in the square," he explained to his dad as he retrieved the shiny object from his pocket.

"What have we found now?" his father asked fondly. "Bring it here. Let's have a look," his father said patronisingly.

"This," Wurie said and opened his clenched fist to reveal the shiny stone in the palm of his hand.

Amadu Bah couldn't believe his eyes; he recognised the shiny object at once. It was a diamond. The stone was a whopper, and a very valuable one at that. His mind started running in every direction, but he retained enough sense to grab the stone from his son's hand and dump it into the right chest pocket of his shirt. He pulled his son closer and asked in a husky voice, "Where did you find the stone?"

Wurie noticed the change in his father's voice and thought he was in trouble. He managed to blurt out, "On the square, while I was playing marbles with Komba."

"Did you show the stone to Komba?"

"No, I didn't. Komba was retrieving a stray marble at the time, and the stone was too beautiful to share. I put it straight into my pocket. What stone is it, Daddy?"

Amadu didn't answer at once. He looked at the boy long and hard and decided not to tell him the truth. He was not sure the boy would keep the secret. When Wurie disclosed where he found the stone, Amadu realised at once it must be the stolen diamond. Diamonds didn't miraculously appear in village squares. The stone must have escaped from Samuka's guts when the Gaandoe split him open. "It's the devil's stone," he said simply in answer to his son's question.

"What is the devil's stone?" asked a worried Wurie.

Dead End Poverty

Amadu Bah didn't answer immediately. Instead, he folded his easy chair quickly and half-dragged the confused child into the house and into his room. He locked the door. Amadu Bah knew that God had finally answered his prayers. He didn't want to mess anything up. If the child let anyone know about the shiny stone, people would put two and two together to make four. Amadu Bah couldn't risk that, and he couldn't risk anyone overhearing them, either. He sat the boy on his bed and kneeled in front of him. "The genies are after you, my boy, that's why they let you see the stone. It's a way to establish contact with you to make you their own."

The boy began to snivel and soon burst into tears. He didn't want to be associated with genies. He had seen what genies did to people they controlled. He had seen medicine men try to revive people when genies possessed them. He didn't like it. Besides, if genies possessed one's body, people would consider that person different from everybody else. Amadu was very sorry to lie to his son, especially because it led to him crying. However, it was necessary to instil fear in the boy and get him to promise not to talk about the stone to anyone. Amadu Bah told his son the genies would do very bad things to him if he told anybody about the devil stone. Amadu Bah then patted the boy on the back and encouraged him to stop crying. He promised him that as long as he, Amadu Bah, was alive, no genie would dare interfere with him.

"Don't worry, my son, you'll be completely safe. However, this must be our secret. You mustn't tell anyone, your mother and best friend included, unless you want the genie to possess you."

"I'll tell no one, Father, not even Komba," the boy replied, still snivelling. "I don't want to be possessed by genies.

"Good," Amadu said, "now wipe your eyes dry and eat your dinner. Your mother must be wondering where you are. And remember: no word of this to anyone. All right, my champion? You don't want a genie living inside you." The boy nodded in agreement. Amadu Bah smiled to himself, confident that he had instilled enough fear in the boy to discourage him from talking about the stone to anyone.

Alone in the room, Amadu Bah spread out his hands in prayer. He retrieved the diamond from his pocket and examined it carefully. It was a magnificent, flawless, blue-white beauty. Amadu reckoned it was eight carats or more. He was going to be rich beyond his wildest dreams if he handled the situation carefully. Satisfied, he secured the diamond in a cigarette tin that he kept in a secret hole behind the earthenware drinking water pot in the far corner of his room. He knew he would have to leave the village. He wouldn't be able to explain his sudden wealth to his fellow villagers if he remained. The answer was to leave—as soon as possible, before his son opened his mouth. After all, he was just a child. But what would he tell his in-laws and friends? He decided not to worry about it. He was sure he would think of something plausible to tell them when the time arrived.

That night, while in bed with Konomusu, he told her that they would be leaving the village soon. Konomusu did not even ask why they were leaving, when, or where they would go. Women in the local community were brought up to accept the decisions of their men without question. All she needed to know was when they would leave so that she could have time to pack their few personal belongings and the meagre commodities in the shop.

"I'll take leave of the chief tonight. And after that, we should be ready to leave at any time. Tell your friends and relatives that my brother has provided me with a new job in Kenema. Please make sure everything is packed and ready. I wouldn't want a delay when it's time to leave."

"You won't be delayed," Konomusu answered lazily, everything will be ready." She turned her back and was soon snoring.

Amadu stayed awake a long time after Konomusu drifted off to sleep. He wondered about the sudden twist of fate. He had mined diamonds for decades and gotten nothing of note. And then a valuable diamond had turned up in his lap, courtesy of the demise of an unfortunate man who tried to get rich. He felt a little guilty that he would be enjoying what someone else brutally died for. *That's life,* he thought, *everyone has a destiny.* Konomusu always reminded him that what was destined for a person would come to that person. She said that whenever he moaned about his bad luck and finances. The diamond was part of his destiny, just as the hard times had been. There was no time for sentimentality. Samuka was dead and wouldn't need the diamond where he was. Amadu Bah was very much alive and needed all that the stone had to offer, all that the stone would unlock for him. Satisfied, he drifted off to sleep and dreamed of the blissful life ahead for him and his family. But not before he silently thanked Allah and the unfortunate, dead Samuka.

26

Most men in the village loved Marie. Conversely, the women in the village hated her. They hated her for blatantly accommodating their straying partners and taking money off them. But secretly, they envied her for her independent and carefree life. Marie was a very beautiful and sexy woman, and it was very difficult for men to ignore her completely. She suddenly appeared in the village one day with Mr K—about three years earlier—and stayed. She was from Koidu. Her family was still living there.

Her father, a pious Muslim, long ago deemed Marie to be dead to the family. He believed Marie had soiled the family name. Just past the age of twelve, and still intact (female genital mutilation was compulsory in her society, but her tribe didn't practice it), Marie was already having sexual relations with grown up men. Some of the men were married. Although she was very lithe, she was very attractive. Most men, young and old, wanted to touch her, fuck her, and make her do things to them they would only keep in their dirty heads otherwise. But she had known that a couple of years before she turned twelve. Her unmarried uncle, Kormoh, made sure she took carnal lessons from him. The frequent sessions of backscratching in his room were only pretexts to get her to pleasure him. His fingers never came out from her tender pussy while she scratched his back, and his hand never stopped rubbing the hard, long thing he took out of his trousers. Afterward, he removed his grubby hand from the little girl's pussy, dripping wet with her juices. He put his contaminated hand to his nose and breathed deeply. After that, he put his fingers to her nose and ordered her to smell them. To Marie, it always smelled like raw fish.

Sometimes, Uncle Kormoh asked her to rub his hard, long thing for him in a special way. Once she started, it made him groan and breathe heavily. After a while, his body performed several jerks, his face transformed into a grimace, and little spurts of white liquid spouted from the big, long thing between his legs. The very first time it happened, Marie nearly bolted from the room because she thought Uncle Kormoh was dying. However, Uncle Kormoh held her so tightly that she couldn't break his grip. She watched him groan louder and more frequently, and then his whole body shivered as spurts of hot, white, sticky liquid sprayed over her childish face. At the same time, his body went limp. He seemed tired as he breathed heavily. The long, hard thing was still up, and it was dripping some of the slimy, white liquid she had on her young face.

"Now clean it up with your mouth," he said, and he forced her head towards the long, hard thing between his thighs.

Marie found herself, unprecedentedly, willing to obey her uncle. When her lips closed on his engorged penis, Uncle Kormoh groaned some more and rubbed her head tenderly. He called her *my baby* and many other endearing names. Marie noticed that the sticky liquid she cleaned up was salty. It also had a unique smell. And she liked it. She loved the taste of it in her mouth.

On the second occasion, Marie realised that, even at a tender age, she could wield real power over her uncle. She stopped sucking and removed her mouth from his penis. Uncle Kormoh moaned with disappointment. "Continue to suck," he ordered.

"No," Marie answered simply, not sure whether she would be slapped for her affront.

"Please just do it, Marie," pleaded her uncle.

"No," Marie insisted, now sure that she had power over her uncle.

"I'll slap you if you don't," Uncle Kormoh threatened.

"Go ahead," said Marie, secure in the knowledge that he wouldn't carry out his threat. If he were going to slap her, it would've come sooner, she figured. Uncle Kormoh had never warned her before; he had always slapped her when he wanted to. But things were different; she felt *she* had the power.

"Okay, I won't slap you. Can you suck the damn thing now?" Uncle Kormoh asked, getting more desperate by the second.

"I said *no,* in case you are deaf," said Marie. She had never spoken to her uncle like that. Under normal circumstances, she would have received punches and slaps from him. He would also complain to her parents, who would deliver more punishment. But she knew Uncle Kormoh wouldn't report her. He had far too much at stake.

"Please continue to suck," Uncle Kormoh pleaded. "Don't stop now. I'll give you anything you want, just name it."

"What did you say?" asked Marie, surprised that her uncle was begging and making her offers. She felt a surge of power inside of her, the power to give pleasure and the power to control. She decided to test the waters more. "What'll you give me if I do it?"

Her uncle withdrew a few coins from the trousers he was still wearing and held them out to her.

"No, I don't want that. If you want me to put my mouth down there, I want two leones for doing it," said Marie, surprising herself.

"Two leones!" her uncle exclaimed in disbelief. "Where do you think I would find that sort of money?"

"Its two leones or I'm going away," declared Marie, sure of the power she held over him. "And if you try to stop me or hit me, I'll tell mother about what you do to me."

"You little devil," Uncle Kormoh said in a defeated voice. "Here, have your two leones and get on with it." He dipped his hands into his pocket and came out with a crisp note, which he handed to a smiling, victorious Marie.

From that point on, Marie never looked back. She felt comfortable doing things with her uncle. At least she was paid for it. Her uncle, it seemed, wanted her all the time. She obliged as long as two leones were in the picture. But she never graduated to full sex with him until she was twelve. He was content with her rubbing and sucking his penis while he lightly fingered her. She also knew her uncle was afraid of being caught. He ended each clandestine session with a stark warning, "Never reveal our little game to anyone. If you do, I'll just kill you."

Marie believed him. Uncle Kormoh was not the only one Marie pleasured. She also offered her services to other men who wanted her. She didn't really do it for the money. In fact, she gave away most of the money she got from her seedy, callous, carnal clients. She simply enjoyed the power she held over men—the power to make them plead, the power to make them give her anything she wanted . . . all for a few minutes of pleasure. When she was twelve, Uncle Kormoh went the full length. He got her to have full sexual intercourse. It was her first time. She loved the experience. After that, she made sure her newfound experience was on the menu when she provided her services to other lewd, sick men.

Of course, her parents learned that she was sleeping around. Several times, they tried to stop her but failed. Her parents didn't even know that her uncle was the one who took her virginity. They couldn't follow Marie around all the time, and Marie had a mind of her own.

Worried that she would get pregnant while unmarried, Marie's father paid Pa Morlai, a man of about fifty, to marry her. She accepted her father's choice without question. She was quickly married off to the gleeful old man who was anxious to lay hands on her sexy, young body.

Marie knew married life was not for her. Besides, Pa Morlai had six other wives. Marie was not prepared to engage in all the quarrels that were the daily engagements of women sharing a single husband. One week into her matrimonial home, Marie ran away from her husband's house, taking her meagre belongings with her. She was determined to go anywhere but her father's house. Somehow, she found herself in Koidu's main motor park. That was where she met Mr K. Their eyes locked, and she knew straight away that Mr K was interested in her. Actually, she knew that Mr K wanted to fuck her. From then on, everything had gone smoothly. To make sure her new benefactor didn't lose interest in her, she suggested they go somewhere exclusive. An hour or so later, Mr K was hooked. He eventually brought Marie to Yengema, even though he knew she was a woman who belonged to no man and every man. Thereafter, Marie became a hot topic and star in the miners' lives.

Marie was one of the first to know that Sahr's gang had washed their gravel, and that a good number of diamonds had been found in it. Marie always managed to get the latest news in town. She had several miner clients who told her anything she wanted to know once she had them in her bed. On that occasion, she was naked in bed with Sumaa, a regular and generous customer for whom she sometimes deferred payment when the going was tough. She learned of the diamond find through him. Having been rocked to cloud seven amid ecstatic sighs and groans by a professional like Marie, he didn't need to be prodded to talk.

"We got thirty-three stones from our pit," he blurted out.

"Wonderful," said Marie cheerfully as she tenderly stroked him where she knew he liked it most. "That means you can afford to pay me all the backlog you owe me. Of course, once you get your share of the money."

Sumaa smiled and stroked her neatly plaited hair. "You know me, Marie, I'll settle every penny I owe you. Don't worry."

"I'm not worried. I know you'll pay. You can't afford not to." She suddenly jumped out of the bed and exclaimed, "I nearly forgot! I've a lot to do today."

Sumaa took the hint and got out of bed. The woman had exhausted him, but he'd held his own, too. He could tell from her response to his piston-like thrusts. She'd urged him to go faster, moaned, and cried out aloud. He had relentlessly poked and pounded into her like a man possessed. He finished putting on his clothes, waved Marie goodbye, and exited the room, puffed up like a victorious gorilla securing the role of dominant male.

By the time Sumaa left, Marie was already devising a plan to capture at least one of Sahr's new boys. They would have money, and it would be to her advantage to bring them out from the cold and into her fold. Mila would be the easier nut to crack, she reckoned. As soon as Sumaa left, she sent one of the children playing outside to fetch Mila and bring him to her house. She knew he was in town because they hadn't started a new pit yet. Pleased with herself, she smiled knowingly as she went back to her room to prepare for the seduction. She would confirm whether the large bulge in his trousers was real and functioning. Confident that Mila wouldn't refuse what she had to offer, she took a quick trip to the river beside the village for a thorough clean up. *The first time always matters; one must be at one's best to trap and make a man eat out of one's hands,* she said to herself as she stepped into the clear, cool water in the women's section of the stream.

When she returned from the stream, an overeager Mila was waiting in her yard.

"A child told me you wanted to see me," he blurted out.

Marie engaged one of her professional smiles, the sort that turned a heart of stone into jelly. Mila's heart catapulted into his mouth, and he was aroused at once. Because he was a sexually starved man, he almost spilled his seed in his trousers. He noticed Marie's eyes were trained on the heavy bulge in his trousers. He squirmed. Embarrassed, he muttered a quick apology that sounded like a bleat.

"Never mind," said Marie, with a knowing smile, surprised that his tool was already up and running at full speed. "Yes, I do want to see you, Mila," Marie continued in a voice that could have seduced a eunuch. "Follow me, please." She entered the back door of her house and went into the semi-dark parlour that was her room. "This is my room. Come inside, please."

She stood aside to let him in first. And then she entered the room swiftly, locked the door behind her, and leaned on it. Mila still had his back to her. He didn't see that Marie had dropped the sole piece of clothing that protected her modesty. She cleared her throat to gain his attention. Mila turned around to face her and discovered a beautiful, inviting, sexy, naked body. The exotic, triangular, black bush that confronted him was the bushiest he had ever seen. And he liked them bushy, very bushy. He stood there, incapable of doing anything but staring. Marie's triangular bush still contained shiny droplets of water. It gave the impression of having diamond-studded pubic hair. And that's exactly how Mila thought of her in his sexual starvation; she was a diamond.

Marie walked the short distance from the door to the bed, sashaying her naked ass in all directions. It was the ruddiest ass Mila had ever encountered, and he desperately wanted his hands on it. He didn't need a second invitation when Marie signalled for him to join her on the bed. With the speed of lightning, Mila found himself in front of the bed. Next thing he knew, his trousers were down to his ankles. Marie admired and massaged his engorged penis. Marie wasn't disappointed. She had suspected that the boy packed a big one, and the proof was in her right hand. There wasn't much difference between what Mila had between his legs and what Samuka had. She knew she was going to love him. She stopped massaging Mila's dick and lay down on the bed, almost spreadeagled, and beckoned Mila to get to work. Even before Mila could start on her, her juices were flowing and transporting her to a state of extreme euphoria.

Mila got naked in record time, as if afraid Marie would change her mind. She didn't. And when he finally entered her, he felt her warm juices flow over his starved penis. The warm, magical pot of pleasure that was her throbbing pussy enveloped and gripped him like it would never let go. They both moaned, and their moans merged just as their bodies did. They formed a ravenous beast with two backs, each taking and giving as much as the other, urgently working themselves towards the inevitable, explosive climax. In his head, Mila was just happy to pump away, oblivious of anything save the warm, female, naked body underneath him. The sweet, sexy noises that purred out of her throat made Mila thrust into her faster and deeper. By the time he really got into it, a moaning, whimpering, and shivering Marie had already come three times. And moments later, when Mila sprayed his abundant, hot liquid inside of her—and then some on her oval face—she felt as if she had been to paradise several times.

Marie could hardly move. She just lay there, stark naked save the colourful beads gracing her midriff. She savoured the pleasure and emotions the boy had triggered in her body. She was satisfied. She didn't have enough strength to get up from the bed, even when Mila, after dressing, was ready to leave. Instead, she waved him off affectionately and asked him to shut the door behind him.

27

We sold the entire haul of diamonds the day after we completed kicking the gravel. Of course, it was Mr K, the local diamond trader and supporter, who bought the stones. Sahr and Mr K took a long time haggling over the price. In the meantime, two gang members were nominated to look after the interests of the gang. In the diamond trade, no one could be trusted. The rest of the gang stayed outside of the room, and from time to time, they heard raised voices haggling and nervous laughter. Eventually, the party agreed on fifteen thousand leones for thirty-three gemstones. The proceeds from the sale of the stones were split three ways, just as Sahr had said in their first meeting. The supporter, Mr K, got a third of the share for supporting the gang. The shovel received a third of the share to maintain food and tool supplies and other necessities essential for mining. The gang itself, excluding Sahr (who would receive a third of the shovel's share), kept the final third of the money.

Everyone was happy and excited. The total sum of five thousand Leones was divided between all members of the gang. Tamba divided the money into eight shares of 625 leones each, and he invited each member to grab a share. Mila and I had never felt prouder as we stood there with big wads of notes clutched in our hands. It was the most money we had ever held in our hands at any one time. We were so happy and proud, we nearly shed tears. We didn't believe the money was ours yet, and we kept looking down at it as if we expected it to disappear at any moment.

"Koidu calling," said Boima in a loud, confident voice. Evidently, having money in his pocket added more bravado to his character. Gang members knew they were effectively on holiday as soon as they received their personal shares. It was an unwritten rule that miners honoured and practised: there would be no work for two consecutive days once the miners finished kicking the gravel, even if no diamonds were found.

"Sure," said Francis, "when do we leave? I've a great hunger down here," he said mischievously, vigorously rubbing his crotch at the same time.

"You have your shares," said Tamba. "It's only one leone to Koidu. Anyone can leave whenever he likes. However, be careful out there: there are too many rogues waiting to squeeze money out of you. As for me, I'll be on my way now." He turned around, and with quick steps, he left the little group. Others began to disperse until Mila and I were left on our own. "We should go to Koidu, too. Today," declared a determined Mila who had already boasted to me about the blissful session he enjoyed with Marie the other day.

"We are going to Koidu, but not just for pleasure," I agreed. Remember Mama Finda? It would be good to meet that nice woman again, at least to fulfil our promise. I know she will be happy to see us."

"When do we leave, then?" Mila asked.

"As soon as we make our money safe," I said. "I say we seek Sandivah out and trust her to keep the money for us. We should only take with us a hundred leones each. The rest of the money we'll leave with Sandivah."

"Good idea," said Mila, "but why take only a hundred? How about 125? Remember, this is our first diamond money. We are going on our first outing to Koidu. Something tells me we will need more than a hundred."

I knew when I was beaten. I knew that Mila would insist on 125, regardless of what I thought. "Okay, 125 it is, then," I said. "Now let's go find Sandivah and get her to keep the rest for us."

By the time Mila and I were ready to leave for the coveted Koidu, the rest of the gang had disappeared. The old boys knew they had to walk the three-odd miles to the main road before they could board a vehicle for Koidu. We set out to walk the distance, but mother luck was on our side. Just a few hundred yards down the road, we saw Mr K on his way back to Koidu. He gave us a lift in the same old jalopy we had ridden in before.

"How do you like mining now that you have earned your first income?" he asked. We smiled happily but said nothing. Mr K could see we were happy, and based on the reports from his headman, Sahr, he knew we were willing to work. We hadn't avoided even the most difficult tasks. He felt lucky to have found us. And he was grateful for Mama Finda's recommendation.

"Are you going to visit Mama Finda at the eating house?"

"Yes, we will," we replied in unison.

"Good for you," said Mr K. "True men don't forget their roots and contacts. I know she would be pleased to see you. In fact, she has been asking me about her two young sons whenever I visit. Yes, that's how she refers to you. Of course, I always tell her you are fine. She will see for herself today," he declared cheerfully. Mila and I remained silent, but we acknowledged the information.

Mr K's banger ate the twenty-five miles to Koidu in good time. We remained quiet and withdrawn throughout the entire trip. Mr K must've wondered why, but he didn't pry. He was happy singing and whistling a well-known, obscene song that he enjoyed. In fact, every time he sang or whistled the tune, he fantasised that he was the great and virile character Hindowa that was mentioned in the song. Hindowa had screwed his way through seventy-seven virgins in one night and still wanted more.

We were not quiet and withdrawn for nothing. By coincidence, a feeling of nostalgia seemed to have descended on Mila and me. We both remembered our parents and siblings, and we even reminisced about the lives we lived before we'd voluntarily disappeared from the village.

Mila thought about his friends and other relatives, about his many girlfriends, about his farm work, about his animal traps, and about the animals they had caught for him. He thought about the river and the early morning, cold dips he cherished. He thought about the little fires in the village square and the people huddled around them. In his mind's eye, he saw Pa Gibril, the carpenter; Saidu Korah, the tailor; and Lansana Kpaka, the mason. Mila even imagined he heard them talking and engaging in good-natured banter. He remembered his wicked stepfather, Uncle Marrah, and a sudden chill shot through his body. And images of his mother, Nyallay; his brother, Jayman; and his sister, Kona, played in his brain. They made him happy. His demeanour, though, was sad.

He knew his mother would still be wondering what became of us. She wouldn't think that we were dead—far from that. Jayman surely would have explained to her that we had run away from the village. Mila's heart bled for his mother. For a moment, he wished he were back in the village, but he immediately dismissed the idea. He knew that, someday, he would return to Simbaru in style: rich, important, and cherished by all in the community. He reckoned his mother would be very proud of him and wouldn't even remember that he had ever left. A tiny smile formed on his lips.

My thoughts were very similar to those of my friend. However, unlike Mila's, mine were interrogative. *How did my parents take it when I left? How about my father, did he think of me as a coward or someone brave who took his life into his own hands?* I knew Joe Weggo would think of me as anything but a coward. He would never think of me as a coward. He had seen me in action all my life, and he knew I was no coward. I knew the old man expected me to take over for him. But take over what? A doomed life of working eighteen hours per day, living in perpetual poverty with a harem of wives responsible for scores of scantily dressed, malnourished children and scores of extended family members. I shivered at the mere thought. I felt better that I'd escaped that life, left it behind me when I did. But it hadn't made me any happier. The thought of Joe Weggo and Massey and the rest of the family made me woefully sad.

Another question bothered my thoughts, but I was afraid to ask it, even from within. *Do my parents think I'm dead?* Tears settled in my eyes and made them glassy. I wiped the tears away quickly. I was determined to be strong. I would persevere through all to succeed, break the cycle of poverty in my family so that future family members wouldn't have to suffer like us. I envisaged myself returning to Simbaru a wealthy man. My parents would be so proud of me. I was sure they would forgive me on the spot. They would forget the torture and heartbreak I'd caused them. In fact, the whole village would be proud of me. My parents would be immensely respected and recognised in a new light. Many other parents would want to match me up with their daughters. All would seek to forge some connection with me, Yandi Lenga, the rich tycoon of the village, the favourite son of the village, the brave man who took his fortune into his own hands, the man who went to war with poverty and returned with bundles of money to spend. I didn't shiver at the speculation. In fact, I liked it and believed in it. Things had already started happening: I'd gained my first diamond money. It gave me immense confidence. A few more hefty shares would probably see me ready to return to the village. I would luxuriate in the glory bestowed upon me. I sighed in my mind. I was determined to make my dream happen. I felt at peace and somehow drifted into a snooze.

The cheerful, boisterous voice of Mr K brought me back to the land of the living in time to hear him say, "The Koidu agricultural and trade show. It starts today."

"I bet it must be an interesting show," said Mila.

"It's a nice show, and the crowd will be huge," said Mr K. "For a couple of days, Koidu will be exceptionally cheerful. You've chosen a good time to make your first visit. You'll get anything you desire as long as your pocket can meet the cost. In Koidu, it's all about money. You have money, you live; you don't have money, you are just waiting to die. That's a fact." He laughed dryly. Mila laughed with him.

"What's an Agri—" I started to ask.

"It's called an agricultural and trade show, Yandi," said Mr K. Mila and I were just talking about it. "It is a festival open to all. There will be celebrations, masquerade parades, music, dancing, spectacular performances, lots of drinks and food, and women."

"Where is this show held?" asked Mila.

"When you arrive in Koidu, just follow the crowd. One way or the other, you'll find yourselves at the show grounds.

"Just like that?" It seemed strange to Mila.

"Yes, just like that. But the place will be overcrowded. If my experience is anything to go by, the place will be absolutely choked," Mr K cautioned. He drove on. After a few minutes, he exclaimed, "We're almost in Koidu! See the nicely dressed people in the roads?"

We looked out of the vehicle's windows. Men, women, and children were dressed in their best clothes, and they looked happy and excited. As the vehicle drove down the road, the people increased in density and forced Mr K to slow the old girl down. A few minutes later, the old jalopy crackled to a stop in front of a bright yellow house. "We've arrived," Mr K announced.

28

At first, we didn't realise Mr K had stopped right in front of the place where we'd devoured our first meal in Kono. But something about the yellow building seemed familiar to Mila, and he said so to me. He seemed to search his mind for it, but the something still eluded him. Suddenly, it dawned on him: "It's Mama Finda's eating house," he said to me quietly. Mila could clearly hear the voice of the smartly dressed woman they had asked about an eating house immediately after their arrival in Kono as if she were saying it right then: *There's a nice one just down this road. You can't miss it; it's painted bright yellow.*

"This is Mama Finda's eating house," Mr K announced to no one in particular. "Why do you think I stopped here in the first place?" He gave us a wide, happy grin. "Down with you two. Run along and see your 'mother'; she'll be happy to see you. But remember that Koidu can be very dangerous."

We didn't need another prompting. In a flash, we were out of the vehicle. In our haste, I nearly knocked a young man over with the vehicle's door.

"Mind that door, you asshole," blasted the young man as he jumped nimbly out of the way to avoid being hit by the opening door. I stammered an apology to him, but that only agitated him more. Instead, he gave me another blast of his colourful language. Mr K burst into uncontrollable guffaws, between which he managed to mimic the young man's word: "Welcome to Koidu, asshole." He continued laughing. Mila and I joined in his laughter. Safely on the ground, we quickly made our way towards the entrance of the yellow eating house in anticipation of seeing our benefactor.

At the far end of the eating parlour, Mama Finda, busy serving a customer saw us as soon as we entered. She immediately dropped what she was doing and ran towards us with open arms, radiant as ever.

"Welcome, Yandi and Mila," she said excitedly in a genuine display of affection. She embraced us both when she reached us, one after the other. She then looked us over as any parent would if a child had been away for a while. "You look good. And you are more mature than when I saw you last."

We could only manage to smile. Although we felt a little embarrassed, we welcomed the warm hospitality. We were pleased that she still remembered us and even called us by our names.

"Hey, everyone," she said aloud to no one in particular, "my sons have just arrived. They've come to visit their mother."

Those who knew Mama Finda well also knew she had no sons. In fact, she had no children of her own. So it was not surprising when a few raised eyebrows were seen. But they welcomed us all the same, and we were thrilled that she considered us to be her children. I was sure Mila and I wouldn't mind calling her *mother* as well.

"I thought you would never come to see me," she said. She was all smiles and looked stunningly beautiful.

"We never forgot you," said Mila. In fact, we thought of you every day. We'll never forget how you helped us. Actually, we've come particularly to visit you and make good on our promise.

"We got our first diamond money, and we would like you to have some of it," I continued. "We really want you to have it."

"Forget about the money," she said with a wave of her hand. "You've just arrived from the diamond fields. I'm sure you must be hungry like wolves. Follow me to my quarters; I'll serve you a hefty meal, and we'll talk only after you've eaten."

In her room, Mother went to a low, two-door cupboard and brought out two bowls full of rice and stew. She placed the bowls on a flowery Formica table at the centre of the room. She brought out a big jug of clean drinking water and filled two enamel cups. "There you are, all ready to go. I knew you were hungry," she said encouragingly as she poured stew over the rice. "I don't want to see a single rice seed in this bowl when you finish eating."

The stew smelled nice. Mila's stomach began to rumble as if triggered by the tasty aroma of the stew. We thoroughly washed our hands under the watchful eyes of our new Mother and fell to. As always, Mila ate voraciously and gained our host's praises. "That's good, Mila. I like the way you eat," said Mother. "A cook will never be disappointed with you. You eat as much as you can, and don't mind Yandi. He is just pecking at his food, no wonder he's so thin."

"I'm a poor eater. I've never eaten as much as Mila," I said defensively.

"You could eat if you wanted to. All miners eat. And boy! Do they eat so heavily!" retorted Mother.

I made some effort to eat a little more while I silently cursed Mila for being a glutton. The guy had a drum for a stomach and could eat a whole cow all by himself. I had never seen Mila willingly deny food, even when he appeared full; he could always manage to accept a taste of any grub on offer.

"That's how you do it, Yandi," Mother said cheerfully when she noticed I was making an effort to eat more. "You should eat more like this." She got up, rearranged her cotton dress, and said, "I'll go see what that girl is up to in the eating house. I'll be back shortly. Don't bother to clean up anything. Just sit and relax after your meal."

With Mother out of the room, I advised Mila that he should curb his voraciousness. "Aren't you ever ashamed of what people might say? You eat like a pig."

"Is food not provided to be eaten?" Mila asked, his mouth full of rice and stew. A piece of meat was firmly clenched between his closed lips and protruded from his mouth. "Just because you don't eat much, it doesn't mean people like us must starve. Eat what you can; I'll eat what I can."

"It is bad manners to be voracious in the presence of your host," I said. "And besides, you could eat slowly and still consume the same quantity."

"Stop your whingeing, man," said Mila. "You've known me from childhood. You know I like food. You're wasting your time and energy on me, my friend."

"Suit yourself," I countered. I was full at that point and had stopped eating. I carefully washed my hands and swung them vigorously to help them dry more quickly.

"Why didn't you simply say you were full instead of preaching? You kill my appetite when you criticise my eating habits," Mila said mischievously, shoving another fistful of rice and stew into his mouth.

I looked at him contemptuously, but I decided not to say anything. By the time Mother came back from the eating parlour, Mila had cleaned the bowl and was hungrily licking the stew off his fingers.

"I see someone is still hungry," Mother teased him. "I could get some more food for you from the eating parlour if you want." Mila declined, especially as my eyes trained on him. However, he thanked his host and proceeded to wash his hands thoroughly while she cleared the bowls from the table.

"So now that you are here, what do you want to do?" asked the host.

"Go shopping. Buy some new clothes and shoes and then raid the town," I said.

"Only we don't know our way around town."

"I'll go with you to do your shopping. As for raiding the town, you'll have to do that by yourselves. You are big boys, and I'm sure you can look after yourselves. Or can't you?" she teased. She finished clearing the eating utensils and proceeded to wipe food spills from the table. Job done, she clapped her hands together and said, "Now then, I'll inform my assistant that I'm going out for a while. Come on, boys, let's go out together. I'll tell her on the way out."

We looked at our reflections in the big, unframed, cracked mirror that was perched against the right wall of Mother's room. We liked what we saw. We were smartly dressed in some of the outfits we bought earlier when we went shopping. Everything we wore was new, from the brightly coloured caps on our heads to the brightly coloured shirts hanging loose over navy blue Wrangler jeans to the black, fake, leather shoes firmly laced to our feet. We'd never worn fancy shoes or socks. Even the cheap, made-in-Hong-Kong, nylon underpants we wore were new to us. Mila and I were used to walking barefooted, or if lucky, with flip-flops. Most recently, we had used the worn-out boots to work in the mines.

We had to practice moving around in our new shoes in the living quarter of the eatery. Mother watched and commented as we walked around in the shoes. All geared up in unfamiliar, trendy outfits, and with money in our pockets, we felt like rich and important people. We were proud of ourselves. We could never have imagined that we would wear clothes and shoes like the ones we had on. For us, it had always been threadbare, khaki shorts or other types of shorts picked up from the mobile, second-hand clothing vendor that visited Simbaru once every month.

Shopping was exciting for both of us. We loved the experience, and with Mother acting as chaperone, we found great values. She had relieved us of our monies and told us that 125 leones each was too much to keep on us. Mila and I couldn't believe the array of goods on display in the shops when we arrived in the town centre. The stores and stalls exhibited all varieties of goods, from clothes and shoes to electronics to mining products to foodstuffs to bicycles and machinery. We admired all the things we saw and secretly wished to possess them. We were like schoolchildren left alone to wander in a sweet shop. We didn't know what to choose or buy. We were completely lost in admiration. Had Mother not been with us, we probably would've bought nothing at all.

Mother executed the shopping like a true professional. Taking the decisions out of our youthful hands, she correctly guessed her "sons" wouldn't know much about shopping. She haggled over prices and shouted, cursed, and wailed to get her way. At the end of the shopping ordeal, she had spent only a small fraction of our money.

"A fine pair you are," Mother commented, smiling in genuine admiration, holding each of us by the shoulders to turn us gently towards the cracked mirror against the wall. It was as if someone had geometrically designed the crack on the mirror: it ran through the windowed surface diagonally (at a 180 degree angle).

"Look at you, the girls will haunt you out there. Better be on your guard," she said as a final verdict.

We could only laugh and shuffle our feet in glowing discomfiture. We liked the pretty woman fawning over us. No one had shown us such open admiration and love since we absconded from Simbaru, and it made us miss our parents. But the feeling was only momentary. *God willing,* I silently prayed, *we will see our parents again soon. Not as they used to see us, but as rich, respectable men.*

"You should be on your way now or you will miss the better part of the celebrations," Mother advised. "Each of you will have twenty-five leones to use on the town. That is more than enough to see to your needs. Off with you now before you miss most of the celebrations."

29

Mila and I marvelled at the crowded streets. We'd never seen anything like it. We dreaded getting lost until we accidentally bumped into two of our workmates. Sumaa and Francis were Koidu veterans, and they didn't mind us cruising along with them. We were happy to oblige. They had been to the agricultural show before, knew procedures, and were great sources of information.

Sumaa was excessively buoyant and talkative as he showed us places. "That is Katacoombay," he said to us, his novice friends, with a lewd grin on his cheerful face. He pointed at a low, blue, sordid house across dusty Yaradu Road. In front of the place, scantily clad girls in various sexy positions could be seen.

"That's where you go if you want a girl. All the girls posing over there are up for it. You can pick any girl you fancy."

"That's all you know, getting laid," said Francis scornfully. "Why not leave the boys alone instead of corrupting them?"

"All the scantily dressed girls you see out there're waiting for men, men who can buy them," said Sumaa, giving no indication that he heard Francis's rebuke.

"Waiting for men to buy them . . . how?" Mila asked. In Simbaru, we paid a bride price. The concept of purchasing women confused me, too.

"The girls belong to no one, but they belong to anyone with money," answered Francis as morally as he could.

"He means, if you want one of them, you speak to her and agree on a price. And then she is yours to fuck!" said Sumaa. "On average, they charge about one leone per client."

Sumaa was being explicit. But there was no harm showing the new boys the ropes, he reasoned. He figured that, the earlier they learned, the better for everyone. Besides he had recently noticed that he and Mila shared a hobby: loving women. Sumaa smiled wryly when he saw Marie take Mila inside her house. Listening at the window, he heard Marie's cries of pure ecstasy, a thing he was never able to bring out of her. He left before anyone could see him, and he never mentioned anything to Mila

Mila was very interested in that kind of talk. He had a feeling he and Sumaa could be good friends. He realised, too, that he shared the same interest. He felt Sumaa was the right, unopposed candidate to learn from, to show him the process of engagement in a whorehouse. He decided to keep a low profile. He would speak to Sumaa privately about visiting the whores.

"So what do we do now?" Mila asked, suddenly changing the topic. I was surprised and bewildered. I thought Mila would continue talking about his vice. He revelled in talks about women and sex. I knew it was too good to be true. I was sure it was a ploy to avoid my criticisms, which he knew would surely come. Mila just didn't abandon talks about the opposite sex.

"We continue to the show, then, unless you have something else in mind," said Francis.

The air was full of festivities. There were all kinds of costumes, and the people's attire was designed mainly out of colourful raffia and other materials. Their carved, wooden masks depicted many values and beliefs within the community. We saw a female costume that featured a wooden mask carved as an exquisite woman: small slit eyes complemented by a beautiful, ridged neck that the Michelin Man could have envied. The carved, black, wooden mask was part of the outfit the woman wore. She was all done up in black raffia, black tights, black pumps, and two black socks to cover her hands from view. A large group of singing women and young girls (accompanied by various local musical instruments, of which the popular shegbura was most pronounced) followed the masquerade. There were no men in their midst.

"That is the Sowei or Bondo Devil," Francis tried to explain. It belongs exclusively to women, and it plays a significant role in female circumcision."

"Yes," I agreed, "we have the same back home. It is said that if a man sees the face beneath the mask, his scrotum will swell up enormously."

"That is true," said Mila. Yandi, do you remember Pa Foray in the village? He had a swollen scrotum to the point that it made him waddle like a duck rather than walk. Rumours say he developed the condition after spying on girls undergoing female circumcision in the sacred Bondo bush.

"Tradition taught us that a lot of masquerades possess supernatural powers. One must really not joke with them," said Francis. "In my village, a Sowei once cursed a man for disrespecting her. Within two weeks, the man's stomach bloated as if he were nine months pregnant. It remained distended up until the time I left the village. Masquerades are a serious business. One mustn't be disrespectful towards them."

We saw other masquerades like the Gorboy, Nafalie, Kongoli, Laniborway, Humui, Ariogbo, and Koskos. All of them wore wooden masks. The masquerades danced from house to house, accepting tokens of money and food that were freely and cheerfully given out by the households they visited.

Wherever they went, scores of excited children followed them. However, they were more interested in taunting the masquerades and their attendants because, occasionally, the masquerades light-heartedly pretended to chase them. On such occasions, the kids ran as fast as possible to avoid capture, squealing in delight and laughing happily. They were ready to return as soon they thought it was safe. And then they went through the same ritual again. They were never tired of playing that game.

The children loved it when the masquerades chased them. But they loved it best when Koskos chased them. Koskos always carried a large whip that he kept lashing on the hard ground, producing terrible noises that instilled fear in both kids and adults. As a masquerade, he had a mandate to strike out at people with his whip, though not with malice or vindictiveness. Koskos was a disciplinary masquerade, and on certain occasions, several operated at the same time, keeping check on other masquerades as well as the crowd.

In order for Koskos to chase after them more frequently, the kids taunted him by chanting "Koskos, buy clothes for me" in Krio. Koskos replied, "Na you backside go feelam." That went on for a while, and when Koskos thought the kids were within easy reach, he would turn round suddenly and chase them for a short distance. He brandished his mean whip before returning to his minders. Even when the children fell over or got a little taste of Koskos's whip, the kids never got tired of playing the game. They came back to taunt Koskos, hoping for another chase. That went on for hours until Koskos retired from the festivities.

Koidu didn't disappoint us. It was everything we'd imagined. We enjoyed the festival, and Mila and I had our first taste of Star Beer, the national brew. Previously, we'd only managed to have sips of the illegally brewed gin in our village. I liked the Star Beer. Mila liked it too. The drink was cold and refreshing even though it seemed to freeze our teeth. Sumaa and Francis couldn't stop laughing when they noticed the effect of the cold beer on our teeth. I thought my teeth were burning and said, "This drink burns my teeth." That was when Sumaa and Francis erupted into laughter.

Between fits of laughter, Francis explained that my teeth were not burning, that it was impossible for my teeth to burn because beer wasn't fire. He explained that it felt like burning because the beer was from a fridge. He explained to us that fridges cooled things no matter how hot they were. On that occasion, the drinks had come from a red, water-cooling Coca-Cola fridge. Mila and I had never consumed water or anything from a fridge before. But we enjoyed the coolness of the drink so much that we ordered two more rounds each before all four of us left the bar.

Navigating our way through a forest of sweaty bodies, we saw strange things: raffia-clad firewalkers with grotesque face paintings, skilful people walking metres high on tight ropes, local conjurers, and many more entertainers. Mila and I couldn't get enough of what was on offer at the festival: we gawked at and admired things we never thought we would see. We knew we would never have experienced them if we had elected to stay in the tiny, impoverished village of Simbaru.

We all enjoyed ourselves in different ways. Mila and I even watched Francis and Sumaa gamble on several types of chance games. They lost some of their hard-earned money. But we were still cheerful and in a festive mood. Francis and Sumaa engaged in playing dice next.

"I want to go to the Opera Cinema," declared Francis as he put more money on the number six, hoping that the numeral would turn up when the dice rolled. It didn't.

"Who is coming?"

"Count me out," said Sumaa. "I'd rather stay with the festival. Cinemas make me sleep."

"I wasn't really asking for your benefit," Francis explained.

"Well just so you know, cinemas are not for me. Maybe Yandi and Mila would like to go."

"Oh yes, I would definitely like to," I said excitedly. Since I first saw the glamorous Opera Cinema, it'd been my secret ambition to go there. Are you coming, Mila?"

"I'm not sure. I'll remain with Sumaa. There is so much more to see, and I want to see everything."

Mila's response surprised me, but it didn't fool me. I was sure I knew why Mila wanted to stay with Sumaa. They had been muttering to each other and dragging their feet since Sumaa pointed out the whorehouse. I knew exactly what those two would be up to.

"Well we'll meet at Mama Finda's, then," I said. "You know where to find Main Motor Park."

There was a big crowd outside of the Opera Cinema trying to obtain tickets to the film by any means. It was pandemonium; tickets to watch Bruce Lee's new film, *Fists of Fury* had sold out. Scheming touts collaborating with ticket-selling staff had bought more than three-quarters of the total tickets on sale. They were now selling them at five times the original price (one leone). Francis and I, after a very hard struggle, managed to purchase two tickets. Keeping close to Francis, I manoeuvred my way through the crowd to one of the entrances to the cinema hall. We presented our tickets at the door and entered the semi-dark hall. It seemed that the film had just started, but because we were coming from outside, it was difficult to spot vacant seats. I'd never been in a hall as large as the Opera Cinema hall. I was impressed from the first moment we crossed its threshold. But I was disappointed with the semidarkness in the hall. However, Francis explained that it was necessary for the hall to be dark in order to see a film clearly.

As our vision improved, I noticed that the hall was almost full and that there were other people looking for vacant seats. Stooped as low as our bodies allowed us to get, and hoping not to block other people's view, we scanned the hall for seats. Angry, rude cries—"Move out of the way, bastards!"—were shouted in our direction. Eventually, Francis spotted a couple of empty seats in the middle tier of the hall. We raced towards them and occupied them quickly, preventing our nearest rivals from taking them. The seats were the folding type; users unfolded them first before sitting in them. The seats independently folded again

Dead End Poverty

when not in use. I didn't observe Francis putting down his seat, so I sat on mine when it was still folded. There were immediate protests from the audience.

"You must put your seat down before you sit on it. You are blocking others when you're seated like that," Francis noted.

Apparently, sitting on the folded seat made me taller. It prevented people behind me from seeing the screen properly. Therefore, I put down my seat and sat in the soft, red, leather chair. The protests stopped almost immediately. The seat was quite comfortable. It reminded me of the chairs I sat on in Sahr's room. I adjusted my position and turned my attention to the film. I struggled to understand what it was about; I didn't speak or understand English. But I was happy just to be in the Opera Cinema and watching the pictures.

As the film progressed, Francis tried to explain what was happening in a very low voice: "You see, Bruce Lee is surrounded by bad men. In a short while, he will spank them all. They will run away in pain with Bruce Lee in hot pursuit."

Francis went to school and could understand some English. Besides, he had watched *Fists of Fury* before and remembered what happened. Francis continued to explain the film to me when he could. I was mesmerised by the supernatural activities being displayed in the film. I was grateful that I had a narrator in Francis.

Soon, it was time for interval; a flood of lights hit the cinema hall. I thought the film was finished when I saw many people heading towards the exits. "Is the film over already?" I asked Francis.

"Not yet," he replied. "It is only interval. People are heading out to buy food or relieve themselves."

"Do we need to go out, too?"

"Negative. Unless you're hungry or want to take a leak. Getting back inside will be chaotic. Besides, your seat could be taken over by another person. You will definitely have to fight for it to get it back. Do you want to go outside?"

"No, I'd rather sit here and get a good look at the hall. I would like to describe it to Mila later."

"Good man," said Francis, "I'm not going outside either. Interval is only fifteen minutes. The film will resume soon."

Roland Charley

People soon started streaming into the hall again. Some were still coming in when the film resumed. I heard the usual angry calls—"get out of the way!"—several times as people returned to their seats. Soon, it became relatively quiet and people settled down to watch the film. Francis and I made ourselves comfortable in our plush seats and continued watching the film right to the credits.

30

Sumaa and Mila headed straight for the warehouse. They wasted no time pairing up with two teenage girls. They were about fifteen or sixteen, judging by their young bodies and pretty faces. One was plump, short, and stocky with a cute, moonlike face. Her face was emblazoned with dark, shiny, innocent eyes that seemed ludicrous with heavy, cheap, red lipstick and other cosmetics. Still, her striking beauty compensated for all other physical shortcomings.

The other was pretty, bubbly, and talkative. She wore similar cosmetics and smelled like the plump girl. They must've applied the same brand of perfume; friends in their line of work tended to share most things. Both girls were kitted in tight bandage dresses with hems that barely covered the bottom halves of their curvaceous posteriors. The dress was so short that almost every movement provoked a flash of their underwear.

Sumaa was the first to see them. They were seated on a long bench under an orange tree that was laden with fresh, ripe fruits. The tree added a sweet, fruity smell to the immediate atmosphere. Sumaa, even before he could meet the girls, claimed one of them as his. Mila was still gawking at the skimpy dresses the girls wore.

"The plump one is mine. I like them plump and beautiful," he said and strolled towards the girls. Mila followed without any comment. Both girls saw Sumaa coming towards them at the same time. They noticed the two young men as soon as they arrived in the compound. Without being too obvious, they had thrown frequent, sly glances at them, hoping that the young men would seek their services. The furtive glances seemed to have done the trick.

"Hello, girls," Sumaa said with a confidence that implied it was not his first visit. "Are you up for some fun?"

The bubbly, talkative girl supplied a flippant answer: "Well you know what they say: no money, no honey. You want honey, you pay money. What did you have in mind?" The young woman was being professional. She knew a lot about men, and most of what she knew wasn't worth remembering. In the flesh trade since the age of twelve, she had experienced lots of abuse, including physical violence. But

Roland Charley

she had to remain in the trade because her parents were dead and her relatives were unwilling to help. She didn't have an alternative. She had taken the only path that guaranteed her food. It was either prostitution or starvation.

"What's your name?" Sumaa asked the bubbly, lanky girl.

"They call me Clara," she answered in her trade voice. "This is my friend, Candy."

"Clara and Candy. Very nice names you have. Candy is sweet. I like Candy," Sumaa declared. He walked over to sit beside the plump girl on the bench.

"I'm Sumaa," he said to the plump girl. "Over there, with Clara, is Mila. He wants a girl, too." And then he said, "Be careful with him, Clara. This is his first visit."

"Trust me, I'll be gentle with him," Clara said with a luscious smile that left Mila wishing they were in bed at that very moment.

Mila's dick had been playing tricks—rising and falling in his new pants—since he set eyes on Candy and Clara. He had to keep a hand on top of his crotch to shield the growing bulge in his pants. Clara was his type, and he was glad he would be having her. Still, he wouldn't have minded the plump girl. There was no chance Mila could refuse a pussy; it didn't matter whether it was a thin or fat pussy. All he needed was a woman who could fuck.

Summa laughed. "That's not what I meant, Clara," he said. "It is not his first time with a girl. It's his first time in a whorehouse."

"Then I'm the right girl for him," said Clara. "By the time I'm through with him, even the army would fail to stop him from visiting me again." She laughed, looked at Mila seductively, gently took his hand, and led him into the whorehouse.

Sumaa and his plump girl followed. At the entrance, Mila noticed a fat, huge, bald man sitting on a chair. There was a lit pipe clenched between his thick lips, and he was puffing on it fervently as if it were his last smoke. The obese man had no top on. Mila observed that the man's entire upper body was ridged, like the Michelin Man he once saw on a poster in Kenema. The man's bottom boasted a big, blue, cotton wrapper that covered his enormous ass, which barely fit in the undersized chair.

"I see you've a customer, Clara," said the fat man. "Can I come and watch?" A raucous laughter rumbled out from deep inside the obese man. "See you shake your skinny ass and all?" And then he guffawed again.

The fat man was the proprietor of the whorehouse. Nevertheless, he commanded little respect from the girls. He insisted on having sex with any girl he fancied in the brothel, free of charge. He thought it was his right because he rented cubicles to them. For some of the girls, the cubicles were home *and* a place of business. They had no choice but to comply when he fancied them. Luckily for the girls, the man's sex sessions were very short. He possessed a staying power equivalent to a mating cockerel. But he told his friends otherwise when he told them about his sexual exploits. The girls, on the other hand, had learned to accommodate him if it meant they could stay in the whorehouse— even though they paid him the daily rent of two leones per cubicle. But the fact that they knew it would be over as soon as it started made them a little more indifferent to pleasuring the fat bastard.

"Fuck you, Smelly Joe," Clara retaliated. Past and present residents of the whorehouse had nicknamed him Smelly Joe because of the permanent, pungent odour his body emitted.

Smelly Joe laughed and said, "No, fuck you. Which I've done many times."

"Don't mind the old pervert," said Clara before turning her attention to the fat man and saying, "A cockerel lasts at the game longer than him. No girl wants you, Smelly Joe. You smell like a latrine."

"Well you'll have a taste of the smell of this latrine tonight," said Smelly Joe. "I must have you tonight or else. You know the score. Make no mistake: you'll have a taste of this tonight." he rubbed his crotch and laughed raucously.

Clara avoided any additional exchange of words with the old trash and led her party inside. The whorehouse was once a warehouse. In its glory days, it stored the goods the rich Lebanese traders sold in their shops. Not anymore, though. The only goods the old warehouse stored at present were female bodies willingly engaged in lewd liaisons with seedy clients who paid handsomely for their time.

Mila counted forty cubicles lined up on both sides of the long corridor in the building. They were available for rent to *rarray girls,* the local name for prostitutes. It was the perfect place for vice girls to ply their trade.

"My room is at the far end on the right," Clara explained. "Candy's room is opposite mine on the left."

Mila noticed the whorehouse only had one exit, the one they just passed through. "There's only one exit," he said.

"Yes," Clara agreed, "that's to guarantee punters don't run away after the deed." She noticed Mila frown. "I'm only joking. This place was a warehouse, that's why there's only one door."

As the quartet walked along the long, dim corridor, Mila heard various erotic groans and moans coming from some of the cubicles. At the same time, he noticed a few men leaving cubicles. Some were still trying to button or zip their trousers. One even came out with the girl he'd apparently bedded, his hand buried deep inside her black skirt. Mila wondered whether the men had any shame at all, and then he remembered that he was one of the shameless men. But he already knew the setting wasn't a place of shame; it was the opposite.

"This is my room," Clara announced. She removed a single key from her bosom, opened the door, went inside, and gestured with the other hand for Mila to follow.

Mila looked at Sumaa, but his attention and groping hands were all over Candy's fat, firm ass. He was squeezing, rubbing, and occasionally slapping it. Sumaa's caresses did not go to waste. Candy was all giggles and wriggles as she tried to open the padlock on her door. She failed several times before she got it right.

"Sumaa," Mila began, "I just—"

Sumaa interrupted without even looking at him. "We'll meet under the orange tree. If you finish first, wait for me there. If I finish first, which I doubt, I'll wait for you there."

By that point Candy had opened her door. Sumaa followed her in and slammed the door. Mila turned and went inside Clara's room. She was already stark naked, lying flat on her back on a grass mattress. Her left hand was slowly massaging her triangular pubic area. In a husky voice, Clara said to him, "Shut the door, please, and come inside." Mila shut the door but didn't begin to undress.

"I don't have all day, man," Clara said. "I've rent to pay. Make yourself ready. And get my money ready, too. It's one leone per each sex session."

Mila counted five one-leone notes, walked over to Clara, and gave her the money. "Is that enough? I don't want to be hurried."

Clara engaged one of her captivating smiles. "You could even stay the night if you wish." She laughed and moved to a kneeling position so that she could reach Mila's fly. She noticed at once that he was rock hard. She also realised that whatever was under the fly was huge. She was pleased. She loved big ones. She drew Mila onto the shabby mattress and started to work on him. As she undressed him, she told him softly, "Your money has been well spent. This will be the best you've ever had."

"Then let's get on with it," Mila said in a hoarse, impatient voice. "Show me what you can do."

He penetrated her, quickly, brutally, like a sex-starved animal. He pounded into her like a piston working an engine in fast gear. Soon, they were making that unique music of sex: groaning and moaning. The sounds were like those he had heard along the corridor, and he liked what he was hearing.

31

"So how was the Opera Cinema?" Mila asked me.

"Why are you asking? You didn't want to come," I replied.

We were cosily nestled in one of the bedrooms in Mother's living quarters. We'd made it home safely without getting lost. Mother, pleased to see us back, immediately set before us a meal fit for chiefs. While we were eating, she asked a series of questions about our experiences in Koidu and the show. She also pointed out our room and the way she prepared it for us. She hoped we would like it.

Mila thought a little wheedling and cajoling might help loosen Yandi's tongue. "Come on, Yandi," he said, "you know you're my brother. What would I do without you? How was the cinema?"

"Tell me what you were up to first," I said. "You tell me that, and I'll tell you about the cinema."

"That's not fair," Mila replied. He was not having it. "I asked first."

"You want to know about the cinema," I said.

"Yes, but—" he began.

"Just tell me, then. No buts," I interrupted.

"You wouldn't want to know," he countered.

"Let me be the judge of that," I said.

"Since you insist, I'll tell you," he said demurely.

"On second thought, tell nothing," I said laughing. "It won't matter anyway. I believe I already know: you and Sumaa visited the whorehouse."

"Wish you were there," he said. Had this nice, slim, beautiful girl. She was up for everything I threw at her. Yet she exhausted me. Wow, she was a real goer. And sweet." He smacked his lips, apparently reliving and relishing the good time he had.

"Please spare me the details," I said with mock horror. "For you, every woman is sweet. I'm sure you'll never come across the vinegar type," I added.

"You asked for it," was Mila's simple reply. "Seriously, though, I wish you were there, Yandi. Sumaa had the plump one. There was no sign of him when Clara—yes, that was her name—finally released me from her amorous clutches. He was not under the orange tree where we'd arranged to meet.

"Released you? I asked. "Don't tell me a slim girl imprisoned the great womaniser."

"Unfortunately, man, she did. She got the better of me in our sexual encounter. The girl just blew me away. But I liked it," Mila said.

"How much did you pay her?" I inquired.

"Five leones," he answered nonchalantly.

"Five leones. You paid five leones for one lousy sex session?" I asked in disbelief. "Were you out of your mind? Sumaa said it was just one leone. No wonder the girl blew you away . . . money, mind, and all."

"We did it eight times," Mila boasted. She wanted it more than me." She said, "There was no telling when she would have someone so generous and so big again."

Unconsciously, he scratched his groin as if to check that the big thing was still there. Mila did that several times before he arrived at Mother's because he couldn't feel anything and wasn't sure his penis was still in his trousers. He felt numb down there and developed the weird feeling that Clara had probably kept it with her. The way she craved it (infinitely, to be exact), Mila wouldn't be surprised if his dick went missing.

"Still, five leones was a lot to give a rarray girl, regardless of the number of times you did it," I said. "At that rate, my brother, your money will soon disappear."

Mila shrugged and said, "The money didn't matter. I got my fill. But to be honest, my fill nearly made me colic. Enough of that, though, tell me about Opera Cinema."

"I'm very sleepy now," I said. "Let's leave it till the morning."

I was annoyed with him for wasting money. Back in Simbaru, five leones was a lot of money, a miniature fortune. My old man would have to sell at least two bags of husk rice to make a similar sum. And there was Mila, giving it away as if it were valueless. To me, it was a blatant waste, and I didn't like it. I agreed that a man had to be with a woman sometimes, but spending five leones on one who sold her bodily merchandise for one Leone was outrageous.

"That wasn't the arrangement," said Mila. "You promised to talk about the Opera Cinema if I told you about the whorehouse."

"No, it wasn't," I said. "Plus, my eyes are now heavy with sleep, Mila. We'll talk tomorrow." I turned round on my side to face the wall and covered my entire body with my cover cloth. I ignored Mila completely; he was still going on about unfairness. The drone of his whinging acted as a catalyst to put me to sleep. "You can't treat me like this; it is absolutely unfair," Mila said, and that was the last thing I heard him say before I fell into a deep slumber.

I woke up to the clattering noise of dishes and the sweet aroma of fresh coffee, apparently homemade. Mila was already awake and had been for a while: his bushy hair was combed, and he was dolled up in a flowery, short-sleeved, cotton shirt. His new towel was draped around his neck, and he looked refreshed. He must have had a good night's sleep. He smiled happily, and I smiled back.

"Well," he said, "I'm waiting."

"Waiting for what?"

"For you to tell me about the cinema. You promised. Remember?"

I didn't argue. I told him all about Opera Cinema, at least the bits I could remember. He was impressed because he kept saying he would definitely go there on his next visit. Halfway through my narrative, Mother walked in with two steamy mugs of coffee. She also carried fried plantains, sweet potatoes, and stew. It smelled delicious.

"Good morning, my sons," she greeted cheerfully. "Hope you slept well."

"Yes, we did," answered Mila, "And thank you for everything."

"What are mothers for," she said airily.

She went over to the single window in the room, drew the cotton aside, and threw the wooden shutters wide open. The bright, early morning sunlight flooded in and gave the room a golden glow. She stood there against the yellow sunrays. She was smiling lovingly at us, glowing stunningly in an illustrated Sir Milton Margai cotton dress. Slim and on the best side of lanky, the woman oozed love and kindness. As usual, she was neat and beautiful—very beautiful. *It's a pity she has no children of her own. She deserves a dozen children, and a dozen children couldn't wish for a better mother.*

"You must have your breakfast now if you want to make an early start on the town. I presume today will be your last day here," said Mother.

I confirmed that it was our last day and said, "We will return to Yengema this evening and head straight to the fields."

"Then go on, have your breakfast," she said. "I'll go back to the parlour to help out with the early morning customers." As she left the room, she added, "And young men, make sure you finish your food."

While we were eating, I concluded my narrative about the Opera Cinema.

"You should've come with us. But you opted for the whorehouse instead," I said.

Mila grinned and touched his crotch involuntarily.

"Leave it, man. Or are you jealous?" he said cheerfully.

We finished breakfast. It was a good breakfast. The coffee was good, too. Mila took back the dishes and cups to the eating parlour while I went out to the backyard to attend to my daily hygiene rituals.

We spent the day in town, strolling from street to street, event to event. We observed all the shops and festivities around us. That time, there was no Sumaa or Francis to guide us. The traffic was terrible. Vehicles were barely able to cruise because of the crowd on the streets. Blaring vehicle horns and sounds from scores of various musical instruments, coupled with the din of happy and excited people, added spice to the agricultural show. Occasionally, a few tempers flared, but other revellers controlled the ensuing confusion quickly. It wasn't an occasion for quarrels and fights; it was a day to be happy, enjoy community cooperation, and relax.

32

Wandering the pothole-ridden, dusty streets of Koidu, we admired and absorbed most of the things we experienced. Soon, we found ourselves at Tankoro, the police station we'd passed on our way to Yengema in Mr K's old jalopy. The building was huge and frightening, especially because we knew it housed arrested illegal miners and other criminals. It was a two-storey concrete monstrosity with a circular base that was painted green. I observed scores of iron-grilled windows high up on the circular wall. Four or five faces peered out of each, scrambling for a better view of the outside world. They shouted, argued, and begged cigarettes and food off passers-by. They spewed obscenities if they got nothing. Just looking at the building terrified me; I'd never been locked up and had no intention of visiting the place.

"How do you find Tankoro?" I asked Mila.

"Impressive," he replied. "It's quite a large building, bigger than any I've ever seen."

"What do you expect? They keep prisoners there. What else do you notice?" I asked.

"Tankoro throws fear into me; it gives me the jitters," said Mila, almost in a whisper.

"You're not alone. It scares me, too," I said.

"So don't get caught in the fields, then," said Mila. "I'm determined not to get caught."

"I won't be caught," I said, "I'm equally determined. Joe Khakis will never catch me."

Mila and I walked past the Opera Cinema. Even that early, the courtyard was full of people. A huge, colourful poster advertised the film for the day. It was the same film Francis and I watched. Mila suggested we buy tickets to the cinema. I declined, arguing that we were supposed to return to Yengema that evening, that it was better to do it the next time we were in town. Mila was disappointed but made no meal of it. We left Tankoro and further explored the town. There were people everywhere. It seemed as if the festivities weren't only confined to the centre of town. There were miniature parties and celebrations going on in most streets. Open bars playing cacophonous music from big speakers acted like magnets that attracted people. Most of the bars were full of young men and women drinking Star or Guinness. Those who couldn't afford beer made do with Omole, the locally brewed gin. Regardless, everyone seemed ebullient as they shook their bodies in various rhythms.

Occasionally, we saw huge, bright yellow dumper trucks laden with fresh earth from the NDMC mines. They were on their way to the processing plants. We also saw trucks full of Joe Khakis in full uniform, probably on their way to raid unsuspecting illegal miners. I wondered how many they would catch given that the town was engaged in festivities and most people were out to celebrate. I hoped the Joe Khakis would take the day off. But they seemed to be harassing poor blokes trying to earn an honest living—not because they loved doing their job, but for the love of the remunerations the sale of arrested illegal miners provided them.

Overall, Koidu was a colourful, vibrant town that was growing larger every day due to the daily arrivals of men of all ages seeking to strike it rich in the diamond fields. Most people in the country knew of Kono and its precious stones. Thus, it was no surprise that the town was overcrowded with hopefuls, just like Mila and me, from all around the country. The reputation of the diamond fields was like a magnet attracting iron filings. The temptation was hard to resist.

The town had electricity and a pipe-borne water supply, even if most people got their water from street taps that the locals called pumps. Indeed, most residents in Koidu used wells for their water supply. There were private taxi services commuting within town or between Koidu and the nearby villages. There were street vendors selling everything from boiled groundnuts to skewered, roasted meats to varieties of fruits and vegetables.

There was one main market in Koidu, and we decided to explore it. A huge space consisting of rickety stalls and tables made up the market. It was overcrowded, noisy, filthy, and damp. Large, swirling, buzzing houseflies hovered over and settled on most of the commodities on sale on the tables. They also frequented the displayed goods on old sacks resting on the damp ground among small heaps of pungent, decaying rubbish. Smoked and raw fish (in addition to stale bush meats) attracted the most flies.

We came across stalls selling clothes, electrical goods and other hardware. I spotted a small transistor radio in a stall. I'd never had one before, but I had always yearned for one since the day Papa brought a radio home from Kenema. I was about nine then, and though allowed to listen to it, I wasn't allowed to touch it. At first, I wondered where the voice came from. There was no one inside the radio, yet it talked; it was magic to me. I had a great urge to find out, but I wasn't allowed to touch it. Father would kill me if anything went wrong.

The urge to find out who talked from inside the radio became an obsession for me. Even when I knew Papa would skin me alive if I messed with it, the urge to find out overwhelmed me so much that I actually tried to find the mysterious person within the radio. It was on a Friday. I remember because Papa's cousin, Albert, was visiting from the city and staying with us. Both Papa and he went together to the mosque for the Friday prayers. Massey and the other women were still out on the farm. It was the right opportunity to fulfil my curiosity. I went to Papa's room and brought out the small, leather-cased transistor radio. Somehow, I managed to tune it to a station that caused it to start talking. I was determined to find out what was inside. I decided to stay on the veranda so that Papa wouldn't surprise me when I was fidgeting with his radio. I removed the leather holder from the radio; the glossy, black box was beautiful. I noticed that a single screw held the radio together. Without hesitation, I commenced unscrewing it. I was so engrossed in the task that Papa and my uncle were standing right by me before I noticed them.

"What do you think you are doing?" my father asked in a very angry voice, grabbing the radio from me and giving me a vicious slap. I felt the sting of the slap and saw flashes. Another was already on the way when Uncle Albert intervened. "That's enough, Joe Weggo. The boy didn't mean any harm."

"I told him not to touch it," Papa said in a mean voice. "Didn't I tell you not to touch this radio?" he asked, shaking a fist at me. I said nothing. He raised his hand again to strike me, but Uncle Albert wouldn't let him.

"Leave the boy alone, please. Nothing happened to the radio, after all," he said in an attempt to pacify my father. Uncle Albert took the radio from him and retrieved the leather case that was still close to me.

"He disobeyed me," Papa insisted.

Dead End Poverty

"Yes, he did," agreed Uncle Albert. "But must you kill the boy for that?" While Uncle Albert was dealing with the radio, Papa went inside the house, still seething with rage. Uncle Albert winked at me and smiled kindly. "What were you doing with the radio?" he asked.

"I only wanted to see the person inside it," I said.

Uncle Albert was amused but didn't laugh at me. "There's no one in this radio, Yandi," he said in a serious tone. In fact, there is no one inside any radio."

"Then why does it speak?" I asked.

Listen, Yandi, the talk or music you hear from the radio comes from hundreds of miles away, from Freetown."

"Freetown? Where? How?"

"Yes, Freetown," replied my uncle. "Freetown's our capital city. A man in the studio in Freetown speaks into a microphone. His voice travels through the airwaves. The engine in the radio captures the voice from the airwaves, and that voice comes out through the radio's speaker."

"I see," I said, not really understanding. I didn't ask any more questions. I knew that there was definitely no one in the radio.

"I should go inside now," my uncle said. "Your dad must be waiting for me. Don't worry anymore about this incident. I'll talk to him. Next time, don't go around dismantling things." He smiled reassuringly, ruffled my hair, and disappeared through the door to the parlour.

But years in the future, I could afford a transistor radio of my own. We went into the shop and asked the price from a skinny Fulani man who kept spitting in the dust. His teeth were yellow, probably from eating too many kola nuts. In a singsong voice that surprised the young men, the Fulani man replied, "Eight leones."

"I'll pay four leones for it," I said. Our trip to the shops with Mother had taught us a new skill: haggling. And I was employing that skill to buy something for myself.

"Do you think I'm here to waste time?" asked the skinny Fulani man. "No trader will sell that to you for four leones. Do you want my family and me to starve?"

"Four leones," I insisted. "If you agree, I'll pay you right now."

The trader swore under his breath and said, "Look, the radio cost me six leones fifty. I'm only getting one leone and fifty cents out of it. Is that too much profit?"

"Four leones or we go to another trader," I said.

"You don't want to go to another trader," the Fulani said quickly. "They are all thieves. They will rob you with your eyes open. Me, I'm the best trader in the market. Come, my friend, give me a better offer and the radio is yours. I'll sell it to you for five fifty."

"No, five fifty is still expensive," I countered, "How about four twenty?"

"This man wants to see the death of me yet," lamented the Fulani trader. I swear by Allah it cost me more than that."

Mila was enjoying the haggling but didn't join in. He just stood there watching us spar as if we were in a boxing match.

"Four twenty," I said, "and that's my final offer."

"Is your friend buying as well?" the Fulani asked shrewdly.

"Yes," said Mila.

"Then make it five Leones each and we've a deal," said the Fulani trader.

"Four twenty," I insisted

"Let's meet in the middle, then. Pay four fifty each and the radios are yours."

"Four fifty it is, then," I said. Could you test the radios now, please?"

"Good," the trader said, offering his hand to shake on the deal. "You'll not regret it." He unpacked both radios and loaded them with batteries he retrieved from a large pile in a carton. He tried one radio at a time, and both radios worked perfectly. "Batteries are not included," he said. "The ones inside are old batteries. You'll need two new batteries for each radio. Each battery costs ten cents. Four batteries will be forty cents."

He removed the old batteries, peeled off the transparent, plastic sleeves from some new ones and loaded the radios again. He tuned one radio after the other to the Sierra Leone Broadcasting Service (SLBS), which was the only broadcasting station in the country. Mende music blared from the transistor radios. It was the infamous Amie Kallon on air. We knew and understood the song well, having heard it several times in Simbaru. Besides, Amie Kallon was a Mende just as we were. For me, the song invoked immediate memories of Simbaru and my folks. It did the same for Mila; there was a hint of yearning and nostalgia in his demeanour and eyes.

I counted five leones out of my stash. Mila did the same. After putting the money together, I handed it to the eager trader.

"Both radios cost a total of nine leones, plus forty cents for the batteries," he calculated. "That gives us a grand total of nine leones forty cents. I owe you ten cents change." He gave me the change and carefully repacked the radios in their boxes before putting them in a bright green, plastic bag and handing the bag to me. "There!" he said, "Enjoy. Thank you."

We walked out of the shop, excited and proud owners of brand-new transistor radios. We explored the market a little further, shopping with our eyes and wondering where the numerous types of goods came from. We found a stall that sold jewellery, underwear, and cosmetics for women. I'd never so much female paraphernalia in one place. Back in Simbaru, and throughout most of the country, it was very rare to see a woman's underwear (unless one was making love or spying on a woman). But one could easily see the thighs and breasts of women; they didn't feel shy about those parts of their bodies. In fact, it wasn't unusual to see naked younger girls. It was a cultural thing that had survived generations upon generations.

An overwhelming desire to buy some feminine items came over me. I wanted to buy something for Sandivah. She had been very nice to us since our arrival, but that wasn't all. Recently, just the sight of her affected my dick. Besides, she was our banker, and buttering her up could only work in our favour. "I want to buy something for Sandivah," I said to Mila.

"That would be nice," Mila said. "However, have you thought of what Sahr will do if he finds out you bought presents for his wife?"

Mila was right. The man had warned us not to interfere with his own. But I didn't think giving Sandivah presents counted as interference. Even if it did, I really didn't care. I was sure Sandivah wouldn't go shooting her mouth off to Sahr that I bought her presents.

"Do you think she will tell him?" I asked.

"I'm not sure," replied Mila as he tried to scratch his ankle. "How would I know?"

"I'm going to buy her things anyway," I said stubbornly.

"Suit yourself," Mila replied. "As long as you know what you're doing."

I picked out four panties of varying colours, a couple of gold-plated earrings, and some cheap bangles. I was sure she would like them.

"I'm sure she'll like those," Mila confirmed without committing himself.

I paid for the items, and we continued to explore the market. We were surprised after going round a corner to see a big, stagnant lake. We went closer to have a good look. The lake was quite big, and like most streams and rivers in Kono, the colour of the water was muddy brown. We later learned that the lake's name was Gbayshan. All sorts of activities were taking place in Gbayshan. Children and adults were swimming along the length of the river, scores of women were washing clothes on the muddy riverbank, and young lads cast fishing hooks relentlessly. The boys were hoping to catch some tiny, bloodless tilapia or other small fish. They knew there was a chance of catching something bigger with a little luck.

The sight of illegal miners in Gbayshan surprised us. We didn't know illegal miners worked in broad daylight in the middle of Koidu. We noticed illegal miners diving into the water to retrieve soil and gravel from the riverbed, which they immediately kicked to see whether what they dredged up contained diamonds. If they found no diamonds, the men dived in again and brought up some more soil and gravel to sift through. We stood there watching them for quite a while: they kept disappearing under the water and reappearing with sacks half-full of gravel.

Seeing the miners at work must have reminded Mila that we needed to return to Yengema that evening. "We should be heading back to the eatery to get ready for our return," he advised. I agreed

33

Mama Finda wasn't in the eating parlour when we arrived, but the hired help told us she'd left instructions for us to meet her in her living quarters. Mother didn't see or hear us coming. We stood in the doorway, watching her, appreciating her, thanking God for directing us to her. She was a good woman. I wondered why she wasn't married. We saw that she'd neatly folded and packed our stuff in the cheap, Chinese travelling bags she'd bought on our shopping spree.

A sixth sense must've warned her she was no longer alone in the space. She turned around to look, consternation written all over her pretty face. But the worry disappeared the moment she recognised us. Her worried face transformed into a dazzling smile. "You scared me," she said with mock horror, but her face retained that sweet, radiant smile, making her look almost angelic. "I wasn't expecting you so soon."

"We decided to come back early," Mila said.

"So that we could return early to Yengema to get a good rest," I added. "We start work again in the mines tonight. I see you've already packed our bags. Thank you."

She said, "I didn't want you forgetting anything. Everything is packed and food's ready. Come on in. Maybe you want to eat now."

"Thank you, we actually do," said Mila, whose eyes had widened in anticipation of the food.

Mother pointed to a few bowls on a small table that were covered neatly by a white piece of cloth. The cloth was hand embroidered in the centre. Each of its four corners were red and green, and bright yellow formed its perimeter. A big jug of water, two enamel cups, and a bowl of water for washing our hands were also on the table.

"Eat well, then," she said. "Who knows, you may be arriving in Yengema after the evening meal. Besides, it'll be sometime before you have such a meal again. I know all about miners' meals. I wouldn't live on them."

While we were washing our hands, she left the room to return to the eatery. The food was good. It was rice and cassava leaf sauce cooked in bright red palm oil. It was overloaded with juicy meat, dry fish, and other enticing vegetables. My appetite was surprisingly good. I matched Mila right to the end of the meal, and he didn't seem to like that fact. It didn't bother me, though; I enjoyed the meal immensely.

Mother accompanied us to the lorry park, our transistor radios proudly in hand and blaring sweet, traditional songs. The lorry park wasn't very far from the eatery. Earlier in our room, where we'd said our goodbyes, she refused the money we offered her. No amount of persuasion convinced her to accept the money. However, in order to satisfy us, she elected to accept a single leone.

"This is all I need from you," she said and cried.

Tears streamed from her eyes and down her cheeks. We could see that she was sad. She didn't want us to leave, but she realised we had to: we had work to go back to.

"Stop crying, Mama Finda," Mila said soothingly. "We are going to be back again soon."

"Yes," I agreed. "Besides, we have some money now. We could come on a Friday when we don't have to go the mines."

The words didn't stop her tears. She cried all the way to the park, carrying our canvas bags in both hands. She refused to let us carry the bags ourselves. In the lorry park, she sobered up a little while we searched for her favourite driver. We found Safia eventually and took a crimson red Peugeot 404 Familiar. There were already some passengers in the car, but Safia needed three more to meet the eight-passenger quota.

"Safia," said Mother, "these are my sons. I want you to drop them at their door in Yengema." I'll kill you if anything happens to them."

Safia laughed and assured Mother that we would be fine. Safia took our bags and deposited them in the boot of the car.

"How much is the fare for both of them?" Mother asked.

"You know the price, Mama Finda," Safia said, laughing nervously.

"Come and see me in the eatery when you get back. I'll have the money ready for you."

"But Mama," I began.

"Don't even start," she interrupted.

I kept my mouth shut. She took hold of our hands and led us away from the car and Safia. "I want you to be very careful in the mines. I hear that accidents happen all the time. I don't want to lose you. I love you. You're the children I never had. If you run into any problems, let me know immediately. You would let me know, wouldn't you?" We nodded.

"I'm ready," shouted Safia. "I must leave now. The car is full."

Mother drew us closer to her and embraced us tightly with both hands. "Goodbye," she said, "go now and take your seats in the car. I'll stay here until you leave."

We got into the far rear seat, which we shared with another young man and an old man with grey hair and a very white beard and moustache. He was dressed entirely in white. He was already snoozing in the hot interior of the car. The young man grumbled that our transistor radios were noisy, so we turned them off. Comfortably seated, we waved goodbye to Mother as Safia engaged gear one to begin our journey. We kept waving to Mother, and she kept waving back. She was still standing there when the vehicle negotiated a bend. She looked crestfallen, anguished by the departure of her "sons." I'm sure she was wondering whether she would ever see us again.

34

We arrived in Yengema just before sunset. We were the first of our gang members to arrive. There were no signs of the rest of the gang; we figured they were holding out on their return until later in the evening. Still, we assumed they would be back to work by night like everyone else. They were old hands in the trade, and returning to work just hours after their arrival would not likely affect their work at all. On the other hand, I was glad we'd managed to return early. We would have ample time to rest until it was time to go to the fields. We put our new bags in our corner of the vast parlour. I opened mine and retrieved the plastic bag containing the gifts for Sandivah.

We found Sandivah in the backyard dishing the evening meal. Interrupting her work, she stood up to greet us warmly with the wooden dishing spoon still in her right hand.

"Welcome back," she said, smiling at us sweetly while adjusting her big boobs with her free left hand. "I hope you had a good time."

"Hello, Sandivah. You're looking good," I said. Her simple adjustment had a great effect on me. At the same time, I gave her the plastic bag containing the four pairs of panties and gold-plated earrings and bangles I bought for her in Koidu. She blushed but said nothing. I noticed deep appreciation in her eyes, perhaps affection. Nevertheless, I guessed she was flattered by the gift. She sat down again and continued dishing from where she'd left off.

"Thank you, Sandivah," said Mila. "We'd a great time. We nearly didn't want to return. Where are the other gang members?"

She shrugged her shoulders and said, "Don't worry about them. They never return early from Koidu. However, they do return just before workers set out to the mines."

"What about Sahr? Is he here?" I asked. At the same time, I clandestinely watched the regular rising and falling of Sandivah's braless assets under her thin, cotton top. The sight aroused me, and I liked the feeling very much. Perhaps I caused some arousal in her, too, but there was no way of knowing.

"Ask me another question," Sandivah replied bitterly. "Sahr never stays in the village when he has money in his pockets. He left on the same day you did. He took that little child slut (who is yet to learn how to wipe her own backside clean) with him."

Mila and I laughed. We believed she was only jealous. However, the way she answered the question made me think that I might have some success with her. I knew I had to approach her in the near future to let her know exactly how I felt about her.

Sandivah was quick, fiery, and to the point with her reprimand: "It's not funny. It's never funny when your husband abandons you for a younger woman. You feel old, useless, and worthless. In fact, you start to believe that you've passed your sell-by date and become undesirable to other men."

We stopped laughing. We stood there awkwardly for a moment. Silently, I was screaming that I desired her all the time. Mila rescued the awkward moment when he asked, "So what news in town, Sandivah? Is there anything interesting to tell us?"

"Nothing much really," Sandivah said. "Amadu Bah, the Fulani trader, left the village with his family to settle somewhere else. He left on the same morning you went to Koidu."

"What happened?" I asked. "Did he find a big diamond?"

"He didn't find any diamonds that we heard of in town. According to his in-laws, his elder brother in Kenema wanted him to work with him to manage some of his shops. Amadu said it was good for him and his family to make a change. He said all the years he'd spent mining diamonds hadn't helped him. Therefore, he was willing to take a chance and work with his brother, a rich trader who owns several shops. So he closed shop, took his wife and little kid, and left town for good."

Unknown to all in the village, the unlucky diamond miner doubling as a petty trader commanded a stone that would make him a very wealthy man. Wherever Amadu Bah ended up, he could be sure that he and his family would live quality lives. Diamond mining had paid him after all, even if another man had to die violently before his payday. In a way, Samuka died to enrich Amadu Bah. His death seemed to have unlocked Amadu Bah's luck.

"The village will miss him," I said. "He was such a nice man."

"He said he would return one day with his family to see his in-laws and friends," added Sandivah.

"Who took over his house and shop?" Mila inquired.

"Do you want to buy it?" I asked mischievously.

Mila just shrugged, but Sandivah answered the question anyway. "He gave it to his youngest in-law, Moiwa." Sandivah finished dishing the food. She had not cooked for the gang because most were still away. We helped her tidy up, and when we were finished, she invited us to eat with her directly from the pot.

"We ate before we left Koidu," I said. "However, you being such a fabulous cook, I'll take a few handfuls. It smells delicious. How about you, Mila, are you up for eating?" I realised it was a stupid question the moment the words left my lips. Mila was always ready to eat.

"Want to bet? Watch me," Mila challenged, grinning wolfishly.

We found some objects to sit on, washed our hands, and ate with Sandivah. I was nervous and kept looking through the open doorway of the house, expecting Sahr to walk in at any moment.

"Why do you keep looking around you?" asked Sandivah before she dumped a fistful of rice and potato leaf sauce in her mouth. She ate in a gracious way. I admired the way she chewed and how quiet she was.

"Sahr may not like it if he finds us eating with you," I said.

Sandivah laughed. "Don't mind him. He's all talk. He never carries out his threats—not usually anyway. But you shouldn't be afraid of him."

"He warned us not to interfere with his wives, that we would do so at our peril," said Mila.

"He warns off everybody who comes to work for him," said Sandivah. "If you ask me, I'd say he's just looking after his interests, frightening other men away from his wives. But at the same time, he goes after other women. He already has three . . . and one in waiting as well. What right does such a man have to tell you whom not to interfere with? Where is he now? I'm sure he's hard at work poking the shit out of his little sluts and Koidu call girls."

Mila laughed naughtily and said, "I would gladly exchange places with him."

"It's not funny," replied Sandivah, though she managed to smile at the same time. "Let's just eat," she said, "And forget Sahr, okay?"

We agreed with her. To me, her smile was like sunshine. I felt like hugging her, squeezing her, and feeling her. But I restrained the urge. We ate in silence, but Sandivah and I gave each other several furtive,

Dead End Poverty

I nearly jumped out of my skin when Sahr greeted me at the door of the big house. My imagination went wild; I believed he'd already learned about my sexual liaison with his wife and was there to confront me. I prepared to defend myself physically or through dialogue. However, his next words took me out of my misery.

"I didn't know you'd returned," he said cheerfully. "It's a clever thing to do. I'm sure you'll be fresh and ready for work tonight." He turned round and started walking into the huge parlour. I followed.

"That's why we decided to return early," I said dryly.

"So where is Mila?" he asked.

"He decided to take a walk in the village," I said.

"Hope you enjoyed your outing in Koidu," he said, readjusting the cord of the bag he had on his shoulder. Apparently, he'd just arrived; the big, silver padlock was still protecting his room door.

"We did," I answered.

"Have you seen Tamba?" asked Sahr.

"Negative," I answered back.

"Never mind," he said curtly as he searched his pockets for the silver padlock's key.

"With the exception of you two, no one else has returned."

He opened his room door. Without another word, he went inside and shut the door behind him. I took a quick look towards Sandivah's door and saw that it was shut. No light was emanating from under the door. I wondered where she was. I also realised how lucky I was. We could've been caught in the act if Sahr had decided to take a walk in the bushes near the stream. He hadn't. I presumed we were safe as I walked thoughtfully towards an empty hammock. However, I was only properly relieved when we set out for the fields with the rest of the gang. They'd arrived in time for us to go to work.

35

The dry season was at its peak, and it was terribly hot. It started in mid-May and went through mid-November. Everything seemed to be dry or half-dry, carpeted with the red dust that was so characteristic of Kono. Only the intermittent downpours of sudden rain, signalling the advent of the rainy season, offered respite. However, the sudden rainfalls didn't last long, and they smelled of dust that had settled in the air, on the houses, and on all vegetation in Yengema. But they were bound to get bigger and more frequent, and we knew they would become an everyday occurrence for the next six months. A person who worked outdoors, which was the case for almost all people in Yengema, would have to work in the rain. Luckily, tropical rains could be quite warm, especially in September. Gangs hurried to dig and complete as many pits as possible before the rains began in earnest.

Our gang worked several more deep pits, but without much reward. Most of the diamonds obtained from the pits were terribly flawed and small. Each gang member received fewer than sixty leones from the sale of the gems from each pit we completed. Mr K was not a happy man, and he complained of spending too much money supporting the gang without profitable returns. Sahr looked morose; he was always miserable when money was scarce. Less money for us meant less money for him and constant pressure from Mr K.

We were working on our last deep pit before the rains arrived in earnest. We worked harder than usual. We came earlier to the fields because we were racing against time to remove the gravel from the pit and wash it. Unnecessary delays would mean the loss of the entire pit to the rain. Eventually, we finished working the pit and concentrated on kicking the gravel. We did that within a record two nights and found absolutely no diamonds—not even the tiny ones. Our hard work had yielded nothing. We were all tired and crestfallen from the experience, but we hoped we would find diamonds in the next venture . . . or the next. Nonetheless, we were happy that we wouldn't be deep mining for several months to come.

Although expected, the rainy season surprised many people. Torrential rain poured from the sky with a vengeance, almost nonstop for three days. And September was still months away. It was early May, and such rain was not really expected. Even then, the rains didn't deter anyone from work.

The rainy season was the time for mudslides and miniature landslides in the mining fields, events that no one wished to experience. When they happened, people sometimes lost their lives. Because they happened a little too frequently, the death toll by the end of the season was often considerable.

It was Friday night. As customary, we didn't have to go to work, but we didn't go to Koidu because we didn't want to spend the money we'd earned. Some of the gang members were already sleeping, others were roaming about the small village. Mila and I were the only two people on the veranda and it was raining heavily. We lay in our hammock without talking, but I could sense Mila was deep in thought.

I was thinking, too: reviewing our stay in Yengema (and diamond mining in particular). It was our second rainy season since we left our original home for the rich diamond fields of Kono. Yengema felt like home, our second home. Over the years, we forged good relationships with our peers and many other folks in the village. We learned to participate in all communal activities, and we were willing to help other people when we had time. We'd become popular in the village, too; men, women, and children knew our names. They accepted us as one of them, especially because we became fluent in Kono, the local lingo. Some villagers even invited us into their homes several times. In short, we felt very comfortable in Yengema. It was as if we were born there. We felt like we were still in Simbaru. Only our parents, siblings, and other relatives were missing. The knowledge of that hurt us at times, but we got on with life.

All the while, we visited Mother in Koidu whenever we could, and she always welcomed us as her sons. We even started to believe that she was our real mother because of the extent she went to see that we were fine and comfortable. She was an extraordinary woman, and our love and respect for her only increased.

In the diamond fields, we were experienced veterans, almost as experienced as our mentor, Tamba, who showed us the ropes during our early days. We'd experienced digging in all three recognised terrains: dry ground, swamps, and water.

Because it was rainy season, mining in the swamps came to a halt. It was too wet to dig diamond pits in the swamps unless we had the aid of a portable petrol water pump to dry out the pits. Water pumps were terribly expensive, and very few bosses opted to buy any. They were equally expensive to run in terms of fuel, oil, and repairs.

Few gangs, therefore, worked in swamps during the rainy season. The underground water and the almost endless rain filled pits in minutes. Unaided, it was almost impossible to mine on such terrain. Gang leaders preferred to have their gangs work on dry ground instead. It was more sensible and cheaper. If a gang wanted to dig for diamonds in the swamps, the only option was to rent a machine from another gang boss who possessed it. It could take days before one was free. Meanwhile, gang members remained idle and ate the same quantity of food. For most gang bosses, it was bad business. They preferred and encouraged gangs to mine on dry ground instead.

Those gangs with skilled and experienced divers among them often preferred to work in deep water. It was a difficult and very dangerous job. Several miners lost their lives collecting gravel from riverbeds, either by suffocating or through drowning. Notwithstanding, many miners continued to risk their lives carrying out the crude processes.

One way of doing it was to use petrol-powered air compressors (locally known as Putuputu), because of the *phut-phut* sounds they generated when in use. The diver wore a small, waterproofed chamber with leads attached to the Putuputu over his head to enable him to breathe underwater. One of the leads acted as a safety device. A diver pulled once if he wanted to surface and twice if he felt he was in danger. Either way, his workmates pulled him up to the surface quickly.

Armed with a Konkordu and a close-knit sack, a diver descended to the bottom of the river for any period of time between five and fifteen minutes. He dug for some gravel, loaded it in the sack, and pulled on the rope to surface. Once a diver was up, ready hands relieved him of the loaded sack and handed him an empty one. The diver then went to the bottom again to continue the process. When he was tired, he came up and exchanged places with another available diver. If none were available, he took a breather and went down again. The downside of the process was that, sometimes, carbon monoxide got into the breathing hose, contaminated the air, and killed the diver.

The other method of digging for gravel underwater—the method practised by most miners—was the *natural method*. It was a slow method, and most skilled divers only spent a maximum of three minutes underwater. It was a more dangerous method than the one involving the crude air compressors. As the name suggests, it was a more natural way of diving: a diver with a long rope tied around his waist navigated down to a riverbed using natural diving skills. His safety depended solely upon how long the diver believed he could hold his breath underwater. The diver quickly dug and loaded as much gravel as he could in sacks, and then he tugged on the rope to be pulled to the surface along with the loaded sacks.

However, a diver sometimes overestimated his endurance below water and drowned for lack of strength and air. Sometimes, makeshift bush ropes tied around the waist of a diver snapped. On such occasions, the diver seldom survived. Yet the urge to find diamonds overwhelmed the risks. Consequently, divers continued to mine the precious pebbles underwater without allowing the accidents to frighten them.

Working on dry ground was a much safer option than working in the swamps or underwater. Consequently, dry ground mining locations were always overcrowded; frequent fights erupted between rival gangs over the right to dig in particular places. Miners from different gangs worked close to each other, creating pits just feet apart, pits that would inevitably merge in the crude crisscrossed tunnels that evolved below the ground. When that happened, everyone encroached. Therefore, the fights for locations above ground didn't matter after all. However, the miners enjoyed the spontaneous fights. With scores of men working in close proximity, boys had to be boys.

Generally, miners dug on small sites everywhere the land was dry. Most chose to work in little plots they claimed instead of the impossible swamps and treacherous rivers and lakes.

As long as miners dug the ground for only a couple of feet, they were relatively safe. However, it was common belief that the best and biggest diamonds were lodged deep under the dry ground (but not as deep as in the swamps). Diamonds from the depths were less likely to be flawed, and they came in exotic colours: blue, brown, white, yellow, blue-white, and a variety of greens. In addition, they were much bigger than most stones from the swamps or underwater mines. Therefore, miners preferred to dig deep within the bowels of the earth to land the big ones. Of course, many miners died using that method.

Dry ground mining was as tricky as it was risky because it involved what the locals called Damakoro pits, which eventually transformed into tunnels. Miners from various gangs dug scores of single, near-perfect, circular holes in locations they'd claimed. The holes ended up being about six feet deep. Only then did tunnelling begin. The tunnels, supported by small sticks, twigs, and leaves, were barely large enough for a man with a sack tied around his waist to squeeze through. They grew until they interconnected in some way, blurring all demarcations and making the scramble by gangs for sites irrelevant.

Because they were crudely supported and the soil was moist from heavy rainwater, the weak pit tunnels were accidents waiting to happen. Indeed, several accidents happened before the end of the rainy season.

At least five members from each gang worked in the labyrinthine tunnels at any one time. Armed with a Konkordu for digging and a Makambo or torch, the first gang member descended into the tunnels through the single, circular hole. He was followed by a second gang member with several sacks, some lighting device, and a shovel with a very short handle. The other three members, also with Makambos or torches, descended into the tunnels, too. They took single-file positions in strategic places along the length of the winding tunnel up to the exit.

As the first miner dug, the second miner with the shovel loaded the loose soil into a sack. When the sack was half-full, he passed it to the third miner. That person passed it to the fourth. The sack continued the journey to the surface until it arrived at the fifth miner. The fifth miner passed it to a sixth one waiting at the entrance of the Damakoro pit. The miner waiting at the entrance transported and deposited the soil near a water source. Two miners were responsible for protecting the gravel from thieves.

The gang changed places when necessary, making sure that every gang member did a fair share of the job. Later during the same night, with designated watchers pointing their bright torches or Makambos at each shaker, the miners took turns kicking the gravel. Left in the open (regardless of whether twigs and leaves covered it), heavy rain could wash away all or most of the gravel. Such an event would mean that the time and effort invested would probably amount to nought.

During our first year, Mila and I experienced dry ground mining and liked it. In fact, the work was much easier than in the other mining methods. We didn't have to dig to reach a unique, greenish-blue soil to excavate the gravel. The soil dug on dry ground, depth and tunnels notwithstanding, *was* gravel. In spite of the dangers associated with dry ground mining, Mila and I felt no qualms with doing it again. We witnessed pit cave-ins that buried miners alive. On some occasions, a few lucky ones were rescued after hours of digging using all equipment available, including bare hands. They lived to tell the tale and worked on dry ground again.

The Joe Khakis were a major problem while dry ground mining. In fact, they arrested more people on dry ground than on any other location. Because miners worked underground, it was very difficult to escape, even when lookouts shouted out early warnings. By the time the unfortunate miners navigated their way out of the tunnels, the Joe Khakis were waiting for them at the narrow exits. If the miners opted to stay below ground, the Joe Khakis would send in a team to bring them out.

Rumour had it that, during one rainy season a few years before we arrived, a dozen Joe Khakis were buried alive from a cave-in triggered by persistent rain. They'd risked following stubborn miners into the tunnels, and that was when disaster struck. All efforts to dig the poor security personnel out failed, and the poor men perished underground. However, their colleagues seemed incapable of learning a lesson. They continued to pursue miners in the tunnels in the hope of making extra money to augment their pitiful wages. The urge to gain a reward was always greater than the risks involved.

It wasn't so much the arrests that bothered the miners as the waste of valuable working time that could be converted into dividends. They knew they were being held only until they received some money. As soon as money changed hands, they were on their way back to the village and the mining fields. However, being taken to Tankoro and sitting on the cold, wet, muddy floor of a truck full of rude, grinning security personnel until the money was paid could take days. It was not good for business, so our boss insisted that we couldn't get caught in the first place; no work time lost, no money to the Joe Khakis . . . the boss would be happy!

In all the different mining environments, regardless of which season, miners were plagued by big, shiny, greenish flies; snakes; tiny insects locally known as mootmoot; and above all, mosquitoes.

The mosquitoes were everywhere in the mining fields, even in the tunnels. The conditions were just right for them to breed unchecked. There were hundreds of stagnant pools scattered all over, and mosquitoes used them to lay their eggs. There was no way to avoid the mosquitoes other than slapping at them. Consequently, the sounds of uncoordinated slaps on certain parts of the body filled the night air like an audience clapping for a very poor performer.

The mosquitoes made the miners sick with malaria. When that happened, sick miners stayed in town drinking jugs of boiled Gbangba, Yubuyamba, and other leaves and roots believed by the locals to cure malaria. Most miners recovered, but malaria was prevalent. A few unlucky ones died and were buried far away from home. No one mourned for them, no family members knew whether they were still alive. It was quite tragic! I wouldn't wish such a predicament on anyone.

In the swamps, the miners had to cope with big, fat leeches that were happy to latch their suckers onto their busy hosts, only for the miners to pull at them vigorously until they fell off. Others used snuff to get rid of them. They were no scientists, but the miners were aware that snuff made leeches fall off their bodies. Nevertheless, others attacked them again in short order.

We were still idling in our hammocks on the long veranda. I constantly wondered whether Mila and I would die mining, most especially when a death occurred. I didn't want to die away from home, lonely and buried in some plot that would be a mining site one day. Before I died, I wanted to return to my village and reunite with my parents, siblings, and people in my community—people who loved me.

"Tell me, Mila," I said, "do you sometimes wonder if we will come out of this alive?"

"Leave that to God," Mila answered. "It's bad luck thinking about death all the time. It becomes quite boring. Think of something else, man."

I ignored him and urged him to answer the question: "Just answer me, please. Do you think we will come out of this alive?"

"Absolutely, yes," he said with certainty. It was as if he were the one to determine our times to die. "We've survived up to now, and we will survive in the future. Don't worry."

36

I wasn't comforted, but I said no more. Somehow, I dozed off in the hammock. When I woke up, Mila was not there. He had disappeared, but I had an inkling where he was: writhing in bed with Marie as long as a rival wasn't with her already. Feeling alone, I came down from my woven bed and entered the big parlour, determined to go to bed. I stepped over bodies as I went to my mat. I was asleep in minutes. It was not a peaceful sleep. For the first time since we absconded, I experienced the dream I'd had in Simbaru. Events in the dream happened exactly as they did then, and with almost the same effects.

Proceeds from dry ground mining that rainy season netted us 362 leones each, not very much for such hard and risky work. We were not happy with the returns because we didn't think it was fair compensation for our labour. But the money was more than what many people earned annually in Simbaru. We could never have earned such a sum in Simbaru. That realisation eventually made us feel a little better.

Mila and I kept sixty-two leones each and gave the rest to Sandivah for safekeeping, making sure we knew the amounts she had for each of us. Making so little for so long, I reckoned we wouldn't be getting too rich soon. Nevertheless, I was convinced that, by the following rainy season, we would have accumulated substantial sums of money.

About six miners perished in the tunnels before that season was over, but nobody did from our gang. I knew Koroma, the albino. His was the last body recovered from the tunnels after a frantic and haphazard digging spree that lasted until noon the next day. As coincidence would have it, his muddy, battered corpse turned up in the mouth of a tunnel close to me. I saw that his eyes had bulged out of their sockets. They seemed to have grown more than five times their normal size. His stomach was as flat as cardboard. It was as if he hadn't eaten anything for days. And the smell—God, it was awful. It wasn't the smell of decomposition. It was the smell of shit mixed with the deathly odour of the wet, red soil. Some people, including Mila, pinched their noses to avoid the stench. I didn't. I knew Koroma. I'd laughed and played with him a couple days before the fatal disaster. I felt I owed respect to his corpse. I was sure it wasn't his fault that he'd emptied his bowels. Anyone under such circumstances would have done the same. I decided that I wouldn't shy away from the smell. Using stretchers made out of poles, twigs, and leaves, volunteers among the miners (Mila and I included) took the six corpses back to the village for burial. Mila, two other miners, and I carried Koroma's dead body. It was a longer trek than usual, and it proved quite difficult, especially with a dead weight for company.

In town, we took the bodies to the men's section of the stream for cleaning. Wrapped up completely in white satin, the corpses were laid to rest in crude, unmarked graves in the village's cemetery. It was a very quick affair devoid of too many rituals. The older miners assumed all six people were Muslims, and according to Muslim tradition, they were already long overdue for burial: they were obliged to bury their dead a few hours after death unless serious circumstances prevented them from doing so. Such was the case with Koroma and his five unfortunate peers.

Koroma, like me, was not a native of Yengema. He'd come from Gardohun to seek his fortune, but death found him first. I stood over his fresh, unmarked grave wondering whether I would be next. Two fat tears fell from my cheeks; I didn't know whether they were for me or for Koroma, my ill-fated friend.

No one officially mourned Koroma. The village was back to normal business soon after the burial. The villagers, accustomed to deaths caused by cave-ins, had since ceased being emotional about them. Besides, the living had to get on with living.

"What a waste! He was very young," Mila said. He sighed sorrowfully on the way back to town.

"He was," I agreed. "He used to be so full of life."

"Do you suppose it could be us next season?" asked Mila.

"Forget that. God, it is bad luck thinking about death all the time. Think of something else, man," I answered, throwing back at him the exact words he had used when I asked him whether he thought we would die in Yengema. The only difference was that I was being hypocritical; only a few moments ago, I'd been wondering whether it would be me next. But I wasn't going to let Mila know that.

Mila didn't say anything. I could see he was hurting from my answer. I don't think he ever imagined that I would answer him with his own words. He shrugged and crossed his arms with his hands clasped firmly under opposite armpits. He didn't say another word until we reached the village. "You know where to find me if you need me," he said grumpily, and he trudged off, presumably to Marie's house.

37

Business was booming for Marie. That meant the mining trade was also booming. The rainy season was the best period to ply her flesh trade. Miners kicked gravel every day, and there was a good chance they had money in their pockets. They could afford to pay the amounts Marie charged for her time. During the dry season, she was lucky to service more than two clients per day. Gangs spent weeks digging a pit, and it took a few more days to wash the gravel. During that period, most of the miners were skint. True to typical miner behaviour, many miners blew their hard-earned funds faster than a prostitute dropped her pants. Without money, they couldn't afford Marie . . . unless Marie agreed to defer payment to the next time they had money.

Marie knew there weren't many native, single women in the village brazen enough to come out as prostitutes in public. Officially, in fact, none had ever dared to come out. The backlash would've been too much to bear. Family members and friends considered such women despicable, and they would definitely disown them or ostracise them from their "respectable" social circles. Nevertheless, Marie was aware that a few single women and even some married women she knew—secretly practiced the flesh trade in spite of the risks. But the men didn't like such women very much. Therefore, the men preferred to go with Marie. Sexually, they believed they expressed themselves better with Marie, and they were able to do what they wanted to do. They weren't burdened with the anxiety of being discovered with a chaste woman who was a prostitute in every sense of the word.

Suddenly, Marie was getting more clients than she cared to accommodate. Not that she couldn't accommodate them all if she wanted, but she'd set a ceiling of five paying clients per day, and she was resolved to stick by it. More customers meant more money. And she wasn't lacking in that department after saving several thousand leones for a rainy day in the false bottom of her earthenware drinking pot.

There was a sixth client, actually, but she had stopped charging him because he was the only one who rang her bell until it rattled.

Mila was a permanent fixture in her sex life, and she loved it. She didn't love him, though; she just liked the sex. They fucked at every given opportunity, place and time notwithstanding. That was all it was to her: fucking.

But Marie couldn't afford to fall in love. It was bad for business. Besides, she had started the game with Uncle Kormoh when she was a mere child, the power to make men do almost everything she wanted for sex. In the process, she had dulled her capacity to really love someone. Marie had never seen him since she moved away from Koidu. She often wondered what became of him.

As far as Marie was concerned, men didn't really love women. Uncle Kormoh didn't love her. Her polygamist of a husband, Pa Morlai, (the man forced on her by her pious father) didn't love her either. In fact, she had no illusions that any of the men she sold sex to ever loved her. Men only wanted one thing: pussy. It was all sex, sex, and sex for them. Men only married or took partners so they could have a warm pussy available to them whenever they wanted one. If it were only to make babies, men could bed any mature woman. But they could not guarantee that they would have that mature baby's mother whenever they wanted her.

Married women and some single women loathed Marie. They couldn't see what she had that they didn't. Yet their husbands kept visiting the loose woman as if some sexual spirit possessed them. They mused that perhaps, Marie's pussy was made of gold and fresh honey. They wouldn't have been surprised if it actually were made of such things given the number of men who bought her services.

Marie knew that many women in the village despised her. When, Mr K first brought her to the village, the women welcomed her warmly and helped establish her. However, upon discovering that she was a prostitute who she slept with their men, their attitude changed. She became the centre of gossip at the riverside, on the farms, and even in the diamond fields. Over the years, she had been involved in many scuffles with other women (and a few men who thought they could take advantage of her). Marie seemed to have won the fight because she was still in town plying her trade. Apart from the occasional scuffles, she assumed she was well.

She was wrong. Most women, including Sandivah, still hated her. All along, for a long time, they had been planning to chase her out

Dead End Poverty

of town. But they were waiting for an opportune moment. Sandivah hated her more than she hated Sahr's future fourth wife, Martha. Sandivah had never forgotten how Marie made her feel in the swamp. She could still hear her saying the words: "I could swear I just saw you shiver. Is something wrong with you?" She also recalled the laughter. The laughter had really annoyed Sandivah. She wondered what right Marie had to laugh at her. She was just a worthless prostitute, and she had laughed at and embarrassed her, a respectable, married woman.

Unknown to Marie, most women in Yengema were planning to teach her a lesson, a lesson they reckoned she would never forget. They hoped it might get rid of her for good. Sandivah had joined her fellow conspirators once she heard about the plan. The plan to get rid of Marie wasn't new; it was an ongoing one that they kept secret. Those involved guaranteed secrecy by invoking the same sacred oath that bound them not to divulge the secrets of female genital circumcision. The women had been holding clandestine meetings in the traditional Bondo bush, the official venue for female circumcision. They were patiently waiting for an opportune time to deal with Marie. They didn't want men to be around when the time arrived. The men, they believed, might be inclined to intervene to save her cheap womanhood for selfish reasons.

Only circumcised women and very young children of both sexes entered a Bondo bush. If an uncircumcised woman ventured into the sacred bush, she would be circumcised against her will. It was forbidden for men to enter the Bondo bush, unless they were invited by the Sowei to do the tasks the women couldn't do themselves. Under such circumstances, the men experienced no negative repercussions. On the other hand, if a man defied the ban and entered the sacred bush or spied on them in the bush, that man would develop elephantiasis of the scrotum and a grossly swollen belly. That man would never recover until his death unless the Sowei intervened and agreed to perform special ceremonies to alleviate the situation. But those ceremonies were very expensive.

Sandivah and several other women were present in one such secret meeting. Also, present at the meeting was Kamanda's young wife, Jenneh. She had gotten married the previous year. Jenneh secretly admired Marie. She loved her lifestyle, her freedom, her glittery jewellery, her clothing, and her carefree nature. She would've loved to be like Marie. But she knew her father would kill her on the spot. She couldn't quite see why the other women hated Marie. Marie didn't force their husbands to do anything. The husbands, with eternally lewd intentions, encroached on Marie's patch. Did it matter, then, whether Marie slept with them? If Marie didn't ply her trade, they would find some other woman to satisfy their sexual hunger.

Jenneh had no idea whether Marie was a circumcised woman. She really didn't care either way. If it were not for tradition and fear of her parents, she wouldn't have succumbed to the practice herself. But she had no choice in the matter. It had been about two years since her initiation into the Bondo society. The experience had left her bitter and in pain. Violated savagely to conform to the ancient practice of genital mutilation, she wouldn't wish the experience on anyone, not even Marie. When she thought about the episode, she could still feel the pain inflicted on her while in the clutches of the Sowei and the sadistic elders of the sacred bush. She believed it was unfair to subject women to such savagery, especially against their wills. She decided to pay Marie a clandestine visit after the meeting. The woman didn't deserve what was coming to her.

"We must teach the whore a lesson she will never forget," Sandivah said bitterly. "We should invite her to the sacred bush now."

"Let's hound her until she leaves the village," said Jenneh. She didn't mean it. She only wanted to divert suspicion from herself when the other women discovered that Marie was wise to their plan after all.

"Have you noticed that she is never a keen visitor to the sacred bush?" asked another woman in the process of fixing a pinch of snuff under her discoloured tongue. The daily use of the stuff over many years had turned her tongue brown and yellow. She savoured the taste for a few seconds before jettisoning a thin string of slimy, brown spittle into the bushes. "In fact, as far as I know, I have never seen her in the sacred bush. That could only mean one thing . . ."

She couldn't finish her sentence; the other women did it for her: "Maybe she's uncircumcised," the women said in unison.

"Yes, she is still a girl in a woman's body," agreed Bondu. An uncircumcised woman is just a girl.

"Let's invite her here, then," Sandivah persisted. "If she turns up, she will get no help. Men, for all their bravado, wouldn't enter the sacred bush to help her."

Dead End Poverty

The women realised they would have Marie where they wanted her if she visited the Bondo bush.

"So how do we get her to the Bondo bush?" asked a tall, thin, heavily pregnant woman with a stooped posture induced by her pair of giant, natural boobs. She loathed Marie with body, soul, and mind. Her husband was a frequent visitor, sometimes immediately after making love to his wife.

"Yes, but how do we get her to the bush," echoed Yei.

"Yei," Sandivah said to her husband's second wife, "you don't get mature women to the sacred bush by dragging them there. You invite them in the name of the Sowei."

There was no love lost between them. Sahr was their cause of disagreement. But Sandivah, until Martha emerged on the scene, was the favourite wife. That was enough to set her rivals, Yei and Bondu, against her. "I'm not stupid, and there is no need to be sarcastic," retorted Yei.

"I didn't say you were," Sandivah snapped.

"That's exactly what you meant, Sandivah," said Bondu.

"So what if I meant th—" Sandivah began.

"Shut up all of you. You're behaving like kids," the thin, pregnant woman interrupted. "We are here to talk about Marie. We don't want any sideshows."

The other women agreed and the meeting continued with Bondu asking, "What do we do if she refuses to come?"

"Then we'll go get her physically," said a fat, middle-aged woman. "And that will be far worse than if she came voluntarily." Her husband was also a recurrent visitor to Marie's den of illicit pleasure.

"Again, the men won't interfere once we let them know that Marie refused an invitation to the sacred bush," said Sandivah. "Not that they're unaware that she is uncircumcised, but few men care whether a woman is circumcised or not. What they see with an erect dick is a receptacle to pour their seed, a pussy to fuck. A baby is better equipped to think rationally than a man with an erect penis; he ceases thinking with his brain. His dick totally assumes the thinking role. I assure you: men will put it in any hole available, even a hole in the ground, as long as they get pleasure from it."

The women laughed and slapped their thighs in response to the joke. When they finally stopped laughing, they concluded the meeting.

They agreed to send an emissary to invite Marie to visit the Bondo bush the following evening (as dictated by the Sowei). The thin, heavily pregnant woman volunteered for the job. No one opposed her. With her in charge, they knew Marie would get the message. There was no doubt about that.

Later, Marie wondered what the Sowei wanted from her, but she also knew she was wasting her time thinking about remote possibilities. Marie knew why she was being summoned to the Bondo bush: she was not circumcised. Her sex life started too early, and most men didn't mind that she wasn't circumcised. Actually, they preferred her uncircumcised. She was different from their wives, and men liked variety, especially when it came to women. She was confident that her secret was safe with the men. They loved touching and playing with her private parts, parts that were either mutilated or completely absent from their wives. She couldn't count the number of times men had complimented her, confessing to her that they got much more pleasure from her pussy.

Perhaps men loved being with her because she was not circumcised. Men liked her that way, but remaining uncircumcised had its own disadvantage: she couldn't go to the sacred bush. Therefore, she had kept her secret, at least from other women, since the day Mr K brought her to Yengema. For an added measure of protection, she left the village for the two weeks during the dry season when the sacred bush initiated girls from as young as five years old. At such times, she always had a woeful story about an ailing aunt, a dead relative, or a sick family member to justify her absence. Some of the circumcised women in the village noticed her avoidance of the sacred bush. Marie was aware that they suspected the truth about her womanhood. But they couldn't prove it. She never even washed naked in the river when other women were present. She always wore her wrapper around her waist.

"You always wear a wrapper when you wash with us," Bondu observed one time when Marie was bathing with them in the stream near the village. "Why?"

"Yes, tell us why," the other women echoed. What are you afraid of? Do you think we will rape you?

"I just don't like to bathe naked in the company of other women," Marie replied, careful not to add fuel to the situation.

For the local women, Marie's explanation was odd: they knew she was a prostitute who slept with their husbands and sons (or any man who could afford her). She was obviously comfortable being naked around others, so covering herself in the company of women was curious. Women with beautiful bodies flaunted their bodies, but the beautiful Marie always hid hers.

"And we've never seen her in the sacred bush," threw in Yay Sata, a thick, fat woman washing her body close to Marie. Yay Sata's bulging skin folds were similar to those sported by the Michelin Man.

"Pressing family affairs keep arising, problems that I must take care of. It's not my fault that things happen to me during initiation periods," Marie explained.

"Hope you'll be there this season," said Bondu. "We'll pray that nothing happens to your relatives this time."

"Hopefully," Marie said. And fortunately for her, they left it at that.

But out of the blue, the Sowei had summoned her to the Bondo bush. She knew no good would come out of the meeting. She had suspected as much from Hawa's body language. She knew the woman hated her because of her man, a hairy, round, potbellied, bald man who could've been mistaken for a gorilla. Marie didn't really like the man, but he paid well and frequented her love nest often. Somehow, she felt sorry for Hawa, considering all the slander her baboon-faced husband had levelled at her while Marie massaged his dick and ego.

Standing at the doorway to her house, Marie stared into the darkness and realised that she was also dark. Her gleam was just about to be eclipsed by envious women bent on revenge because she sold her body to their husbands. She didn't think she was doing anything wrong. It was just commerce: she had the goods, and they had the money. Everybody was happy, it seemed.

But not everybody was happy. Try as she might, Marie couldn't come up with any plausible reason or explanation for the summons. To her, it meant only one thing: her secret was out. The more she thought along those lines, the more convinced she became. The village women knew she was uncircumcised.

Somehow, she knew that her long stay in Yengema, a place she had considered her home, was coming to an end. But what had she achieved? She had money, but she didn't really have any friends—at least no one she was close to. Even the men she slept with were not her friends. They came to her because of her pussy. They were clients, and she wouldn't depend upon them, especially given the fact that her problem was associated with the sacred bush. Generally, men were in awe of the Bondo bush. They knew better than to mess with anything that bore its signature. Marie realised she would get no help from them and wondered what she should do. She wanted to remain in Yengema, but she didn't want to be circumcised. She was convinced that wasn't what she wanted. Being different attracted the men. Besides, she didn't want to undergo the excruciating pain involved in the process. Circumcision wasn't for her; she didn't do it when she was small, and she wasn't going to do it as an adult. She knew that she wouldn't willingly attend the summons to the sacred bush.

She also realised instinctively that she would have to leave Yengema. But she didn't know where to go. She wondered what would become of her if she stayed and refused to attend the summons. She knew what would happen and didn't want to think about it. But she had to come up with a plan soon. The following evening wasn't next year. The thought spurred her into action. She went back into the house and into her room. She found Mila lying naked in the same place where she had left him after one of their hot sex sessions.

Marie said to him, "Dress up, Mila, you're leaving now."

"What should I do about this?" he asked, pointing to his engorged monstrosity of a penis. He grabbed her hand and attempted to draw her to the bed. "Come on, love, this won't take long."

Marie yanked her hand out of his grasp and said, "I'm not joking. Please leave now. I want you to leave now; I want to be alone."

"Is anything wrong? What have I done?" asked Mila.

"Nothing's wrong, and you haven't done anything. I just want you to leave," Marie said, picking up his clothes from the floor. She threw the clothes at him on the bed. "Please dress up and leave now."

Mila obeyed. While he was putting on his clothes, his mind went into overdrive. *Why is Marie behaving this way? She's always wanted to be in my company, and she even begs me to stay the night when I'm not out in the diamond fields. Is she pretending she isn't angry with me even though she is? But she can't be angry with me. I don't remember doing anything wrong to her. She'd been happy before the knock on the door, just after we finished fucking. She'd been all smiles, willing to go along with every bedroom trick I threw at her. What could've changed within such a short period?* He couldn't come up with an answer.

His clothes were back on, and he moved close to Marie and slapped her bottom hard. Normally, Marie would have giggled, taken his hand, and helped him massage her backside. That always led to a sex session, even if they'd just had one. On that occasion however, Marie didn't giggle or help his hand to massage her pert bottom. "Not now, Mila," she protested. "Please just go away and leave me alone," she said, firmly removing his roving hand from her bottom.

"Okay, I'm going." Mila knew when he was defeated. May I come to see you tomorrow, then?" he asked in his most seductive voice.

"You may," Marie said without emotion, "but I can't guarantee that I'll be here."

"You are going somewhere?"

"Maybe."

"What time will you be back?"

"I don't know."

"Then I'll keep checking till I find you home."

"Yes, you do that," Marie said lazily.

From her veranda, Marie watched Mila until he disappeared from view. She felt sorry for him. She didn't love him, but she liked him. She wondered whether she would see him again. She had no idea. She sighed heavily. As she turned around to get back into her house, she heard a female voice calling her name. Her first reaction was one of terror. She thought the angry women had decided to come for her sooner than later. She hastened to get into the house.

"Marie," the female voice called out again, "please wait. I want to tell you something."

That time, Marie recognised the voice and stopped. Jenneh came out of the shadows and onto the veranda. She quickly led Marie into the house. "Please come inside quickly and shut the door," said Jenneh in an anxious, low voice. Marie obeyed. Jenneh sat on Marie's bed uninvited.

"Why? What's the matter," asked Marie. "What's wrong?"

"You are," said Jenneh. "Listen. Please don't interrupt me."

Marie remained standing. She wondered what the young woman wanted to tell her. Whatever it was, it was important or urgent. Otherwise, Jenneh wouldn't have risked going inside her house.

If someone saw her and told her husband, only God knew what punishment she would be subjected to. The men came freely without hindrance, but they didn't want their wives anywhere near Marie. *What gross hypocrisy!* Marie thought.

"They're coming to get you," said Jenneh

"I know," said Marie lamely. "Hawa was here awhile ago."

"I don't know if you are circumcised or not. I don't care. However, if you answer the Sowei's command and go to the Bondo bush uncircumcised, you will wish you'd never been born. All the women are against you. This time, they want to prove if you are a real woman. If you aren't, they'll chase you out of town. If you refuse to go to the sacred bush, the women will come to get you. God knows what they will do to you. There is no escape from this. If I were you, I would pack up and leave the village in secret. That's all I have to say." Jenneh rose up from the bed and headed towards the door.

"Thank you," Marie said. "I'll never forget this. Thank you." She touched the girl on the shoulder as she neared her.

"I like you, Marie. I'm not like the other women. I don't know why they hate you so, and I don't know why being circumcised or not matters. I admire you, and I want to be like you. You are a nice person," Jenneh said and smiled coyly.

"Thank you," Marie replied.

The girl was quite young, about fourteen, and already married. She didn't know what it involved to be like Maria. On impulse, Marie decided to compensate her informant. "Wait here a minute," she said. Marie moved past the girl to her earthenware drinking pot with the false bottom, removed a handful of notes, and handed the money to Jenneh. Jenneh refused to take the money, but Marie insisted.

Finally, she relented, took the money, clenched it in her left hand, and prepared to open the door to get out.

"Wait," said Marie, "let me have a look first. You never know who's out there." She opened the door and looked outside, straining her eyes to see properly in the dark. She saw a male silhouette passing by and recognised that it was Kamanda, Jenneh's husband.

"Hiya, sweetheart," Kamanda greeted Marie when he recognised her. A knowing smile spread across his face. "Expect me tomorrow. The usual time," he said.

Marie laughed and said, "Off with you. And goodnight, you sex pest. Your young bride must be pining for you." She watched Kamanda until the darkness swallowed him. She was glad she had decided to check. Jenneh might have walked right into her husband.

Marie saw no other person in the immediate vicinity, so she went back inside and gave the all-clear sign to Jenneh. She did not, however, tell her that her husband had just passed her front door. She reasoned that it didn't matter because Kamanda was going in the opposite direction from his house. Besides, telling Jenneh would have spooked her more. Jenneh was out of the house in a jiffy and on her way, praying silently that her husband wouldn't notice her absence. In a moment, she merged with the darkness, and the dark and the young bride became one.

For quite a while, Marie stood in the centre of the room feeling angry and defeated. Her demeanour was sour, her attitude vindictive. At that moment, she could have murdered her adversaries with her bare hands without hesitation. She would have relished the act, too. She sat on her bed with her head in both hands, thinking deeply, trying to discover a solution to her predicament. But no matter how hard she thought, she came up with the same answer: she had to leave the village.

The notion of leaving had been in her mind since Hawa's visit. The thin, pregnant woman hadn't disguised her loathing and abhorrence for her. In fact, Marie had understood from Hawa's body language that she would respond to the Sowei's call at her peril. Therefore, Jenneh's visit to warn her of her impending plight had only reiterated the fact that she needed to be on her way. If she were ever in doubt that the village women were bluffing, young Jenneh's visit definitely made her mind up. The girl had been very brave to risk the wrath of the other women and her crazy husband. Marie hoped she wouldn't get into trouble over the matter, and she was glad she insisted that Jenneh accept the money she offered her.

"I must go away," Marie heard herself say.

That spurred her into action. She jumped up from the bed and retrieved a red suitcase from the top of a table in one corner of her room. She threw the suitcase on the bed and opened it. Save a hoard of cheap, glittering jewellery (made out of copper, silver, and a variety of exotic beads in every colour and size; a few metal and plastic bangles; and a couple of bottles of nail polish and other cheap cosmetic accessories), the suitcase was empty.

There was not a single item of clothing inside. Her articles of clothing, though few in number, were numerous compared to the amount owned by the local women. Her clothes were neatly hooked on nails around the room. She looked around the room, choosing which pieces of clothing to take with her. She would travel light, but she didn't know where. She was more inclined to opt for Koidu, her birthplace. Fortunately, Koidu was only a short distance from Yengema. It was not the ideal place, but it was a place for her to clear her head and decide where to start a new, honest, respectable life. But she doubted the thought as soon as it popped into her mind. Men would still find her attractive, regardless of where she set up shop, and she loved the power she had over them.

She wanted to get away from Yengema, to put a great distance between her and the sad, despicable, conniving women plotting to mutilate her genitals. Koidu would be her starting point. It would be the ideal place, and there was the possibility that her clients from Yengema would still visit her when they were in Koidu. The jealous women of Yengema thought they'd won, but Marie knew better.

But she wasn't sure whether she should visit her family in Koidu. The question hit Marie like a thunderbolt. From that fateful day when she ran away from her geriatric husband, she hadn't heard from or seen any of her parents or relatives. She thought it was strange that she hadn't encountered a family member in Koidu given its proximity to her. At first, it troubled Marie. Bouts of sadness overwhelmed her whenever she thought of her family. Sometimes she cried. However, she had managed to suppress those feelings, and over the years, she'd succeeded. She stopped thinking about and yearning for them. The more she established herself in the Yengema community, the less she thought of her family and other relations.

Marie walked around the room, unpinning her best clothes from the nails on the hall and hanging them over her left wrist. She took them to the suitcase and packed them neatly, one after the other. It was an agonising process for her. She couldn't help feeling sorry for herself. Emotions overwhelmed her, and she felt tears running down her high cheekbones. She didn't wipe the tears away. She was glad she was crying. She loved many things about Yengema, but she was on the verge of losing it all. In fact, she believed she had already lost it. Maybe that was why she was crying. When one lost something one loved and treasured, one always yearned and cried for it. It was okay to cry. She had lost Yengema and had to cry. She never thought she would leave Yengema for any reason, but a bizarre group of vindictive women had changed all that. Yengema was no longer her home; she was no longer welcome there.

With a heavy heart, she packed the last of the clothes on her wrist into the red suitcase. She added a couple of shoes, bedspreads, and toiletries to the case. Satisfied that she had all she needed in the case, she snapped it shut. She went over to the door and pulled on it. The door was securely locked. She turned around and headed to the far corner, where she had the earthenware pot with the fake bottom. She retrieved all the money from inside and took it back to the bed. She sat on the edge of the bed and laid the money out according to denomination. By the time she was finished, notes in neat piles surrounded the red suitcase. It resembled a giant money cake with an equally giant suitcase cherry in the middle. The money amounted to well over six thousand leones, but Marie didn't count it. She gathered all the money and dumped it in her big head tie, making sure she left some out for her immediate use. She arranged the money neatly in the headscarf, folded the edges over the notes, tied it nicely, and put it back on the bed.

Marie dropped the wrapper she was wearing, exposing a plump and round bottom and a bushy pubic area. She was stark naked. She retrieved her pants from the floor in front of the bed and put them on. She took the green and yellow headscarf from the bed and tied it securely over her ample bum, which became instantly enormous. She tugged at it vigorously, but the headscarf with the money inside stayed in place. Next, she wore her wrapper over her improvised money belt and believed that her money would be quite safe where it was. She was set, all ready to go. Her suitcase was packed, she was dressed for her escape journey, and she had money to use. All she had to do at that point was wait until the village went to sleep.

When she thought the time was right, she would slip out and walk the few miles to the main road. She wouldn't be afraid. She had walked that road alone several times before. With the suitcase still on the bed, Marie stretched her body along it, trying to relax as she prepared mentally for her journey into the unknown.

In her dream, Angry women chanting her name, accompanied by melodies emanating from empty food tins and bottles, were chasing her. Some were asking whether she believed in her womanhood. "We will kill you," they said. Marie ran as fast as she could. To run faster, she kicked out her flip-flops from her feet and sprinted along the path leading to the main road. But the faster she ran, the more it looked like the angry women were gaining on her. She looked back to see how close they were. They were close enough for her to recognise that they were being led by Hawa, the tall, thin, pregnant woman with the massive boobs. Marie wondered how such a heavily pregnant woman could run like that. Regardless of the weight and the bobbing of her jugs, the woman kept going. *She will actually kill me if she gets me,* Marie thought. She increased her speed. It was a mistake. She lost her footing and tumbled heavily to the ground. Hawa was on her in record time. Crouched over Marie, her massive jugs hanging down and swaying like pendulums, she was nearly smothered. The other angry women arrived soon. Everyone was having a go at Marie's unprotected body. She curled herself into a ball, ready for the worst. She was practically dying of fear. The angry female mob was assaulting her unprotected body. In her pain, flashbacks of her life in the village played out in her mind like a film. She saw herself in the old jalopy, arriving in Yengema with Mr K. She was a pretty teenager, and she had already decided how to earn her keep. Kamanda, her very first customer, flashed before her eyes, followed by Samuka, the dead diamond thief. They passed through her mind's eye in rapid succession. It was now Sahr passing through, and then Komba, and then Lavally, and then Kemokai, and then some elders of the village including Yaya, keeper of the Gandoe. Finally, she pictured Mila, her most recent conquest. She even saw Jenneh, the Good Samaritan who risked her well-being to warn her. Marie even saw herself woefully packing her things into the red suitcase. A heavy kick landed in her abdomen. The flashbacks immediately disappeared, replaced by bolts of pain that ran through every fibre of her body. But she was still conscious.

"Let's initiate her in the Bondo society here and now," she heard Hawa suggest. Get the razor blade ready!

"Spread her open. Let me mutilate her, show her what it takes to be a real woman." It was Hawa again. "By the time we finish with her, she will run away from a man when—"

Suddenly, Marie opened her eyes. She was sweating and expecting to see angry women. But there were no angry women. She was still lying by the red suitcase on her bed. Marie couldn't tell how long she had been asleep. However, she knew it was very late. The area was quiet save a few barking dogs and the sounds of night creatures.

She got up and went to the door. She opened it and peered outside. It was dry. It was not raining, and she didn't think it would rain. There were no black clouds in the sky heralding a downpour. The moon was out. That was unusual but not impossible during the rainy season. The whole atmosphere was enveloped in a flood of pale, bluish light.

She listened carefully, but she didn't hear a single human voice. She didn't think angry women were lurking in the shadows, either. She shut the door and returned to the bed. Marie retrieved the suitcase from the bed and held it in her right hand. It wasn't heavy and wouldn't be a deterrent to her speed. She stood there for a good while, gazing at everything in the room and thinking about all the fun she had had there. A sad feeing came over her. But sad or not, she had to go. She shot one last look at the room, turned around, and walked briskly to the door. She opened it and walked out into the moonshine with the red suitcase held firmly in her hand. She left the door ajar. There was no point in shutting it. She was leaving and didn't want any of the things she left behind.

Outside, she recited a short prayer and took her first step into the unknown. However, she was sure that she would never return to Yengema. Her life there was over; she was heading for a new one. And how that life might turn out to be would depend entirely upon the natural asset between her legs. Instinctively, she rubbed her crotch with her free hand as if seeking assurance that it was still there. It was. On the outskirts of the village, she turned around to take a quick look at the town she had called home and sighed before continuing her journey. She was leaving the sleeping town of Yengema behind her— perhaps forever.

38

Mila raised the alarm that Marie had disappeared. Indeed, he had checked on her several times, as he had promised. The first time, he found it odd that Marie would leave her house door open when she was nowhere in sight. He simply peeked inside and shouted her name several times. But he didn't get an answer. However, he did notice that, in her room, the red suitcase usually on the table and some of her clothes that used to hang on the wall were gone. He then shut the door and left, wondering where Marie could be at that time of night. He returned twice more that night, but Marie never returned.

Mila was worried. Worst case scenarios about what could have befallen Marie played out in his mind. *Could someone have kidnapped Marie?* He didn't believe that. *Had a thief broken into her house and forced her to go with him? Alternatively, had she simply gone away?* Mila couldn't understand why Marie was missing. So he did the only logical thing he could think to do: he reported to the town chief that he was worried Marie was missing, that something could have happened to her.

"How do you know she is missing?" the chief asked.

"She is not in her house. Her suitcase and some of her clothes are missing," Mila replied.

"Maybe she went to Koidu. Have you thought of that, young man?" suggested the chief.

"She has not gone to Koidu," Mila said with a little impatience. "I know; I was with her until nightfall."

The chief smiled knowingly and said, "Aren't you always with her? Don't forget, news travel fast in this village. Anyway, we should wait until morning. If she's still not home, we will do something."

The chief was finished with him. Mila didn't like the chief's handling of the matter, but he didn't want to argue. He returned home and crept quietly onto his mat, taking great care not to wake his sleeping mates. He was still thinking about Marie when sleep overtook him.

We woke up to the news that Marie had left the village for good—never to return. "Marie's gone for good," I heard many people say. The rumour spread like wildfire among the residents of Yengema. Maina, the halfwit who'd delivered the news of Samuka's diamond theft, also brought the news of Marie's departure. Apparently, he'd been coming back to the village from the main road after a visit to Motema. Maina never paid any transportation costs. He walked everywhere he wanted, unless a kindhearted driver gave him a lift.

Mila and I were together when we heard about Marie. He was shocked and devastated, but not because of Marie's safety. To think that he wouldn't be shagging Marie any longer hit him like a sledgehammer. He had taken it for granted that his sex life was fine and settled. Marie had demonstrated that she liked him, if only for the sex. She was also the only woman who had matched his sexual voracity, taking everything he could throw at her and giving back as much as she was given.

For the rest of that day, the normally cheerful Mila was moody and easily irritated by things that never seemed to bother him. He even pulled out of work that night, claiming that he was sick. Not for a single moment did he stop thinking about and missing Marie. He asked questions of himself that he couldn't quite answer, taking the blame for not seeing it coming when Marie's demeanour changed after their last sexual escapade. He was sorry that Marie was gone, but he also knew that he had to replace her with another woman as soon as he could. For Mila, life without sex was like drinking tea without sugar. Regular sex brought out the best in him.

Sandivah, thinking that we didn't know Marie had departed, told us the news enthusiastically, almost revelling in it. "I'm extremely happy that prostitute left. All women in this village should be equally happy. Marie was a homewrecker."

"Did she wreck your home?" Mila asked a little heatedly.

"Not exactly," Sandivah replied. She was being candid and spoke plainly. "But she was fucking our men. And then they refused to fuck us."

At that point, I intervened. I tried to avert any ensuing argument.

"Sandivah, do you know why she left?" I asked.

"I do. And so does any circumcised woman in town," she said.

"Why did she leave? I was not expecting this, and it genuinely surprised me."

"We invited her to the sacred bush in the name of the Sowei. Pretty though she was—favourite of all cheating men—she was uncircumcised. She was a little girl with adult clothes on. Yet shameless men still slept with her. It is against the customs of our community to sleep with an uncircumcised woman. But men do whatever they want." She stopped and looked at us in triumph.

Mila moved away from us and lodged himself in a hammock. He didn't want to hear what Sandivah had to say about Marie. To him, Marie was fine; no amount of character assassination was going to make him change his mind about her. Besides, the woman was his pleasure pot. He knew that, because she was gone, he would be starved sexually.

"Still, why must she go away?" I asked Sandivah. "She lived here for years. You did nothing. Why now?"

"We wanted to chase her out of town, to get her away from our men. Was that too much to ask? Lucky bitch, someone must have warned her. I hope we catch that traitor. Anyway, I wish Marie had stayed to receive what was coming to her."

"Like what? What did you have in store for her?" I asked.

"Ganging up on her to circumcise her by force," answered Sandivah promptly. "Only God knows if she would have come out of it alive. But I doubted it. Judging by how angry we were with her, she probably would not have survived. She would have become another casualty of the sacred bush, another statistic."

"You mean she could have died or been killed in the sacred bush if she'd attended?" I asked in disbelief.

"You are absolutely right," Sandivah said. "Nevertheless, her guardian angels seem to have been wide awake." And then, pretending to be jealous, she asked, "Anyway, why are you so interested in her?"

"Just curiosity," I said.

Sandivah gave me a sweet smile and whispered, "I'm glad you never went to her. I'm glad you came to me, a real woman in every sense."

"I'm glad, too," I said. "But we mustn't talk about that here. It's too risky."

"Well I'm off to meet the other women in the sacred bush. I know they are jubilant. Let's meet tonight at our usual place. This news had made me extremely horny. I feel like celebrating, don't you?"

Dead End Poverty

"Okay. I'll be there," I said.

She looked at me seductively, and then, with an exaggerated sashaying of her provocative, bouncing bum, she went to meet her cronies in the Bondo bush.

Weeks after Marie left, the village women were still happy. They even organised impromptu celebration dances to mark the occasion. The Sowei herself, in her black raffia costume and exquisite mask, joined in the festivities. For nearly a month, Marie was the hottest topic in the village. Gossip about her prostitution and uncircumcised genitalia died down gradually after some time. She was seldom mentioned in conversations after a few months.

It had been busy for the miners, too. Like rats, they scurried in and out of the crude maze of inadequately supported, poorly lit, underground tunnels. They were intent on retrieving as much gravel as they could. Sacks went into and out of the mouths of scores of Damakoro pits. At first glance, it was as if the earth was ejecting the dead from its bowels.

Even though it was the rainy season and the soil was quite moist, it was still very hot and stuffy underground, making the back-breaking work more difficult. Miners stayed below until heat, humidity, or tiredness overcame them. At that point, they exchanged places with other gang members.

Mila and I were in the thick of it all, encouraged by the recent diamond finds. We were averaging about thirty pieces per night. However, the majority of them were small stones under one carat. Regardless, small stones in big quantities fetched profitable returns. As it was, we stood to gain money every Friday when we sold the gems we found to Mr K.

And every Friday, we travelled to Koidu to add more money to our growing stash, which Mama Finda kept for us, and to pursue our private interests. On such occasions, I always made time to go to the cinema. I had become very drawn to the cinema, and I enjoyed the films even though I didn't speak or read English. But I realised that pictures by themselves told stories, and I managed to comprehend the films that way. Sometimes, Mila came with me to the cinema, but visiting the whorehouses around town was his preference. He was a happy man when we were in Koidu, but he missed Marie when we returned to Yengema.

Sandivah was no longer our banker because I had become uneasy with her keeping our money. Considering my sexual involvement with her, I was afraid we would lose all our money if Sahr learned that I was sleeping with his wife. So I convinced Mila to have Mother be our banker, but only after I let him know I was sleeping with Sandivah.

"You conniving devil!" Mila exclaimed jauntily. "You beat me to her. I was intending to have her for myself."

"What? In addition to Marie?" I asked with mock horror. At the time, Marie was still living in Yengema, unaware of the plot to chase her out of town.

"And anyone else available," Mila said with a wicked grin. "You know me: I can cope with any quantity."

I didn't say a thing. Nor did I laugh.

"Seriously, though," he said, "under the circumstances, Mama Finda is a much safer person to give our money to."

The discussion ended there. We relieved Sandivah of her role as our banker that same week, but we compensated her with the princely sum of ten leones. She was over the moon when she got the money. She also asked us not to mention it to her husband because he would surely take it from her.

As the days passed by, after Marie left, Mila gradually accepted the fact that Marie was gone for good. He knew there was nothing he could do about it. He realised he had to move on and find another regular sex partner. He was determined to forget Marie, so he threw himself into work, doing more than what was expected of him.

Somehow, Mila and I found ourselves working side by side in the humid tunnels. There were other miners all around us digging and shifting gravel to the surface. The miniature tunnels had merged to form a vast network of underground passageways. Notwithstanding, all gang members managed to bring up their gravel from the mouths of their original Damakoro pits. It all depended upon teamwork. I was doing the digging, and Mila was loading bags with gravel that went up the human chain until they reached the surface. After that, they were carefully deposited on top of a growing pile. The empty bags went through the reverse process until they reached Mila or any gang member who found himself in that position. Lighting, of course, was poor. We had to work carefully or risk mutilating ourselves with

Dead End Poverty

the ever-sharp Konkordu. Breathing, too, was difficult. And talking, though necessary, was kept at a minimum.

"You reckon we will discover diamonds in the gravel?" I asked Mila.

"What do you think?" he answered back. "I'm sure there will be a few leones in it for us just as soon as we wash the pile. Why do you ask?"

"No reason. I just wanted to chat."

"Wrong place, though," he advised. "Talking is a distraction, and you have the Konkordu."

We didn't talk again. We worked in silence, but we could hear the din of other people talking. Soon, it was time for us to go back to the surface. However, it was not to be. Loud buzzing sounds emitted from several cow horns at the same time. Soon, we heard people bellow, "Joe Khakis! Every man for himself!" It was just the lookouts warning us that the security forces had arrived to raid the dry ground. An almighty confusion broke out as miners from every tunnel abandoned everything to run for to the surface. In their quest, miners pushed and shoved, falling over and trampling each other. Some were stuck in the narrow tunnels and blocked several escape routes for others. We also knew that all the miners who were above ground (and those nearest the mouths of the Damakoro pits when the warning came) would have escaped to safety.

Being at the lowest level of our tunnel, Mila and I knew we would never make it to the surface in time to escape the raiders. We were sitting ducks, awaiting the hunters.

"What do we do now?" asked Mila.

"Put out all the Makambos and torches. Stay where you are," said a gang member.

We put out all the sources of light and hoped against hope that the Joe Khakis wouldn't find us. Plunged into pitch darkness, I felt like I was buried alive. I thought, *If this is how dark the grave is, then it is a terrible thing to die.* I was afraid, especially as the darkness echoed the one that crept over me and my troubled thoughts.

A bright light penetrated the darkness in our tunnel. We heard a commanding voice say, "I know you can hear me. Come out now if you know what is good for you." I didn't hear any one talk or move. The tunnel was quiet as a tomb.

"Security personnel are guarding every entrance of the Damakoro pits," coaxed the same commanding voice. "There will be no avenues of escape for you this time. Come out now before I lose my temper!"

Still, no one responded. I noticed that we were huddled together, hiding as much as possible from the light. I also observed several reflections of light in the adjoining tunnels. I began to believe that the security personnel did have every pit entrance covered. I thought it might be better to give up. I might avoid being manhandled by greedy security personnel known for unprovoked violence.

"I'm coming out," a miner shouted.

"We are waiting," shouted back a voice.

"Now you have betrayed us all," said someone among us.

There was movement, and we heard a miner following the light to the entrance. A couple of minutes later, we heard an agonising cry. It was proof that the security personnel had their man and were wasting no time intimidating him into total submission. It was all about control.

"Where are the others? How many of you are down there?" It was the commanding voice again. He was shouting at the top of his voice through the Damakoro entrance, but we could barely hear him. "I know you're there. Come out now, or we will start going to town on your mate," the voice threatened.

But it was not a threat. Our mate started shouting in fear and agony. He didn't stop because the Joe Khakis were raining baton blows on his head and body.

"I'm going out," I announced to no one in particular. "If we don't give ourselves up, they'll definitely harm our mate."

"I'm with you, then," agreed Mila. "Let's go out."

Only two others agreed with us. They were the only two people beside us in the tunnel. That meant every one of the five people from our tunnel was accounted for. The fifth man was, at that moment, suffering from at the hands of the Joe Khakis.

"We are coming out. Four of us," I shouted. "That's all of us down here."

"We are waiting," the voice cried faintly.

It was our turn to follow the light. Hands linked in a chainlike manner, we probed our way to the surface, unsure of what treatment awaited us. One by one, the Joe Khakis yanked us out of the mouth of the tunnel. And as each of us landed on the wet soil, vicious kicks, swear words, and baton blows welcomed us. Bludgeoned into submission, the security personnel found it easy to tie our hands behind our backs with some rough nylon ropes. They then forced us to sit down among several others they had captured before us. I reckoned that there were about seventeen of us. The Joe khakis had made a good killing, and they were happy. I could tell by the glee in their voices that they would be getting lots of money for us.

The Joe Khakis left their trucks on the main road. We had to trek to reach them. The two miles were agonising, especially because we had our hands tied behind our backs. Those whose steps faltered were subjected to kicks and blows, spurring them to walk faster. And because it was night, a lot of us missed our steps. We couldn't keep our balance, and we ended up receiving countless blows to our bodies. By the time we reached the main road, most of us were bruised and sore.

The Joe Khakis pugnaciously threw us into two trucks. Thick, hard boots landed on each of our backsides as catalysts to climb into the high vehicles quickly. I reckoned that sacks of rice or cocoa would have fared better. The drive to Koidu was slow, bumpy, and very uncomfortable. Whenever the trucks encountered one of the thousands of potholes, our bodies bounced like balls. If we cried out, we got kicks for our efforts. Thus, I was relieved when the trucks grumbled to a stop at the entrance of the police station. The Joe Khakis threw us out of the trucks in the same way they'd boarded us, and most of us ended up falling in the giant puddle in front of the station. But we were quickly made to stand up and march into the station. After that, we went through the charge office and into a waiting cell.

The Joe Khakis threw all seventeen of us into the cell without any food or water. The cells door clanged shut with a thunderous noise that seemed to echo throughout the building. A key rattled in the lock, and I heard the door lock click. Plunged into total darkness, and none of us in the mood to talk, we jostled each other to retain the most comfortable position in the tiny cell. I couldn't even discern the whereabouts of Mila, it was that dark in the cell. But I knew he was inside. I shouted out, "Mila!" Someone immediately asked me to shut up. I didn't get any response from Mila.

The cell was small, and I believed it was meant for just a few people, probably not more than seven. For hygienic purposes, there was a filthy, smelly bucket in one of the corners of the cell. The floor was wet with what could only be urine. The smell of ammonia was overwhelming in the tight space. By the look of it, no one had emptied it for a long time. I tried to hold my nose, but my elbow hit someone in the face. "Watch it, pal," he yelled. After that, I gave up and resigned myself to smelling ammonia and shit.

It was the first time Mila and I had been locked up. My first impression of the experience was gross apprehension. Seasoned veterans had relayed strange stories of what happened in cells, from serious rows to gang rapes. I wondered what was going to happen to me and Mila. I didn't want to fight or be raped.

I feared rape the most. In our culture, if a man had a sexual relationship of any kind with another man, he was considered an abomination. It was the same throughout the country. Even hugging another man attracted serious repercussions from the Simbaru community. But there were no cells in Simbaru, and men were held together for periods of time. I heard that men engaged in sexual activity with each other in the cells, that they poked each other in the anus with or without consent. In the cells, it was survival of the fittest. One looked out for oneself. I decided that I would fight to the death if anyone tried to rape me. And I meant it. I would definitely kill anyone who tried anything with me.

My fear, however, proved unfounded. All of us in the cell came from the same village, worked together, and knew each other fairly well. Therefore, it was highly unlikely that anyone would make an attempt. According to stories I heard, such things normally happened among strangers. Outsiders didn't recognise each other and felt little or no compassion for each other. However, if someone among us tried it, shame and forced exile would be the reward. There was even the possibility that some vigilante would murder him. Women would look at him with scorn, and none of them would be willing to have him as a husband or boyfriend.

Strangely, we knew that the police never did anything about prisoners raping other prisoners. All they cared about was ransom money.

I spent the night in the cell standing upright. I presumed the others did the same due to the urine and stale shit on the floor. Hardly anyone slept-standing amid the concentrated stench of urine, shit, and body odour ensured that we didn't. The mosquitoes attacked us in droves, biting every exposed area of our bodies. When they were full, the mosquitoes buzzed about. If we were to believe the folk tale of the mosquito and the ear, they talked in our ears to remind us that, though we were considerably bigger and fatter, they were still alive. Throughout the night, many of us urinated on the cell floor. The cell was too dark and crowded to look for some dilapidated bucket in the corner. Besides, even if it were possible to see the bucket, chances are that it was overflowing with urine and feces; a tiny bucket couldn't cope with waste from seventeen inmates. Therefore, the cell floor became the preferred option.

At last, it was morning. Faint streaks of morning light penetrated the high, narrow, barred windows of the cell. Mosquitoes, gorged and bloated on our blood, disappeared to sleep peacefully in some dark area. They left us to cope with the itching induced by their bites and the ever-increasing stench in the cell.

"This place is not a cell, it's a latrine," someone complained. I was sure it was Mila. I recognised his voice.

"Are you okay, Mila? Can you see me?" I asked, my spirit lifting immediately. The first part of my question was a rhetorical one; I knew he was fine, but he responded anyway. Luckily, no one told me to shut up. "Glad to hear you, Yandi," I heard him say. "Yes, I am fine. No, I can't see you. It's still quite dark. Are you okay?"

I couldn't answer his question because I heard the sound of a key in the huge, metal cell door. Everyone was silent; we could have heard a pin drop if the cell's floor were a normal floor. Unfortunately, it wasn't; it was layered with shit, urine, and grime. The door opened slightly. A police officer in a black beret hat with the silver police emblem on the front popped his head through the slightly opened door. The silver emblem glittered in the dim, early morning light. "Make way for Mr K's boys," he instructed. "I want them out now!"

There were some movements within the cell: inmates contorted their bodies as Mr K's boys squeezed through the entrance. By the time I was out of the door, which was slammed and locked promptly, I found four people from our gang waiting outside. Apparently, a member of our gang had been apprehended above ground before us because there were only four of us in the tunnel. We were glad to be out, but everyone one reeked of human waste.

The police officer who let us out pinched his nose. "You stink like a latrine," he said in a ghostly, nasal voice. "Move your asses down the hallway to the charge office. Now!"

We didn't need to be told twice. We scampered towards the office, leaving a horrible aroma of human waste in our trail. There were a few officers standing by the huge, semi-circular desk, and some more folks were sitting on wooden chairs at wooden desks. Huge piles of files and papers littered every desk. The moment we walked into the charge office, the officers pinched their noses and gestured to us that we should continue outside to the huge roundabout in front of the building.

We emerged a sorry sight. The stench from our bodies reached the vendors long before we appeared outside. They immediately started protesting that we shouldn't go their way. The police officer instructed us to head for the trees that were yards away from the roundabout. We trudged along with our heads bowed in shame and embarrassment. As we neared the trees, I recognised Mr K's old Land Rover. And for the second time that morning, my spirit was lifted. I was sure freedom was at hand.

As cheerful as ever, Mr K jumped out of the driver's side of the old jalopy to welcome us. Dressed in his usual style of contrasting colours, he said, "You smell like shit and rotten eggs combined." After that, he burst into raucous laughter. "Get into the back of the vehicle; I won't have any of you sitting with me in the front for all the money in the world," he declared.

We hesitated because the police officer was still with us. Mr K seemed to understand our predicament instantly. "Oh, him," he said, pointing to the officer, "everything is being taken care of. Get into the back and keep the tarpaulins down. I don't want to smell you more than I can manage. God, you stink worse than skunks!"

That time, we didn't hesitate. We quickly boarded the vehicle when the officer walked back to the station. The front door of the vehicle slammed shut, and the engine came to life. A moment later, we were on our way back to Yengema as freemen. We knew money had changed hands to acquire our freedom, but we were not keen to learn the details.

39

From the main road, the feeder road leading to Yengema was narrow and extremely windy. Palm tree trunks functioned as crude bridges over the streams and swamps that vehicles and pedestrians crossed every time they got to or departed from the town. In most areas, overgrown twigs and long elephant grass reached into the road to brush over and against the sides of passing vehicles. The road was completely bald where vehicle tyres encountered the ground. A steady stream of green shrubs thrived between the tyre-worn, bald areas of the road. The bare areas terminated in a clear space right in front of the village.

Mr K was negotiating the road. The engine groaned with every change of gear, which was rather too frequent because of the layout of the road. In the back of the Land Rover, we hardly spoke to each other. The small space stank of shit and urine, and with the tarpaulins down, it was as if we were still in the Tankoro cell. Although the rear tarpaulin of the vehicle was slightly raised to allow ventilation, the disgusting smell was still overpowering.

From the main road, it was just a few miles to Yengema, but the journey seemed to last longer because of the bad state of the feeder road. It was full of potholes, and erosion had washed out the soil on the bald part of the road, leaving deep gullies that forced vehicles to sway violently from side to side as if they were about to tip over. As if that were not enough, unscrupulous miners had dug pits close to the road in search of precious stones.

I heard the engine whine sorrowfully as if grieving for the time when the vehicle was new. Evidently, we were climbing a hill, and the old jalopy was doing its best not to disappoint its driver. The wheels encountered the gullies in the road, throwing us from side to side so much that we had to hold onto the metal frames supporting the tarpaulins to avoid falling off the two long benches that served as seats. It was the same going downhill, maybe slightly worse: the vehicle went a little faster and swayed just as much.

We were surprised when the vehicle stopped in the middle of the bush. "Why have we stopped," asked Dowu.

"How the hell would we know," said Sumaa. "We are all here at the back."

"Get your smelly asses out here!" shouted Mr K. His words were followed by a hollow, metallic *clang* that reverberated throughout the entire vehicle. Mr K had just slammed the driver's door shut. We streamed outside to discover that Mr K had stopped by the last of the two streams before the village. "Clothes off. Give yourselves a good wash. I have some clothes and soap for you in the cab," Mr K continued. He went around the front of the vehicle, opened the passenger side door, retrieved a yellow bag, and threw it to the nearest man. "The soap is inside as well. It is cheap soap. Get your own fancy soap if you want to smell nice. Judging by the way you stink now, I am sure that would take you some time." He laughed merrily as he slammed the door shut. "I'm off to the bush to attend the call of nature. I want everyone ready by the time I get back. Please don't waste my time."

The stream's water was nice and surprisingly warm given the fact that it was the middle of the rainy season. Although a harsh soap, it cleaned our bodies very well, especially when used with a bunch of tough lemon grass for scrubbing. The local soap was manufactured using caustic soda, palm oil, and burnt wood ash. Everyone set out to clean his body as much as possible. Soon, it seemed like everyone was acceptably clean; the foul aroma that had stuck to us had disappeared.

As we washed our soiled clothes and shoes, none of us was ashamed of being stark naked. We didn't deliberately stare at each other's private parts, either. Again, the soap came up trumps: the smell of shit and urine evaporated from the clothes. Later, we opened the bag of clothes that Mr K provided and found that each of us had fresh clothing among the contents. We quickly changed into the dry, clean clothes. The clothes were actually ours, which meant that Mr K had taken the trouble to ask our free gang mates in Yengema to supply him with our clothes. However, his foresight hadn't included spare footwear or underwear. It really didn't matter, though. It was just delicious to be clean, dry, and warm.

Fully dressed, we returned to the vehicle, raised all the tarpaulins, and cleaned the back with bunches of lemon grass. Mr K returned just after we were finished, and he was impressed we thought to clean the back of the Land Rover. The vehicle smelled of sweet lemon grass instead of stale shit and urine. We pulled down the tarpaulins again to keep the dust from entering the vehicle when it was on the move.

We made it into Yengema town square in less than a quarter of an hour. There were very few men of working age around the square at that time. They were probably catching some sleep to prepare for the night's work. As usual, women and children sat comfortably under the shade of the big mango tree. They were engaged in work, banter, and play. Their attention was on the old jalopy well before it arrived in the square. Mr K made sure of that by beeping the horn musically as if we were important people visiting the town. From the back of the vehicle, we heard Mr K slam the driver's door and shout at us to disembark. As we alighted from the vehicle, he couldn't resist bragging to the audience at hand: "I brought my boys back as I said. See?."

"Mr K! Mr K! Mr K," the little group under the tree chanted in admiration when they saw us descending from the vehicle. They knew he was a vain man, that he revelled in praise. He allowed the chanting to go on for a while before he raised one hand for silence. When he achieved the silence he required, he put his hand in his pocket and produced some small notes. He walked towards the oldest woman in the group and handed her the money. "Buy something for all of you, including the children," he said. The chanting started again when he walked back towards us.

By that point, other people, attracted by all the fuss, started appearing from the nearby houses. Sahr was among them, and I could see the relief on his face. He walked up to Mr K and pumped the man's hand several times in appreciation. He thanked him at the same time.

When Sahr was done, he came to us and jokingly asked whether we had enjoyed our stay in jail. No one answered him. Still, he herded us back towards his big house.

That same evening, we returned to work in the tunnels. Everyone was telling stories of their encounter with the Joe Khakis the previous night. Of course, many of the miners glorified the ingenious tactics they used to escape the raid. For the miners who were caught, the stories concentrated on the horrible confinement of a cell.

"I could hardly breathe," I heard Mila say to a workmate. "I had my hand over my airways for most of the night."

"Welcome to the clan, then," said Tamba. "You are now a full-fledged miner. You never become one until you experience Tankoro."

Mila laughed and started to say, "And to think that the cells stank like—"

"Please spare us the details," Boima said. "Some of us have been there so many times that we have lost count. We know the cells like the back of our hands."

Tamba agreed with him but said, "However, as you've seen, we always come back." Mr K would never let us rot in Tankoro. He needs us if he's to realise any profits from his investment. It's in his interest to get us out as quickly as possible."

"All these cell talks depress me," grumbled Dowu. "Can we talk about something else?"

"Like what?" I asked.

"Like the unguarded gravel we left last night, like the tools we left behind in the tunnels," Dowu replied.

"The gravel is fine," said Tamba. "I came back last night when I thought it was safe and retrieved and hid our tools. I also safeguarded the gravel."

We were all glad to hear that. We didn't want to lose our precious gravel. We had lived like moles to bring it to the surface. Besides, if we lost it, we would only wonder whether there were diamonds in it.

"We may not be digging more gravel out tonight," explained Tamba. "We will wash all the gravel we accumulated last night. It's quite a big pile—more than I expected it to be. That won't take us the entire night if we work fast. We will go home soon after we finish the task. At least we'll have some time to rest after last night's raid."

I was looking forward to returning to town early. I was secretly hoping to lure Sandivah into some dark area for a quick fuck. Lately, we'd been getting bolder and careless, getting together at every opportunity we had, even when we knew it was brazen and dangerous. In our first few sex sessions, we were concerned that someone would catch us in the act. But the concerns faded with every successful sexual liaison. In fact, our lust for each other far outweighed our worries. Otherwise, we wouldn't have taken the risk. I wondered what would happen if Sahr caught us.

We'd even done it in the big parlour one Friday night when everyone else was in the village square enjoying a variety of masquerade dances. At that time, in one of the dark corners of the huge parlour, Sandivah raised her Lappa over her bum and revealed that she wasn't wearing anything underneath. Thus, I had access to her hairy, wet pussy. In my haste, I fumbled a couple of times before I was able to penetrate her. The sex was quick. I climaxed in record time, and anxious not be discovered, I got out of her with sperm still dripping from the tip of my dick. However, I rated it as the best sex I had ever had. Afterward, we returned separately to the village square. There were no indications that anyone had even noticed our absence.

We finished kicking the gravel just as a pale, floating moon appeared in the cloudy sky, partially illuminating the mining site and its surroundings. It wasn't raining yet, but there were strong indications that, even with the moon around, rain would undoubtedly fall before it was morning.

We had only taken in seven pieces of diamonds from the huge pile of gravel, but they were all larger than half a carat without a single flaw. Tamba showed us the stones after we washed up and were ready to return to the village. They were beautiful stones, and we were pleased with the return. The lot would yield good money, and we were happy about that. We figured we'd be getting ready to visit Simbaru sooner than we expected.

In town, we went to Sahr's place and Tamba knocked on his door. "Who is it?" asked a woman. I recognised the voice immediately, it was Sandivah's. Instant rage and jealousy overwhelmed me, but the feeling disappeared quickly when I realised I was being a fool. Sandivah was not my wife; I was only a thief and needed to be grateful for what I was able to steal. All the same, I wasn't happy about the situation. Sandivah opened the door and looked quite tantalising.

"We want to see Sahr," said Tamba.

"At this time of night?" asked Sandivah.

"Let them in," growled Sahr from the bed. "And Sandivah, wait outside until I call for you."

Without a word, Sandivah obeyed. As she was coming out the door, our eyes met. She winked at me, but I didn't wink back. I deliberately let the others enter the room first, and as she passed by, I pinched her ample bottom. She turned around quickly to give me a sweet, reassuring smile. I didn't acknowledge the smile either, especially once I noticed that she wasn't wearing any underwear and the area I touched was wet. Sandivah had just had sex, and there was more to follow. I felt jealous again, but I followed the others inside wordlessly.

"So how was it?" inquired Sahr.

Tamba removed the crumpled white paper containing the stones and gave it to Sahr. "It's all in there," he said.

"How many stones are in here," Sahr asked as he tried to unravel the crumpled paper without spilling the diamonds.

"Seven clean stones, each over half a carat," Tamba replied calmly.

Sahr readjusted his position on the bed. He opened the crumpled paper and reached for his torch, which was nearby. He flicked it on and trained the light on the stones in the paper. They returned a brilliant spectrum of colours. They were clean, as Tamba claimed, and he was also right about the weight estimation. "I agree, they are very nice stones," said a broadly smiling Sahr. "Good work, my boys! Thank you!"

We were pleased with his reaction, and he seemed very satisfied. His whole demeanour had changed. I guessed he was already calculating his expected share. "I have to say that we got better stones this time," Sahr continued. "However, we cannot sell the stones yet because it is only Wednesday. We'll bring more gravel out tomorrow night, and if we find any more gems, we'll sell them all together on Friday when Mr K arrives." He carefully folded the white paper around the stones and put the packet in a green plastic cup on the table by his bedside. After that, he switched off the torch. "This time, boys, you will have a lot more money to spend in Koidu. Go now and have a good rest. You all verily deserve it."

"We will," said Tamba. "Goodnight."

I was the last one out. I noticed Sandivah was standing by the left side of the door, but I passed by without looking at her. Strangely, it didn't seem to bother me that she'd just had sex. Somehow, the knowledge aroused me.

"You can come back inside, woman," I heard Sahr say.

I knew then that any hope of a meeting with Sandivah that night was gone. I followed Mila with a heavy heart to our sleeping spot. I watched him prepare our mat, and when he was done, we both went to sleep immediately. The following night, we went back to work in the tunnels. For more than half the night, we removed gravel. Just as

Dead End Poverty

the pale moon broke through the dense, rainy season clouds in the sky, Tamba deemed we had enough gravel to commence kicking. The gang members in the tunnels brought up all the tools.

"Mila, Yandi, and Boima: you are the first set to go," said Tamba, handing each of us a shaker. "Francis, Sumaa, and Samson: you are the watchers. Use the Makambos and torches at the same time for more lighting and better visibility. Dowu and I will load the gravel in the shakers. We'll exchange places every half hour. Good luck to us all."

The three of us, armed with shakers, descended into the miniature lake of muddy, water. It was colder than I expected, and a little shiver went through my body. Everyone was in position, and the work started in earnest at that point. Throughout the night, we kicked shaker after shaker of gravel, but we didn't find a single gem. The work became a lacklustre affair; we were now resigned to the notion that we would not find anything in the remaining pile of gravel. A couple of hours later, we finished washing the rest of the pile but found nothing.

It was still night when we set out to return to the village. It proved to be tiring because we were disappointed. It took longer than usual for us to arrive. We'd hoped to add to our earlier collection, but it wasn't to be. Mila and I went to bed immediately, as did the others. I can't remember how long I was asleep, but I woke up with the sense that I had to urinate or I would burst. I got up quietly from the mat and meandered my way through several sleeping bodies that were snoring in various tones. When I finally got outside, my bladder could hardly hold the urine any longer. I had to run the few yards left to the latrine, fumbling with the fly on my trousers as I went. It was semi-dark inside the latrine, but from experience, I knew where to go. I sprayed in that direction until my bladder was empty. I enjoyed instant relief from the pains in my bladder. As I turned to go outside, though, the door opened. Sandivah entered and shut the flimsy door behind her quietly.

"What are you doing?" I asked.

"Shh," she hissed, putting a finger over my mouth for a moment.

She removed her hand from my mouth and raised her Lappa up to her armpits with one hand. She then took my hand with her free hand and rubbed it against her naked, velvety, black bush. My brain stopped functioning rationally. The rage and jealousy that overcame me at Sahr's door was nowhere to be found. At that moment, nothing else mattered. Not even her husband. All I wanted was to fuck her. I turned her roughly against the door to take her from behind. After a fumble or two, I hit the jackpot. I entered her savagely, enough to cause a small, popping explosion in her pussy. In the confinement of the little toilet, the popping noise was quite loud. I was afraid someone would hear it. But it really didn't matter to me. I fucked her quickly and efficiently. A while later, I sprayed my warm seed into her hot, throbbing pussy while she gyrated and rubbed her firm ass all over my groin. She waited until my spasms passed away. Without a word, she straightened out her Lappa, opened the door slightly, peeped outside, and disappeared in a jiffy. I expected a voice, Sahr's voice, to challenge her at any moment. The challenge never came. I waited a while before walking out of the latrine. After that, I went back to sleep.

It was Friday, and we'd just finished eating the big bowl of palm oil soup and rice that Mama Finda set before us shortly after our arrival in Koidu. It was a delicious meal, and we were quite hungry, having gone without a meal before our sojourn. Mother was one proud woman, proud as a peacock. She exhibited that pride from her vantage point directly above us while we ate. "You could have some more if you want," she offered.

"Yes, please," I said.

"Bring some more of the same food for my sons," Mother shouted to one of her kitchen helpers. And then she turned her attention to me. "I am amazed at your appetite today, Yandi," she observed.

"That's because this is the most delicious meal I've eaten for a long time now. It's really a great meal. Thank you, Mother."

"He's hungry because he has a special job to do in the village," Mila quipped, laughing at the same time. "That's why he's so hungry, Mother."

If looks could kill, mine would have exterminated him instantly. But the jolly joker didn't even flinch at my hardest look. "Mila's a joker, Mother," I said, defending myself lamely. "Don't pay any attention to him. He thinks I am like him."

"Stop it, you two," Mama Finda reprimanded. "Look, your food is here. You'd better eat it before it gets cold. While we were eating, Mama Finda fired questions at us. She had never asked us so many questions. It was as if she were trying to know us afresh. "You never told me where Simbaru was," she said

Dead End Poverty

"Simbaru's just a little village not far from Kenema," Mila answered.

"Kenema? Where the big diamond office is? That's where Mr K goes to sell his diamonds. I've never been there though. Are your parents alive? Do they still live in Simbaru? Do you miss them?"

I answered all her questions promptly: "Yes, our parents are alive and still living in Simbaru. Mila's father is dead, but his mother, Nyallay, and Jayman, his little brother, still live in the village. My father, Joe Weggo Lenga, and my mum, Massey, are still alive. Yes, we intend to return when we make enough money. Yes, we miss Simbaru and would miss it more if it weren't for her kindness. Yes, one could easily travel to Simbaru from Kenema; it is an easy town to find.

Mother asked many more questions, and by the time we were through the second helping, I believed she knew more about us than anybody else in the whole of Kono. We helped her clear the dishes and return them to the eating parlour. After we washed our hands, we let her know that we needed to talk with her in private. She led us to her private quarters. "What can I do for you, sons?" she asked, concern showing in both her eyes and voice.

"We brought some more money," I said calmly. "We sold some stones today, and we got a thousand leones each."

We removed the money from our pockets and laid them neatly in two piles. Mother was impressed with the money. "You are becoming rich men fast," she said without malice. "It's unbelievable. At this rate, you will be returning to Simbaru soon. Your parents will be very proud of you."

In our presence, she counted every note. And when she was done, she nodded in agreement and said, "We have two thousand here. Do you want me to keep it all? Have you got any spending money?"

We told her that we still had some of our spending money from the last diamond sales. Still, she insisted that we replenish the money with fifty leones each.

"You never know when you might need money for an emergency," she reasoned.

It was good advice. We accepted fifty leones each. We offered her another fifty each, but she vehemently declined. "I have my own money," she said. "Besides, you may need it more than me. Do you know how much money each of you has now?"

We told her we didn't want to know; that we trusted her completely. We explained that we knew she would never cheat us. That brought tears to her eyes, and she hugged both of us tightly. "My sons, my sons, you're really my true sons." she cooed. When she finally released us, we took our leave and headed straight into town. I went to the cinema, and Mila went to the whorehouses.

Later that same evening, we returned to Yengema. It was a beautiful evening, and there were no signs of rain in the sky. When I had the opportunity, I gave Sandivah ten leones. She was genuinely happy when she accepted the money.

"I'll meet you in the coffee bushes tonight," she offered.

"Can't make it. Have to go to work, remember?"

"Just before you leave for work, then. I'll be there."

"I will try to be there," I said.

She looked at me seductively, smiled, and sashayed her nice, big bottom until she vanished from view.

"What are you staring at?" asked Sahr sombrely.

Apparently, I had been so preoccupied with his wife's ass that I hadn't noticed his arrival.

"Nothing," I said.

"She does have a lovely ass, doesn't she? Sahr said,

"I don't know about that," I said, feeling fear and embarrassment at the same time for getting myself into a tricky predicament.

He laughed happily and said, "Keep it up, boy. Just keep your eyes and hands off. You continue like that, I will have no problem with you." He laughed again and walked off, seemingly satisfied that his scare tactics were working on me.

I said nothing. I walked off in the other direction. *What a pitiful, selfish man,* I thought, *he preaches, but he doesn't follow his own teachings. If only he knew I was screwing his wife at every chance.* I wondered what he would do. I figured he was stupid to believe that while he was in bed with one wife, the others were waiting for him. Sahr had complemented her bottom, but he didn't know I had seen and fucked that bottom. Sahr needed his head examined; he was deluded. *You are not the only one enjoying Sandivah's ride; I will be right there beside you, taking rollercoaster rides on her sexy, rounded bottom. Trust me,* I thought.

Still, Sandivah and I were willingly inviting trouble. The risks we took became more and more prone to discovery. I wondered why we hadn't been caught yet, why we hadn't even heard any rumours about our relationship. Perhaps it was just paranoia on my part. Maybe there was nothing to worry about. But the village was small. I didn't believe my fornicating with Sandivah would go unnoticed for much longer. Just seeing the woman not only made me horny, it made me lose my inhibitions and rationality. I was constantly exposing myself to potential dangers. Sahr looked quite mean. I knew he may even kill for his wife, so I vowed to be more careful.

I walked up to the village square where some miners were putting finishing touches on whatever they were doing to prepare for the night's work. I stayed for a while, chatting with some of the guys. After a while, I left, intending to go back to the big house. Against my will, I took the path leading to the coffee bushes. Sandivah was waiting for me. All doubts and fear were immediately confined to the back of my brain. My only thought was of the half-naked woman in front of me. I pulled my pants down and joined her on the bed of twigs and leaves she had constructed. I wasn't disappointed.

40

As November approached, the rains became sparser by the day. It was pleasant to see the subtle sunshine gradually replace the rains. The sunshine lasted most of the day, but sometimes, light rains that lasted no more than a few minutes interrupted it. However, as soon as the rain stopped, the weather was nice again. Rain when it was sunny caused exotic rainbow arcs to appear on the white, blue, and grey African sky. Everyone enjoyed the spectacle; kids chanted a special song every time the rainbow arcs appeared, believing that it would bring them luck. Although the sun shone, it was cold. Being November, it was the beginning of the cold, dry harmattan winds, which usually occurred during the dry season. At that time, especially at dawn, little fires (with groups of people huddled around them for warmth) sprouted up all over town.

Even the landscape began to change into the brown monochrome that was so characteristic of the dry season. With the dry, cold wind of the harmattan acting as a catalyst, the vegetation around the village and beyond became brittle, creating the perfect environment for bush fires.

Soon, the rain ceased completely. The streams started to shrink in volume and flowing speed. Even the little stream near the village that had flowed with fast currents was shallow, calm, and lazy, so much so that its flow was nearly unnoticeable. It created the ideal setting for the women to go fishing for freshwater foods, including shrimp, crabs, snails, and prawns. Armed with Bimbeeys (local fishing nets), and Piyehs, (local fish holders made out of rattan and shaped like Coca-Cola bottles), women and children could be seen chattering with excitement on their way to the rivers near the village. They hoped to catch anything from crabs to fish to frogs to water snakes. They would use them to prepare meals for their families and the miners.

The little boys used hooks; fishing rods made of sticks with lines attached; and worm bait to fish in the deeper areas of the river. The middle-aged and elderly men laid carefully woven fish traps (locally called Bumbui) on the riverbeds to trap fish. Once a fish went inside, there was no way it could get out until the trapper or someone else retrieved the trap. The catch would eventually end up in some meal.

After a long period of hunger, farmers started to harvest more crops. Rice was the most important crop cultivated by the farmers; it was the staple food of the entire country. The subsistence farmers had endured the lean times, and they were happy that the time of plenty had arrived. In the evenings, women and children streamed back from the farms and into the village with big baskets of husk rice, kola, cassava, coffee, cocoa, and, red palm fruits on their heads. The palm fruits, ultimately processed into palm oil through some complicated method, produced oil that was used in food, soap, body lubrication, and fuel for local lanterns without shades. If the harvest was plentiful, the excess palm oil was sold to raise cash for clothes and other things needed for the family.

The dry season was the time of plenty. It was the time of festivity for all in the community. Young people in the area faced weeks of initiation into secret societies that signified the coming of age. The boys were initiated into the strict Poro society. The girls were initiated into the Bondo society. A big ceremony preceded the end of each initiation. There was an open invitation for everyone, including outsiders, to patronise the celebrations and make them a success. At the end of it all, ceremonies for the female initiates of marrying age began. They usually married older men who sponsored the initiation of the brides. The marriage ceremonies could last for days and involved feasting, lots of music, and dancing. But the length of each celebration depended upon who was hosting it.

Save a few, male initiates were usually not old enough to marry, though they could become betrothed to a girl. Marriage rites were deferred until those couples came of age. Boys and girls of marrying age did not stay single for long; custom dictated that they marry as soon as possible to avoid unwanted pregnancies and children. Pregnancy outside of marriage was the ultimate disgrace, and most families didn't condone it.

Varieties of storytellers, fortune tellers, magicians, and other entertainers visited Yengema and the nearby villages. People drifted from town to town in an attempt to attend all the celebrations. It was nearly impossible. The locally brewed alcohol, Omole, which was very potent, was free in the season of plenty. Most people indulged in drunkenness every day. Such people stayed in the same village for a long time because the drink tended to null their desire to drift to other celebrations in other villages. Sometimes, men and women stayed because they encountered new sexual partners. Regardless, the celebrations were always a big success, marred only by the inevitable disputes arising from accusations related to sex with other people's wives. But those accusations were usually settled with fines. Life would continue, and all would be well again.

Mila and I joined in the celebrations, but we still went to work on the dry ground every night. Unless it was a Friday, miners didn't take days off during the celebrations. The hope of riches beyond imagination lured us into the fields to dig for more gravel. However, during the initiation and marriage celebrations, our gang went to work earlier than usual so we could return to town early, join the celebrations, find time to sleep, and get ready for work the next day. Tamba pointed out that such a routine was normal practice. It was a good arrangement, and Sahr didn't argue with it. Some miners, because of overindulgence, didn't make it to the fields sometimes. No one really minded because a miner only got a share of the proceeds if he was at work when gems were found. No work, no pay—it was the unwritten policy of the trade. Mila and I were determined to make money, so we tried our best to avoid being absent from work. Still, we enjoyed the celebrations.

It was in the nearby village of Njolavulahun that Mila was caught in the act with someone's wife. The town square of Njolavulahun was packed with people when we arrived that night. We were hardly ten minutes on the scene when Mila told me that he'd found a girl who was willing to shag him.

"Be careful," I told him, "you hardly know anyone in this village. This girl could be married. And her husband might be watching her."

"Get some fun in your life man," Mila said. "Remain that way, and you'll enjoy nothing out here." He was gone before I could answer back.

I remained in the square to watch various performances around the big bonfire specifically made for the event. Periodically, people threw more dry logs into the fire to keep it lit.

The first time I noticed the girl was when she rubbed her posterior against me in her quest to get to the front of the little crowd in the square.

"Sorry," she said, smiling as if she were sunshine.

"Never mind," I said.

"You must be new here. I haven't seen you before." She raised her face to look at me properly.

"I come from Yengema," I said.

"Oh," she said, "what's it like over there?"

"Same as here," I replied.

"It's boring standing here," she noted. I would like to show you something if you come with me."

"What do you want me to see?" I asked

"Follow me," she said. "My name is Jatu, and I come from Koidu." Without waiting for a reply, she turned around and began forcing her way through the crowd. When we came into the opening, she took hold of my hand and asked, "What's your name?"

"Yandi," I told her.

Still holding my hand, she led me along the dark passages of the village. I followed blindly. As we turned a corner, we saw a little crowd gathered not far from us with a couple of Makambos in their midst.

"Let's go the other way," Jatu suggested.

By that point, I fully understood what Jatu wanted from me. Although I wasn't keen, I didn't want to hurt her feelings. Besides, she was quite a lovely girl, and the excitement of having someone different was becoming overwhelming by the second. Just as I made up my mind to go along with her, a voice from the little crowd near us stopped me in my tracks.

"I didn't know she was married. She said she wasn't married."

It was Mila's voice. I was certain. "I can't continue to go with you," I told Jatu. "It seems that my brother is in trouble."

"What do you mean you can't go with me?" she asked with agitation in her voice. "You followed this far, and now you can't go with me?"

"You don't understan—" I started to explain.

"Screw you," she said, pushing me away. "You men are all the same, leading a girl on and getting out at the last minute."

"I didn't lead you on," I protested.

"Yes you did, you stupid dickhead. Go screw yourself," said Jatu. She quickly turned around and headed back the way we'd come, sucking her teeth with her tongue in a show of great contempt towards me.

I went over to the small crowd quickly. Peering over the shoulder of some men, I saw Mila sitting on the floor in his underwear. There was also a girl sitting on the floor a few yards from him. She was the girl he was with.

"You want a woman?" a tall, dark man asked. "You should have brought your own. That's my wife. I'll take you to the chief, and you'll pay heavily," the man threatened.

"Sir, that's my brother," I said over the heads of the men. Mila heard my voice and was glad to see me. He was bleeding a little just above a swollen left eye. I assumed that the angry husband had inflicted that on him when he caught him in his bed with the girl.

"So you're his brother, eh? Then come right here to the front. Make him come to the front," ordered the tall man.

A few people forged a way for me, and I came face to face with Mila. He seemed very relieved to see me.

"Is this goat your brother?" the tall man asked me.

"Yes," I said.

"Did you ask him to sleep with my wife in my own house?" He didn't wait for me to answer. "You know, I could have killed him there and then."

"I am glad you didn't kill him, Sir," I said.

The man seemed not to hear. "I caught him right on top of my whore of a wife, completely naked. He didn't even notice when I entered the room. He was busy pummelling into my wife as if he paid the bride price for me. I had to lift him up off my wife."

"I am very sorry," I said. "We—"

"God, the bastard is big," the tall man interjected for the benefit of the crowd he was playing to. "When he got off my wife, his enormous monster was dripping wet from her juices."

At that point, the man's voice nearly broke as he thought about what Mila's enormous penis could have done to his wife. "My God, this bastard will pay. Trust me, he'll pay," the man threatened.

"Isn't there anything we can do to resolve this?" I asked.

Dead End Poverty

"No," he said, "I am taking him to the chief. And you know what? She is the chief's daughter; let's see what he'll have to say about this."

I was not ready to take *no* for an answer. I pleaded with the man and asked him in the name of God to let me talk to him in private. Unbelievably, he agreed.

"Moiwa, don't let him escape," he said to the fat, bald man with clothes in his hands, clothes I recognised to be Mila's.

"Not on my life," the fat man replied. "This piece of shit is going nowhere. Take all the time you need."

The tall man and I moved away, putting a considerable length of space between the crowd and us. We stopped under a coconut tree.

"What do you want?" he demanded.

"How much?" I asked instinctively. I'd learned from the boys that most husbands accepted money for that sort of crime. Going to the chief meant they would receive only a fraction of whatever fine would be levied.

Without hesitation, he replied, "Fifty leones would be fine.

"God Almighty, do you think I am Jemil?" I asked. (Jemil was a well-known Lebanese diamond trader, supposedly the richest man in the country.) I don't have such money. I could give you fifteen if you like."

"Please don't insult me," he said, "that's not why I am here."

"But even if you take my brother to the chief, he will only be fined, and the chief will share part of that fine, too. Everyone knows that, I suppose."

"Fifty leones or no deal," he insisted, pressing his luck. "This case is different. It was in my own bed, and don't forget: she's the chief's daughter."

"I'll pay twenty, then. Because she's the chief's daughter," I said.

"You're full of contempt," he growled bitterly. "Fifty or nothing," he persisted.

"Leave it, then," I said, pretending to lose interest. I started to walk away and said, "We'll have to go to the chief, I suppose. I presume you'll come out better off," I added sarcastically.

After a few steps, he called me back: "Don't be so hasty. Your brother has committed a hideous crime against me. It was even within my right to kill him when I caught him in my bed. But I didn't. Now you don't want to pay good money. He fucked my wife, man. In my own bed. And I caught him on top of her. What if it were you? Would you accept such a meagre sum?" The man was almost pleading: "Let's settle for forty."

"Forty's still too much. I'll settle for thirty. That's twice as much as you would get if you went to the chief. Take it or leave it, that's all I have."

The tall man's shoulders drooped in defeat. He knew it would be better to get the money directly from me. The chief, his supposed father-in-law, would definitely deduct a court fee. "Give me the money, then," he said, stretching his right hand outwards. He was disappointed that he'd failed to squeeze more out of me. I withdrew some money from my pocket, counted thirty leones, and put the rest back into my pocket. He took the money. "You're a hard man. You have all that money, and you refused to compensate me properly," he said bitterly. Please add some more. No amount of money compensates for the shagging of your wife, especially when you catch the man responsible in the act, in your own house. Have some sympathy, man."

"You're wasting your time," I said. "You'll not get a penny more from me. If you don't want the money, please give it back."

"I didn't say that. I only—"

"You're wasting your time," I said again, "And mine, too."

The message got through at last.

"Please don't mention the amount you've given me," he said. My friends would want a bigger share if they learned about the true sum." I assured him he didn't have to worry. We slowly walked back to the little crowd.

"Give him back his clothes," the tall man said to the fat, bald man. "He's free to leave." Standing right in front of Mila, he said, "If I ever catch you with her again, or any of my wives, you'll be a dead man. It's not a threat. I mean it."

Without any argument, the fat man threw Mila's clothes at his feet. When Mila began to put on his clothes, the tall man grabbed his wife by the arm and hair and yanked her up. "Keep moving, he ordered. I am going to kill you tonight. By the time I am through with you, you'll wish you'd never be born." He delivered a heavy slap to her left jaw. We heard the girl yelp in pain and terror. By the time Mila was fully dressed, the little crowd had already disappeared.

Dead End Poverty

We didn't return to Njolavulahun town square. We headed straight for Yengema. The moon was bright, the night was dry, and it was a lovely time to walk. "What on earth did you do that for? Why would you shag another man's wife in his own bed?" I asked. "You owe me an explanation."

"She said she wasn't married," said Mila. "How was I to know that she was married, that we were doing it in her husband's bed?"

"You are supposed to figure that out," I snapped. "Your manhood is going to get you killed someday. Can't you just resist women, or at least choose the trouble free ones?"

"Look who's talking," taunted Mila. "Why can't you resist Sandivah? Or do you think I don't notice your reactions when she's close by. Your manhood will kill you first. And if it doesn't, Sahr will."

"So that's how you thank me for rescuing you?" I asked.

"I would've done the same for you, Yandi, so don't keep moaning," Mila replied.

I didn't answer. As we walked along the moonlit path, Mila's words haunted my mind. Mila was right: Sandivah and I were fools to think that our secret was safe. I had to be more careful. Better still, I had to break off the relationship. But Sandivah would be angry if I dumped her. I didn't know what she would do. An angry woman is unpredictable like a cat trapped in a cupboard. Sandivah, in her anger, might decide to tell Sahr about our illicit liaisons. I would end up in the same trouble I was trying to avoid by dumping her. I was in a real dilemma, a predicament that required thinking before I could make a decision. It was much easier to think about dumping Sandivah when she wasn't present. The effect of the woman on me was incredible. Just thinking about her was enough to trigger an erection. I wasn't sure I could resist the urge to fuck her when we were alone. I knew then that I would let events take their course. If I got caught, that would be my fate. Sahr could have a field day with me. However, I had to tell Sandivah that we needed to be much more careful. People were watching, and they could see us. And when they saw us, Sahr would definitely know about it.

We arrived in Yengema to find the celebrations still going on in the town square. The log bonfire was burning as bright as ever. The musical instruments and the voices of the singing men and women drowned out every other sound.

"I'll stay in the square and have some fun," said Mila. He hadn't said anything since he last spoke to me.

"Just make sure you don't fall into similar problems," I cautioned him.

"Fuck off," he said. "You are not my dad."

"I know, but I'm the closest to family you have around here, Mila."

"Does that give you the right to criticise me?" asked Mila. And then, in a more conciliatory tone, he continued: "Look, whatever happened has happened. I regret it. I appreciate your help in the matter. I hope we'll put that behind us now." Without another word, he walked past me and headed towards the square.

I decided to go home and sleep. But for a few men sleeping, the huge parlour was empty. As I was arranging the mat, I heard Sandivah's door open. I turned my head in that direction.

"Oh, it's you," she said. "I saved some food for you and Mila," she said as she walked the short distance from her door to where I was arranging the sleeping mat. Everything deserted me at that moment. My legs became weak, and I felt a terrible pain of want in my groin. I looked around quickly to see whether any of the men on the mats were awake. As far as I could judge, they were fast asleep, snoring the night away.

As if she understood what was happening to me, she whispered, "Go to the usual place. I'll meet you there soon." She walked back into her room and shut the door. Moments later, she came out with a medium-sized bucket in her hand.

I finished arranging the sleeping mat in record time and announced loudly, "I'm going back to the square." Outside, I took the road to our meeting place. I didn't have to wait long, Sandivah emerged from the bushes, and she was as sexually hungry as I was. We didn't talk as we attended to business. When we were spent, she laid her head on my chest for a short while, breathing softly with contentment.

"We have to be more careful, Sandivah," I said to her. "People are taking notice."

"Nobody knows about us," she said, "but I'll be more careful."

"You better go now, before Sahr finds out you're not in your room."

"Sahr went to Koidu late in the evening," she revealed. "I wouldn't be here if he were in town."

She took hold of my hand and rubbed it on her great boobs while she massaged my dick with the other. When she was sure I was hard enough, she got up and sat astride of me, manipulating my throbbing dick into her body.

Afterward, she was the first to leave. I stayed in the moonlit bush for quite a while before I ventured to make the trip back to town. I finally understood that there was no way I could leave her. Nevertheless, Mila's words still haunted me. I decided to leave things in the hands of destiny; what would be, would be. I was sure I would be ready.

41

Once again, we were deep-pit mining in the swamps, as we did during every dry season. The Makambos were burning bright; they provided enough light and visibility for us. It was our first pit in the swamps that dry season, and it was already proving different from any I'd been involved in before. For starters, no water oozed from beneath the ground to flood the pit as the digging progressed. That was unusual; water always flooded the pits after the first few feet. We'd been digging for a little over two weeks—and the pit was over six feet deep—yet the pit didn't flood. We were baffled. The pessimists among us speculated outright gloom, but the optimists forecasted hope and success.

It all began with Francis and Dowu. They were down in the pit. In a low voice, almost a coarse whisper, Francis voiced his fears about the state of the pit: "I'm sure we are wasting precious time on this pit," he said. "We might find nothing in it."

"That makes two of us," replied Dowu. "Why is there no water in the pit? All the pits closest to us are constantly flooded."

"All I can say is that it is a very odd thing," Francis said. "I haven't seen the likes of it since I started mining. It's odd, very odd."

"Come on, guys, stop yapping and dig," said Samson. He was standing on the second tier closest to them in the pit. "What are you whispering anyway?"

"It's about the pit," returned Dowu. "I believe we are wasting our time."

"Why do you think that?" asked Tamba. He was standing like the rest of us, close to the mouth of the pit. Apart from digging and shovelling the earth out of the pit, there was nothing else to do.

"The pit has not flooded since we started digging," piped in Francis. His body language demonstrated that he had lost hope in the pit. It seemed as if he was digging just to avoid letting the team down. "Something must be wrong with it," he added woefully.

"Do you know what is wrong with it?" asked Tamba. "I believe that this pit will be a productive pit, regardless of the absence of water," continued Tamba, trying to keep high spirits in the camp.

"Maybe the water is being blocked by a chimpanzee's ass," said Francis calmly.

"Or not at all," said Tamba. "Or not at all," he repeated. "Aren't you happy that there is no water in the pit yet?" If the pit were flooded, we wouldn't have dug this far by now. I'm sure there's nothing wrong with the pit."

"But what if there is a chimpanzee's ass in the pit after all?" asked Boima.

Tamba looked at him sharply and said, "This is not good for morale at all. If you believe we'll hit a chimpanzee's ass, you are free to leave. And that applies to the rest of you," said Tamba with some steam in his voice.

No one left. But no one offered any other ideas, either. No one was going to leave after two weeks of back-breaking work. No one wanted to be on the losing side. If anyone left and the pit proved productive, it would be his loss, he wouldn't get his share.

"We don't have all the time in the world," said a calmer Tamba. "Please resume digging. If you think you are tired, then you may exchange places."

Francis and Dowu remained in the pit and continued to dig for a little while more. Mila and I relieved them soon after. Mila and I were the last pair to work in the pit before Tamba decreed it was time to go home. In a single-file formation, we started on the long, windy path back to town. We were unusually quiet; we had a premonition that nothing good would come out of the pit. I guessed that each of us predicted doom and gloom.

The following night, Tamba and Sumaa were the first pair to descend into the pit. About twenty minutes after they started digging, Sumaa's shovel hit something hard. The sound of metal scraping against stone reached us clearly. "I think we've hit the chimpanzee's ass," he announced. "Our worst fear has come true."

"Are you sure? Don't be too hasty in your proclamation," Tamba admonished.

"Maybe it is only a small boulder that we could remove."

"Not on my life," returned Sumaa. "This is no small boulder; it's a chimpanzee's ass. With a small boulder, some flooding would have occurred. I know a chimpanzee's ass when I encounter one. Make no mistake about it, Tamba, we've hit bad luck!"

Tamba said nothing. He frantically dug in a particular area, away from where Sumaa had hit the stone. Before long, his shovel made the same scraping noise of metal against stone. He moved to another area and dug but got the same result. He tried one more time in a different area, but still got the same result. "Sumaa is right," Tamba finally conceded. It's a chimpanzee's ass."

"What do we do now? All our hard work was for nothing, then," grumbled Boima.

"We stop work on the pit as of this moment," Tamba replied. He took his shovel and started to climb out. Sumaa followed him.

"Nearly three weeks work—gone. So much energy wasted," Sumaa lamented.

"Sorry, but there is nothing we can do about it," said Tamba sympathetically.

"Yes there is," said Mila.

Tamba and the others laughed at him. "No, Mila," Tamba said, "we can't do anything about it."

"I think we can," I said, supporting Mila's claim.

"What do you have in mind?" asked Dowu.

Mila waited until Sumaa and Tamba climbed out of the pit before he answered. "We could set a fire on it."

"Set a fire on it?" Tamba asked doubtfully. "What good would that do?"

"It would make it easier for us to break the stone," said Mila. "The heat from the fire will cause the stone to crack in places. We could then pour cold water over the blistering boulder and take it from there to break up the chimpanzee's ass gradually. But we will need plenty of dry wood to create the sort of fire I have in mind."

"Are you sure it will work?" asked Tamba. "Have you tried it before? Have you ever done it?"

"I've done it many times," replied Mila. "If we heat it long enough at high temperature, we will definitely break the rock down." But it will take hours to heat the stone, and as I said earlier, the procedure will require lots of wood for the fire."

"And we must do it during the day," I said. "We can't leave a fire burning at night in these dry conditions. We might inadvertently set fire to the entire area."

Tamba thought for a moment and then asked again, "Are you really sure it will work?"

"It will work," I said with confidence. "We did it several times in Simbaru."

"I say we go for it, then," said Tamba. "What do you think?" He was asking the rest of the gang members.

"Good idea," said Dowu.

"There's no harm in trying," said a philosophical Samson. "If it works, it would be all the better for us. If it doesn't, we would only lose a few hours."

Everyone agreed that we should implement the firing method. As there was nothing more to do in the field for the rest of the night, Tamba suggested we clean up and return to the village.

"Everyone must be ready to leave after the dawn prayers," he said. "Collecting dry wood should not be a problem. We have loads of it littering the fields. We will light the fire on the chimpanzee's ass as soon as we collect enough wood."

"We must also bring a couple of pickaxes to break the stone," said Mila. "Only a pickaxe can properly do the job."

"We already have a couple or more of them in our tools cache," said Francis.

"Anything more?" asked Tamba.

There was nothing more to add, so Tamba said, "Then let's head back to town. We have an early start in the morning."

We had the fire going early that morning, having left the village for the fields immediately after the dawn prayers. The fire burnt very well. It was a great fire. Mila and I supervised the fire's creation so that we could achieve the maximum temperature. We could feel the heat fifty yards away, from under a breadfruit tree where we'd sought refuge. It'd been burning for over five hours. Fortunately, there was very little wind, so the heat from the great fire was able to exert itself on the chimpanzee's ass fully. Soon, we heard the stone cracking from the expansion the immense heat caused. Some miners from other gangs, intrigued by our idea of burning the chimpanzee's ass were hovering around us under the breadfruit tree. They asked us questions about the technique, and we tried to provide eloquent answers. For their part, they seemed very doubtful that the method would work.

"I believe you're wasting precious time here," said Boss Kai.

He wasn't a boss over anyone; it was just a nickname, but he insisted everyone call him Boss Kai. He wasn't married and had no children. He was just an ordinary miner like most of us. However, he was a very big, thick man. He was about six and a half feet tall, and he was immensely strong. With a few more inches of growth, he would've become a giant. In fact, most people called him a giant behind his back. His size and strength induced fear in people. There were even rumours that he once killed a leopard with his bare hands. Scars on almost every part of his body seemed to be proof that the man had tackled a big cat. Anyway, Boss Kai himself was there to authenticate the story if someone was brave enough to bring up the story around him. But Boss Kai was a gentle giant, never going out of his way to bully people. Because of that fact, he was much respected by the villagers.

"Do you really think this will work?" continued Boss Kai. He was standing right by my side, easily dwarfing me.

"It won't work," said Mattia with confidence, as if he had tried the procedure before. Mattia was an old man, over sixty years old. He started mining as a young man, and he was still at it. After all those years, he was as poor as when he first started.

"Didn't ask you, Mattia," Boss Kai said. "What do you know about it, anyway?"

That prompted some men to rib and laugh at the old crone. Mattia laughed along with them. Anger had long ago disappeared from his emotions. Nothing seemed to get under his skin. Some people accused him of being a *dieheart,* as the locals referred to someone who never got angry.

"Will it work, Yandi?" asked Boss Kai again, having waited patiently until the laughter died down.

"I am sure it will," I said simply.

"I have never seen anything like this," said Boss Kai, "and I have been in the mines for nearly two decades. If it were something that worked, I would've seen it before now."

"Maybe people never thought of the idea," said Tamba. He was close by, and judging by his expression, he didn't welcome the negativity from Boss Kai.

"There're many things we don't know about in life," Tamba continued. "We learn them as life progresses. I believe the procedure will work. Yandi and Mila are so confident about it."

"Dream on!" retorted Boss Kai. "I'd better be getting back to my pit before I get into trouble—you know my gang supervisor."

Everyone laughed. We were all aware of his boss. He was the exact opposite of Boss Kai: a small, thin, and weak man. Yet his courage was commendable given his squeaky voice. He wasn't afraid to speak his mind to his gang members, Boss Kai included.

"I fear no one," Sillah would say. "What could anyone possibly do to me? Kill me? Go right ahead, you'll be doing me a great favour. All my sins will just be transferred to you."

As if on cue, we heard his squeaky voice shouting for Boss Kai. "Where is that big lump of a man? Don't you realise we have work to do, Boss Kai?"

"Just coming over," Boss Kai shouted back.

"Well be fast about it before I kick your fat ass," Sillah joked.

"You won't," said Boss Kai, bemused by the idea of Sillah kicking his ass.

"Why?" asked Sillah.

Boss Kai smirked and said, "Because your feet wouldn't reach my ass." Everyone laughed. Boss Kai was still laughing as he quickened his pace towards his pit. It wasn't far off.

We let the fire burn for another three hours, adding fuel as needed to keep the temperature high. The hotter the fire became, the more cracking we heard from the stone. When we were satisfied that the fire had burned long enough to serve its purpose, we didn't add any more fuel. Starved of fuel, the fire diminished in size and intensity. Before long, only hot embers remained on top of the chimpanzee's ass.

"What do we do now?" asked Tamba.

"Put buckets of cold water over the hot coals to put the fire out and cool the boulder. The cracks in it will expand more," Mila explained.

"But we should go back to town after putting out the fire," I said. "No one could cope with the heat in the pit. The boulder will be very hot, even after pouring water on it."

Mila agreed. And because we were the experts, Tamba listened. "Then we must go home as soon as the fire is out. Get the buckets and start pouring water in the pit immediately," said Tamba.

I was both hopeful and worried about the experiment on the chimpanzee's ass. Deep down, I knew it would work; nevertheless, it didn't stop worrying me during the night. I shared my concerns with Mila. "What if it doesn't work?" I asked him softly in the safety of our sleeping mat.

"It'll work," Mila reassured me. "Stop worrying your head for nothing."

"How do you know?" I asked. "If we get it wrong, the boys aren't going to like us."

"Tough luck for them, then," said Mila. "But you worry too much. It will definitely work. I've no doubts about that. Just go to sleep, will you?"

And that's exactly what I did. I didn't wake up until Mila nudged me to say that it was time to leave. I worried about our experiment throughout the long walk to the mines. But that time, I didn't let Mila know.

We were back at the mines very early the next morning. Tamba had acquainted Sahr with the procedure we were employing to defeat the chimpanzee's ass. The idea had intrigued him so much that he wanted to see things for himself. Unlike our fellow gang members, he had seen the possibility in the technique immediately. He believed that fire was the most definitive weapon; it wrecked almost everything it encountered.

I beat everyone to the pit. My fears evaporated as soon as I peered over the edge and looked inside the pit. The boulder was visible in the bright morning light. There were several big, open cracks in the rock. But exactly how deep they were remained to be seen when we employed the pickaxes. Pleased with what I had seen, I let the others know: "There are many big cracks in the chimpanzee's ass," I shouted out. "We might be able to get rid of the rock after all."

The others came running. They caught up with me, Sahr leading the way. After looking, they seemed impressed. "I knew it'd work," said Sahr. He was as enthusiastic as the rest of us.

"There *are* cracks in the rock," exclaimed a happy Sumaa, grinning from ear to ear as if he were personally responsible for the presence of the cracks.

"You guys are geniuses," continued Sumaa, slapping my back. In his enthusiasm, he also gave me a bear hug.

"A large piece of the rock is even separated from the mother stone," observed Sahr.

"Yandi, your idea looks like it worked," said Tamba in his cool tone.

"It doesn't look like the idea worked, Tamba. It worked marvellously," declared Mila.

"When you have cracks like that in that monster down there, it means that the heat from the fire succeeded."

"I will go down the pit to check," offered Francis. And before anyone could say anything, he descended into the pit. He tentatively touched the rock a couple of times and then declared that it was cool enough to tolerate. "It is still lukewarm, though," he warned.

"Never mind the temperature. We'll start work on it as long as it is not scalding hot. Get the pickaxes; let's start chipping at that rock now," said Tamba.

"The pickaxes are here already," said Dowu, who had just arrived with the tools.

"Which two of you want to go first?" asked Tamba.

"Yandi and Mila should have the first go," said Sumaa. "That way, we'll learn from them how to chip at the cracks to destroy the boulder." Everyone agreed.

Mila and I descended into the pit and started chipping at the cracks in the rock, starting with the piece that was almost separated. A few heavy blows dislodged the piece of rock from the original rock. While I was breaking that into smaller pieces, Mila attacked other cracks in the rock. The rock steadily disintegrated with every assault from our pickaxes. The rock had burned out better than we expected. I hoped it would be like that to its core. Working in pairs as usual, we exchanged places frequently because the work was hard and exhausting.

Sahr, not being a patient man, took his leave to return to town as soon as we began work on the pit. He'd only stayed for about half an hour as he watched us chip at the boulder, which disintegrated slowly but steadily. Sahr knew the job would take a long time, and he'd obviously seen enough to believe that we would eventually realise gravel from the problematic pit. He'd seen how easily the rock was disintegrating, and he was confident that the gang would conquer the stone. He seemed satisfied with what he had seen, and he decided his presence wasn't needed after all. "Update me on the pit's condition when you get back to the village," he said to no one in particular. "Good luck to all of us." And then he was gone.

We used buckets to remove the smaller chips of stone from the pit. Bigger and heavier pieces passed from hand to hand on their way out of the hole. Removing the chipped rocks helped clear the pit to allow further chipping. As usual, we exchanged places throughout the course of the operation, and the chimpanzee's ass kept diminishing. It was a difficult job. Sometimes, we encountered areas in the boulder that were very difficult to penetrate. It seemed as if the heat hadn't had any effect on those areas.

However, with our dogged determination to destroy the rock, we made a breakthrough. Mila and I were in the pit again when it happened. At first, it oozed through the base of the chimpanzee's ass. Mila noticed it first. "Water is coming up into the pit," he announced.

I looked down at the base of my feet. Sure enough, the dry stone we'd been chipping at appeared a little wet. We knew we were close to victory, and we chipped away with renewed vigour. With each stroke of the pickaxes, more water flowed into the pit, making it flood faster. On several occasions, we stopped chipping at the rock in order to get rid of the water. When the water level dropped, we continued to chip at the remainder of the disintegrating boulder. Eventually, most of what was once the giant boulder disappeared to provide ample space for us to go after the gravel. At that stage, Tamba declared that we had to stop work to continue the following night. After all, daylight was turning into darkness fast. He was happy with our progress. "Well done, everyone. And thanks," he said with genuine sincerity. "But for Yandi and Mila, we would've forgone the pit. Our time and effort would've counted for nought. Now we have some hope. You have Yandi and Mila to thank for that. You must be feeling happy. Good luck to us tomorrow night."

We weren't feeling happy. In fact, we were elated. I was already thinking about the money we would derive from the pit as we walked back to town. I assumed others were, too. The prospect of removing gravel was certainly a catalyst to start one dreaming about money and all the things that could be bought with it.

That night, curled up near Mila in the cocoon of my cotton blanket on our sleeping mat, the dream disturbed me again. It was the same as the others I had experienced, the same threatening, black cloud; the same fearsome, malevolent face; the same python grip on my ribs; the unconsciousness; and the fear.

42

We derived very little money from the troublesome pit with the chimpanzee's ass. It was not that we didn't discover diamonds; rather, we discovered better and bigger stones than I had ever seen. They were beautiful, flawless stones we could've sold for thousands of pounds. But as fate would have it, everything concluded in a way we never imagined.

We succeeded in removing all the gravel in the troubled pit in one night. There wasn't much gravel in the pit, and we were sure we could wash the whole lot in one night. Sahr didn't come with us because, as he said, he had something important to do. Tamba supervised us as usual, and the work went well. But unfortunately for us, more than halfway through the pile of gravel, we found no diamonds in the concentrates that we examined meticulously. We were beginning to believe the gravel would prove to be barren.

"I've found something in the shaker," announced Dowu with an edge in his voice. He was already on his way out of the water. "It's quite a big one."

"Bring it out, then," said Sumaa. He'd been moaning loudly that the gravel was useless, that we wouldn't find any gems in it.

With the Makambo flames flickering up and down around us in the cool night breeze, Dowu put the stone in Tamba's outstretched hand as soon as he got out of the water. There was still mud on it, but Tamba could see that it was definitely a diamond. Tamba used the edge of his shirt and a little spittle to clean the mud off the stone.

"Someone, pass me a torch," he said.

I passed him mine. He flicked it on and directed it to the palm of his left hand. "It's a beautiful stone," he said. "My first impression is that it is a flawless, blue-white, almost six carats. Everyone, come and take a look."

We did. Huddled around him and excited about the find, a couple of gang members voiced their opinions.

"This'll make us some tidy sum," suggested Boima.

"If we find more like this, we'll be rich men in our own rights," said Sumaa. "I told you we'd find diamonds in the gravel." He forgot that, before the find, he'd been the grumpy one, moaning loudly about how the gravel was useless. Fortunately, no one reminded him.

"If you intend to discover more of this," said Tamba, clenching his hand into a fist over the gemstone, then you must return to work. Meanwhile, I'll keep the stone."

Everyone returned to his position and work resumed. Soon after, Boima made another find: a stone a little bulkier than its predecessor, but equal in every other characteristic. Tamba kept the stone in the same paper with the earlier find. Boima continued to wash the gravel, but he indicated he was tired after a while. An eager Mila replaced him. He kicked his first load of gravel, and with the concentrates still in the shaker, passed it to Francis. Francis deposited the concentrates in a designated area and passed the shaker back to Mila. We crouched around the concentrates, carefully rummaging around with the hope of discovering more precious stones.

We all saw the stone at once. It was staring at us from the top of the glistening concentrates. Tamba snapped it up and examined it under the flame of a Makambo. "It's a fine stone, I believe." He said and took a torch out of his back pocket to examine the stone again. "It's not as big as the first one, but it's not smaller than the second stone, either. It's a good stone."

We examined the rest of the concentrates, but we found no more diamonds. At that point, Tamba announced, "I must go to the bushes for a shit."

"So that's why this place was stinking," Sumaa teased.

"But not as much as your mouth," Tamba said in retaliation, but with good humour.

Several of us laughed. "Just go," said Sumaa, "or you'll be doing it right here. No one wants to smell your shit."

"Francis, you're in charge," said Tamba. "If the gravel yields any more diamonds, keep them until I return. There is very little gravel left, though. I'm sure we will be finished here soon." Tamba hurried into the bushes, seeming very pressed to unload the bulk of whatever was in his stomach.

We continued kicking the gravel. We found a dozen more diamonds, but they were very small ones, worth almost nothing. The gravel diminished rapidly, but Tamba still hadn't returned. Boima was getting concerned. "He has been out there for a long time now," he said.

"Who?" I asked.

"Tamba, stupid," Boima said.

"He must be shitting stones or irons," said Samson.

"This is no joke," said Boima. "He has been gone for a while now. How long does it take someone to shit?"

"Maybe he dozed off," offered Dowu.

"Sitting on shit?" I countered. "That would be most unwise. Someone must go look for him."

"Let's wait a little while more," said Francis. "If he doesn't turn up, we will send two people to go look for him."

By that point, the gravel was almost finished. Those at the shakers were kicking the last remaining loads. It was almost time to go home, but Tamba still hadn't returned.

"Boima and Yandi," said Francis, "Take a Makambo and go search for Tamba."

We headed in the direction in which we saw Tamba disappear into the bushes. We searched the area, loudly calling out his name, but there was no response and no Tamba.

"I hope nothing has happened to him," I said.

Boima agreed: "This is very unusual; it's not like Tamba."

We looked around a bit more, but we couldn't find him. We returned to the pit to let the others know. "Did you find him," asked Francis as soon as he saw the flames from our Makambos. We were still several yards away from the pit.

"No," Boima shouted back, "We looked everywhere, but we couldn't find him."

When we arrived at the pit, we noticed that they'd finished washing the gravel in our absence and cleaned the tools as well.

"I am getting worried now. Where did Tamba go?" said Francis.

"Aren't we all worried?" asked Mila. "What if a snake bit him? What if he's lying unconscious or dead somewhere out there?"

"Or maybe he fell into a pit," suggested Sumaa.

"Or maybe he has done a runner," I said in a quiet tone.

"You don't know Tamba very well," said Francis. "He would never run away."

"How could you even think of that? Tamba's an honest man, and that's why Sahr appointed him as our supervisor. He would never run away," Francis concluded, shaking his head.

I didn't say a word. But looking at the faces of the other men, I noticed that they were confused. I'd sown the seed of doubt, and it was beginning to grow quickly.

"And he has our diamonds," said Dowu, as if he just remembered. What if he has really ran away with our diamonds?"

"Shut up, Dowu," said Francis. "Tamba would never run away with our diamonds. He knows the rules. He knows the score. He knows what happens to a diamond thief."

"Only if the thief stays long enough in the fields or the village to be captured," I said.

"What if he decided to run away straight from here to the main road? He could be anywhere by now. So how would you apprehend him?"

"He didn't run away with the other diamonds we found before," Francis pointed out. He has always been in charge of our diamond finds, and he has never even tried to run away. Why should he run away now?"

"Very true. But we've never found diamonds as clean and valuable as the ones he has with him now, wherever he is," Dowu persisted. "I just wish he would come back with the gems."

"All I can say is that we must all go looking for him in the bushes," said Mila. "Arguing among ourselves won't solve the mystery of Tamba's disappearance."

That ended the argument. With everyone armed with a Makambo or torch light, we headed back into the bushes. "Pair up and spread out," said Francis. "That way, we'll cover a bigger area. We'll all meet again at the pit when we finish the search."

"What if we don't find him," asked Boima.

"Let's worry about that after the search," Francis replied.

We didn't find him. For over half an hour with inadequate lighting, we scoured the bushes and high elephant grasses. We also searched the old pits to no avail. We looked everywhere we thought he would be, but we still couldn't find him. It was futile to continue the search, especially because we were tired. Thus, we elected to go back to the pit.

"I told you he'd scarpered with our diamonds," I said to no one in particular.

"He must be miles away now. No one will ever catch him. I can't believe Tamba stole from us."

"He may have just gone back to town. I said it before, and I will say it again: Tamba is not a thief," said Francis.

He was trying to neutralise the effect of my accusation. Somehow, I felt sorry for Francis. If he really believed that Tamba went back to town, he was the most naive among us. However, I knew Tamba was his friend and had been his friend for years. It was difficult for him to believe that he could actually abscond with our diamonds.

"Without telling anyone?" asked Sumaa. "He was going to toilet man, not to town. He was supposed to have been back ages ago. Where is he, then?" he asked scornfully.

"Yes, where is he?" echoed Mila.

"We are wasting time here," said Dowu. "We must go to town to find out if he's there."

We realised he was right. We started for town, but the conversation continued. "I know he won't be there," I said. "By now, he could be anywhere. My instinct tells me that that is the last we will see of Tamba."

"Shut up, Yandi," said Francis. "I am sure Tamba will explain everything to us when we meet him in town." That was how confident Francis was; he trusted Tamba to a fault.

"Keep dreaming," I retorted angrily. "The bastard's ran away with our gems, as you will eventually find out. Grow up, Francis. Tamba saw an opportunity; he took it."

"Then he's up for the crocodile," said Samba.

"If they ever find him," said Mila. "Like my brother said, he could be anywhere by now."

43

"He put me in charge, said he was going to toilet and would be back soon," Francis explained. "He never came back. We searched everywhere, but we couldn't find him."

A sleepy Sahr became fully awake when he heard that Tamba had disappeared with the diamonds we discovered in the gravel.

Sahr was shocked. He trusted Tamba fully; he had always trusted him. Tamba had never given him any indication to the contrary. But somehow, he knew Tamba was gone with the stones. Although he didn't want to believe it, instinct told him to. "Have you checked his room yet?" Sahr asked.

"We already did," said Francis. "He wasn't there. No one in the village has seen him, either."

"How long since he disappeared?" asked Sahr.

"It's been a few hours now. Maybe close to four hours," said Sumaa.

Sahr scratched his scalp as he realised that Tamba could be long gone. Four hours gave him a huge advantage. "Did you find any more stones apart from those with Tamba?" he asked.

Francis retrieved the folded paper containing the diamonds from his chest pocket and gave it to Sahr. "There are twelve small pieces in there. Peanuts compared to the three stones Tamba absconded with."

"Were they big stones?" asked Sahr. He put the folded paper containing the diamonds into his pocket without even inspecting them.

"The biggest one was almost six carats, and that was according to Tamba," said Francis. "The other two were smaller, but both were more than three carats each."

Sahr almost choked. "Are you sure?" he asked between fits of coughing triggered by the revelation.

"Positive. I'm absolutely sure," said Francis. "We all saw the stones. They were blue-whites and completely flawless."

Sahr groaned. The latest revelation added to his misery. "That's a double whammy for me! Wasn't it enough for the diamonds to be big? Did they have to be blue-white, too? His mind started racing. Why am

I so unlucky? I've waited all these years for the big one, and when it finally came, some son of a bitch I thought I trusted ran away with it. I'll personally kill that rat when I catch him. Sahr's expression changed to burning anger.

"Are you okay, Sahr?" asked Boima. He was afraid the man was going to have a heart attack.

"I am okay," said Sahr, recovering himself quickly and flashing a smile. "We must find Tamba quickly. I believe he has ran away."

"But where would he go?" asked Dowu.

"Where else but Koidu," said Sahr. "It is a big town, and he could easily blend in and hide there forever if he wished. We must go to Koidu to look for him."

We departed for Koidu immediately. It was close to dawn, and some people were already awake in the other villages along the way to the main road. Sahr spread the word among the villagers that Tamba was a diamond thief and a wanted man. Sahr said that he had to be apprehended if seen in the vicinity to face up to his actions. Sahr said the same to the chief in Yengema. He went to see him just before we left, and the chief had promised to send a search party into the bushes around the mines again.

The search for Tamba was futile. It had seemed futile before it even started. First, too much time had elapsed since Tamba absconded. And unless he was dumb, he would be putting as much distance as he could between himself and Yengema. Second, assuming that he was in Koidu as we believed, the chances of finding him were minimal. Koidu was an overcrowded town, and thousands of people graced its streets daily. In addition, there was the daily influx of people from the nearby villages who came to shop or conduct other business. Plus, there were the hopeful miners. Nevertheless, Sahr refused to acknowledge the obvious.

In Koidu, Sahr immediately took us to see Mr K. Fortunately, he was still in bed when we knocked at the front door of his big house. A slim, young girl of around thirteen, evidently still sleepy, managed to open the door for us. "What do you want," she asked sourly.

"We want to see Mr K," said Sahr.

"My dad is still in bed. I can't wake him up. No one wakes him up when he is—"

"It's alright, Fifi," said Mr K's familiar, booming voice. "Let me deal with this."

Without a word, the girl left and was replaced by a towel-clad Mr K.

"Oh," he said, "it's you." Surprise was written all over his jolly face. "What in God's name are you doing here this early with the gang? I hope you've brought me some big stones. Come inside." He threw the door wide open.

Sahr went straight for the jugular and didn't mince his words. "Tamba has run away with gems from the pit," said Sahr.

"You must be joking!" Mr K said, even though he knew the man wasn't joking. There was no other reason for him to be in his house at that time. He just didn't want to believe the information. He'd known Tamba for years, and he had come to respect and admire him for his honesty and tenacity in relation to work.

"It's true," said Sahr softly. "According to the boys, he ran away with three immaculate, blue-white stones, all above three carats."

Mr K was speechless for a moment. His mind was doing some calculations. *Three flawless, blue-white stones, each above three carats. That would be over a hundred thousand leones, roughly.* He felt his anger rising.

"Did you hear me, Mr K?" asked Sahr. "The biggest stone was approximately six carats. The boys said so. They said Tamba himself acknowledged the size—"

"Say no more, Sahr," interrupted Mr K in a quiet, terrible voice. "I'll personally skin that scum of the earth alive when I find him. Oh! The things I'll do to him. He will be passionately calling for the crocodile before I am through with him."

"What do we do now?" asked Sahr.

"Let me change into proper clothes," said Mr K. "I'll tell you what to do when I get back."

We watched him disappear into a room. He came back a few minutes later looking smart but odd in his combination of clothes. "Now let's go," he said.

In his Land Rover, he explained that we would conduct the search individually to cover large areas. "But we must start with all the motor parks first," he said. "A man running away would need a vehicle to get him out fast."

For the whole day, we searched everywhere we could in Koidu town but found no trace of Tamba. Because Mr K had a vehicle, he drove around for the whole day searching the streets. He couldn't find Tamba either. It was late evening, and we grudgingly acknowledged that we would never find Tamba. We knew he was long gone from the area, and that we should get over him and move on. Besides, we were all tired, hungry, and longing to get back to Yengema.

Mr K drove us back to Yengema, and throughout the journey, he kept describing what he would do to Tamba if he caught him. Tamba hadn't surfaced in our absence; the information was delivered even before we asked for it. The entire village knew that Tamba had stolen diamonds.

Sahr sold the remaining small diamonds to Mr K before he returned to Koidu. We pocketed about seventy-five leones each. Mr K assured us that he would keep searching for Tamba, and that he would spread the word among associates. "Don't worry," he said, "Tamba's now a marked man. To me, he's already dead."

But to me, he wasn't already dead. If anything, his life was just beginning—the exciting part of it—and it wouldn't be a dull one with all the money he would get for the diamonds. We returned to work as usual and began a new pit. We felt bad that Tamba had cheated us out of gems that could've earned us substantial sums of money. Nevertheless, I was secretly happy for him. Working in the mines was back-breaking, especially if you had been doing it for years with nothing to show for it. Tamba had taken the easy and dangerous way out. But I questioned whether it was dangerous. He had simply walked the stones out of our reach, out of Sahr's reach. Unless he was damned, he wouldn't ever be caught.

Tamba wasn't caught. Mr K's extensive searches and Sahr's threats and swearing against an absent Tamba yielded nothing. Eventually, even Sahr accepted the loss. "This will never happen again," he said one night when we were all on the big veranda, planning where to mine next. "No one will abscond with my diamonds again. That son of a bitch is the last one to do so. It'll never happen again."

"How will you prevent it from happening again?" asked Dowu.

"I'll be keeping the diamonds myself," said Sahr. "From this moment on, I must be there when we are kicking gravel. No gravel should be washed in my absence."

And so it was that Sahr was with us that night in the mines. We'd removed all the gravel from our new pit, and he was with us to oversee the kicking. By the look of it, I calculated we would spend nearly three nights washing the gravel. We'd recovered abundant gravel in the pit, and it was piled in three large heaps under a lone palm tree.

Three nights later, the gravel was washed. We discovered sixteen stones of various sizes and colours. The majority of them were flawed, but there were a few flawless ones as well. We sold the stones for a total of 16,500 leones. Mr K had to return to Koidu to get more money before he could complete the deal. Each of the six remaining gang members received a little over nine hundred leones. No one had yet replaced Tamba.

We were still entitled to the usual days off after completing work in a pit. We used the opportunity to visit Mother in Koidu. We added to our growing pile of money that she was keeping for us. "You boys should be thinking of going home now," she said after we handed her the money for safekeeping. "You have managed quite well in this short period. You must go visit your parents. They must be heartbroken for you. You must go home."

We assured her that we were seriously thinking about doing just that. That seemed to satisfy her. After painting the streets of Koidu red, Mila and I returned to Yengema. On the way, we talked about Mother's advice. She was right. It was nearly time to return to Simbaru. We had money, more money than our parents had ever earned or seen at one time. We agreed that we should go home.

Back in Yengema, we immersed ourselves in work once again. There wasn't enough time left to do another pit in the swamps. The rains had already started, and dry ground mining was the ideal option open to us. Some other gangs still opted to work a last-minute pit in the swamps before the rains came proper. But Sahr decided we should go back to dry ground mining the same pit we'd worked in the previous year, the same pit from which the Joe Khakis had arrested us.

44

For early rainy season, the rains were too severe and persistent. And they were complemented by rumbling thunder and lightning. Dark rain clouds continually on the move covered the skies most of the time, and their sculpture-like, irregular shapes kept changing like amoebas. Relentlessly, the rain poured every day and night. Wetness was everywhere. Even the little river near the village was close to overflowing. The villagers recalled that it had been ten years since it rained so hard. Nevertheless, the rains didn't deter people from engaging in their everyday chores.

The decision to return to dry ground mining instead of staying in the swamps turned out to be smart. The daily volume of rainfall made it impossible for anyone to work in the swamps. Even with machines, it would have been extremely difficult to extract excess water from the pits in the swamps. Too much excess water forced those who opted to do one more pit in the swamp to abandon their work and take up dry ground mining.

Every night, Sahr joined the gang at work—not because he wanted to, but because he had no choice. We kicked gravel every night, and he didn't want another person absconding with gems we found. There was also a change made to one sector of our work methodology. Instead of piling gravel to kick it in one go, we washed it as it came from the pits. One gang member was responsible for loading the gravel in a shaker, and another person (under the watchful eyes of Sahr) proceeded to wash it. After working for a couple of weeks on dry ground, we hadn't realised a single diamond for our effort.

Sahr didn't like our results, and I suspected he was already getting tired of his new role. He expressed his honest feelings after every check. "Bloody nothing again," he said after another meticulous but futile search of the concentrates. His lit torch (we couldn't keep the Makambos lit in such wet weather) would swing in every direction as he gesticulated with his hands. "At this rate," Sahr continued, "we won't be finding anything. Bloody diamonds. Trust me, they are real demons."

And so it went on, night after night; we removed gravel from the ever-dangerous underground pits, but we found nothing when we washed it. It was frustrating and tiring, especially when other gangs around us seemed to be getting something out of their work. I wondered whether we would find anything at all and expressed my doubt to Mila and the others. "I am not sure we will find diamonds here," I said. "We have been working for nearly three weeks now."

They all agreed that they were sceptical of getting diamonds from the current endeavour. "We should relocate," suggested Sumaa.

"That's out of the question," said Sahr.

He must've overheard Sumaa even though he stood a good distance from us. No one asked why, and he didn't offer any reasons or explanations. That was the end of the discussion. We carried on with the job, but there was a resigned feeling within the gang. We were all thinking that we wouldn't make much money until the next season. The state of the underground pits didn't help. It was much wetter below than the previous year. Wet sludge intermittently dropped off the walls and ceilings of the dark, narrow, dingy tunnels and onto the floors. A number of minor accidents, none of which resulted in a fatality, had already occurred. Moreover, when accidents happened, people started thinking that they could be next. The incidents preyed on our minds as we scurried between the tunnels digging and loading gravel into sacks. Yet the carrot was too tempting to allow our fears to stop us from obtaining it. Therefore, we banished our demons to reclusive areas of our brains and carried on with the job. We hoped for and wanted the carrot, the biggest one we could find. That was why we were mining in the first place.

Still, the rains came. Eventually, it was almost impossible to work the tunnels. Excess rain from above ground seeped through the earth and streamed through the narrow, circular, Damakoro pits. The rain partially flooded the tunnels, making them potentially dangerous. Sahr ordered us to take a couple of days off work. "The tunnels are extremely dangerous," he said. "Let's watch how the rain goes, and if it gets any better, we can resume work."

Personally, I thought he was frustrated and needed a break, especially because our luck hadn't changed at all. Behind his back, we blamed him for our unlucky stretch. We assumed that he was the one with the bad luck. When he wasn't with us, we had found diamonds without much struggle. However, since he joined us in the fields, we had found absolutely nothing.

Mila, other gang members, and I spent the days off idling and dozing in hammocks on the big veranda of Sahr's house. On our second day off, there was nothing to do. It was also raining as if God had decided to drown the earth. Naked children ran excitedly in the warm rain, shouting and chasing after each other. Their anxious parents, from rain-protected verandas, called on them to be careful while they remembered their own childhood antics in the rain.

"This rain will never stop. I feel trapped," Mila complained. "I don't like being idle." He was lying in a hammock near mine.

"I agree," I said, "but there's nothing we can do about it. "We have to wait it out."

"Doing what?" Mila asked quickly.

"How about remembering home, treating ourselves to some nostalgia. Would you like to remember the loved ones back in Simbaru?" I asked. "Sometimes, I miss them a lot and wish I was right there with them. I miss the village people, the early morning fires, and the gossip around them."

"I miss my mother and my brother," said Mila in a strained voice. "I even miss the elders, even though they tried chasing me out of town."

"Then we must go back as Mother suggested," I said. "We have money, more money than our parents ever possessed at any one time."

"That's right," Mila agreed. "Our parents will be especially glad to see us. To them, it will be like we are returning from the dead."

"So are you for it, then?" I asked, though I knew what his answer would be.

"Do I want to go? Are you kidding?" he said. "I've wanted to go back since the day I left."

"Then we must go after the rainy season ends," I said. "It will be dry season, and that's the best time to be in Simbaru. We'll tell Sahr we're going home to visit come the dry season."

"I am looking forward to it," said a solemn Mila. "I'm seriously missing Simbaru. I miss the women, the lifestyle, and all the people."

"Except Uncle Marrah, of course," I said.

"You've got it," said Mila, "Except my wicked stepfather. He never even enters my thoughts. The man is a leech, hanging onto all my dead father's belongings, bossing everyone around."

"He's still your stepfather," I said.

"Tell me about it," he moaned, but he smiled for the first time since we started talking about home.

It was nice to reminisce in the hammocks; we remembered the farms with the endless chores, our traps, and the tasty dishes our mothers prepared from the animals that they snared. We remembered the river and our early morning dips in its cold water. We remembered the healthy fish it provided us. The elders and their kangaroo courts penetrated our thoughts, too. Later, we both fell silent. I presumed Mila was engaged in private thoughts as well.

I thought of my father, Joe Weggo. I thought of Massey, my mother. I thought of the rest of the family. I felt guilty and sad that I left them so suddenly. I knew I shouldn't have run away like that without saying a proper goodbye. Above all, I should have sought my parents' permission to leave, even when I knew they would've vetoed it. My parents likely went through hell. And for all I knew, they were still devastated and heartbroken. Added to their woes would be my unexplained disappearance, the state of not knowing and not getting closure. I was sure they blamed themselves for failing to protect me.

I knew Joe Weggo would've used his fortune telling and witch doctor skills to try to understand what happened to me, to us. I was convinced Mila's family would've depended upon him to come up with plausible answers. He would've used his ancient, almost yellow cowry shells and small, mysterious bones to learn our location or determine whether we were still alive. I could see him in my mind's eye: he was sitting cross-legged on his praying mat with the Mecca picture in a semi-dark corner of his holy room. He was casting the shells and bones, scrutinising them meticulously for several agonising seconds or minutes before attempting to interpret what the spirits said.

Anxious family members would watch him quietly, anticipating any grunt and shaking of the head that meant negatives or positives in their quests to learn what became of us. "The spirits say they're not dead," I imagined him saying. "They say they are alive but very far away from this land. They cannot tell us whether we will see them alive again, but they do say that we should not lose hope. They will make money wherever they are." Yet I knew that, even in their negativity, my parents and extended family hoped against hope that we would finally return one day, back to the village unharmed.

I thought about Massey and her tasty meals. Oh, how I missed them! I thought of the unreserved motherly love she bestowed upon me and the children of my father's other wives. Kindness exuded from deep inside my mother, complemented by strength, courage, and loyalty to my father and the family. Though a woman, she was the next most powerful person in Joe Weggo's clan. The children and other wives of the household obeyed her in all circumstances, except when her husband vetoed her commands. I thought of the last words she said to me before I embarked on my journey. Although she had no idea I was leaving, she had prayed for me, showed me affection, and tried to make sure I was well fed. "May God save you," she'd said, touching me affectionately on my upper arm. "I hope you're all right. You're not hungry, I suppose?"

I felt sad and wished I were close to her. Being her only son, I wondered how my absence had affected her. I felt sorry for the agony I'd put my mother and the rest of the family through. I was determined to make things right upon my return. My little thought-provoking engagement had only made me more resolved to go home at the end of the rainy season. I was sure Mila was determined, too. I turned my attention to him for the first time since I engaged in my personal thoughts. He was fast asleep in the hammock, curled up like a baby and snoring lightly to the gentle sway of the hammock. I envied him. The only thing that would bother him were his dreams. I sighed and repositioned myself in the hammock to get more comfortable. I hoped I would fall asleep and be peaceful like my friend.

45

In the fields, on the Monday night after the two-day break, Sahr abruptly announced the condition of one of his wives. "Sandivah's pregnant," he said. "Another hungry mouth to feed is on the way. And that bastard Tamba had to run away with our diamonds. But for him, I would be loaded with no money problems."

To hell with Sahr and his financial worries, I thought. As far I was concerned, he could become the chief of all paupers. Sandivah was pregnant! That was news to me. Sandivah was my girlfriend, and I never even suspected that she was with child. Call it naiveté on my part.

But I had seen her getting paler, refusing food, and throwing up almost anything she ate. I asked her what was wrong with her, but she smiled and said she was just a little sick. That fever, according to her unsuspecting husband, had miraculously become a baby in the womb. I wondered whether the baby was mine. I had sex with Sandivah more often than her husband did. Sahr had three wives with a fourth on the way, and each wife was entitled to his services for three nights only. The more I thought about it, the more I was convinced that the baby was mine. I wondered what would happen if Sahr noticed it looked like me when it was born. Regardless, I had an urgent reason to return to Simbaru. I didn't want to risk the wrath of a jealous husband.

"Congratulations!" I said. "We're happy for you."

"Yes, we're really delighted with the good news," said Mila. "When's she due?" Something instinctively told me that Mila asked the question for my benefit.

"Thankfully, soon," said Sahr. "She said she was a little less than six months pregnant, though I think her baby bump does not correspond with the estimated time."

A little less than six months pregnant? I'm sure the baby is mine. Within the last seven months, Sandivah and I engaged in regular sex when she wasn't with her husband. That means more sex than she had with her husband. Sahr was with her for only three nights per week.

"But as things are," continued Sahr, "it will not be easy to have a pregnant woman on my hands. Money is tight. Very tight. I'm sending her and her children to live in her mother's village until she gives birth."

That was news to me, and I didn't like it. I was glad we were in semi-darkness; my face would've betrayed me. Pregnant or not, Sandivah was my sole source of indulgence. If her husband sent her off to her mother until the baby arrived, it meant no sex for me for a long time, unless I quickly forged a relationship with another woman.

"There's something wrong with the pregnancy, though," I heard Sahr say. "I'm suspicious that I didn't make my wife pregnant."

"Tell me about it," said Dowu. "Don't tell me some invisible ghost was humping her while you watched," he teased and laughed raucously.

Some of the boys were amused, and laughed nervously. I didn't laugh. I was thinking. And I was worried. Sahr just confirmed that he didn't make his wife pregnant. If he believed he didn't make Sandivah pregnant, it stood to reason to assume he had a suspect in mind. In fact, I had a feeling he'd already identified me as the culprit.

"It's not funny, Dowu. I'm sure I didn't make Sandivah pregnant. For six months now, even though Sandivah came to my bed when she was due, we didn't have sex. I haven't had sex with any of my wives," said Sahr.

I was worried. *Does Sahr already know I was the other man in the picture? I refused to doubt it. If he did know, would he be so calm with me in his sights?*

"I've been performing Kattacha for exactly six months now," continued Sahr. "I don't need to tell you about that. You know the rules."

Kattacha was a ritual ceremony performed to cleanse the body and ward off all evil spirits, sickness, and bad luck. One of the main conditions for successful Kattacha was that the performer could not indulge in any sexual activities with a woman until eight months after the process began. Sandivah never told me that Sahr was performing Kattacha. Yet I was sure she knew he was. She would've wondered why he was not sleeping with her and asked questions. Not that Sahr was obliged to supply answers, but the swiftest and surest way to keep her from asking more questions—some of which could be embarrassing—would be to speak the truth. I was inclined to believe that Sandivah knew about it. *But if she knew, why didn't she tell me? Unless she thought*

I wouldn't sleep with her if I knew the truth. That must be it. I willed myself to believe that was the case, I thought.

"Before I send her packing to her mum," Sahr said, "she must tell me who made her pregnant. I am sure it wasn't me. She must tell me on Friday."

That wasn't good news. It would be doomsday for me. I would meet my end on Friday, and we were halfway into Wednesday night already. My downfall and possible confrontation with Sahr was arriving faster than I ever expected. He was going to pressure Sandivah to reveal her lover. That lover was me. And upon our arrival in Yengema, Sahr warned us not to interfere with any of his wives. *God forgive me. What am I going to do? I must speak to Sandivah before Friday, even if I have to move heaven and earth.*

"Hilariously, I already know who made her pregnant," continued Sahr.

Sahr knew he was lying. He didn't have a suspect yet. It was just a ploy to get the culprit worried and cause him to make mistakes or confess. No one commented, but we all looked at each other as if our faces would reveal the guilty party. I felt guilty inside as I went through the charade of looking at the others. Only Mila knew that I could be the man who made Sandivah pregnant, and I had no doubt that my secret was safe with him.

"I've known for quite a while now, but I have no evidence to confront him," Sahr lied again. "Now I have evidence in Sandivah's pregnancy. I didn't bleeding fuck her into that condition, but come Friday, I will know the culprit. God help him then. By the time I am through with him, he won't know what hit him," he threatened.

"Are we going to do any work tonight, or are we just going to talk about Sandivah?" asked Mila. He didn't like the threats the boss was making, especially because he was aware that his best friend, his brother, was unquestionably the culprit that made the man's wife's pregnant.

"Everybody, let's get to work now," Sahr instructed, assuming his professional role once again. "Mila is right. We should be doing some work instead of procrastinating. We've wasted much time already; I don't feed you to be idle. Get on with it, you bloody time wasters," he complained.

"You wasted the bloody time, not us," retorted Sumaa. "You were the one moaning about not making your wife pregnant, that another man—"

"Just get in the bloody tunnel, you squirrel, before I physically dump you in there myself. And that goes for everyone supposed to be down below," said Sahr.

"There'll be no need for that," returned Sumaa, "I am going in now." With only his head visible at the entrance pit, Sumaa took a parting shot at Sahr: "Talking about tunnels! Some well-hung hunk took a real fancy poking your wife's tunnel." He quickly disappeared down the pit. He laughed as Sahr playfully threw his torch at him, uttering sexual obscenities about Sumaa's mother and sisters. We could hear Sumaa's pleasant laughter coming from below like a voice from the grave.

"I am going to kill that monster someday," said Sahr, taking the few strides needed to retrieve his torch light.

No one took his threat seriously. They knew it was an empty threat; Sahr was always vowing to kill somebody, but he never did. Three other gang members and I followed Sumaa down the tunnel. I was immensely grateful to Mila for his timely intervention, and I thanked him in my heart. Every second was torture to me while I stood there listening to Sahr going on about his damned suspicions. Thus, I was very happy to hide my anxieties within the dingy tunnels. Not that it freed me permanently from the problem, but being out of Sahr's sight and being engaged in work gave me a little respite. It was all right to hide behind work in the tunnels, but I knew that, at some point, I would be forced to reckon with the inevitable. I would have to take responsibility for my actions and suffer the consequences. I dreaded the moment, but I was determined to deal with it when it arrived.

46

Thursday morning was sunny and bright. Even before we arrived from the fields, the sun was already up and shining. There were no traces of rain clouds in the sky any longer. One would have mistakenly thought that we were in the first weeks of the dry season instead of the rainy season. The village was suddenly lively again, and everyone was going on with their daily chores with some springs in their steps. Men, women, and children returning from or going for their early morning dips saluted each other merrily.

It was a beautiful morning, but for me, it was overshadowed by the fear of being found out as Sandivah's lover. I didn't join the others washing in the river. I remained on the veranda, lying in a hammock, my eyes and ears on the alert, anxious to see or hear Sandivah. I was desperate to see the woman.

"Sahr says you should come," said a tiny voice below the hammock, startling me. It turned out to be Sandivah's six-year-old daughter. She was the only one who called both her parents by their first names, and they didn't seem to mind.

"Okay, I am coming," I said, but I was filled with fear immediately. "Where's your mum?" I asked the child while ruffling her untidy, tangled hair as we went along to meet her father.

"In the room with Sahr. They are both waiting for you," said the small girl.

They are both waiting for you, I repeated silently in my head. Trouble had arrived. I had to face it. It wasn't going to go away; it was here to stay until it was resolved. I took a deep breath and knocked on Sahr's door, expecting the worst. The small girl pushed the door open and announced, "Yandi is here."

"I know you're very tired this morning after having worked all night," said Sahr. He always went straight to the point when having a conversation. "But I really need your help and hope you are not too tired to refuse."

Sandivah was sitting in one of his red leather chairs, the first signs of her swelling belly already visible. Her left leg was rested on the cushion of the chair, enabling me to see a bit of her rosy, sturdy thighs.

As usual, I felt a tinge of stimulation down below. The woman never failed to induce a reaction in me.

"Yes, Yandi, Sahr needs you to help me," she said. "I must pick up some things from the farm, heavy things that I couldn't carry." She touched her belly delicately. "They would be too much for me in my condition."

Sahr looked at me directly. He smiled knowingly and said, "So you see, Yandi, we must help the woman. That's where I need your help, young man."

Help the woman? What an anti-climax! I was expecting Sahr to maul me, and here he was asking for my help! It was all getting very confusing. "Well I am really not very tired," I managed to say, relieved that it wasn't what I'd expected. "I am willing to help. Sandivah has been like a big sister to us since we arrived. Besides, she feeds us every day."

"Thank you," said Sahr. "Sandivah will tell you the things to bring back from the farm."

"When will you be ready?" asked Sandivah.

"I am ready when you are," I said, and I took my leave.

Just before I walked out the door, she said, "I will come out in a moment. We will head for the farm. If we return sooner, it might give you some chance to sleep before you go to work in the evening."

"Why didn't you tell me you are pregnant?" I asked Sandivah as soon as we were a safe distance from town. Before then, I had been engrossed with ensuring that Sahr was not following us. I was still convinced that the trip was designed by Sahr to catch me. Sandivah assured me that Sahr was still ignorant about our relationship, but I refused to believe her. Consequently, she thought I was being paranoid whenever I backtracked down the path or looked anxiously at the bushes to see whether anyone was had hiding there.

"You're not my husband. Why should I?" Sandivah replied simply. "I just didn't want you to worry yourself too much. And you may have stopped sleeping with me if I did."

"You should've told me all the same," I insisted.

"You know now," she said. "I am sorry I didn't tell you, but I'll tell you this: you made me pregnant. Without doubt, you're my child's father. It would be wishful thinking to believe another man is responsible. Sahr was actually performing Kattacha at the time I conceived. He religiously kept to the rules. I know because he didn't touch me. Why do you think we got to meet so frequently? But there's really nothing to worry your cute head about," she concluded. And then she flashed that bright, encouraging smile of hers that always melted my heart.

"But I am already worried. Still, I am not angry with you," I said, "Your husband knows he didn't make you pregnant, and he is going to find out who did. According to him, he knows who made you pregnant. I am really worried."

Sandivah laughed merrily and contemptuously. "Fishing," she said. "My poor husband was just fishing in muddy waters. Relax. You mustn't worry about nothing. I am Sahr's wife, and as far as I know, he made me pregnant—Kattacha or no Kattacha. A married woman does not give birth to a bastard."

Customarily, as long as a married woman didn't confess to being impregnated by a lover, traditional law maintained that the child was the husband's. That held true even if there were striking similarities in the child and the suspected lover. Everything depended upon the woman. If she didn't say a word, the husband had nothing to work with. Like it or not, he would be forced to accept the child. If he didn't, the community would punish him.

"Just deny everything if you're ever confronted," said Sandivah with unbelievable confidence. "Leave everything to me, and we'll be fine. Trust me. My mouth is sealed even if he gives me the thrashing of my life. I'll never name you as the other man. It'll forever be our secret. So you see, there's really no need to worry. Besides, I know how to deal with Sahr; he's my husband, after all."

"Are you sure about that?" I asked. "I've seen other women punished until they divulged the name of their lovers."

"Not me. Not this woman," she said with conviction.

My instincts told me to believe her. I decided to go with my instincts. "Well," I said, "if you don't want me to worry, I won't."

"That's more like it, my big man," she said and touched her bulging stomach tenderly. And then she sighed. "You're this child's father, but no one will ever know," she lamented. "I would've liked the whole village to know, but I'm a married woman, another man's wife. Of course, I love you more than him."

I was touched. I never realised Sandivah loved me so much. Throwing caution to the wind, I drew her towards me and placed my hand over her belly. "I will always be this child's father," I said, "and I love you, too."

Sandivah raised her head and looked at me intensely. "Do you really love me as you profess?" she asked tenderly.

"Without any doubt," I answered promptly.

"Then let's elope," she suggested.

Her words caught me by surprise. It was the last thing I expected, and I felt my face crumble for a moment.

"Just kidding," she said quickly, disappointed but trying hard not to show it. She must've noticed the surprise and apprehension on my face. I felt sorry for her. I wanted to do as she asked, but I was sure it wouldn't work. Besides, Sandivah had other children. Where would she leave them if we eloped? In addition, I was young and not ready yet to be tied down by a woman or kids. I also knew that I was in Yengema for a reason: to make my fortune. Nothing was going to stop me from achieving that goal, not even a woman who was carrying my child. Regardless, I felt sorry for the woman. I was in love with her, but that was not enough for me to elope with her. I was in Yengema for the family I left in Simbaru. My parents wouldn't be too happy to be presented with a daughter-in-law from another tribe who already had children from another man. It just wouldn't work.

"You know we can't do that," I said in a soft voice.

"No, we can't. Don't you think I know that?" she asked. "I just got carried away, but as I said earlier, I was just kidding. Don't mind me and my silly ideas."

We didn't talk much after that. It seemed as if the words about eloping had dampened our emotions and enthusiasm to talk to each other. I decided not to bother her, and she didn't bother me. We were just two silent people walking towards our destination, each engaged in private thoughts.

"We are almost at the farm," she exclaimed happily. She then started to walk much faster towards a thatched shack that passed for a farmhouse. "I'm feeling very hot and could use the shade and coolness of the farmhouse."

By the time I arrived at the farmhouse, Sandivah was comfortably seated on one of four big logs that were placed against the inside of the four sides of the shack. In the middle of the shack sat a big, strong, makeshift, rattan basket that held two plastic containers, each containing five gallons of bright red palm oil.

Pointing to the basket, Sandivah said, "That's what you have to take to town. Are you up for it?"

"That's child's play," I boasted, "I can carry three of those to town at the same time."

"My big strong man," she said. and at the same time lifted the cotton Lappa over her tummy. She wasn't wearing anything else underneath. "It's still hot in here. I can't believe it's rainy season."

"Cover up," I said, "someone might've followed us." Even as I was saying that, I felt my groin stir. My dick began to grow steadily in anticipation of fucking her.

"So I no longer make you horny?" she teased, rubbing herself down below at the same time. "Is it because my stomach is swollen?" I wanted to fuck her there and then, but instead I said, "Far from that. It's just that Sahr or anyone could walk in on us. Someone may have followed us. You never know."

"No one followed us," she said a little heatedly. "Sahr didn't follow us. He had to go to Koidu to squeeze some money out of Mr K, money to give me for when I go to live with my parents."

"Why didn't you say so before?" I asked in a husky voice that surprised me.

"Come here," she said, and she got up from her log seat to spread her cotton Lappa on the ground of the shack. Come and get some sweet honey."

I got rid of my clothes in record time. She was still trying to arrange the wrapper so that we didn't have to do it on the rough ground. Her posterior was directed towards me. She bowed to straighten the Lappa and exposed a wet, pink, slit. My body went mad. I couldn't wait any longer. I moved towards her quickly, aimed my erect dick at her slit, grabbed her around the waist, and drew her closer. Soon, I was deep inside of her and pumping away, oblivious to any prospective danger. Penetrating her in such a savage way caught her by surprise, but it didn't stop her from responding in an equally lustful fashion. She accommodated all of me and matched me stroke for stroke.

"Fuck me to your heart's content," she advised. "This may be the last time we fuck, probably for a long time to come. Remember, I will have to stay with my parents till the baby arrives . . . and way beyond that."

"Then shut up and let me get on with it," I said, and I continued pounding until I poured all my juices deep inside of her. The muscles in the walls of her pussy contracted rhythmically over my engorged dick until the last drop of sperm was milked from it. I slowly disengaged from her, causing her to moan sweetly. I was breathing heavily but not tired. My engorged appendage became flaccid and pointed towards the ground, but I still wanted more of her.

"That was quick," she complained. And then she turned her head to smile at me sweetly.

"I haven't even started yet," I said and grinned. "Now get down on the Lappa and get ready for a marathon session."

"Your words are my commands, my great master," she said, and then she slowly and seductively took her favourite position. She was lying on her back with her legs almost spreadeagled. Her pussy was completely exposed. Her thick, black, coarse pubic hair sat on top of her red, open slit. Her pubic hair was like a monarch sitting on a throne. I quickly got beside her, and we started fondling each other in all the right places. We were both groaning and moaning, driving each other into a sensational frenzy. We did not have a care in the world. In fact, at that moment, no one else existed. When the right time arrived, I entered her and made love to her passionately but tenderly until we were both totally spent. We dressed up, sat side by side on one of the logs, and talked for a long time. We said our premature goodbyes, frightfully aware that it would be a long time before we saw each other again.

It was past midday before we were ready to return to the village. Sandivah helped me put the rattan basket of palm oil on my head. Carrying a load of ten gallons of palm oil was no easy feat. I knew the load was heavy, but I was sure I could carry it all the way to town. I made a head pad out of palm leaves and grass to alleviate the pressure on my bare head. When I was sure the load of palm oil was balanced on my head, I broke into a light trot towards town. Sandivah trailed behind.

"The sky's getting dark. I think it's going to rain," said Sandivah.

I had the load on my head, but I could still see the sky ahead of me. The sky was getting darker; pockets of thick, black clouds were moving slowly across the skyline and drowning the sunlight. The fine weather we'd enjoyed on our way to the farm was disappearing fast. "We must walk faster," I said. "Are you up to it?"

"You're the one carrying the load. You should be worrying about yourself," she said.

"You are on, then," I said with a note of challenge in my voice. I began trotting faster.

"I'll be right behind you, me and your baby," she said.

Yes, you and my baby, I repeated silently, my heart swelling with pride.

Midway to town, the black clouds became more ominous. The day suddenly turned into dusk. Heavy winds blew against the palm trees and long elephant grass, and we heard barrages of thunder. Bright flashes of lightning illuminated the sky in spectacular ways. It seemed that God was giving us a special fireworks show. I heard the cries of monkeys anxiously cackling and calling on their young ones to head for shelter before the rain fell. The cries of other anxious animals and birds added to the cacophony. It was going to be a huge storm. I hoped that we would reach the village before it started. Trotting even faster, I shouted to Sandivah to increase her pace.

"Just keep going," she said, "I am right behind you."

"It's not only going to rain," I said, "there's going to be a storm."

"I know. I have eyes and can see for myself," she said.

"You've got legs, too," I teased. "Make them walk faster, or the storm will catch us on the way."

She didn't reply. I didn't engage her in conversation again. The storm was bearing down on us and it was getting more difficult to hear each other. The intensity of the wind and rumbling thunder were steadily increasing. We kept on going until we were on the outskirts of the village. When we crossed the stream close to the village, we were relieved to learn that there were only a few hundred yards more to walk. However, just as we were entering Sahr's compound, the sky opened. Rain fell in thick, heavy, furious drops, drenching our clothes and bodies instantly. Nevertheless, we were glad we made it. In the shelter of the big parlour of the house, Mila helped me put down the rattan basket of palm oil where Sandivah wanted it. He stood there looking at me accusingly. There may have been a glint of jealousy in his eyes. I pretended not to notice.

"Thank you," said Sandivah, "And lots of thanks to you, too, Mila. She disappeared into her room swiftly after that.

47

"You must say who made you pregnant," said Sahr, "because I didn't. I'm sure of that."

A rain-filled Friday afternoon turned out to be the potential doomsday for me. Sandivah had to reveal the name of her lover, and regardless of her reassurances that she wouldn't reveal my name in the discussion, I was still very nervous. The town crier had gone round the village announcing that there would be a court session immediately after the Friday prayers. Despite the rain, people filled the big, round hut with the low walls that stood in the centre of the village. The structure served as a place for community meetings and court sessions. As per custom, most people didn't leave the village to work on the farms or in the diamond fields on Fridays. Friday was also a day for settling disputes and engaging in celebration, depending upon what the village and elders had on the agenda.

The seven elders in charge of the case sat in a separate elevated area. Sandivah and her husband sat on crude rattan chairs a short distance from the elevated area. They faced the elders. There were loud murmurs within and around the courthouse until the elder ordered silence. When the people were quiet, one of them spelled out the charges levied against Sandivah.

"Your husband says he didn't make you pregnant. Who did?" asked the elder with only one good eye. Rumours had it that he lost an eye when a cobra spat in his face when he was a teenager.

The question made me more apprehensive than ever. It was the decisive moment: I was going to learn whether Sandivah would involve me or not. Arms akimbo, Mila stood close by me and watched the procedure with interest. He didn't miss my uneasiness.

"Pull yourself together," he said, "she has not named you yet." He smiled, and somehow, that smile helped me settle my nerves.

"He did," said Sandivah, pointing to the man beside her. "I know he did. Would I mistake my own husband for another man?" There were murmurs and sniggers in the courthouse, but it didn't take long for an elder to call for order.

"I didn't," countered an exasperated Sahr. "I have been performing Katta—"

"It's either you shut up, or we fine you and drop the case," reprimanded an elder in a long, blue, flowing gown. Turning to Sandivah, the elder asked, "How did he make you pregnant if he was performing Kattacha?"

"Simple," said Sandivah, smiling with confidence, "he slept with me. We fucked a few times before his Kattacha."

Sahr didn't answer immediately. Sandivah's response shocked him. He didn't expect her to make their sex sessions public. *The woman is a liar,* Sahr thought. Something told him that the woman might outfox him after all. And that was disturbing.

"Answer the woman," ordered another elder. He was a tall, thin, scrawny, bald man dressed in European clothing. "Is the woman right? Did you have sex with her before the ceremony?"

Sahr fiddled with his clothes and answered in an almost inaudible voice. "Yes, I did, but only before the ceremony. I never slept with her again when I started the ceremony. God is my witness."

"Then it's possible that you made her pregnant. Why did you bring this woman to us, then?" asked the tall, thin, scrawny, bald man. "We want to know."

"Because I don't believe I made her pregnant," Sahr insisted. "She told me herself that she was less than six months pregnant. I couldn't have made her pregnant because I was five months into the ceremony."

The elders consulted each other. They agreed that Sahr had a point. If he hadn't slept with his wife for five months, and she was about six months pregnant, it was obvious that someone else had stepped into the husband's role. "How come you are almost six months pregnant?" The elders demanded.

"I don't want to say," said Sandivah.

"But you must say," said the elder in the flowing, blue gown, "or we'll rule that your husband is telling the truth."

Sandivah took a deep breath. She pointed at her husband and said, "He made me pregnant. We even did it during the ceremony. He broke his Kattacha, and he slept with me several times during the ceremony. He didn't abstain from sex at all, as he's now claiming. I didn't want to bring this out in public, but since my reputation is at stake, I have

Dead End Poverty

no choice but to do so. Am I lying, my dear husband?" she asked with a smug face.

The crowd gasped. The people knew no man should sleep with a woman during Kattacha. Sahr jumped up from his rattan chair and confronted his wife. He was apoplectic, but he managed to keep the anger under control. "She's lying. I never did; I never slept with her during Kattacha," he said.

"You must pay two leones to the court for interrupting," said the elder in the European clothes. "We warned you earlier."

Sahr sat down, clearly angry at the turn the case was taking. He was angry because the woman was lying. And on top of that, he had to pay a fine for interrupting. He started to regret bringing the case before the elders.

"Can you prove that she isn't telling the truth?" inquired another elder.

"Unfortunately, no, but I know I didn't make her pregnant."

"Do you have a suspect in mind?" asked the same elder.

"Negative. But I know I didn't make her pregnant. And I never slept with her during my Kattacha ceremony.

Sandivah was right: her husband was just fishing. The man himself admitted that he didn't have a suspect. I was greatly relieved, but I felt sorry for Sahr. His case was fast turning against him.

"Unfortunately, we can't prove that, either," said the same elder. "These things take place in secret and between two people."

The spectators roared with laughter. Sahr wanted the earth to swallow him there and then. The incident would make him lose face with the villagers and the elders. Desperately, he tried one more time to make the elders believe him. "I really didn't make my wife pregnant," he said without conviction.

"We're wasting time here," said the elder in the European clothes. "Sahr has no suspect; he can't prove he didn't sleep with his wife during Kattacha, and his wife insists he made her pregnant. Based on the evidence before us, I think we should decide this case now. Both swore before the case commenced that lightning should strike them dead if they lied to the court."

"Well said, my brother," stated the elder in blue. "I am sure we all agree with you." He looked at his fellow elders, and one by one, they nodded their heads in agreement. After that, the elders engaged in muffled deliberation as the audience looked on. It took a while before they agreed on a final decision.

"Sahr and Sandivah," began the man in the flowing, blue gown, "us elders have reached a verdict. Based on the evidence before us, Sahr has no suspect and cannot prove to us that you didn't sleep with your wife. Therefore, we're forced to conclude that you made your wife pregnant. We have no doubt because no one else stands accused."

"And we also want to make it clear that you must take care of the child when it arrives; otherwise, you'll be answering to us," said the elder in the European clothes. "If there isn't a suspect, the husband is deemed the father." The elder resumed his seat.

Another elder was on his feet at once. "You've wasted the time of this court," he said to Sahr. "You shouldn't have brought the case to us without proper evidence and a suspect. For that, this court will fine you a total of thirty leones."

Sahr groaned. He didn't have thirty leones to spend on court fines.

"And that's not the end of it," continued the elder. "You broke the sacred rule of Kattacha. You know what to do. Yaya already knows you broke the rules. He'll be expecting a hefty sacrifice and a big fine. And don't forget: you owe this court thirty-two leones."

Sahr crumpled. He acknowledged that he'd foolishly put himself in an impossible position: he had lost face in the village and was going to lose a substantial amount of money, too. And all of that because of the stupid, horny cow that was his wife. *The woman couldn't keep her Lappa round her thighs even if it were tied with chains and padlocks. I really didn't make her pregnant*, he said in his head. *But who would believe me? I've lost the case and must bear the consequences.*

"I know," said Sahr, and I won't forget. I'll see Yaya as soon as possible and do the right thing."

"As for you, Sandivah," continued the same elder, "you have no case to answer. That's not to say that you aren't guilty as charged. However, as we can't come up with proof, we'll give you the benefit of the doubt. You're free to go. Court is adjourned."

Angrily shoving people out of his way, Sahr left the courtroom, muttering threats, swear words, and obscenities under his breath. He walked away from the courthouse quickly. He was steamed and ready to explode at the slightest provocation.

Sandivah followed her husband slowly as she walked towards the house. She shot me a quick, knowing glance. The rest of the crowd dispersed as well, the majority of them intrigued by the outcome of the case. They were wondering who was telling the truth.

As Mila and I walked back home, I realised it had stopped raining completely. The sun had even managed to break through the clouds to bestow a warm, golden glow on the village and its vegetation.

"You're a very lucky bastard," Mila said, slapping my back playfully but painfully enough to draw a grimace from me. "You got away with it, you sly fox!"

I just smiled. Watching the whole procedure as a spectator instead of the culprit, I realised how unpredictable a woman could be, especially when in love. Sandivah was a living example: she'd lied shamelessly to protect me, the man who made her pregnant. Nevertheless, I was glad that she'd diverted trouble and shame away from me. But I didn't know whether I could trust such a woman, let alone elope with her. I figured she might do the same thing to me. And then I felt happy and relieved that her husband was sending her away.

Sahr was angry and ranting. We could hear his voice before we arrived at the house. Sandivah had arrived, too, and she was standing a safe distance away from her ranting husband. She watched him as he brought out her things from her room and dumped them unceremoniously in the large parlour. He accompanied each load he dumped with some derogatory words directed at Sandivah.

"You will not sleep in this house tonight," said Sahr. "You're going to your parents."

"But I'm not packed yet," Sandivah protested lamely.

"Can't you see? I'm doing it for you already, you stupid, smelly whore." Sahr was trying to insult the woman off the face of the earth. "And if you open your mouth one more time, you'll regret it. You're lucky to be pregnant, or you wouldn't be standing there talking."

Sandivah started to cry, but it didn't deter Sahr. He was intent on bringing out all her belongings. She moved onto the veranda and continued to cry. Her children joined her, but they didn't fully comprehend why their mother was crying.

"Yandi," said Sahr, "go get me Sumaa, Samson, and Dowu. Tell them I need them here fast. And you, Mila, help me get that rarray girl's things ready. She's definitely leaving my house today."

I left to follow orders. On the veranda, Sandivah was still crying. I stopped by her and uttered a quick thank you. She smiled, looking radiant as if she hadn't been crying at all. I started to move, but then I realised that she would be leaving soon. I had some money on me, and I withdrew the large sum from my pocket and handed it to her. She tucked it into the folds of the cotton Lappa around her waist, thanking me with her eyes at the same time.

"That may come in handy," I said, and I went to look for the boys. I noticed that it had started raining again, although not heavily. I was fortunate; I found Samson, Dowu, and Sumaa huddled over a game of cards. I gave them the boss's message, and we all walked back to the house together. Sandivah was no longer on the veranda. She had returned to the parlour, but she was still crying.

Sahr was still ranting when I arrived with the boys, but he stopped for a moment to give them instructions. "You will accompany this witch back to her parents' village. Do you understand?"

The trio nodded in acknowledgement. "When will that be?" asked Sumaa.

"As soon as her things are put in order," said Sahr, pointing at the untidy pile. "Tell her parents that she can't return until I send for her or come for her. If they ask you questions, you know nothing."

"We will," Dowu replied.

"Now help pack these things and be on your way; otherwise, you won't be able to make it back here tonight," advised Sahr.

A while later, everything was packed. It was still drizzling, but Sahr insisted that Sandivah and the boys set out immediately, the rain notwithstanding. The three men carried the bulky packages on their heads and led the way. Sandivah, still crying her eyes out, carried a heavy load on her head as well. She was dragging her children along, and the children were obviously upset that the rain was making them wet and they were leaving their father behind. Sahr couldn't resist a nasty parting shot at his wife: "Go in pieces. And as far as I'm concerned, you can fuck all the men in your village. Abominable woman!" he said.

48

We were in the middle of the rainy season, and the rains kept coming steadily (albeit not very heavily most of the time). We had to work in the rain. There was no avoiding it; even the farmers and their wives and children did their work in the rain. Sometimes the rain relented for a couple of hours, but it always started up again.

"We must try to remove as much gravel as possible tonight," said Sahr. "I have noticed that we've been getting lazy."

It was Wednesday, just over a fortnight since Sandivah left, and we were in the mines. Morale was low, and we weren't happy. We were not very enthusiastic about the work, either. Our efforts hadn't paid off for quite a while. In fact, we wondered whether the rainy season work would earn us anything at all. We even devised ways of wasting time instead of investing it to remove and wash gravel. Without gravel, though, there would be no diamonds. We were standing under a leafy tree taking temporary shelter from the rain. Fortunately, the rain wasn't one accompanied by thunder and lightning.

"We will do our best," said Sumaa, "but it is difficult working in the tunnels when it's so wet. We don't seem to be finding anything. Everything is just so muddy and sticky down there. It's very difficult to excavate."

"Just load the bags with soil, wet or not," said Sahr. "You're forgetting that everything down there is gravel. I want four people down there now."

"Do you think it is safe to work down there tonight?" asked Mila. "It is still raining, just like it was a week ago when Boss Kai was killed in the pit collapse."

"How would I know? I am not a surveyor. But are others not working down below at this moment in spite of the tragedy?" asked Sahr angrily. "Don't worry. Anyway, what happened to poor Boss Kai won't happen to any of you."

Sumaa, Samson, Francis, and I, equipped with the tools and bags we needed, descended into the tunnels and commenced work. As usual, we changed places after reasonable periods of time. By the time I came up from my third trip, we had enough gravel piled up by the water source. In response to Sahr's instructions (and under his watchful eyes), Mila and Boima began kicking it.

Sahr showed me a small, flawless stone they'd recovered from the gravel just before I came up. "I'm sure there is more of this in that pile," he said.

I agreed. Sahr let me look at the stone for a while. It was shone brightly as the light from the torch reflected off its surface. *If only it were bigger,* I thought. *Still, little stones are better than no stones. And as Sahr said, there might be more of the little gems in there. That's good for us because we haven't earned substantial money for quite a while now. Even small diamonds will boost the morale of the gang and make the members a little richer. I know Sahr needs the money; he constantly complains about being broke due to the fines he incurred and the cost of the sacrifice to Yaya.*

"We have a large pile, and it's still raining," I said to Sahr. "Unless we bring the others above ground to help kick it, we won't be able to complete the job before daybreak."

"Then go down there again," said Sahr. "Tell them that we don't need more gravel, that they should all come up to help wash the gravel."

With Tamba's dramatic exit and his replacement not yet secured, there were only six of us to kick the big pile of gravel. One man was loading, and the other one kicked. They both worked close to each other so that Sahr could watch the shakers and make sure nobody swallowed or hid a gem.

The first concentrates of pebbles and stones from my shaker yielded six tiny, clean diamonds, each considerably smaller than a carat. I reckoned that we would need fifteen to twenty such stones to make a carat. Still, diamonds were diamonds, and they were expensive; many similar stones put together would sell for many thousands of leones. I was happy I would be making some money from the night's work. Concentrates coming from the other two Shakers also yielded similar stones, and everyone felt hopeful that the night's work would be worthwhile. All of us were happy to work once we smelled money. Sahr seemed to be the happiest; he smiled from ear to whenever he was handed a collection of stones. "I think we hit a spot. Diamonds are concentrated in this particular pile of gravel. We must dig in the same area tomorrow night."

Shaker after shaker yielded diamonds of different sizes, colours, and qualities; some of the stones were hardly bigger than a small pebble. They were almost like large grains of sand. Before long, we were more than halfway through the gravel, and Sahr had collected over two hundred small gems from our efforts. He was a happy man. "Put some more effort in," he said encouragingly, "there's only a little more gravel left. And judging by what we've discovered so far, there may be more than a hundred diamonds in it yet."

We obeyed. The little pile started disappearing quickly, and we handed over more diamonds to Sahr. Everyone played their part, and work was going well. It seemed that we would be returning to town sooner than later.

It was my turn to work at the shaker. Just as I handed over the first concentrates for examination, someone called out, "Joe Khakis! Run for your life." Pandemonium broke out as the wet diamond fields full of miners below and above ground erupted into action. Nevertheless, I heard Sahr shout, "Run! Every man for himself! But take what you can with you. We'll meet in the village."

"Follow me, I shouted to Mila as I jumped out of the water to run to safety. My vision was a little blurred due to the falling rain. Dawn was just breaking, and it provided ample light. Our gang ran away in various directions to make it more difficult for the Joe Khakis to catch us. Running wasn't new to Mila and me: we always ran in Simbaru, chasing squirrels and other small mammals until we caught them. In less than a minute, Mila and I had cleared the open mining field, and we were running into the bushes to disappear into the long elephant grass. That made it even harder for the Joe Khakis to catch us. We didn't want to be arrested again, so we continued running—wet to the skin, totally drenched—until we were sure no one was chasing us any longer. Afterward, we made our way back to town, happy that we wouldn't be guests of Tankoro again.

Everyone from our gang survived the raid, but as we learned later, several members from other gangs (some of whom we knew quite well) were arrested. I assumed they were lodged in one of the hot, congested cells. And I knew they'd be suffering from the stale, acidic odours emanating from several days worth of human waste. They would be waiting patiently but anxiously, secured in the knowledge that it was only a matter time before they could return to the village and continue mining.

We were all on the big veranda, feeling as wet as a river and cold. We were still wearing our drenched working gear, and it was still raining heavily. Thunder rumbled every few minutes, accompanied by lightning that seemed to flash all across the sky.

"We should go back to the fields to finish kicking our gravel, there may be a good number of diamonds inside," Francis suggested. "The Joe Khakis will be gone by now."

"In this weather? You must be out of your mind," replied Samson. "Besides, the Joe Khakis might still be there; they've been known to stay and wash abandoned gravel themselves."

"Samson is right," said Sumaa, "if we go back now, we might walk right into them. Whom would we blame if we were caught? Besides, there wasn't much gravel left. Not enough to risk our freedom."

"What are you guys talking about?" asked Sahr as he came out of his room. He was clean, dry, and wearing warm clothes.

"Francis reckons that we should go back and finish washing the remaining gravel because there might be more diamonds in it," said Mila.

"That's out of the question," said Sahr. "No one should go back; it could be dangerous, and the weather is very bad."

"Since when did rain stop us from mining?" asked Francis bitterly.

"We're not going back," said Sahr emphatically. "However," he continued, "since you seem very keen to return, you're free to go. But don't expect anyone to get you from Tankoro."

"I just thought that, since the gravel was yielding so many diamonds, we should—"

"Never mind," said Sahr. "we'll wash it tonight when we get back. If the Joe Khakis washed it in our absence, we'll just dig for more. And we know exactly where to dig." Pointing at us with an outstretched hand, Sahr continued: "You are all in your wet working clothes still. You will be sick if you don't wash and change into dry clothes soon. It's still raining, so you won't have to make the trip to the river. Come and see me afterward, when morning comes proper."

Once clean and dry after a good scrub in the rain, we returned to the big veranda for the meeting with Sahr. He emerged from his room smiling brightly. The moaning Sahr from the previous night had transformed because he was confident that his money woes would soon disappear.

"Last night was good for us," he said. "I didn't have the chance to tell you about the diamonds we found because of the raid. Altogether, we got two hundred and nine small diamonds. We found another three pieces that likely weigh close to or over half a carat each."

He withdrew a balled, white paper from his trouser pocket to show us the stones. Clustered together in the confined space, the diamonds were a beautiful sight to see. I had never seen so many diamonds together like that. They glittered and threw shiny rays in every direction as Sahr stirred them with one of his fingers.

"When do we sell?" Sumaa demanded.

"Tomorrow. Friday," he said. "Mr K will arrive tonight, but we will be at work. He'll spend the night anyway, so no worries there. We will sell the diamonds then, and everyone will have some money in his pocket."

"Then you better keep the stones in a safe place before they get lost," I said.

"Good idea," said Sahr. He folded the white paper around the stones and put it back in his pocket. "You'd all better go to Yei to have breakfast. Eat well; we'll be working harder tonight. As for me, I'm off to sleep."

49

The following night, it was pouring rain when we returned to the fields. Everyone was wet to the skin. Fortunately, the rain was warm and we didn't feel very cold. Sahr had decided to stay home to wait for Mr K, but he made us realise that Francis was in charge.

"I hope he doesn't do a runner like Tamba, that dog," Sahr said. "But I'm sure you won't let him. Remember, Tamba taught us a lesson, and that is still fresh in our minds. Don't let him out of your sight, even if he wants to attend to go to the toilet."

"Since you don't trust me, Sahr, you must come with us," Francis replied as we left the shelter of the veranda and headed for the fields.

"Just go," Sahr said, "but be sure you do a good job. Bring me more diamonds."

Even before we arrived in the fields, disappointed gang members returning to the village informed us that the tunnels were too flooded to mine, that it was impossible to work, that they were going back to the village. They said that, unless we were very lucky, we wouldn't find any gravel left behind from the previous night. Though we believed them, we wanted to see things for ourselves. Thus, we trudged along until we arrived. There wasn't any gravel at the site where we'd piled ours, and it seemed to be the same situation for other gangs. We could hear swear words coming from all directions.

The Joe Khakis, true to their nature, had stayed to kick the abandoned gravel left behind by the fleeing gangs. They even confiscated all the tools they found. We weren't surprised, but we were furious with them. They were thieves. They were supposed to maintain the law, but their greed for money surpassed their loyalty to the job and the government.

I turned to Francis and said, "I wish you'd returned last night to kick the gravel. You would've been in Tankoro by now."

Samson agreed: "You're a very lucky bastard. The Joe Khakis would've been glad to have you; they would have forced you to kick the gravel for them. And they would've still taken you to Tankoro."

We all laughed nervously at Francis's expense, but he didn't take any offence. Instead, walking in the thick sludge created by the rain, he crossed over to the tunnels, switched on his torch, and directed the bright light into one of the Damakoro pits. "It's true," he said, "the tunnels are flooded."

We hurried over to him and saw that the tunnels were flooded. Every Damakoro pit seemed to be full of water, so I could imagine what it would be like deep below ground. Unless one was a diver, one wouldn't be able to work down there.

"I can see the water. It seems to be rising. We cannot work here tonight," said Francis. "In fact, it will take a few days before we work in the tunnels again."

"So what do we do now?" asked Dowu.

"What else?" replied Mila, "We should just go back to the village."

"That's exactly what we will do: go back to the village," said Francis.

When we knocked at his door, Sahr was surprised that we'd returned so early. "Stay in the parlour," he advised after noticing that we were dripping wet. "What happened? What're you doing here at this time?" he asked.

"The tunnels are flooded. We can't work. Other gangs can't work either. And like us, they have also returned to the village," Francis answered.

"You should've stayed to kick the remaining gravel from yesterday night," said Sahr.

"The dirty, greedy Joe Khakis stole it and kicked it, including all the tools they could lay their hands on," said Mila.

"That's too bad," lamented Sahr, "I was hoping we would add more gems to our collection. Never mind, though, what's done is done."

"So where's Mr K? Has he arrived yet?" asked Boima

"That was something I was going to speak to you about," said Sahr. "Mr K didn't come. He sent someone over to tell me not to expect him, that he couldn't make it tonight because he had an important task to complete. However, according to his messenger, he will be here first thing in the morning. There is no cause to worry; you are still going to be rich men tomorrow. Allow me to return to sleep now. Tomorrow will be a busy day." He turned around to go back into his room, but he stopped just before he went inside and said, "And if I were you guys, I would go get out of those wet clothes now."

It rained through the entire night, and I suspected that the next day would also be a wet one. Surprisingly, Mila and I woke up to a dry morning. We entered the empty veranda, chose our best hammocks, and climbed into them to wait for breakfast to be served. I enjoyed the fresh, sweet morning breeze that blew onto the veranda, courtesy of the flowering fruit trees nearby. I took long breaths of the sweet, aromatic air and found it to be very refreshing. I shut my eyes to enjoy it more, but I was interrupted by the entrance of four members of the gang.

"Is Mr K arriving this morning?" Mila asked, directing the question at the boys who had just joined us.

"He arrived very late last night while we were still in the square gambling," replied Boima. "His Land Rover is parked right in front of his house. He must still be sleeping."

"Is Sahr aware of Mr K's arrival," I asked.

"No, I am not," said Sahr from the doorway leading onto the veranda. He was dressed in a long, white, flowing gown. "Who said he arrived?"

"I saw him arrive late in the night," said Boima.

"Then you better go get your breakfast and be back here soon," said Sahr. "Mr K is a very busy man. I am sure he will be here soon to take care of business."

Yei, Sahr's second wife, had prepared Gari, a carbohydrate dish derived from cassava, and palm oil for breakfast. It was delicious, and we all thanked her heartily after the meal and went back to the veranda. Mr K was already there, deeply involved in conversation with Sahr. When he noticed our arrival, he stopped the conversation to address us directly.

"I heard that you've done very well these few days," he said with a big smile. "Sahr said you found hundreds of pebble diamonds. "Having only a few of them is worthless, but when there are a lot, they can be worth a few pennies." He looked at Sahr and continued speaking: "The boys are here. If you are ready, perhaps we can start the sale now."

All six gang members and Sahr took part in the gem sale. We left Sahr to do the business side of things. We were just there to look after our interests and certify that we weren't being cheated. After a marathon haggling session, Mr K agreed to pay 18,500 leones for the 209 small diamonds. He paid 4,800 leones for the bigger gems.

I was elated. I suppose all of us were. It was the first time since Mila and I took up mining that a diamond sale had brought us so much money. As was customary, we divided the money equally between the supporter, the shovel, and the work gang. The gang's share amounted to a little over 7,760 leones. Because Sahr derived his share from the shovel, each gang member was poised to receive nearly 1,300 leones. Earlier, we believed that we wouldn't make any profit from our work. We were happy. After Friday prayers, Mila, the rest of the boys, and I left for Koidu. We felt like the richest men in the land.

Mama Finda was very pleased to see us. She suspended all that she was doing and spent time with us. "It's been some time now since I last saw you," she complained with mock anger. "I thought you would never come."

"We had so much work to do, and the rains didn't help either," said Mila.

"We're here now." I said and smiled, "We brought you some more money to add to the pile."

"I told you that you were going to be rich, but you didn't believe me," said Mother. "Do you know how much money each of you has with me already?"

"We don't need to. We trust you with our money and our lives." Mila knew how to make Mama Finda feel happy and proud. "If one can't trust his own mother, who can one trust?"

"Thank you, my sons," said Mother. "However, I am a bad guest. I haven't fed you yet. What would you like to eat?" We told her.

During the meal, we revealed to Mother that we intended to return to Simbaru temporarily to reunite with our parents and relatives.

"Good of you to still want to do that," Mother stated. "I've seen people who came here as young men and are now old men. They never returned to their homes or their families. They prefer to die out here, especially if they haven't been able to make it or led wild and extravagant lives. Some wasted money on women, drinking, and gambling. I really do admire you boys for your tenacity. When do you want to leave?"

"As soon as the rainy season is over," replied Mila.

"Then you haven't got much time," said Mother. "In a little over a month, the rainy season will be over. You must start shopping now for anything you might want for yourselves, your parents, and your relatives."

"You're right Mother," I said.

"When do you return to Yengema?" she asked.

"Tomorrow evening, I suppose," I said. "Why?"

"Then we'll begin shopping as soon as possible," said Mother. "In fact, as soon as you finish eating, we'll set out for the shops. You must tell me all you want to buy when we get to the shops."

"But first we must give you the money we have on us," I said. I withdrew two large bundles of notes from my pocket. Mila did the same. Mila and I subtracted one hundred leones each and gave mother the rest for safekeeping.

Mother left us eating while she went back to the eating parlour to tell the kitchen help that she would be in charge while she was out. By the time she returned, we had finished eating and tidying up the food bowls and the table.

"We can't take all this money along," said Mother as she entered the room. "I'll have to keep most of it with the rest of the money."

Mama Finda walked over to the far corner of the room where three wooden trunks sat on top of each other on a strong table. She groaned as she tried to lift up the topmost one. I quickly went to her aid and pushed her aside. "You shouldn't lift heavy objects while we are here with you," I said. She watched me move the two top trunks to reveal the third one. I moved away when she came to the box. She searched for the right key to the big, rusty padlock from a bunch of jingling keys.

The trunk was nearly full of money: neatly packed notes of various denominations in numerous stacks. The notes occupied three quarters of the trunk. On top of the notes, there were two plastic bags that I presumed contained money as well.

One was blue and the other was green. We were gobsmacked; we knew it wasn't possible to earn all that money during our time in the mining trade. I realised Mama Finda was a rich woman; no wonder she didn't take money from us. There must've been twenty thousand leones in that trunk.

"Come closer," Mother said, "Your money is in here, too." She took both plastic bags out of the trunk and held them out for us to see. "These are your monies; each bag contains a little over six thousand leones—that's what you've given me so far."

We didn't know we'd accumulated that much money, but we were very happy. *We now have a little over seven thousand leones each— we are rich men in our own rights,* I mused. We knew we shouldn't procrastinate any longer; we needed to leave for Simbaru as soon as the season was over. She opened the bags to deposit the money we'd given her. She kept the rest for shopping. She padlocked the trunk again, and Mila and I put the other two trunks on top of it. She thanked us and told us it was time to go shopping.

Although it was not raining, Koidu was still muddy. Except for the few tarmac roads in the town, all other roads were full of potholes of varying sizes. Dirty, brown rainwater festered in the potholes, some of which were as big as a car. It was quite difficult to walk on the muddy streets while dodging the potholes and avoiding being splashed with muddy water by careless taxi drivers. Occasionally, we heard pedestrians exchange abuses with inconsiderate, speeding drivers for splashing dirty water on them. Regardless of the mud, I noticed that many people walked barefoot or with flip-flops. The flip-flops sprayed more watery mud on their clothes every time they moved. Fortunately, we had our canvass shoes on, but they were muddy before we were halfway to the market.

Because it was a Friday, the market was exceptionally full. So were the Lebanese and Fulani shops. Like Mila and me, hundreds of people (most of them miners) were out in the streets shopping, utilising the fruits of their labour. Many of them carried huge cassette recorders in their hands. We saw brand names such as Sony, Aiwa, Panasonic, Conic, and Samsung. Loud music blared from their favourite radio stations or favourite cassette tapes as if they were in a competition to determine whose set played the loudest. Some people even carried the damn things on their heads, singing along and dancing to the melodious sounds. The sound of heavy bass so associated with and loved in Africa was always present.

Mother hired a taxi to take our shopping home. We weren't interested in shopping; we knew Mother would take care of that. So we just stood by, watching her joke, haggle, swear, quarrel, and cry to get her way with the traders she encountered. The three of us couldn't fit in the taxi because of the quantity of goods we had. Both the back seat and the boot of the car were full with things, so we put more on Mama Finda's lap in the passenger seat.

"You'll find me at home, then," said Mother as the driver started the engine of the car and engaged gear one. "You could stay in town if you want to, but please don't get into trouble. Koidu can be as dangerous as it is fun," she warned.

The taxi drove off with Mother. She waved to us, and we stood there waving back until it we couldn't see her any longer. Because we didn't have any goods to carry, we decided to explore the shops and the big market. It was difficult to negotiate the dense human traffic to get to the part of the market we wanted to see. We had to jostle and squeeze our way through, but not without being cussed at, squeezed, and jostled.

Seemingly contained in one area, the jewellery shops displayed cheap, attractive, traditional, and imported jewellery in numerous designs. There were gold-and silver-plated earrings, bangles, necklaces; glass beads; copper earrings; and much more.

"I am going to buy jewellery for my mum, my sisters, and my father's wives," I said, and I led the way into one of the shops.

There was no customer in the shop; the Fulani shopkeeper, in an immaculate, white, flowing gown and a white hat immediately came over to serve us.

"How can I help you," he asked with a welcome smile spread across his jolly face. "I've got everything you need; just tell me what you want."

"We want to buy some jewellery for our families," said Mila.

"Then you've come to the right place," said the jolly Fulani as he went behind the glass counter. "Have a look and choose all that you want. After that, we'll talk price."

By the time we were through looking, we had chosen over thirty items between us. The Fulani shopkeeper placed them on the cracked glass counter in two piles. "Are you sure this is all you want?" he asked.

"We may want more, but let's settle the price first and pay for the ones we have chosen so far," I said. "How much will each pile cost?"

The Fulani scribbled some strange characters on a small notebook he held in his hand. He appeared to make some calculations, and then he said, "Each pile of jewellery will cost you twelve leones and fifty cents."

We were no longer strangers to the market; we knew how it worked. All the traders, no matter how encouraging or kind they were, always tried to fleece their customers if they could get away with it.

"Do you think we pick money from trees?" Mila asked. "This jewellery is not worth even half the price you've quoted."

"I swear by Allah—" the Fulani began.

"Leave Allah out of this," I said. "We know that technique already. Tell us the real price."

We continued to haggle over the price until we reached the handsome and satisfactory price of eight leones and fifty cents per pile.

I counted out my share of the money and paid for the items. Mila did the same.

The Fulani shopkeeper wrapped the jewellery in two paper bags and handed them to us. "Please come again some other time," he said to us as we prepared to leave. "Are you sure you want nothing more?"

"No, thank you," said Mila, "but we might come back in the future." We walked out of the shop and into the muddy, noisy street.

"What do you plan to do now that we've finished shopping?" I asked Mila.

"You know what I plan to do," he said with a twinkle in his eye. "I'll go to the whorehouse, of course, to see Clara and Candy."

I hadn't had sex since Sandivah left. Hearing the names *Clara* and *Candy* was playing tricks with my manhood. I was very tempted to go with Mila and told him so.

"Join the club," he said. He seemed pleased and bemused. "I thought you were holiness itself and wouldn't indulge with rarray girls."

"It's been hard without Sandivah available to satisfy my sexual needs," I confessed. "I masturbate when I desire a woman."

"Scrap the moaning," said Mila. "It's you who doesn't want to sleep with women. Look at me: I've slept with over six women in Yengema alone, all under the noses of their husbands. I don't starve due to lack of sex. Just come to the whorehouse with me. Candy will be very good for you."

We found Candy and Clara outside of the whorehouse, which meant they were free. After we established prices, Clara and Mila led the way inside. His right hand was already grabbing Clara's protruding, gyrating bottom. Clara was giggling like a teenager in love. Candy and I followed closely behind, but I kept my hands off her plump, luscious body because I was shy. Though willing to try out the whorehouse, I wasn't willing to display open love for a prostitute. But Candy had other ideas; she unexpectedly grabbed my crotch and gave it a tender squeeze. I jumped back in surprise. "Ooh," she crooned, feigning surprise, "the one-eyed snake is busy growing in there already."

Mila was surprised to see a younger man at the entrance of the whorehouse. Clara introduced him as Kalala. Kalala is everything that Smelly Joe wasn't. "Kalala doesn't force himself on any of us, and he's much more considerate when it comes to paying the rent," Clara explained.

"Where's Smelly Joe," Mila asked.

"The old pervert died," said Candy, "and I'm happy he kicked the bucket. He won't be contaminating my body any longer."

"How? When?" asked Mila.

"He died a couple of weeks ago in his sleep," said Clara. "The fat, smelly bastard kicked the bucket just as I predicted whenever he forced himself on me. How relieved I am he died."

By that point, we were at the end of the long corridor of the whorehouse. The girls' cubicles were directly opposite each other, and we waited patiently while they tried to unlock the padlocks.

"Don't wait for me when you're done," said Mila. "With Clara, I never know when I will leave." Clara giggled, obviously pleased with the compliment.

"I didn't intend to." I said. "Your lust is insatiable. Spend the night if you want to; it won't bother me."

"We'll meet at Mama Finda's," said Mila, "unless you decide to stay longer, too."

By that time, Clara had the door open. They walked inside with Mila's hand still planted firmly on her bum. The door closed with a bang, but I heard Mila tell the girl to take her clothes off immediately.

Candy opened the door. Pulling me behind her, we went inside. I shut the door behind us. There was no chair in the tiny room, but she gestured that I should sit on the grass mattress on the floor. Her clothes were off in no time, and she stood before me, completely naked save some coloured beads around her waist. I was surprised to see her exquisite curves. They aroused me immensely, and I started to undo the buttons on my shirt.

"I wouldn't have you do that," said Candy, shaking her head in disapproval. She sat on the mattress near me, took my right hand, and put it on one of her big boobs. "Do nothing," she said. "I'll do all the work. I'm going to give you a treat you'll never forget. Just relax and enjoy it." She tenderly nibbled on my left earlobe as she removed my clothes. I obliged. Hours later, I woke up to see a naked Candy lying by my side. I didn't know when I'd fallen asleep.

"You slept," she said calmly. "I thought it would've been cruel to wake you up. You looked immensely tired, and I decided to leave you alone."

The sex was quite good, better than I had ever had with anyone, including Sandivah. I remembered that we'd done it twice in quick succession. And then we went again, and that last one really blew my mind. It was the third session that made me tired. She had encouraged me and boosted my sexual prowess with her sexy cries, so we both worked tirelessly until I collapsed on top of her. I was spent, incapable of doing anything more. I must have fallen asleep on top of her because I didn't remember getting off her. Fully in charge of myself, I got up to get dressed. But then she drew me on top of her again. Before long, my dick was hard and throbbing. That time, we had slow, passionate sex. She cried out and moaned lovingly, hugging me tighter and tighter as I screwed her wet pussy as if it were the last pussy I would ever fuck. And when we finally came together, we didn't know whether we were on earth or in heaven.

Minutes after we finished making love, I got dressed. I didn't want to risk another session with her. "I must leave now," I said. I had a hand in my right pocket, and I was looking for some money to pay her. The going price was just one leone, but I gave her five. I knew why Mila had given five leones to the prostitute that first time instead of the lower price they had agreed on. I had criticised him then, but I didn't feel like criticising myself for doing the same thing. As far I was concerned, she deserved more than five leones; she had pressed all the right buttons.

She thanked me, told me she enjoyed my company, and asked me to come again soon. I told her I might just do that because I had really enjoyed myself. She laughed, and I could see that she was happy she'd pleased me. I knew I would be seeing Candy again in the future. She was quite a woman.

"Did my friend knock on the door while I was sleeping?" I asked her.

She shook her head. "Your friend comes here a lot, and Clara always keeps him for a long time."

"Then I must go now. But I'll be back."

She gave me a hug, held open the door for me, and closed it as soon as I was out. I thought it would be apt to knock on Clara's door to see whether Mila was still in there. I decided against it and walked briskly along the long corridor to the outside. To my surprise, it was already night. It wasn't raining, but the sky was dark with rain clouds. I couldn't believe it; I had spent hours with Candy. I decided to go straight to Mama Finda's before she started getting worried. It was quite dark when I arrived at the eating house. Mila wasn't home yet, but I wasn't surprised. I was sure he was still mattress wrestling with Candy back at the whorehouse. Mother was right behind the counter serving hot meals to customers.

"Happy to see you. Where's Mila," she asked as soon as I got close.

"He decided to stay in town a little longer," I lied.

"I hope he'll be okay. Koidu is not a safe place at night. There are too many crooks and bad people out there," she said with real concern.

"I'm sure he will be okay," I said. "Mila is a big boy; he knows how to take care of himself."

"I guess that's true," she replied. "He's big and strong. I'm sure he can take care of himself. By the way, are you hungry? Your food is ready; you know where to find it. As you can see, I am very busy right now."

"Thank you, Mother," I said, "but I'll wait for Mila so we can eat together. I'll go take a wash now. Maybe Mila will arrive by the time I am finished."

"Be careful in the parlour," she warned, "the place is full of stuff. I didn't realise we'd bought that many things. I haven't had time to put them in a permanent place yet."

"Don't worry," I said and headed towards her living quarters, "I will place them properly while I am waiting for Mila. Just tell me where you want to put them and consider it done."

"Thank you, my son," she said, readjusting the Lappa round her waist. "You may put them in one corner of the storeroom; it is almost empty."

I couldn't believe what we'd bought—more accurately, what Mother had bought on our behalf. There were huge piles of male and female clothing, clothes for kids, different types and sizes of shoes, four cassette recorders, bags, and a lot more. I was very grateful to have her in my life.

Mila arrived just as I finished packing the shopping goods into the storeroom. "I thought so," he said as soon as he saw me.

"What?" I asked.

"That I'd find you here," he said. "I couldn't find you anywhere when I finally mustered the courage to get away from Clara."

"I wanted to tell you I was leaving, but I didn't want to disturb you and Clara," I said.

"You did well," he said. "We would've never opened the door to you anyway; we were far too busy doing better stuff." He laughed and asked, "What were you doing in the store room?"

"Packing our shopping goods properly," I replied. I didn't realise until now that Mother bought us so many things. Come and see for yourself."

Mila peered into the storeroom and seemed satisfied. "We will have to buy more things yet," he said. "These won't be enough for everyone in our families."

I agreed. "How about we eat now," I suggested, and I led the way towards the food on the table. "I have been waiting for you for quite a while now."

"I am famished after my sex marathon," he said as he followed me out. "Clara made sure I got hungry. Boy! She really worked me out; I'll not be having a woman for a while yet." We both laughed.

50

After an uneventful journey, we arrived in Yengema late in the evening. We immediately sensed that something wasn't quite right in town. There weren't many people moving around. It was strange considering the fact that late evening was a busy time for the village: it was when women prepared the evening meals, when miners left for work in the fields, and when children screamed and played hide-and-seek. The few people around seemed inhibited if not preoccupied, and in a few houses, we could hear the wailing of women and children. Overall, there was a melancholic atmosphere draped over the town and its people. Even the few bulbs powered by petrol generators seemed to refuse to shine brightly; instead, they offered dull, orange light in protest (or in harmony with) the gloomy mood of the town.

"Why does everybody look so morose?" Mila inquired as soon as we entered the big veranda in Sahr's house. Boima and Sumaa were the only two people on the veranda, and they were not relaxing in hammocks. They were strolling up and down the veranda, and they looked very serious. Clearly, something was preying on their minds.

"We've a big tragedy on our hands," said Sumaa in a voice that was hardly audible. It was a tremendous contrast to the boisterous attitude of the Sumaa we knew. "The underground pits north of our own collapsed on Friday night, killing more than eleven miners," Boima explained bluntly. "Six of them were from here, this village. Five were from the neighbouring village of Sando."

We were shocked that so many people had lost their lives in the accident, but Boima's blunt answer reminded us how dangerous our job was. I was scared, and as if that weren't enough, the dream I had in Simbaru just before we left manifested in my mind. It didn't help the situation; I was suddenly more afraid. However, to allay the fears that engulfed me, I asked, "What happened?"

"It's the bloody rain," complained Sumaa, wringing his hands in pain, feeling sorry for the loss of so many lives. "Too much rain caused the pits to collapse. It rains in this place as if there are holes in the sky."

"Is everyone accounted for, then?" Mila asked.

"Yes," said Boima, "everyone but one. No one has seen Moquee since. But for the quick thinking of the gang leaders to alert the village in time, many more would have died. We spent Friday night and part of Saturday digging for survivors and dead bodies."

"All able-bodied men immediately went out to the scene to help when we heard the news," said Sumaa. "Some of the bodies recovered were horribly damaged; they were not pretty to see. It was a really gruesome affair."

"Do we know anyone who died?" I asked.

"Very unlikely," Sumaa replied. "We know now that eight of the dead were relatively new men. The five from this town were buried on Saturday afternoon, soon after the recovery of the bodies."

"It's very sad," said Mila with genuine feeling. "They are dead forever, their hopes gone with them. Nevertheless, that's the nature of the job. It could've been us, you know."

"Please stop talking like that," I protested.

"Why should I?" said Mila. All of a sudden, he was angry: "The tunnels are death traps, accidents just waiting to happen. With the haphazard ways the tunnels are constructed and the poor supports to the roofs and sides of the tunnels, I am sure we will be seeing quite a few more cave-ins before the rains stop." It was a chilling prediction.

"Mila is right," Boima said. "We work in very dangerous conditions, exposing ourselves to extreme dangers, not even knowing whether we will come out alive when we go in each night. This latest incident has really got me worried."

"This would throw fear into any miner," said Sumaa. "But give it a few days. Every miner will be back in the tunnel pits, dangerous or not, as if nothing had happened. We are lured by greed and the hope of striking it rich. Our lives mean nothing when we go down there."

"Aren't you scared, Sumaa?" asked Mila. "You mean this incident doesn't scare you at all? You must be made of concrete."

"I'm scared and not scared at the same time," said Sumaa. "But what's the use? Scared or not, we'll still have to go back to the tunnels unless we decide to quit and abandon the quest."

Mila turned his back on him. That type of talk wasn't what we wanted to hear. Although there was truth in it, it was very depressing, especially for me. Considering that my father, the great witch doctor and fortune teller of Simbaru, had seen danger in my dream, my fears weren't unfounded. It was alarming that my life could be in danger. My father was seldom wrong. I decided to try to change the topic. "Where's Sahr?" I asked.

"He must be in his room," said Boima. "You know, Sahr supervised the whole rescue and recovery attempt. You could see that he was extremely touched by the tragedy."

"I saw him wipe tears from his eyes when he thought no one was looking," said Sumaa. "The man is not as tough as he makes out to be," he concluded sympathetically.

"Mila and I will go to see him now," I said, beckoning to Mila to come with me. Obviously, I'd failed to divert attention away from the tragedy. I'd set myself a tall order. I wondered, *Who in his right senses could ignore such a tragedy?* It was wishful thinking, and I felt ashamed. The disaster would be the town's hottest topic unless something more spectacular or tragic happened during the interim.

Sahr appeared to be asleep on his prized red sofa. The plush sofa accommodated all of his large frame. He stirred when he sensed people were in the room with him. "Have you heard the terrible news?" he asked as soon as he recognised us.

"Sumaa and Boima just told us," said Mila. "It's very sad news."

"It is very sad business," said Sahr as he readjusted his lanky frame into a sitting position. "Some of the dead were just your age. They were too young to die. What a waste!"

"Indeed, it's quite a waste," I agreed. "I can't help thinking that it could've been us. I mean, we are exposed to the same risks night after night."

"Do you think so too, Mila?" Sahr asked quietly.

"Yes, I do," answered Mila flatly. "I have to say, I'm really worried now."

"Don't tell me you boys are afraid," said Sahr, "Because if you are, you're definitely in the wrong profession."

Sahr gestured for us to sit down. We did so and waited for him to start talking. He remained silent a little longer, and then he began to speak. "Listen carefully to what I have to say to you," he said. "I'm forty-six years old, and I've been in the mining trade since I was thirteen." He sighed and rubbed his left palm over his shiny, shaved head. Before now, we didn't know Sahr's age or how long he had been involved in mining. Thirty-three years was a long time to mine with nothing substantial to show for it. No wonder he got so bitter at times.

"Within this period," Sahr continued, "I have directly or indirectly witnessed hundreds of cave-ins. I've seen many hopeful, young men lose their lives or become permanently injured, but I'm still here. I'm alive and not permanently disfigured. I've seen many friends die before my own eyes, and believe me, it hurts. It makes you ask questions and re-examine yourself. I mined in tunnels for over twenty years before I became a gang master, so I know the risks. I don't blame you if you worry or fear for your safety. As a veteran, I can tell you that a miner's survival depends upon three things: God, hope, and luck. Let me ask you something. Do you believe in God, hope, and luck?"

"We do believe in all three, but this tragedy has been too much for us," I said.

"I know that, too," said Sahr. He cleared his throat and continued: "When you decided to travel to Kono to mine diamonds, to get rich, you depended upon God, hope, and luck. So far, God hasn't let you down. You've been lucky to earn substantial sums of money, and you hope to earn more. Who or what do you think has seen you through all this?" he asked.

Without hesitation, we both answered: "God." We believed in God; He had always been part of our lives and would continue to be part of our lives. In Simbaru, the existence and power of God was instilled into children as soon as they demonstrated that they could understand. After that, worship became obligatory; otherwise, one would anger the head of the house, normally the father.

"You're damn right," said Sahr. "God takes care of you every day. He knows when, how, and where you'll die. When He calls you to meet Him, you don't have a choice. You'll have to go. God has called the eleven that died in the tunnels. Their time arrived, they died. People die everywhere, and you don't always have the pleasure of choosing how, when, and where. I just want to say to you that your faith must not waver. While you were in Koidu, a car could've killed you, but it didn't happen. Why? Because your time hasn't arrived yet. Try to believe that your time hasn't arrived yet. Depend upon luck to get what you desire, and leave your protection to God. So there really is no reason to be afraid. Whether you fear or not, when the time arrives, you die. Go think about what I've said to you. Maybe it will help you overcome your fears. Remember, no one is forcing you to do anything. You may leave now. Goodnight. Incidentally, we start work again tomorrow night. Be ready to leave with the gang if you decide to continue mining."

Somehow, Sahr made us feel less scared. We decided to think about things just as he'd suggested. There was no one on the veranda when we emerged from Sahr's room. I'd intended to laze around in the hammocks and hoped that Mila wanted to do that, too. However, with no one on the veranda, we decided to go straight to bed instead. We carefully arranged our sleeping mats and curled up under our covering cloths to keep the cold and mosquitoes out. Before long, we were fast asleep. It was as if we had never been upset or worried.

51

We returned to the mines a couple of days after the disaster as boisterous, hopeful miners despite the fatal cave-ins in the tunnels. It was as if the cave-ins never happened. We attended to our chores as we talked and argued. Nevertheless, it was impossible not to notice the apprehension under the bravado we pretended to exhibit. I was full of anxiety at the thought of going into the tunnels again. And I suspected the others were worried, too.

The tragedy made us realise that we were pawns in the cruel mining game. It was possible that a similar calamity could befall any of us at any time. Regardless, there we were, excavating tons of heavy, moist gravel from the bowels of the earth. It was a chilling, sobering thought, and it frightened me. I felt a cold tingle at the base of my spine as Suma's words came echoed in my head: "Give it a few days. Every miner will be back in the tunnel pits, dangerous or not, as if nothing had happened. We are lured by greed and the hope of striking it rich."

How correct and poignant his words proved to be! I mused, *Have we really been enticed by sheer greed to be in this life-consuming place? Just for the prospect of striking it rich and living luxurious lives?* I wondered long and hard, yet I couldn't come up with the right answers. However, I understood that life had to go on regardless of anything. The dead were already dead and could do nothing profitable in the land of the living. The only thing the dead could do was appear as apparitions to scare those who believed in ghosts. The living, by contrast, still had lives to live. I was part of the living; I was alive and wanted to keep it that way.

Suddenly, the urge to abandon diamond mining overcame me. It was as strong as my compulsion to return to Simbaru as soon as possible. I yearned to be among my kinsmen, to live with my relatives once again, to enjoy the idyllic village life devoid of sudden deaths in godforsaken pits. The urge to go back home didn't beleaguer me for long; the drenching rain and the constant digging in the tunnels didn't allow it to.

It had been exactly two weeks since we returned to work in the fields after the catastrophic loss of lives in the tunnel pits. The rains fell heavily, almost infinitely, despite the fact that there were only a few weeks left in the season. Regardless, gangs indulged in the hard, dirty work with great enthusiasm, especially as word went round that the precious stones were materialising in every sack of excavated gravel. That meant that the site had transformed into a spot, a place abundant in diamonds.

Infectious, exceptionally happy grins suddenly gripped us. We went in and out of the crude, weak tunnel pits, retrieving as much gravel as we could. We knew that a spot translated into money in our pockets. It also meant that greed overcame reasoning. Safety precautions lapsed and accidents happened.

Awareness that the tunnels were repaying us with more diamonds than before encouraged us to work longer hours, to take unnecessary risks, to dig further into the bowels of the earth without erecting appropriate supports for the heavy earth above us. "Deeper is where the diamonds are" became the popular maxim in both the fields and the village. Consequently, all gangs burrowed deeper into the earth. The more diamonds we recovered, the deeper we dared to go. And the deeper we went, the more we exposed ourselves to risk.

Our boss and protector, Sahr, was a highly cautious man. Yet he was exceedingly excited about the gems we were pulling from the tunnel pits. He encouraged us to go deeper. He, too, had thrown caution to the wind. It seemed that only the gems mattered; not only to him, but to all of us. Everything else became secondary. And when Fridays and we got our money, no one seemed to think about the potential dangers in the tunnels. Our thoughts were focussed only on money.

Mila and I continued to make weekly trips to buzzing Koidu, and on each trip, we added to the growing pile of money that Mother was keeping for us. We knew we could buy anything we desired, from common commodities to rarray girls. It was no wonder that we believed the pleasures we derived from having money somehow compensated us for our risks. On the trips to see Mother, Mila and I filled her room with our purchases. We were preparing for our return to Simbaru. She was concerned that we were buying far more than we needed and voiced her feelings. "You really must stop your buying spree now," she complained whenever we returned to the eating house laden with plastic bags full of goods. "Don't you think you've bought enough? At this rate, you will be taking the entire Koidu market to your village!"

"This is our last shopping," we replied to pacify her and allay her worries.

"That's exactly what you said last week," she reminded us, giving the impression she was cross. Actually, she maintained a benign smile on her lovely face.

"And look where we are now," she continued, "still shopping." She abruptly left the room then, unsuccessfully feigning anger. Mila and I were bemused, and we sheepishly smiled at each other.

Mama Finda was a wonderful woman, and in her own way, she was very pretty. She was still of childbearing age. It was possible, she would have a child of her very own one day. Such a child would be extremely lucky to have her as a parent. She had demonstrated to us, her adopted children, how loving, caring, and unselfish she could be. She had taken us under her wing from day one. The woman was so instrumental in our lives that I occasionally believed she was my real mother. It was safe to assume, judging by his disposition around her, that Mila considered felt the same way. We would definitely miss her when we returned to Simbaru. And I knew she would miss us.

Back at the mines, the pits became deeper. We were rightly convinced that the precious stones would be in every load of soil that we removed from the bowels of the earth. Everyone had smug smiles on their faces. Everybody was happy. Some miners were willing to work day and night to make more money. Never had I seen so many diamonds in such a short period of time. I reckoned there wasn't a gang that couldn't boast of handling at least a hundred gems from each night's work.

By that point, news of the discovery in the Yengema fields had spread to the surrounding villages, as far as Koidu town. Yengema was a rich town, and as was the case with every rich town, people came to try their luck in every conceivable way. Freelance miners who had no respect for ownership, protocols, or authority invaded the little town and mined wherever they thought fit. They were hard men; roughnecks few people bothered to confront directly. They revelled in their status, and trouble followed them wherever they went.

Starry-eyed yullamen dressed in flamboyant clothing, including our very own Mr K, appeared every morning to buy the glittering stones from the various gangs that they supported. Hawkers selling everything from food to mining equipment also arrived; they were guaranteed in the knowledge that they would make even more money than usual selling their overpriced goods.

Bawdy, rowdy career prostitutes (most missing teeth from rough and violent living) also found the rich town suitable for their flesh trade. They knew from experience that they would make good money before the spot was exhausted. Men (miners particularly) always wanted women, especially when their pockets were full of money.

The little town was overcrowded in no time. People rented every available sleeping place in the village. Even the courthouse and the mosque could not escape the influx of people pouring into the town. They bunked in those buildings during the night, but they woke up at dawn to allow the buildings to function. Sahr also cashed in on the influx of people: he charged the new arrivals to sleep in the hammocks on his big veranda and in his huge parlour. There were hardly any additional accommodations left; yet more people arrived every day, hopeful to earn significant chunks of money while the spot remained prosperous. Rickety, makeshift shacks of sticks and mud with thatched roofs quickly became part of the panorama of the village. Property owners were just trying to make some easy money.

The NDMC security personnel, the Joe Khakis, came, too, but only as far as the mining fields. They increase the number of raids, rigidly determined to earn as much money as possible.

And thieves came, too. They stole everything from food in the village and farms to gravel in the fields. With Mr K in town buying our diamonds every morning, Mila and I had considerable sums of money in our possession before each Friday. We worried about the money until it was safely in the hands of Mother in Koidu. Stealing cash became rampant among the miners and hustlers. With Sandivah gone, we had no other trustworthy people in the village to keep our cash for us. We had seen grossly dishonest people cheat others out of their hard-earned cash through deceit and other scams.

For Mila and me, Sandivah was the only trustworthy banker in town. Sandivah had proved to be reliable and honest; she wasn't a cheat, even though she was poor. Once she went to live with her parents to have the baby, we had no desire to seek out another banker in the village.

Consequently, we kept our money with us at all times, deep inside our trouser pockets, securely wrapped in waterproof material to protect it from the rain or the water in the tunnels. For us (and scores of other miners), our bodies were the safest places to keep money. Even when we slept, we kept money on our bodies, putting it down our trousers, right over our groins. To make sure the money was harder to get to, we zipped or buttoned up our trousers properly and firmly drew a belt around our waists. Unless one slept like a dead man or was asininely drunk, it was impossible for anyone to get at it.

52

The projected time for our return to Simbaru drew closer, but the rains refused to make way for the dry season. It was raining as if the rainy season had just begun, but the month of November, which officially heralded the beginning of the dry season, was almost upon us. Dark, cloudy skies returned, and the music of thunder and lightning became a regular occurrence. Heavy and sometimes torrential rainfall drenched the village and the mining fields almost every day and night. It was odd. It seemed the weather would continue until Christmas.

Nevertheless, even the nature of the rains didn't deter people from going about their daily chores. They knew there was money to earn, and everyone wanted a share of it. Men and women happily moved around in their wet clothes that clung to their bodies and revealed nearly perfect silhouettes of their bodies.

Women in their wet, thin Lappas drew several lewd comments from the men because their clothes revealed more than they bargained for. The men could see perfect silhouettes of boobs, pubic areas, vaginas, and backsides. The women loved the attention, and they revelled in it when they realised they were still attractive to other men, even younger men.

Mila, Sumaa, and I—like other men—made it a habit to sit on Sahr's big veranda just to gawk and whistle at the women in their wet clothes.

"Look at that one with the massive bum," Mila might say. "I could do a lot with that. See how her bubble ass judders? And the groove . . . it's so big my sideways palm could pass right through it without touching the cheeks."

"That one must have a very fleshy vagina," another man might say, pointing out a passing woman. "I can bet my life on it. It's plainly there for all to see. Look at the swollen mound under her clothes. She shouldn't have bothered to put clothes on. It's as if she were stark naked. God, to think what I could do with that right now almost makes me swoon."

We uttered comments like those on a regular basis because it rained daily. The daily spectacle of the sexy, wet women made me think frequently of Sandivah, and I yearned for her sensual warmth and affection. However, thinking about Sandivah also made me think of the child. Sahr had shared the good news with us one morning that Sandivah had given him a son, a child that was biologically mine. The realisation left me numb whenever I thought about it. I thought, *Who wouldn't want to have his own offspring?* Having children was testimony that one was a real man, a virile, functioning man. I had proved my manhood with the wrong woman, and it would likely remain a secret forever. I wanted to shout from the top of a roof that I had a child, my first child, but I couldn't. It would only make matters worse. Sahr would pounce on the opportunity to sue me. He would try to take me for every penny I possessed. He would even make me pay back his court expenditures and the fines and the money needed for the sacrifice. It would be pointless to try anything.

Nevertheless, I resolved that, no matter what happened, I would play some part in the child's life, albeit secretly. I would clandestinely visit Sandivah so that I could give her some money to take care of *our* baby before I returned to Simbaru. I mentally noted that I would discuss the idea with Mila.

While we leered at wet women during the day, many miners, most of them immigrants, were at work in the tunnels. Mining became a constant activity, regardless of the frequent raids. However, before long, even the raids dwindled. The Joe Khakis elected to mine the precious stones for themselves. They knew they would make more money that way than by accepting paltry bribes. Of course, that arrangement only worked due to a mutual agreement between the yullamen and the security men. Both parties recognised that the Joe Khakis needed to show they were making arrests for the benefit of their NDMC employers. Consequently, they took several miners to Tankoro every day, but all of them returned to Yengema before dawn without the need for bribery.

With such a surge in the mining population, it was inevitable for mudslides and cave-ins to ensue. It was only a matter of time. Already, there had been reports of several mudslides and cave-ins that had severely injured miners. Even that news didn't damp the enthusiasm and hope of the miners; excavations went on as usual. Every stroke of the Konkordu, every shovel of earth removed, increased the risks for the miners. However, the hope of striking it rich overshadowed the risks. They reckoned that God would protect them. Most of them fervently believed in God, the omnipotent, omniscient, and only deity. The miners were ready to accept whatever fate God had in store for them.

It was very difficult to have a private conversation in Sahr's big parlour without being overheard by someone. The space was overcrowded at every moment. People were constantly waking up to go to work and coming back to catch some sleep. Of course, the din of snoring, talking, laughing, and farting was nearly deafening.

"I can't hear you properly," said Mila, indicating the same with rapid finger circles close to his right ear lobe. "This place is like a marketplace," he complained.

I was asking him what he thought about my intention to visit Sandivah before we left. I gestured to him that we should go outside. I took the lead and Mila followed. As usual, there was a great downpour outside. The veranda was packed with people. We managed to get to one of the far corners and stood facing each other. "I was saying I intend to pay Sandivah a visit before we leave. What do you think?"

"Are you mad? What for?" asked a surprised Mila.

A few heads turned in our direction indicating that Mila had spoken a little too loudly.

"Keep your voice down," I whispered hoarsely. "If I wanted everyone to know my business, I would've been shouting it from the rooftops. Anyway, she has my child."

"Your child?" said Mila almost disdainfully. I knew he didn't mean to scorn me, though. "That isn't your child, my brother. You illegally sowed in another man's farm, watered another man's garden. You have no claims to the harvest. It's as simple as that. Unless you want your pocket cleaned out by Sahr, you shouldn't go near Sandivah."

"I have no intention of claiming the child," I said in defence. "I just feel that I ought to give her some money to take care of the boy. I may not be his legal father, but I know I am his biological father. Sandivah said so herself, and I believe her. I have no reason not to believe her; Sahr was performing Kattacha when Sandivah conceived. And above all, he took his wife to court and publicly declared that he didn't make Sandivah pregnant."

"If I were you, I wouldn't visit Sandivah. Suppose you find Sahr in her village when you visit her? He may put two and two together; you may end up in court for fornicating with his wife."

"I just want to go see the boy and provide some money for his upkeep," I said.

"Sahr's the boy's father in the eyes of traditional law. Let him pay for his own child's upkeep. After all, we are all in the money now." Mila wasn't giving up easily.

"I owe it to Sandivah and the boy," I said firmly. "My mind's made up. I will go and see Sandivah. I wouldn't feel good if I couldn't see them before I left. Besides, we don't know if we'll ever return to this place. You see, I have to see them. I really don't believe I have a choice."

Mila finally relented and agreed to go with me, but he couldn't hold back his opinion about the trip. "I still think it's a bad idea, that we might run into trouble."

"You worry too much," I said, patting his broad back in assurance as we started to vacate the veranda. "It will be fine. Trust me."

The visit proved to be fine. It was on a Thursday morning when Mila and I set out on foot to Sandivah's village. A light, intermittent rainfall forced us to open and close our umbrellas several times before we arrived. It was also on that day that Sahr chose to travel to Koidu to replenish food supplies and tools. It seemed that my guardian angel was awake and looking down on me favourably. With Sahr gone to Koidu, there was no way our paths would cross in Sandivah's village, which wasn't very far away.

By midday, we'd arrived. Our first impression was that the village was deserted. Eventually, we saw a few lazing geriatrics on the verandas of some of the huts. We also saw children playing in the dust under a big orange tree laden with fruit. We saw a few chickens taking leisurely dust baths, and a few more scratched the ground with strong claws. The chickens seemed to ignore the playing children as if they weren't there in the first place, and they only ran a couple of feet if the kids got too close. An old woman with white, woolly hair pointed us in the direction of Sandivah's house, but it took some time to coax the information out of her because she was partially deaf.

We found her in a detached kitchen with a thatched roof. She was pounding rice grains into flour in a big mortar coated with dark grime from years of use and neglect. A child I strongly suspected was mine was strapped to her back. The child bobbed up and down as she pounded with the stout, heavy, carved stick she was using as a pestle. In his hand was a cob of boiled corn, and he was gnawing on it and cooing happily as if wanted to convey to his mum that he was enjoying his meal. When she noticed us, she stopped pounding but kept the pestle in the mortar with one hand. She stood transfixed, her other hand clasped over her mouth in surprise. She was staring at us as if we were ghosts. Nevertheless, those same eyes happily told us that she was thrilled to see us. She couldn't quite believe we'd come to see her—or more precisely, that I'd come to see her. She took her hand away from her mouth and gave us a sweet smile before removing the pestle from the mortar. She carefully leaned the stick against the mud wall of the kitchen.

"What are you doing here?" she asked with the attitude of one overtly pleased to see an old friend. "Please, let's go to the veranda. I never thought that you'd—"

"Come to see you?" I interrupted. "You thought wrong, then. Here we are."

She didn't respond. Instead, she led us onto the veranda of the main house. A couple of long logs lined the wall of the veranda. After we sat down, she took two small calabash containers, scooped water from a big, black pot, and served us the cool liquid. It was only after we drank that she resumed talking.

"Where's Sahr?" she asked with a little shake in her voice. "Does he know you're here?"

"Daft question, Sandivah," said Mila with a guttural laugh. "Are you kidding? We can't afford for Sahr to get a whiff of our visit to this village."

"I know," said Sandivah. "I'm very happy that you are here, though."

Mila knew the lovers wanted to talk, and he decided to give them some space. He stood up and vacated the veranda before either of us could protest. In his wake, he said, "I'll just explore the village, maybe talk to some of the old crones. You won't miss me."

Sandivah and I looked at each other, shrugged, and let Mila go without objection. I shouted after him that he shouldn't be gone long. He acknowledged that he heard me by waving his hand over his head.

Sandivah stood up and came closer. "You still haven't told me the whereabouts of Sahr. Where is he?"

"He's in Koidu, shopping for food and tools," I said. "Where're your parents and your other children?"

"They are all on the farm. Everybody in this village, except for the geriatrics and the very young go to the farms. In this household, it's just Joe and me, until they return at dusk or much later."

"Who's Joe," I asked. I was alarmed and stood up. I thought Joe might be a hostile relative who would tell Sahr about our visit. That would be a disaster. It would be hard to explain our presence in the village given the fact that I believed Sahr knew about us.

Obviously amused by my inquiry and reaction, Sandivah laughed. As she did, she revealed a set of clean, white teeth. It was one of the attributes that drew me to her amorous heart in the first place. When her melodious laughter stopped, she said, "Haven't you guessed yet? Joe's right on my back. He is your son. I named him after your father." She fumbled with a knot on the Lappa that held the child and transferred him adroitly from her back to her hands without much effort.

I stared at her, speechless. The revelation left me emotional. My feet nearly buckled under me; somehow, I managed to stay up. Although I'd suspected that it was my son on her back, I wasn't prepared for the bluntness of her revelation. I was thrilled but equally sad. I was thrilled that I had proved I was a real man, but I was sad that I would never publicly claim the boy. Nevertheless, the sadness didn't dampen my spirit. I was eager to see the boy properly, eager to hold him in my hands, even if I never held him again. I was excited to hear his cries and feel his little, warm body throb against mine. I couldn't wait to hear his little whimpers and feel his tiny heartbeat on my chest.

"Don't you want to hold him?" Sandivah asked, handing the child over to me. He was still gnawing at the boiled corn.

I held the child gingerly, afraid that that I would break his bones; he was so small and tender. I stared at his face for a few moments and felt so proud that I was holding my own offspring in my hands. Tears of joy trickled down both my cheeks. Sandivah saw my tears but elected not to comment. Instead, she lectured me on how to hold the child properly. "Relax and hold him comfortably," advised Sandivah.

"He won't break in two." She smiled and helped me hold the child properly. "See? He's got your nose and eyes."

I'd never actually had a close look at my nose and eyes, so I couldn't quite see the resemblance she was referring to. But I didn't care about that when I had a creation of mine—of ours—in my hands. He was eating and gurgling and smiling contentedly as if he knew he were in his father's hands. I just murmured in agreement. Because I was afraid that I might drop the child due to my excitement, I decided to sit down.

Sandivah sat close to me. "I thought I'd never see you again," she said. "I thought that you'd forgotten about me and didn't care about the child you put inside me. Not a day passed without me thinking about you, Yandi.

"I am here now," I said, ruffling her neatly plaited hair with my free hand. I always wanted to come, but I was afraid of Sahr and your parents."

"My parents?" she asked in disbelief. "What do my parents have to do with it? They don't even know you. Why should you be afraid of them? Besides, even if they knew you were my lover, they'd never tell on their own daughter. You've nothing to fear from them." She looked at the child that I held close to my chest. "Joe's asleep; he must love you carrying him. I'd better put him to bed."

Minutes later, she called me into her room. The boy was sleeping on a mat at the foot of a clumsy affair that passed for a bed. She gestured for me to sit on the bed. She sat down close by, and her nimble hands loitered near my crotch.

"We mustn't—" I began.

She put one finger on her lips to tell me she didn't want to talk. She stood up, and with a simple movement of her hand, she stood stark naked before me. "Would you rather talk or have this?" she asked, pointing to her bushy crotch. She turned her body around provocatively so that I could see what I was missing. I didn't need a second invitation. By the time I had my clothes off, I was as hard as a concrete brick.

Afterward, with both of us fully clothed again and the child still enjoying a deep sleep, we talked. "But why do you have to go," she asked, refusing to understand that I needed to go back to Simbaru to see my folks.

"I have already told you: I need to see my folks. It's been several years since I left. You know my story. My mum and dad don't even know that I am alive. I want to end their torment. I want them to know that I am alive. I must go Sandivah; but trust me, I'll be back."

"I don't like this one bit," she said. "You must swear that you will come back to me and our son."

"Of course I will come back. I swear by Allah that I will be back." That seemed to placate her anxieties.

"I believe you, my strong, sexy man, but I will kill you if you run after the girls in your village," she said, feigning jealousy.

"What girls? There are no girls in my village, only women," I said and laughed.

"Just try it and you'll see," she threatened.

"I won't. Why would I do that when I have a sexy beauty waiting here for me?" To change the topic, I added: "I have something for you."

"What's it?" she demanded.

I put my hands in my pocket and removed a big wad of notes. The money was my share for the week. I tried to give it to her, but she recoiled from my outstretched hand as if I'd shown her a spitting cobra. At the same time, she waved half-raised hands in front of her face to indicate that she couldn't accept it.

"I can't take it," she said. "It's a lot of money. I've never had that kind of money. No one has ever given me that much money. No, I won't take it."

"You have to take it," I insisted. "I'll be leaving you and my baby very soon. I want to help as much as I can to care for him. The money is for you and the boy. I know Sahr never gives you enough money for anything. This will come in handy."

"But I can't take it," she persisted. "You must take the money with you; it will help your parents better."

"I have more than enough to make them happy," I said calmly. "Please take it, at least for the child. I'll be going on a journey. One never really knows what happens during a journey. I don't know what's waiting for me back home. You must take the money."

"Nothing will happen to you," she countered. "You'll go and come back to us whole. You'll suffer no mishap. Remember, you've already promised to come back to Joe and me."

"It was just talk. I know nothing will happen to me," I agreed, "but you must take the money." I extended my hands towards her once again.

Sandivah stood there for a moment, still hesitating to take the money. She looked directly into my eyes, and I saw gratitude and admiration. At last, she sighed and took the money from me. "Since you insist, we'll take it. You are a kind man, and I'll always tell our son about his true father," she said. She raised the grass mattress on her bed and hid the money within the folds of clothes underneath.

"I am very happy that you took the money. It'll come in handy. Don't waste it; Sahr will not be giving you much. Now that he has money, he believes it's the best time for him to marry. He's preparing to marry his betrothed, Martha. You know he has been promising for years. He says the right time is now. You'll soon be four wives in total if the extras are not counted."

"I don't care," Sandivah said with conviction. "I have you, and that's all the more reason that you must come back to us. Besides, an additional wife for Sahr will be good for us: we'll spend even more time together." She clasped me in a tight embrace and continued to talk. "Mila's out in the village. No one's home. The baby's quietly sleeping, and you are going away soon," she said hoarsely. "Don't you think you owe me a thorough goodbye? The first time wasn't enough."

Without saying a word, I swept her off her feet and put her on the bed carefully. In a moment, she rolled out of her cotton Lappa. I was in a frenzy to take off my clothes, and I was getting harder and stronger with each item I took off. I was almost consumed by an animal lust. I took her roughly. I pounded strong and deep into her willing pussy, and she cried out my name in response to the raw pleasure. Eventually, our sex juices mingled, creating an explosion so sweet and tender that I thought I'd died and gone to heaven.

We remained in the bed. We were both exhausted, but we still held hands to allow the last lovemaking currents to pass through our bodies while we smiled at each other. A short while later, we got up to put on our clothes. We noticed that Joe had woken up. That was not surprising given all that shouting. He was lying on his back, playing silently. I took the child in my hands, and we all went outside.

Mila was waiting for us on a log on the veranda. "I could hear your cries while you were at it," he said with a knowing grin. Sandivah covered her face with her hands in embarrassment. "The smell of sex is overpowering on you two. Lucky for you, it was old Mila and not someone who had sympathy for Sahr. It would not have gone well. It's goodbye time for you now, lovebirds. Yandi and I must be getting back to Yengema. We've been lucky so far; you never know who could be popping up here. Besides, it's back to the tunnels tonight.

After a very tearful goodbye, Mila and I began the homeward walk. Again, we had to trek in the rain with only our flimsy umbrellas to keep us dry. I wondered whether I'd ever see Sandivah and my son again. It was all in the hands of destiny. I left it at that, but I was very pleased that we'd made the visit, especially because I was able to hold the seed of my loin for the first time.

53

It was unbelievable the way Yengema had changed just weeks after the discovery of the spot. The population explosion became a huge challenge for the chief and elders in terms of executing law and order in the village. Regardless, strangers arrived every day. There were three times as many strangers in the village as there were residents. There were very few elders to oversee the law and dispense appropriate punishments. Thus, the town more or less ran itself.

Yengema suddenly became a rich, bustling, vibrant town, but it also paid a big price for that success. The excessive influx of people with different traditions, customs, and dispositions triggered a series of unwelcome events in the village. It still rained every day, so it was difficult to undertake construction work to house all the newcomers. Nevertheless, the bushes around the village were hastily cleared and haphazardly developed by hopeful landowners expecting huge rents. They provided the much-needed accommodations for some of the new population, but many more slept anywhere they reckoned they could get sleep. Some people slept in the undeveloped bushes, in empty farm shacks, and in other makeshift shelters.

Overnight, no one needed to travel to Koidu to buy anything. Traders dealing in everything from foodstuffs to mining essentials sprouted up all over town. They sold goods at three or four times the price that one would pay in Koidu. As if that weren't enough, hawkers went around the town harassing people to buy their low-quality stuff. Nevertheless, people didn't mind; the town was rich. Almost everyone, including women and children, had money to spend.

With a multitude of single men present in one location, it was only right for there to be enough women to entertain them. Indeed, there was no shortage of women: prostitutes continued to invade the town with the hope of making money by selling their bodies. Competition was fierce among them, even though they were often friends. Frequent brawls erupted over especially generous clients. Sex was all around the village. The invading prostitutes made sure they did everything to lure the men, and they were ready to drop their pants in any place that was out of the public's view. It wasn't unusual to see men and women going into and coming out of the bushes and latrines together.

Surreptitious drinking parlours established by opportunists plied their trade unhindered, despite the fact that the town was predominantly Muslim. Men and women smoked everything that could be smoked and drank everything with alcohol in it. Many abused their drinks, annoyed others, and got into drunken fights that resulted in serious injuries and a few fatalities. It was stupefying to watch the drunks around the village. Most were too drunk to notice their alcohol-or drug-fuelled behaviours. Their filthiness compromised the daily norms of the residents. Some people in Yengema indulged in alcohol and drugs before the discovery of the spot, but they did so in secret because they didn't want the rest of the residents to know about their vices. Thankfully, no one paid attention to the new breeds for long, except bored kids and rarray girls. The kids craving excitement taunted the drunks to provoke a chase, and the rarray girls tried to rob them of their money once they had them on their own.

With so much money going around, gambling was rampant. Pockets of people gambled day and night in different locations. Professional gamblers, most of them rugged characters, were willing to relieve foolish, greedy miners of their money. The rogues even created impromptu credit facilities with 100 per cent or higher interest rates to encourage losers to borrow more cash to go after their losses. When losers couldn't afford to burrow, they were encouraged to sell their belongings at considerably reduced prices in order to rejoin the games. If they won, they had the right to buy their property back at inflated prices. If they lost again, they tried to borrow more money, sell more of their belongings, or steal the money. If they couldn't do any of that, they returned to the fields to dig for more diamonds that they would exchange for money.

Filthiness was another price Yengema paid for its diamond success. Filth was everywhere. It was in and around the houses, the square, and the nearby river. People threw rubbish about haphazardly. Slowly but surely, the volume increased. The rain became a catalyst for their rapid decay, and it helped them release their pungent odours.

The few latrines in the village couldn't cope with so many people. Some were already full or on the brink of being full. People had to find alternative latrines, and the nearby bushes became an open toilet.

Some people even defecated close to houses if they could get away with it. It was not surprising to see big mounds of feces around town in the mornings. With the rains still pouring, such sightings were disgusting. Very few people bothered to clear the mess, even if it was near their house. They hoped that the rain would clear the filth, which it sometimes did. It was even more disgusting if one stepped foot in the feces; one would smell like a latrine, and one's mates would have a field day.

Even the small river near the village used for drinking and cooking was polluted with feces and rubbish. Before long, the unmistakable stench of human waste overwhelmed the town. The extremely dreadful odour forced most people to pinch their noses in order to minimise the smell as they went about their daily business.

Nevertheless, life continued in the village. In the eyes of the people, the merits of the spot to Yengema far outweighed the demerits. Smelling unpleasant odours was nothing compared to everyone making money.

If the town was overcrowded, unruly, and filthy, the mining fields fared even worse: they were muddy and chaotic. Hundreds of miners covered from head to toe in mud did everything in the mining process at the same time. The pouring rain helped to wash some of the filth off their bodies, but the soft and squishy mud under their feet covered them up again. It was impossible to avoid crashing into someone. People were constantly on the move from one point to the other, and they were ready to correct careless miners if they left their gravel or set of tools unattended.

There were no real toilets in the fields. The surrounding bushes and the long elephant grass became a massive toilet. The acidic smell of urine, accompanied by the smell of stale and fresh excrement were the first odours to grace the nose from as far as five hundred yards away. Men had to dodge mounds of decaying feces all the way to the tunnels. However, no matter how careful the men were, bad luck normally kicked in. Somehow, they would miss a step or two and plant a foot in a disgusting, smelly mound of feces. Even so, it didn't really bother the miners. They knew it was worth stepping in gigantic mounds of anything for what they expected to get in return.

Before the spot, everyone adhered to the unwritten rules, organisation, and order in the fields, but the influx of so many people changed all that. Overnight, loyalty and order disappeared. Such virtues were instantly replaced by selfishness and greed. Anyone could do anything and get away with it. People could dig and retrieve gravel from anywhere in the tunnels or fields. When it started, a few of the original gang members still working in the tunnels opposed the practise and fought to keep what they considered was rightfully theirs. Consequently, people fought over everything. They fought over tools, over where to mine, and over the water used to wash the gravel. Even down in the narrow tunnels, men quarrelled and fought, sometimes causing the fragile, weakly supported structures to collapse, which inflicted serious injuries on many. Nevertheless, after numerous unnecessary fights, some of which were nearly fatal, the miners realised there was enough for everybody. They opted to concentrate their efforts on getting the precious stones out of the earth.

Even the old law prohibiting diamond theft seemed absent. The Gaandoe hadn't been used since Samuka was tortured and murdered on it. The advent of the spot changed the way the miners looked at the Gaandoe. The Gaandoe was not a deterrent against theft. Miners stole gems without hiding that fact. There was no way to police the men; it would have been a futile endeavour. There were far too many people concentrated in one place. Most of them were freelancers who didn't belong to any gang and refused to obey any regulations. The diamond fields had become an insane work site. Gangs even resorted to taking their tools back to town to protect them against theft.

Mila and I remained loyal to Sahr, as did the rest of the men in our gang. Even when we knew that it paid better to work on our own, we respected the mining traditions. However, many miners opted out of work gangs and succumbed to the fascinating lure of going solo to earn more money. We still worked as a team in the tunnels and stuck to our dusk-to-dawn shifts. The only difference was that no tunnel belonged to anyone anymore.

"This place is full of diamonds," said Mila, as if it were news to me. We were soaking wet in the relentless shower, kicking gravel, picking out several gems in various colours and sizes from our overused shakers. "I wish we weren't leaving for home soon," he continued. "We could stay for another month and earn more money. What do you think?"

"I'm determined to go home," I said quietly. "We already have more money than we ever dreamed of. For me, our return is long overdue. I am determined to leave in two weeks' time, just as we agreed."

"I was only kidding," Mila said with a laugh. "Even if we wanted to stay, it would be impossible. Mama Finda would search sky, land, and sea to find us and send us home."

"There you are, then," I encouraged him. "We don't need more money. What we need is love and a sense of belonging among our own people, our kinsmen."

If it were up to Mama Finda, we would've been in Simbaru already. She'd tried to convince us to leave before the end of the rainy season. "The spot had earned you a lot of money," she'd said solemnly on one of our Friday visits. "Take it and go back to your parents. I'm sure they've been very worried all the time you've been away. Going back now as rich men will do them proud and make them very happy. To your folks, it will be like you've been born again. It will be like their sons have returned from the cold, hard grip of death. You must go home."

We promised her that we would go in two weeks' time, when the rainy season was officially over. We told her that we'd promised Sahr to stay until the end of the rains, and we expected to honour that vow. We told her that another two weeks of work would add several thousand leones to our growing money pile, that the money would come in handy to help the people of our village.

She'd settled for the counterargument, but she insisted that she would arrange for a chartered transport to take us to Simbaru when we were ready. She reckoned that, with all the things and the considerable sums of money we would be travelling with, it would be more convenient and safe for us. We didn't argue with her. Mila and I liked the idea of two missing or presumed dead youths returning as rich men in grand style to the village from which they'd unceremoniously absconded. For me, it had a nice ring to it.

"Nothing surpasses the pleasure of a rich man being among his own people," Mila agreed, "except sex, maybe."

I laughed, relieved that our schedule to leave in a fortnight was still on. We continued kicking gravel until it was our turn to excavate gravel from the tunnels again. Sumaa and Boima joined us below the poorly lit tunnels. The unyielding rain and vast human traffic to and from the tunnels created heavy, sticky mud that clung to our bodies like a second skin. The moment we went below, we were standing and crawling in a foot of the stuff while we worked. And more sludge fell from the roofs of the tunnels as we worked. The tunnels had always been dangerous, but they were ten times more dangerous because of the rain, overcrowding, and lack of proper safety precautions.

It was nearly impossible to dig with spades or Konkordus. Our hands became the ideal tools to scoop the heavy, soggy mud into buckets. Even then, we only put small quantities of the muddy gravel into the containers for easier transportation above ground. However, instead of passing the buckets from one person to the other as we usually did, we took them up ourselves. That procedure took longer because of the constant collisions with people in the dimly lit tunnels. Some collisions were so severe that they knocked miners down into the slimy mud. Because some people refused to be civil and give way to one another on the way to the top, some men got stuck at the mouths of the tunnels and elsewhere. It was the same scenario every night, but the diamonds kept coming and putting more money into our pockets. Moreover, we trudged back to town every morning to try to get some rest in our huge, communal bedroom that was Sahr's parlour.

Regardless of the continuous din of droning voices, heavy snoring, and smelly farts, we managed to get some sleep whenever we returned from the fields. Besides, we were so tired that our bodies refused to cooperate even if we wanted to stay awake. And so it happened that, while I was having one of those knockout bouts of sleep, I had that dreadful and depressing dream again. It happened in exactly the same sequence as the first time. But there was a horrible twist to it: I didn't have time to muster my strength to put up any resistance. With one huge, hairy hand, the malevolent, grotesque face held me firmly by the throat and raised me up until my feet were dangling off the ground. When my eyes levelled with his, the face grinned in an evil manner. He squeezed my throat, slowly suffocating me, killing me. He kept repeating the following sentence in his ghastly, hideous voice: "This time you are dead—truly dead—just as your father predicted you'd be."

A few people, including Mila, were standing over me when I woke up. As my eyes went from one person to the next, I noticed that they were all looking at me quizzically, probably thinking I was possessed or insane. I didn't say a word. It was not that I didn't want to; rather, the dream had left me so rattled that I couldn't speak. The creature's hand had held me until I saw myself die in his hand. I'd clearly seen him discard my lifeless body on a mound of rubbish.

"It's that dream again, isn't it?" Mila asked.

I nodded. I didn't trust my voice.

"It's no dream," said one of the men towering over me. "He's possessed by evil spirits."

"Shut your big gob," said a young man who was dressed completely in red. "How do you know he's possessed by evil spirits unless you are an evil spirit yourself?" he asked for good measure. Others laughed and rained more scorn on the unfortunate man.

"Come," said Mila, offering me his hand so I could get up. "Let's go somewhere quiet where we can talk. It's only a dream; you shouldn't let it upset you so much."

We walked away from the house and towards the little stream near the village. We found a suitable place to sit under a very leafy tree in a reclusive area on the bank of the stream. The ample leaves protected us a little from the drizzling rain.

"But it was so real," I said. "I saw my own dead body thrown on top of a mound of rubbish."

"Don't be ludicrous, my brother. The dream wasn't real. No dreams are real," Mila said. I knew he was trying to comfort me and allay my uncertainties.

"When I first had the dream in Simbaru, Papa said it meant I would be in great danger. He said I might die. I am starting to believe him now. I just saw my own death played out right in front of me, and you tell me I am being ridiculous. Remember, my father is a fortune teller and witchdoctor, so there must be some substance to his interpretation."

"Maybe so, but what is there to fear now," questioned Mila. "In a few days, we'll be returning home to be with our families and loved ones again. We will leave Yengema and the diamond fields behind us. We will be back in Simbaru. Cheer up and look forward to the joy of meeting your folks."

"I will try to cheer up, but I'm still worried. The dream looked real this time, more than any other time. It really worries me, but just as you've suggested, I'll try to cheer up."

"That's the spirit," Mila said, and he playfully slapped my back as he stood up. "We're getting wet out here. Let's get back to the house. We still need some more rest before we leave for the fields this evening."

54

The dream didn't prey on my mind while in the diamond fields that night. It didn't worry me on subsequent nights, either. If anything, it made me more confident and brave. Suddenly, I didn't believe in all that witch doctor and fortune telling stuff. I felt like a new man. I didn't exactly know why I felt like that, but I became happier and more satisfied. If Mila noticed any change in me, he didn't say so, but he was surely glad to see me the way I was.

Another Friday arrived. We were in Koidu visiting Mother. As usual, we gave her our weekly earnings, but we kept some as spending money for when we went out on the town. Over a meal of cassava and goat soup, Mother updated us about the transportation she'd arranged. "Safia, the taxi driver, agreed to take you right to your village if you give him directions from Kenema," she said.

Over the years, we'd come to know Safia very well. It seemed like yesterday when Mother made him take us back to Yengema. I remember that day well. It was after our first Friday visit to Koidu. I could still see Mother standing in the middle of the road, waving in the wake of Safia's car as it sped away with us. Safia was a nice, funny, chirpy character, and we were glad that Mother had chosen him to take us to Simbaru.

"We agreed on 600 leones," continued Mother. He charged a lot more than that, but I haggled to bring the price down."

I wasn't going to argue. Mother had excellent haggling skills. I would bet all the money I'd earned from mining that she got us the best deal.

"That's a reasonable price," said Mila. "We're happy to pay that. Thank you very much."

"Thank you, Mother," I said. "What would we do without you?"

"You can do fine without me," she said. "Everything is under control now. We've packed your luggage, your money's safe, and your transportation has been arranged; you shouldn't worry about anything. Run along and take a walk in town. You only have a week left before you leave. By this time next Saturday, you will be well on your way to Simbaru. I don't know yet how I will take it."

Mother's advice was good. We left the house and walked along the muddy street towards the town centre and the market. "What do you think we should do first," I asked Mila.

"Hypocrite, as if you don't know what we'll do already," he said. "Come off your horse and stop pretending. I know you enjoy it there."

I laughed. The whorehouse had become a regular stop on every trip we took to Koidu town, mainly because of Clara and Candy. We had become accustomed to having them, and they were so sweet and gentle, always willing to please in every way. Mila was right: I enjoyed being with plump Candy most, but I enjoyed being with skinny Clara, too. It was just that I preferred a little more meat on my women. I'd been with other women in the whorehouse, but none of them came close to the sexual prowess and expertise of Clara and Candy. Maybe that's why I always returned. In fact, sometimes I visited the girls alone and had both of them send me to cloud nine.

"The whorehouse it is, then," I said, still laughing. "Clara and Candy, here we come."

"I'll miss them when we leave," said Mila.

"Liar," I said. "You only think of them when you are on top of them."

"Out of sight, out of mind," said Mila. "And I've been thinking," he continued, "this is the last time we will be with them. Each of us should have both of them together." He smiled mischievously.

"You're a mind reader," I said. "We should do just that, but we should go drink and smoke first. I do better in the sack when I drink and smoke weed."

"You are on," he said. "Clara and Candy won't know what hit them tonight."

We entered the first cannabis parlour. We'd been to that particular one before, and we both liked it. The place was noisy and packed full of young men and a few women. Almost everyone was smoking something. However, the coagulated, musky, sickly smell of djamba overwhelmed all other odours. We stood by the counter and ordered and paid for our drinks. The four small parcels of djamba were included in our order.

"It will take a little while for the parcels to arrive," said Slim, the barman. He winked at us knowingly as he dragged on the huge, glowing wrap of djamba in his mouth. His physical frame left no one in doubt as to how he'd come by his name; he was like a beanpole. But he was a cheerful, talkative beanpole who seemed to enjoy his work.

By the time the djamba arrived, we were already on our second bottles of Star Beer. Within a couple of minutes, we each had glowing cigarettes of the stuff between our lips. We became hooked on the stuff since Tamba first gave us a cannabis cigarette. Mila and I had enjoyed the relaxed and stress-free feeling we derived from the substance. We'd learned to prepare and wrap the cigarettes, and we were experts at the craft. We'd become regular smokers, too, and we smoked two to three marijuana joints every day.

"More beers over here, please," shouted Mila, his voice distinctly audible over the din in the room.

"Coming up at once," Slim shouted back cheerfully.

I don't remember how long we stayed in the bar. We enjoyed our time smoking, drinking, and flirting with the few girls available. It was almost dusk when we left. Mila and I were singing drunkenly as we headed for the whorehouse. I also remember stumbling and falling twice, Mila helped me up on each occasion. We stopped to urinate in the gutters a couple of times, swaying drunkenly and dangerously over the gaping mouth of the deep trenches. By the time we reached the whorehouse, the drizzling rainfall had helped clear our heads.

Regardless of the rain, we found a few girls standing outside with cotton Lappas over their heads for protection. They were trying to cajole the few men in their midst. As we walked towards the brothel, a couple of the girls detached from the group and approached us. They were hoping to find some business.

"We're all ready for you, sweethearts," said one of the girls as she shifted the cotton Lappa to reveal a beautiful face. She twirled around to display a killer figure and a well-rounded bottom.

"Don't waste your time on them," advised a second girl. Apparently, she recognised us as frequent visitors. "They're Clara and Candy's men. They'll only look at you if Clara and Candy aren't around."

"Who said they can't fuck another woman?" asked the girl with the well-rounded bottom. "No man is one woman's man. Isn't that true, hunkies? If you wish, both of you can have me at the same time." She twirled around again, wriggling her ass in such a way that Mila and I instinctively rubbed our crotches.

"See what you'll be getting? And that's only from the outside," she boasted.

I don't know if it was all that drink and djamba, but Clara and Candy evaporated from my thoughts. Mila and I looked at each other, and somehow, our thoughts clicked. I believed he wanted her, too. Besides, Mila and I had never had a girl together. I figured it would be a nice experience. We were tempted.

"Show us to your room, then," said Mila.

"Shall I come, too?" asked the girl who'd recognised us.

"What for?" asked Mila, "You heard your friend: she will service both of us. And I believe her."

Dejected, the girl started to return to the little group in the rain. I called her back to give her some money without even looking at the denominations of the notes. She smiled brilliantly, murmured a thank you, and walked away.

"What do you think you're doing, Emma?" demanded Kalala, the young whorehouse manager, son of Smelly Joe.

"Clara and Candy will kill you when they know you've taken their men."

"No, they won't," said the diminutive, pretty, and feisty Emma. "Who's going to tell them?"

"Me, of course," said Kalala, striking his chest for emphasis, "Unless—"

"Unless what?" demanded Emma.

"You know the score," said Kalala. "Play along, and you'll have no trouble."

"Yes, I know the score. But one word from you to them about this, and that sorry penis you're so proud of will vanish. I showed you my little knife before; I won't hesitate to use it on bullies and my enemies."

"I am not your enemy," protested Kalala, a little uncomfortable about the way things were unfolding in the presence of others.

"You will be if Clara and Candy learn about this," Emma said. She moved closer to the table at which Kalala sat, took his chin in her hands roughly, raised his head up to meet her penetrating eyes, and said some words in a firm, cold voice: "You'll be a good boy. I trust you." And then she ruffled his hair and turned around abruptly to lead us to her cubicle.

"To do the both of you, it will cost ten leones for short time and thirty leones for the night—the whole night, if you fancy."

Mila counted out thirty leones from his own money and handed the notes to the girl. She took the money and put it away. While she was taking off her semi-wet clothes, she contemplated her action: *I have taken Clara and Candy's regulars. I am sure they will hear of it, and they will take their revenge. But I will be ready for them, come what may.*

Brothel girls forged strong friendships to protect themselves from other girls who might be tempted to bully them. The groups looked more like gangs, and they protected and attacked other girls as was necessary. If a girl offended a member of one such gang, she'd offended the entire gang. The gang members would wait patiently until they were able to corner the culprit, and then they would beat and scratch the offender until someone appeared to help the unfortunate victim. Sometimes, nobody came along.

Yes, they will certainly take their revenge on me. Emma was still reflecting on what she was about to do. *But I will be ready for them, me and my sharp friend hiding in my hair. I have seen such attacks several times, but I have never experienced them personally. I really don't care. We are all commodities for sale in the marketplace where customers buy anything they fancy. Why should one trader attack another when a customer decides to buy the same goods from another trader? Besides, what makes anyone think that a customer belongs to one trader? Customers are for all traders, and Candy and Clara's regulars have decided to buy from me tonight. So be it. Besides, they pay good money. They didn't even haggle over the price I put on my pussy. To hell with Candy and Clara; I have a living to make.*

In minutes, Emma was completely naked and stood right in front of us, her bushy groin glistening from the single light bulb above her. "What do you want me to do for you? Or what do you want to do with me?" she demanded. "I see you're still wearing your clothes. There isn't much I could do with you with your clothes still on. Come on, then, let me help you out of them," she said seductively. "I'm going to give you a long, sweet night."

Emma was very direct. She had an exquisite figure. And standing there naked, it looked even better than I'd assumed. She was beautiful in every way. As she began to take off my clothes, my excitement mounted. I knew that Mila and I were going to experience something we had never experienced before. It was going to be a long, sweet night, just as Emma had said. I was looking forward to it with glee.

We left very early in the morning, saturated with sex but tired and groggy from lack of sleep. Emma was true to her word: she'd given us a long, sweet night that made Candy and Clara disappear completely from our thoughts.

55

"You must never frighten me like that again," said an indignant Mother. "I had people scouring Koidu for you. I thought something bad had happened to you. Thank God you're safe and sound."

"We're sorry," I said, "we just got carried away with our new friends." My head was pounding as I spoke. The beers and djamba in the bar were taking their toll. I felt cold, too, because we were wet.

"You two look like wet, hungry chickens," she said, her demeanour shifting instantly to that of the caring, loving, and concerned mother. "You must get out of those wet clothes at once. I'm sure you'll be dry and warm by the time I bring you some hot pepper soup." She left the room, and groggily, we started to remove our wet clothes.

"I've a good mind to keep you here until you're ready to leave for your village," said Mama Finda. We were hungrily gulping the hot pepper soup she'd prepared for us.

"The way you're going on, I don't trust you with yourselves. I don't know why you insist on going back to Yengema. You already have more money than you ever imagined."

"We already told you, Mother," said Mila with his mouth full of meat from the soup, "we promised Sahr and the gang that we would stay until this Friday. Besides, earning a little more will only help us." She only sneered at us because she knew what we were really worth.

"Mother, you must accept some money from us," I said, trying to take her mind off the topic of returning to Yengema.

"That's out of the question," she protested. "I appreciate your gesture, but you and your family might need it more. Besides, I might be a rich woman for all you know. I don't need your money, young men. I am your mother, and I should be giving *you* money."

"But we want you to have it," said Mila.

"The topic is now closed," she said. "I don't want to hear anything more about it." She took our empty bowls away. When she returned, she stood looking at us for quite a while; we squirmed under her gaze. Finally, she asked, "When will you come back from Simbaru?"

Mila and I had never really spoken about that topic since we planned our departure. We were returning home. We'd been away for years, missing. They probably thought we were dead. I wasn't sure what to say. Deep inside, I knew we'd return at some point in time. Mama Finda was one woman we would never forget. However, as to when we would return to Kono, we didn't have a clue. *Should I lie or tell the truth?* I thought. I decided to tell the truth: "We have no idea," I said. "It's the first time we are going home after over four years. Our parents won't let us leave so soon, especially after the way we disappeared from Simbaru.

She nodded her head. "I know. In their position, I wouldn't let you leave so soon after returning home." She came closer to us and held our hands. "Yandi, Mila," she continued, "I love you and will always love you. Out here, I am your mother and will remain your mother, even in your absence. I'll be missing you when you leave. Nevertheless, never forget that you have love and shelter waiting for you here." And then she let go of our hands.

As she said that, I noticed tears trickling from both eyes. Mother was crying, and it was upsetting to see, especially because we felt there was little we could do to console her. I know she wanted children of her own, but God had not granted her any yet. She'd filled the void within her with us, and while it lasted, she had acted every bit the mother to us. But we were leaving, and I presumed the void was returning.

"Please don't cry, Mother," I said. "We'll only be gone a few months."

"I am not crying," she said. I am happy; my tears are shed in happiness." She tenderly took our hands again. "I have news for you—good news. You are going to have a little brother or sister. I am pregnant. At last I am pregnant again after a very long spell."

I got up, and in one swoop, I took her off her feet and into my arms. I jumped excitedly around the room, and she kept telling me to put her down. Mila just stood there, grinning happily from ear to ear as if he were the proud father.

"We' must be careful for the baby," she said. "Too much excitement won't be good for it."

I put her down immediately. "We are really very happy for you, Mother."

"Yes we are," said Mila. "How far are you gone?"

I haven't menstruated for over twelve weeks. I know I am pregnant because I get morning sickness almost every morning. Plus, there are the cravings. It's like the last time I got pregnant years ago.

"There, you see," I said. "As we leave, God is replacing us with someone you can love, cherish, and spoil just as you did us."

"You are the first to know," she said. I haven't told anyone yet, not even the father. I want to be very sure that this is a real pregnancy before I tell other people. But as you'll be going away soon, I thought it right to tell you now."

"Who is the father?" I blurted out the question before I realised it was out of my mouth.

"Old Boss Kai is the father of my unborn child. He is a good man, and I am sure he can provide for the child. I would be asking him to stop mining, move away from Yengema to stay together."

That was a surprise to us. Who would have thought that wily old Boss Kai had been involved with her? The man had several women around town and boasts of it in the mines. Mother was only one of them. Still, he had been able to make her pregnant; that was the one thing Mother had wanted after her misfortunes.

"I am sure he'll be a very good father," said Mila.

"Good father or not, I'll still have my baby. I will raise it alone if he refuses to help," Mother said. "On top of that, I will still have you young men. When will you come back from Yengema?" she asked abruptly.

"We'll be on the first available transport on Friday," I said. "Saturday will be a busy day. I'm so excited we're going back home."

"We would like to spend an entire day resting in preparation for our journey," said Mila. "We will be here on Friday."

"That's settled then," Mother said. I've kept you talking quite a while. I'll leave you now to get some sleep. Safia will reserve seats for you to Yengema." She went out and closed the door behind her.

56

On Monday evening, we were once more trekking along the familiar footpath to the diamond fields and tunnels. It was our first time returning to the tunnels since we returned from Koidu. Sumaa, Mila, and I were among many people walking on the footpath, which had widened considerably due to the significant increase in traffic. It wasn't unusual to experience a few jostles on the footpath; people traffic was heavy at all times, and everyone was in a hurry. It was as if people were trying to fulfil some challenges upon which their lives depended.

"We'll miss you dearly when you leave," said Sumaa. "It won't be the same without you guys. I really wish you weren't leaving," he lamented.

"We'll be back soon," said Mila. "How many times do I have to reassure you? We'll miss you guys, too."

"That's true," I said, wiping the rain off my face with my hand. We'll be back soon, just as Mila said. We want to come back sooner and earn more money before the spot disappears."

Sumaa sneered at the explanation. "If you really want to earn more money, why are you going when the spot is most profitable? How do you know it will still be there by the time you return? Why not just stay until the spot stops producing."

"Because it's been years," Mila said. "Our folks don't even know our whereabouts or whether we are alive."

"Well just make sure you come back as soon as you can," he said. "You guys have been great to work with. Where is your village, by the way?"

It's called Simbaru, and it's not very far from Kenema," I said. "Kenema is a great town; we passed through there on our way to Kono."

"Where is Kenema?" asked Sumaa. "I've never been there before, but I would love to go there when the spot goes away."

"So where is Sahr?" I asked, changing the topic. I didn't want to encourage Sumaa to ask more questions about Kenema. Mila and I didn't know much about the town anyway. "I haven't seen him since we returned from Koidu," I continued.

"He left immediately for Kenema after you people left for Koidu," said Sumaa. "He said he had some business in Kenema. He was very excited. I am almost sure he had a lot of money in that blue bag he was carrying with him. I haven't seen him since, but I am sure he is on his way back by now."

"I am certain he went to buy a car," said Mila. "Just about a week ago, he told me he would use some of his money to buy a car, which he'd run as a taxi."

"No wonder he carried that sort of money with him," said Sumaa. "I hope he was careful with it. There are far too many dangerous thieves around here; they could easily kill for money. As for Kenema, I hear that's where the professional criminals are."

"Let's hope so. Come Friday, we'll be leaving; whether he's here or not," I said.

"No need to fret," Sumaa said, laughing. "Sahr loves money too much; he won't stay away for long from the mines. He knows far too well on which side his bread's buttered." He laughed again, and that time we joined in. To laugh at Sahr's expense wasn't a regular thing because he always lost his temper. He became violent at times. However, he wasn't around, so we could afford to laugh.

"Do you know his betrothed, Martha, has eloped with one of the miners?" asked Sumaa as he laughed scornfully. "What was the poor girl supposed to do? She was betrothed to him, but after so many years, Sahr neglected to go through the formal ceremony and pay the bride price. Now a younger man is humping her instead. And for nothing: no bride price and no parental consent."

"Is Sahr aware of this?" I asked.

"Yes, he knows all about it," said Sumaa. "He said he didn't mind. He said that, with the money he has, he could get any woman he wanted. In fact, he said he was going to marry three more women to add to his harem. You know what, I believe him. He's the type of man who'd do just that. To him and many others in this community, having more than one woman is a sign of prosperity."

"The man's plain mad," said Mila. "What will he be doing with six women? Does he want a quick death?"

"Look who's talking," I said. How many women did you have going at any one time back home? You always had two or more, and I didn't see you complaining."

Mila laughed and said, "But I didn't have six women."

"But put together, you must have slept with more than ten women in Simbaru," I said. Anyway, let's drop the subject now; we are almost in the tunnels."

As usual, the pits and tunnels were very muddy, extremely overcrowded, and eerily noisy. Although it wasn't raining, the sky was still black. A pale, shy half-moon struggled to penetrate the dark clouds. The moon succeeded on some occasions, but it became concealed again moments later by the ever-moving, black mass. When it succeeded, the moonlight threw an eerie hue over the mining fields. The vegetation and people looked like ethereal creatures from another world.

Mila and I were the first pair from our gang to go underground. The state of the place was beyond comprehension. Light from Makambos revealed to me that people in their haste to remove as much gravel as possible had deliberately taken some of the crude supports that held the interconnecting tunnels in place, thereby making the pit tunnels death traps when the inevitable cave-ins occurred. The tunnels could collapse at any time. I knew that and suspected that every miner knew that. Yet we kept going underground for the money. But some of us had more money than we could have ever hoped for, yet we couldn't get out of the pit even when we knew it was dangerous. *Why do we keep going back?* I wondered. Though the underlying reason was money, everyone had certain reasons that made them come back to the pits.

Altogether, the rewards for the night's work were thirty-two diamonds of different colours and sizes, but none above one carat. We agreed to let Francis keep the stones. We weren't very tired when we returned to town on Tuesday morning because we knew we'd earned money.

When we arrived, the town was awake and functioning despite the fact that it was early in the morning. We found a large, serious crowd in and around Sahr's house. Some were wailing and some were standing idly with terrified faces. Some were talking excitedly. I immediately knew that something wasn't right, that something terrible had happened to someone.

Ludicrously dressed as usual, Mr K saw us coming. He immediately left the people he was talking with to talk to us.

"My boys," he began, "sad news, extremely sad news."

"What's wrong," asked Francis. "Why are all these people here?"

"Something happened to Sahr. A horrible thing," said Mr K.

"Where is he? What happened to him?" I asked.

"He's dead," said Mr K.

"You must be joking," I said, refusing to accept the sad news even though I knew it was true.

"Sahr is dead?" asked Boima in disbelief. No one wanted to believe the news.

"Unfortunately, it's true," said Mr K. "Sahr's really dead. I wouldn't joke about such matters. They found him yesterday at dusk. He was on the road between this village and the main road. Someone had slit his throat for his money. He was going to Kenema to buy a car. He never arrived in Kenema. Poor man."

"Who killed him? Did they catch him?" asked Boima.

"They didn't. They haven't caught anyone yet," said Mr K. "I doubt they ever will. This town is overcrowded, full of strangers and dangerous people. Whom would you catch for the crime? Unless someone was caught red-handed, no one will ever catch anyone."

"Where is the body?" asked Francis.

Mr K pointed towards Sahr's room. "They've already prepared it for burial. We'll bury him as soon as the imam prays for the cadaver. Do you want to see him?"

Sahr was on his bed and wrapped in a white, satin shroud. Only his face was exposed. It was as if he were asleep. The cut on his throat wasn't visible; someone had ensured that the shroud kept the gruesome cut out of view. I stood there with the rest of the gang looking at him, feeling sorry for him. I knew it could've happened to any of us. Death struck very near, and I was afraid. After a while, I couldn't bear to look any longer. I left with Mila in tow.

"How many stones did you get last night," asked Mr K. He'd appeared quickly and waylaid me. I looked at him in disbelief, but I wasn't surprised. The diamond business was a cruel one. Even death didn't interfere with it. Sahr was dead, so he was no longer useful. Life had to go on. The Mr Ks of the world still needed to earn money. "We got thirty-two pieces, all less than one carat. All the stones are with Francis," I stated.

"We'll do business after the burial," he said. "I'll be waiting."

"The man has no soul," said Mila, "And I think he has no respect for Sahr. He shouldn't be talking business at such a time. At least he could've waited until the poor man was interred. Do you think he's made out of concrete?"

"It's only the nature of the business," I said. "Sahr's dead now; he's of no use now. Dead men don't bite, you know. Mining will continue long after Sahr is buried, long after we're buried, and long after anyone is buried."

"I know that," said Mila. "But this was Mr K and Sahr. Remember how close they were?"

"Tell me an occasion when mining or the trade in diamonds stopped because of accidents or deaths," I said.

He shrugged and said, "It's just that Sahr's death is so shocking, I suppose."

"Maybe I can claim my child now that Sahr's dead," I said. The words had come out of my mouth, but I couldn't believe I said them.

"Claim which child? Now I know you've lost your mind," said Mila. The elders of this town, Sandivah's family, and Sahr's family will crucify you. Don't even entertain that idea."

"Forget it," I said. "It was just wishful thinking on my part." It dawned on me that I was no better than Mr K; the dead man wasn't buried yet, and I was already plotting to take a child away from him. I sighed within. I realised that we were living in a dog-eat-dog world.

"It had better be wishful thinking," said Mila, "because I don't intend to wait a single day longer than planned. If you try it, you'll stay to face the music alone."

Sahr's wives, children, and gang members joined Mr K and a small group of people. We accompanied Sahr's body to the cemetery just outside of the village. Sahr was a Muslim, and Muslims buried their dead a few hours after death. Sandivah did not turn up. I wondered whether she had even learned of her husband's death.

57

True to his word, Mr K conducted business immediately after the funeral. He paid handsomely for the thirty-two stones, and as usual, he divided the money equally among us. It didn't matter that Sahr was dead, he still got a third from the shovel's share, which Mr K elected to keep and pass onto his family.

"I am sure you'll be up for work in the mines tonight," said Mr K. "We mustn't let a death affect our business. As you know, the spot—"

"We will be there," said Francis, deliberately interrupting the man, "Right, guys?"

No one objected; we were far too tired, shocked, and upset about Sahr's premature death, a deliberate act of cold-blooded murder with no culprit. We returned to Sahr's big house and found that the crowd had almost disappeared. All the hammocks in the veranda were engaged, but there were a few empty areas in the huge parlour to steal some sleep. We immediately took advantage of the opportunity, but it was impossible for two people to use any of the free spaces together. Consequently, I ended up by myself, in a corner very close to the late Sahr's room.

In the moments before sleep overcame me, I thought about the futility of life. We were mere mortals without control over our lives or deaths. Yet we behaved as if we had such control. We made long-term plans when we couldn't even tell whether we would be alive in the next second. I mused, *Will I be the next casualty? Will it be Mila? Someone else in the gang?* There was no way to know; it was beyond me. There wasn't really any point in worrying about things I couldn't control, but I still worried, especially when death struck so close to me. Sahr was dead; it was his destiny.

I wondered what my destiny would be. Joe Weggo, my father, always said that every man went through life according to what God destined for him. I believed him. Sahr couldn't have known he was going to die when he left for Kenema. Yet he died. It was his destiny. We all had destinies, and we all had to see them through before our inevitable appointment with death. Suddenly, I felt no more anxiety about my life. What would be, would be. It was a decree from God, and He would not entertain any appeals. For the first time that day, I felt peaceful and satisfied. I don't know when sleep finally came to me. The dream, my usual dream, chose to usurp my sleep again that afternoon.

The thick, black cloud with the malevolent, disgusting face wasn't there. It seemed to have assumed Sahr's face, but not as I knew his face when he was alive. It was a terrible face; larvae-like objects crawled out of it from little holes full of blood and yellow pus that stank like burst sewage pipes. He was wearing a blood-soaked, white scarf around his neck. His Ping-Pong ball-sized eyes protruded well past his forehead; they looked more like giant insect antennae than eyes. The terrible figure stood above me and started to talk in a different language. Strangely, I understood what he was saying.

"I knew you were sleeping with my wife," Sahr's face said in a chilling voice. "You made Sandivah pregnant, and then both of you made a fool out of me."

"I am sorr—" I began.

"Shut up and listen," the evil face commanded. He touched the scarf around his neck. "Your death will be worse than mine. I am going to do it myself." Sahr's horrible face really seemed to be enjoying the talk. "I will cut your throat slowly with a blunt knife until you die," he threatened. "You're never going to see your home and folks again. Do you want to see the knife that will kill you?" he demanded.

"No, I don't want to die," I shouted, but the face suddenly developed a hand that was wielding the biggest machete I had ever seen.

"You'll die anyway," said Sahr's face.

One of his hands held me tightly, almost suffocating me as he tried to slash my throat with the big, blunt machete. I fought back and succeeded in freeing myself from the evil creature. But Sahr's face was too quick for me. He grabbed me, threw me down, and sat on top of my belly. Slowly, he began cutting my throat with the blunt weapon. I felt the first blood—warm but slightly sticky—trickling down the side of my neck. I knew I was dead and gave up.

Strangely, I woke up from the horrible dream at the same time that I gave up hope of surviving. I shifted to a sitting position and watched the people around me. Most, including Mila, seemed to be asleep, but some were awake and active. I heard them conferring about events in the fields and the sudden death of Sahr. Little did they know that I had just woken up from a nap that involved the dead man. I reckoned my dream had not disturbed anyone because no one stared or asked me what was wrong.

I remained sitting for quite a while, replaying the dream in my head. *What did it mean? Why should the damn dream assail me during a nap? Why was Sahr's face prominent and hostile towards me? Was the dream or Sahr's face trying to warn me of impending danger? Why was the dream repetitive? Why did it vary slightly whenever I experienced it?* Those were just some of the many questions that preyed on my mind, but try as I might, I failed to come up with answers to any of them.

One good thing about the dream was that it didn't make me fearful anymore. In fact, if anything, it made me stronger and buttressed my belief in destiny. Nothing would happen to me unless God willed it. Dream or no dream, I was alive, healthy, and wealthy. And in a few days, I would return home to meet the family I missed so much.

Cheered up by my positive attitude, I got up and folded my sleeping mat before sticking it in the corner closest to the late Sahr's room. After that, I went out onto the veranda. Fortunately, a few hammocks were available. Evidently, some sympathisers and residents had departed to pursue their daily affairs. I jumped into a hammock and made myself comfortable, but I didn't sleep anymore. I remained there, thinking of and feeling sorry for Sahr. He was buried under cold, heavy earth.

58

For half of Monday night, we scooped gravel from below and brought it to the surface until Francis decided it was time to kick it. Fortunately, it wasn't raining at that moment, but in the tunnels and above ground, the earth was still a bit wet and chilly. It was the type of chill that heralded the harmattan season. The muddy, brown water source we used to kick the gravel was cold and could become quite uncomfortable if one spent a long time standing in it.

"We must kick this gravel as quickly as we can," said Francis. "You are well aware of the antics of the Joe Khakis."

"As if we need a reminder about them," said a disgusted Boima, "they don't bother to mine their own diamonds anymore."

"These days, they prefer arresting people and taking the stones for themselves," said Mila.

"They're bastards; their mothers must have slept with donkeys," said Sumaa. "By the way, don't let your attention lapse; they may come at any time."

"They will not get our stones even if they come," said Francis in a sly manner.

"What makes you think that?" asked Dowu, vigorously shaking the gravel and skimming off the big pebbles from the top of the concentrates. "They'll take diamonds as long as they find them on you."

"So don't have them on you," said Francis. Just keep them somewhere off your body. They'll never find them unless you tell them."

"That would be the day," said Mila, amused. "I'd never tell them, even if they tried to force me to. I'd rather go to jail. At least I could buy my way out."

"Still, we mustn't underestimate the Joe Khakis. They can be very persuasive with their truncheons," I said.

"My friend told me the Joe Khakis took all sixty diamonds they toiled for the other day. He said they didn't just take the stones, they beat them and threatened to kill them if they told anyone.

"Forget the Joe Khakis," said Samson, engaged with the other shaker. He was standing knee-deep in the water, side by side with Boima. "Let's just try to finish washing the gravel."

An hour later, the pile of gravel was gone. We were ready to return to the village. Francis revealed that we found twenty-eight stones in total, and that lifted our spirits. Later we sold the stones to Mr K and divided the money in the usual way. That time, however, Mr K kept the shovel's share. Sahr was dead and wouldn't need it. His family needed it, but Sahr's right to receive some percentage from diamond sales ended after he was buried. It was pay as you go in the diamond business; there was no charitable angle to it.

We were on the verge of returning to the field Tuesday evening when we learned from people coming from the mines that the Joe Khakis had raided and forcefully confiscated every diamond they found on the people they apprehended.

"The Joe Khakis were so satisfied with their pickings that they even let the miners go," said a thin, bird-like man with a stiff upper lip.

"They even had the impudence to urge us back to work," said a short, stocky man with the physique of a gorilla. "As if that weren't enough," the man continued, "they became sarcastic and told us they wanted to seize more diamonds from us on their next raid. I wanted to strangle the bloke who said that, but I couldn't. There were far too many of them to attempt something like that. Nevertheless, I would've loved the feeling of my hands around his skinny throat as I choked him to death. I would've enjoyed his frantic spasms as he kicked to cling to dear life, to survive. And above all, I would've been saturated with heavenly bliss when his dead carcass fell at my feet, motionless and fit for nothing but scavengers."

While he described the way he wanted to kill that unfortunate man, the short, stocky man with the physique of a gorilla acted through the entire procedure. His hands and facial expressions changed depending upon the intensity of the murderous action he was engaging in at the time.

"And just after the raid," said the thin, bird-like man with the stiff upper lip, "a couple of cave-ins occurred. There were no fatalities; we were able to dig the trapped men out before they asphyxiated. You should've seen the poor guys; they couldn't stop thanking their saviours."

"Are we leaving or not?" asked Francis a little impatiently.

We looked at each other but said nothing. I knew everyone was digesting the news of the cave-ins. Cave-ins were the miners' worst fear; every miner wondered whether it would be him the next time, whether he would come back alive.

"Don't tell me the Joe Khakis scare you, or that you are scared you'll be buried." He laughed scornfully.

"I am scared," said Mila. "I've really begun to fear and have premonitions about something bad happening to me in the mines."

That was news to me. I didn't know Mila was afraid, that he was having premonitions. I couldn't believe it. He was the one who kept me going back to the tunnels, so I never realised he was afraid. He might have been afraid all those times he assuaged my fears, but he'd kept his composure to give me comfort and security. It was my turn to allay his fears. Since the daytime dream, I'd ceased being afraid. That was probably why news of the cave-ins did not bother me. "What are you afraid of?" I asked Mila.

"Everything," he said. "I just have this persistent bad feeling."

"That you are going to die?" That you'll be buried alive in the tunnels? Come on, man, don't be a wimp. Nothing is going to happen to us, I assure you."

"How do you know?" Mila asked. "It happened to people today, but they were very lucky to survive it. Not all of us may be so lucky."

"We have to go to the mines," I said softly. "We will be letting the gang down if we don't. We promised to work with them until it was time to return to Simbaru. We should honour that promise."

"There's no reason to fear, Mila," said Boima. "If you are meant to die, you'll die anyway, come what may. See for yourself: some men were buried alive, but they survived; their mates dug them out."

"You're right," said Mila quietly. "Maybe I am just overreacting to the news of the cave-ins."

"That must be it," I said quickly, taking advantage of his diagnosis. "You must've overreacted, that's all."

"So shall we leave now that we've gotten Mila to change into a man again," said Sumaa. "He has been full of fear like a woman confronted by a madman." He laughed and slapped Mila's back playfully. "I thought you were made of stone and concrete."

"Leave it, Sumaa. Every man is afraid, and some circumstances force a man to confront his fears to see whether they'll consume him or he'll overcome them." Mila said. He rubbed the palms of his hands together and made a loud, single clap. "What are we waiting for? Let's get out there and make some more money."

We trooped out of the veranda with Mila leading the way. Almost immediately, it started to rain. It was a very mild rain, the type that could be persistent but never really got heavy. At the mines, we worked through the night as usual, but there were no reports of cave-ins on the entire site. We also expected the Joe Khakis to pop up at any time during the night. They never did. At dawn, we headed back to the village with great relief. We had sixty precious stones for our efforts, and we were all safe.

59

At breakfast, we ate some delicious porridge prepared by Yei. Later, after selling the stones, Mila and I slept through Wednesday morning. Fortunately, I didn't experience the dream that time around. No horrible creatures tormented my sleep. I patted my stomach and was relieved to feel the object under my clothes.

After two night's work, we had a lot of money on us. Keeping it safe caused us some anxiety. Thieving had intensified in the village, especially in sleeping areas where tired miners were the main targets. But one couldn't always resist sleep because of thieves. People just invented ingenious ways to keep their money safe.

Mila and I had ours wrapped in several plastic bags. We stashed them in the original raffia bags we'd brought from Simbaru. We took the bags with us everywhere, and we even slept with them under our clothes. We took no chances; to reach our money, one would have to remove our clothes. Unless we were intoxicated, no one could do that without us knowing, not even if we were sleeping soundly. I saw Mila pat his stomach, too, but his expression did not change. I smiled, knowing that our money was safe.

"What are you smiling for?" he asked. He got up to start folding his sleeping gear, and I followed his example.

"This," I said, patting my stomach again. "It's the first place I check when I wake up. I am not really worried that anything will happen to it, but I like to be sure."

"Mine's here as well," said Mila, patting his stomach again. "We've been very lucky. Look how much two night's work has earned us. We're truly lucky."

"Yes, we are," I agreed. "It's going to be a very happy homecoming for us. We could buy the entire village if we wanted."

"True. But we have to make it out of here yet—safe and sound."

"Now you are being pessimistic again," I said. "You've always been the optimistic one, even getting into arguments and fights when people were pessimistic. Where's is the old Mila?" I took my sleeping gear and stored it in the corner by Sandivah's old room.

"It's just that I have this foreboding feeling that refuses to go away," Mila replied, bringing his gear with him so he could store it in the same corner, on top of mine.

"What foreboding feeling? The same one you had yesterday?"

"Of disaster, of death. Death is hovering like a pair of evil halos over our heads," he replied without hesitation.

"Come off it," I said light-heartedly, "I thought we settled this yesterday. Why are you bringing it up again? We are not going to die. End of story."

"How do you know?" he asked.

"I just know," I said. "At least I believe so."

"Don't tell me you've now become a fortune teller like your father," he said laughing.

It was good to see him laugh, and I laughed with him. "I have," I said. "I'm a fortune teller like my papa if you believe in that stuff. Does that make you feel safe?"

"Only a little," he replied. "But hey!" he said with a sudden change of demeanour. It's Wednesday night! We only have to work the mines tonight and tomorrow night, and then it's goodbye, Yengema.

"There you are," "I said. "How pleasant it is going to be when we arrive in Simbaru. I bet they will mistake us for ghosts at first. A few will need a lot of convincing before they acknowledge that we're not ghosts."

"But we would be ghosts to them," said Mila. "After all these years, letting them believe we were dead—no messages, no clues to indicate that we were still alive since we disappeared from the village. And then all of a sudden, we'll reappear in the village as rich men. They have the right to think of us as ghosts."

"I guess you are right, my friend. They will eventually come around when they see that we we're going nowhere, and that we don't behave like apparitions," I said.

"But we've been away a long time," Mila said, as if I needed someone to remind me.

"Dinner is ready," I heard Sumaa say very close to us. We hadn't noticed him arrive, and his voice startled us a bit. "We leave for the fields immediately after the meal," he continued.

We followed him towards the backyard. We saw that the others had already started eating. We quickly washed our hands and joined in. We could not afford to miss out; we needed ample fuel to tackle the heavy night's work ahead.

There was no news of landslides or cave-ins when we arrived. It was raining slightly, but the sky was getting darker with the appearance of heavy rain clouds. Thunder rumbled and flashes of lightning dominated the atmosphere. It was unusual, especially because it was nearly the end of the rainy season.

"I am sure it's going to be a wet night," said Francis, aware that he was stating the obvious.

"The more reason not to waste time getting the gravel out," said Samba, taking a bucket and a Makambo. "Anyone want to follow?"

Sumaa, Boima, and Samba took up his offer. They trooped into the tunnels. Soon, the gravel started arriving, and we wasted no time kicking it. Every thirty minutes or so, we exchanged positions so that one person didn't have to do the same thing for long. By midnight, Mila and I had been in the tunnels twice, but when we came out the second time, it was raining as if we'd been taken back in time to the middle of the rainy season. Unusually, the moon had come out and lit up the field. Everything was extremely wet and muddy, and the constant squelches of feet plunging into and out of ankle-deep mud was very irritating.

"It has never rained this heavily at this time of year since I came to live in Yengema. And that's a long time now," said Francis.

"At this time of year, we should see the cold harmattan wind blowing, punctuated by outbursts of very hot sunshine. It's quite strange these days—the weather, I mean," said Samson.

"How many stones have we realised?" I asked. "With this sort of drubbing from the rain, we deserve a great haul."

"Forty-two and still counting," said Francis. "I reckon we'll hit a century by the time we finish. Pity you guys are leaving on Friday. You would have earned much more money."

"Don't even start," said Mila. "We have enough money already. Come Friday, we will leave to go back home."

"And we'll be back sooner than you expect," I added, hoping to avoid talk of us never returning.

"I could do with some help at the shakers," said Samson. He was knee-deep in the muddy water, drenched by relentless rainwater. "My back is killing me."

I waited for him to get out of the water and took his place. Mila offered to load gravel in the shaker for me as needed. By the time someone replaced me, we'd added another seven stones to our growing stash of gems. It was going to be a very successful night, and I was glad I was there.

"It's your turn to go below," shouted Francis above the din of the rain and thunder. He was referring to Mila and me. I noticed that Sumaa and Boima had just come up from the bowels of the earth.

"Samba's waiting for you to join him below," said Sumaa. "You better hurry; I don't want to be here the entire night in this terrible rain. It hasn't stopped since it started, has it?"

"Judge for yourself," said Francis. "You're above ground now. Not that you wouldn't know it's raining when you are in the tunnels, some rain will always trickle in."

"Be careful in the tunnels," warned Sumaa as Mila and I headed into the tunnels. They are a bit flooded, more than they were since the last time you were in there. You'll need a little more effort to excavate the gravel."

"Thanks for nothing," Mila shouted back. "We know that already."

Mila went through the Damakoro pit first, and when he was in, I passed him the lighted Makambo. I was just about to go through the mouth of the tunnel when I heard the loudest thunder I had ever heard. It was followed by sheet lightning that turned the entire field into bright daylight for a second or two. But that wasn't all, the lightning had struck some palm trees, and despite the relentless rain, the palm trees caught fire. The rain put the flames out soon after, leaving the crowns of the palm trees smouldering and venting smoke into the air. Mesmerised by such a spectacle, I stood there for a moment. After, I followed Mila into the tunnels. Even with several lit Makambos in the tunnel, it was a little dark. The squelching of our feet made the tunnel even eerier. I noticed that some props supporting the flimsy roof of the tunnels had shifted due to the floodwater and slimy mud. Regardless of the noise from the rain and thunder, I noticed that I could still hear faint voices coming from above ground.

Because Mila had descended into the pits first, he decided to scoop the gravel while I passed it up to the next man on its short journey to the top. Soon, we were churning out buckets of gravel, but it was extremely difficult under such conditions. The sludge was the most difficult to negotiate; it required great effort and skill to retrieve gravel from the water and mud. I wasn't surprised when Mila requested that we change positions a quarter of an hour after he started scooping.

"I think you should have a go now," he said to me. "If I continue any longer, I'm sure I'll break my back. The damn gravel is quite heavy."

"It should be; it's wet mud and stones," I said and laughed. I handed him my lit Makambo when I replaced him.

"You've carried heavier things than a bucket of gravel," said Samba. He was standing a little beyond Mila. "What about that heavy woman I saw you with the other day? Remember? She was bigger than an elephant and must've weighed a ton."

"If I were you, I would keep my bloody mouth shut," said Mila, laughing. "Boy! That was some corpulent woman. But don't be fooled by her giant frame, she moved like a machine. Boy, what a woman!"

"What fat woman, Mila?" I asked. "You never mentioned a fat one to me."

"I was going to tell—" he started.

A great roll of thunder interrupted him. Even from underground, we could tell that it was huge. It rocked the supports and roofs of the tunnels. For a few seconds, I had my heart in my mouth, convinced that the tunnels would collapse. Mila and Samba and a few other miners close to us must have had the same conviction because they frantically directed their Makambos and torch lights in our direction to examine the state of the tunnels.

"They'll hold," said Samba.

I assumed he was right because we heard similar confirmations from other miners. The intention was to reassure us so we would continue mining.

The thunder only rolled once and stopped, but we knew it was still raining heavily above ground. We could tell because the level of flooding in the tunnels was gradually increasing. We weren't afraid that the water would take over the tunnels completely, though— that would only happen over a very long period of time. Because we didn't hear any more monstrous claps of thunder, we returned to the business of excavating the gravel. Soon, bucket found their way up to the top. After scooping another ten buckets of the stuff, I began to feel exhausted and said so. Samba offered to take over.

"Just come out of there so that I can take your place," he said. He passed his Makambo over to Mila.

It was while we were exchanging places that we heard a faint rumbling sound coming through the tunnels. We stood there wet, cold, tired, and transfixed as we listening to the strange sound. From above, we heard some commotion: voices shouting at the same time, full of panic and fear.

"It's the tunnels. They are crumbling on us," shouted Samba as he turned around and tried to run for the exit. "Run for your lives!"

We realised then that we were in real danger. The rumbling noise suddenly became louder, and we felt it closing in on us fast. It was devouring everything and leaving disaster in its wake. By that point, cries of pain and despair could be heard over the rumbling as the flimsy supports that once held the tunnels together gave way.

We didn't need to be told twice. We bolted behind Samba, scrambling to get to the surface before the tunnels crumbled on us. It was a futile endeavour because we were trapped. Loads of miners like us were scrambling to get to the surface, and everyone was looking for an available exit to try to escape. It was like a miniature battle in the darkness, but no one was going anywhere. We were stuck. Bodies blocked the way as people shoved and jostled to get to the exit first. Some were trampled upon when they fell into the sludge.

Fortunately, Mila and I were closer to the entrance, just behind Samba. We were optimistic we would make it to the exit before our tunnel collapsed. But that hope was soon dampened. The entrance to our tunnel had already crumbled, our way out was blocked by a great mound of wet earth. Unless we dug through it, there was no way out.

"We must take another route," said Mila with a trembling voice. "We're surely going to die here. I don't want to die," he lamented.

"We can't take another route," I said, feeling strangely calm. "There are a few people in our way."

"What shall we do then, just give up and die?" asked Samba.

"Let's just tell the people behind us that that this entrance is blocked, that there is no way through. Maybe they'll begin to turn back," I said.

"This entrance is completely blocked," Samba shouted with all his might so that others could hear. The rumbling sound was getting louder.

"How do we know you are not lying?" asked a voice behind us.

"What would I be doing here if there was a way out? I would've been long gone," said Sumaa. "We have to find another way. Keep moving."

Amazingly, the miners started moving away in the opposite direction. They fell over each other to get to another entrance first. Seconds later, we started moving, too, but the rumbling sound seemed very close. For the first time, I was worried. For a split moment, I began to feel that we might not make it out of the tunnel. But I discarded the feeling and kept moving. Without warning, little chunks of wet mud began to fall on our heads, and people panicked and tried to run away to nowhere. In the process, they stumbled against the flimsy supports of the tunnel and displaced some of them. At the same time, the rumbling noise changed its pitch, and before anyone could make some sense of what was happening, the mud roof of the tunnel came crashing down on us.

60

Complete darkness overwhelmed us when the mud roof buried us. It was pitch dark, so black that we couldn't see each other. For a moment, stunned by the impact of the heavy mud on my frail body, I didn't realise where I was. When I did, I heard cries of anguish impregnated with naked anxiety. I heard terrible squelches as trapped men wriggled their bodies to get free of the mud that had buried us. I assumed that several of us were still conscious and alive. I don't know why I felt others were alive, but I was glad to be alive.

The mud had buried me up to my armpits, leaving my hands and head free. I tried to move my body, but the heaviness of the wet tunnel mud wouldn't let me go. I soon discovered that movement was making me sink further into the sludge. I stopped moving my body in order to conserve my strength for when I would need it. I lay there confused, not knowing what to do and scared out of my wits. But the dream came to mind immediately, as did the interpretation my father had supplied. His words—"It means you'll fall into danger and may even lose your life"—came back to me distinctly as if he, too, were in the tunnels.

Meanwhile, the sobs and cries of anguish and despair from other trapped miners filled the dark tunnels. One had to shout if one wanted to be heard. Suddenly, I heard someone very close to me calling out my name. It was Mila; the voice was unmistakable. That gave me a boost. Mila was alive. I called back to him: "Are you alright?" I asked.

"I can't move my body," he complained, his voice still feeble. "Only my shoulders and head are free. I don't want to die."

"You're not dying. We're not dying. You mustn't worry," I said. "As we speak, I am sure that people are trying to get us out of here."

"I hope so," said Mila. "I really do hope so."

I was ashamed of myself. I reckoned that I'd been very selfish. I had only thought of myself since the earth caved in on us. I hadn't spared a single thought for my friend and brother. *How could I have been so self-centred? We were supposed to be looking out for each other, yet I hadn't thought about him and how he was faring until now.* All the same, knowing that he was alive gave me renewed hope. By that point, my eyes were accustomed to the darkness and could discern some objects around me. "Don't worry," I said again to Mila, "they'll dig us out. We'll be out of here even if it takes days. And we will still be alive."

Mila didn't say anything, but I heard him sobbing. I decided not to notice and paid more attention to my surroundings. As my eyes roamed the dark tunnels, I noticed something silvery right above me. I winked my eyes several times and looked again. I was sure it was a ray of light, but it seemed very far away. As I looked away to focus on the black tunnel floor, I noticed a faint light penetrating the mud just an arm's length from me. I suspected it could be a torch light. I stretched out my right hand towards it and realised that I could reach it. I tried to grab the light, but my fingers brushed against a clenched fist cradling the light. I yanked the light from the muddy fist, and it came free easily. The man did not move.

Firmly held in my hand, I directed the torch towards the static man. He'd been completely buried when the tunnel roofs collapsed. In the process, he had put his hands high into the air, probably for protection, and he was stuck that way. I knew immediately that he was dead. I quickly removed the light from the man to prevent others from noticing. I don't know if anyone observed that at least one person was dead, but if they did, they kept silent. They were far too worried about their own plights.

I used the torch to look around myself, and I realised that Mila, a few others, and I had been very lucky. Just yards from us, the tunnel roof had caused carnage. No one in that particular location had survived the crash; the sludge had completely buried everything in its path. If Mila and I had taken another couple of steps in that direction, we would've been dead men, dead like the man right next to me.

I turned the light towards Mila's voice. The light wasn't very intense; it seemed as if the batteries were running out fast. However, I was able to locate Mila after a few frantic waves of the torch. His face was smudged with sludge, but I was still able to see the intense fear on his face. It was so intense that I thought he was contorting his face. Like me, only his head and shoulders were above the sludge. He was motionless, and for a second, I thought that he had died. But he soon raised his head to continue wailing.

"Mila," I called to him, trying to placate him, "I am sure we're not going to die in this hole. They'll get us out. You should stop crying and complaining to conserve your strength. And make sure you don't move too much because you'll only sink deeper."

"Get me out of here, Yandi," he implored. "Please get me out of here. I don't want to die."

"I will get us out of here as long as I still have breath in me," I said in a solemn voice. "Just stay calm. At least we have some kind of light now. We can find out whether there is any way out. Everything's going to be fine; you must stay calm. Would you do that for me, for us?"

Mila nodded his head in agreement as he tried to wipe some mud off his face. I removed the light from him and pointed it upwards, towards the disintegrated tunnel roofs. I was hoping to find a way out. I was surprised by what the light revealed. The tunnel roof was just a couple of feet above us. Two sturdy tree trunks that used to support the roof had saved us. Apparently, the long trunks had crossed each other when the mud roofs caved in. Unbelievably, the trunks and other debris had fallen on vertical supports where we were, forming a sort of safe haven for us. A lot of sludge had passed through the tree trunks and other debris, enough to bury us up to our armpits, but a lot had been stopped by the trunks and the debris as well.

I moved the light around the roof several times, expecting to find something that would give us hope, but my actions seemed to be in vain. I refused to give up. We were still alive in the tunnels, that meant that we were breathing (albeit with difficulty), and if we were breathing, air was coming through from somewhere. I searched above us again, but I still couldn't find where the air we were breathing was coming from. The torch itself was emitting a light that barely exceeded a glow; the batteries had nearly run out. I decided I would take one more look before I switched off the torch. I found nothing.

We were wet, cold, tired, and hungry. The temperature kept dropping. The airflow in our space became sparse, making it more difficult to breathe. By that point, it was a little quieter in the confined space, but the occasional cries of fear and despair continued to pierce the eerie serenity. Some of the men were resigned to their fates.

I had lost track of time. I didn't even know whether it was day or night. I didn't know how long we'd been buried. I must have dozed off or fainted, but when I was conscious again, I noticed a silence that hadn't been there before. Fortunately, I still had the torch clasped in my hand. I fumbled with it in the great dark until I located the control to switch it on. It seemed brighter than when I had last used it. I moved it around in our makeshift crypt. What I saw alarmed me: most of the men I saw had their heads on their chests. They appeared to be immobile. I noticed that I was finding it difficult to breathe, and I realised that the air supply was running out fast. It was no wonder heads were nestling on chests. I quickly pointed the light at the area where I had last located Mila. I saw him immediately. His eyes were wide open in fear or shock, but his head was moving. "Are you all right?" I asked.

"What do you think?" he asked, his voice trembling. I figured the trembling was caused by the immense drop in temperature or fear.

I didn't say anything more to him, but I was satisfied that he was alive. I turned off the light and settled into my confinement of mud. We were waiting blindly, hoping against hope that we would be rescued. Meanwhile, the density of the mud was gradually compressing my body to the point that it became a little painful.

Being fully awake in our relatively quiet tomb, I started seeing my village and relatives in my mind's eye. I saw my father coming from the farm with his machete firmly grasped under his armpit. His long, flowing attire swept the dusty ground behind him. I saw my mum, too. She was as beautiful and lovely as ever with that everlasting smile firmly implanted on her face, a face that was full of kindness, compassion, and love for her family and associates. I saw the other wives of my father chattering and gossiping, engaged in different chores. I saw the sudden silence that descended on them when they knew their husband had arrived home from the farm. I sighed and felt sorry for myself. It was possible that I would never see any of them again, and that made me sad. Still, I didn't stop thinking about them.

My mind roamed to Simbaru's village square. It was exactly as I had left it. I saw the early morning fires around which sat Pa Gibril, the carpenter; Saidu Korah, the driver; Lansana Kpaka, the mason; and others. In my mind's eye, I walked along the path to the river where Mila and I used to take our morning dips and fish. I saw the elders of the town who used to torment Mila for his womanising, and I saw the complete hopelessness that we'd escaped from. *Has it all been for nothing?* I wondered. It had turned out to be a great success for us.

We'd made money and were just days from returning to Simbaru like heroes after a war. But all that money didn't matter when we were stuck inside the bowels of the earth. In fact, apart from the little sums we had in plastic bags near our groins, the bulk of the money was with Mother, Mama Finda.

Mother! I thought, and my heart sank. *Will she ever know that we perished here?* She would be completely devastated when she learned about our deaths. The poor woman would only go back in time and relive the torment of losing a child. And then I remembered she would be having another child soon. That brought me some relief. She was potentially losing us, but she was gaining another child at the same time. Death was giving life in the same way that seeds would rot before growing into new plants. I was glad she had our money. If we perished, the money might come in handy, might help her raise her child. Of course, Mama Finda was already a rich woman.

At that point, I thought I heard faint voices, but I wasn't sure. They didn't seem to come from within our confinement. They seemed to come from above us. I didn't know whether I was hallucinating, though. I listened again, but I couldn't hear any voices. The air supply was getting critical, and I chalked it up to that. My mind was a bit foggy, but it was still capable of roaming and contemplating the neighbourhood.

I saw Sandivah with my child, Joe, firmly strapped to her back. She was crying. Furious tears ran down her cheeks as she did her chores. I felt sad. I didn't know why was she crying and wondered whether I was the culprit. I would never know. And my boy would never know his real father. I knew I might never hold the boy in my hands again or lust after the beautiful, lithe figure of his mother. My parents, too, would never see or hold him as their grandson. All of a sudden, I started to understand the futility of life. It was just one big lie. You made plans, you executed them, but you had no power to save yourself when death called. I wondered why humanity worried so much. I sighed, not knowing the answer. At the same time, I thought I heard voices again. I held my breath and listened carefully. That time, I was sure they were voices. They were trying to rescue us.

Thrilled, I shouted into the darkness, "They're coming to get us. I can hear voices; can you hear the voices, Mila? Listen carefully."

Dead End Poverty

"I hear nothing," said Mila. Several other distressed voices corroborated his words.

The fact that a few of us were still alive boosted my spirits. I had been of the opinion that some had died or fainted given the silence that had overtaken the makeshift tomb prior to me shouting.

"It's very cold. I can hardly breathe," a voice said from the thick darkness. "We are surely going to die here. No one is digging for us. I can't hear any voices either."

No one responded. Quietness returned, and everyone nestled back into the sludge grave. Try as I might, I couldn't hear the voices I believed I heard before. I became disappointed again. It had become frightfully quiet. I presumed everyone was privately engaged in unpleasant thoughts about what death would mean. Perhaps they were reliving the good times. I was sure that anyone in our position would compellingly reflect on his life, especially if the person believed death was the only way out.

I knew Mila was thinking about his family: his mother, his brother, the village, our boyish antics, and a host of other things. The list was infinite. I knew he could be blaming me because I had planted the idea of our adventure in his mind in the first place. There was no time for blame, though. We were in a mess, a potentially fatal mess. All that mattered was conserving our energy and strength to keep ourselves alive until someone rescued us—if they were going to.

Silently, I prayed for God to have mercy on us and save us if he so wished. However, I doubted that we would last long enough to be saved; the air in the cache was almost stale, and breathing had become twice as difficult. Soon, there would be no air available. I started to think that Mila was right after all: we were going to die in a hole not fit for animals. No one would ever identify our graves. It saddened me. Nevertheless, if it was God's choice to have us die in the tunnels, we would have to deal with that fact.

My thoughts returned to Simbaru. The dream dominated everything else, including silhouettes of my parents, villagers, and the farms. It replayed in my mind like it never had before. It accurately revealed every version of the dream I had experienced in chronological order from the time I first had the dream in my impoverished veranda room back in Simbaru. Surprisingly, I wasn't afraid at all. I found myself welcoming what was supposed to—according to my father's interpretation of it—end in death. Strangely, I was relieved. And I believed I even managed a smile at the irony of the years spent trying to forge a better life for ourselves and our families.

The air supply in the collapsed tunnels was getting dangerously low, and I began to feel the effect. Consequently, I started manipulating my air intake, hoping that the air would last longer. Even though my mind was getting a bit foggy, I thought I heard voices and faint thudding sounds. I listened carefully and knew it was no hallucination: people were trying to dig us out, but they seemed to be a long way from us.

"They are digging for us," I cried as loud as I could manage. "Listen carefully. You'll hear voices and sounds of digging."

"I can hear something," said someone whose voice I didn't recognise. "But I am not sure we will be alive when they find us. I can't even breathe properly."

I couldn't breathe freely either, and I presumed that was the case for all of us. We were slowly suffocating in the tunnels. I called to Mila several times, but I got no answer back. I panicked. I thought Mila might be dead. I didn't want to think like that, though. Perhaps he was asleep or had just fainted. Whichever it was, I was worried about him. I remembered the light and tried to switch it on again. It was then that I realised it had fallen from my hand. Franticly, I put my hand into the mud and tried to locate it in the darkness. I couldn't find it, and my movements seemed to be sending me further into the sludge. I stopped moving and resigned myself to what was going to happen. That time, I had no doubt in my mind that we were going to die. The air flow was almost zero, and the rescuers, if there were rescuers, were still a long way from us.

For the first time since our incarceration, I felt tears running down my cheeks. But it wasn't for me. It was for Mila, for our parents, our relatives, our adopted mother, my son, the futility of life, and the anxiety of dying. I also felt dizzy, and at the same time, the memory of the dream came to haunt me again. The sludge took the place of the thick, black cloud that sped towards me. Even in the darkness, I could see features: the distinctive, grotesque, malevolent face in the mud. It was changing colours like a chameleon on the hunt, but I knew it was hunting for me. And when the replay of the dream reached the point where the aura of the malevolent face coiled around me, I started experiencing that pain. I attempted to wriggle my body to avoid the immense pain, which made me sink further into the sludge. The mud was squeezing my ribcage with such intensity that I cried out. I heard no sound.

The lack of air and immense pain started to take their toll on me, and my eyes started to get heavier, making me see things beyond the dream. I saw our village at dusk time. My mother, Massey, was outside in the backyard. She was in the thatched-roof kitchen, dishing out the food she had just finished preparing. It was my favourite, and I felt like I could smell it inside the tunnel. She looked as beautiful as I remembered, and I concentrated on her round, kind, smiling face.

Joe Weggo, my father, was relaxed on the back veranda. He was in his favourite hammock, slightly swaying from side to side, feigning sleep but not actually asleep. He was dragging idly on his lit pipe and exhaling the smoke at regular intervals.

I saw the river that Mila and I had bathed, played, and fished in: its silvery, cool water was meandering its way to an unknown destination. Perhaps, like us, it was seeking things that would enrich it further. I saw the chattering monkeys and colourful, chirping birds that lived on the banks of the river and in the forest. I saw them come out of the bushes to steal food from the women's baskets, and I clearly heard the commotion as the women attempted to chase them away.

By that point, I was struggling to breathe. Not one person had made a sound in the tunnels, even as the rescue sounds got stronger. I really didn't care whether I was going to be rescued, but I was immensely concerned that the lack of air was becoming more painful. It was depreciating by the minute. And it didn't help that I was still being crushed by the mud; it was squeezing my ribcage to its breaking point, just like in the dream. I knew I was losing consciousness, but I tried to struggle even though I knew it wouldn't help.

Suddenly, a great turmoil erupted in my brain. Most events I had experienced started to play out in my mind at the same time, but not in chronological order. Haphazard flashes of my most memorable events zoomed past into my mind with such speed that I was unable to decipher them accurately. I gave up, but the pictures kept replaying. They were driving me crazy. I vigorously rubbed my eyes with my muddy hands, hoping that the images would go away. Strangely, they departed as quickly as they came, along with the sudden confusion that had overwhelmed me. I was peaceful and stable, but I was still running short of air. The tunnels were as quiet as a grave: I couldn't hear any voices, grunts, or movements. Several times, I called out Mila's name, but as before, I got no answer. I feared the worst, and I felt fat tears running down my cheeks. If Mila was dead, I was responsible. I had sold him on the idea of leaving Simbaru in the first place. Tears continued to roll off my muddy cheeks.

In a short while, I started gasping for air. The people working to reach us were hard at work, voices and digging sounds were getting louder, which meant the rescuers were getting nearer. But I believed that they would never reach us in time. I knew that I was going to die; I was doomed. Nothing was going to save me from my plight. Silently, I said my last rites (as my father had instructed me to do if I ever found myself in a fatal situation). Having done that, I felt my whole body flush as if someone had just pumped water through it. I shuddered and kept myself still as I took what I reckoned were my last breaths. Unconsciousness slowly took over my body. In the last moments before I blacked out, I saw my father and mother solemnly waving goodbye from the veranda of our home. I saw Sandivah with tears in her eyes, my boy Joe firmly strapped to her back. She was calling me and asking me not to go away. She said, "Please don't go. We need you now more than ever. And we love you."

The End

Lightning Source UK Ltd.
Milton Keynes UK
UKOW05f0427080114

224153UK00001B/55/P